ONE STUBBORN WOMAN. TWO DETERMINED MEN.
ONE STOLEN NIGHT.

Kat refuses to give in to her mother's demand to marry a man she can't stand. After years of trusting no one with her heart or her body, she wants to be swept off her feet, to experience complete surrender, if only for one night.

Tristan has lusted after Kat for years. She's the woman he wants to put between him and his best friend, Adam, and he's finally making his move. He'll steal her away from his brother, who doesn't deserve her. Then he and Adam will give her exactly what she needs.

Now ready to take control of her life, Kat moves to Philadelphia to open her own law practice and to risk giving her heart to the two men who opened her eyes to desire.

Tristan and Adam are determined to keep Kat close and win her heart. But work dangers and family obligations conspire to tear them apart before their fragile relationship has a chance to grow into something stronger.

Will Kat, Tristan and Adam be able to build a strong foundation for their lives together? Or will everything they've worked so hard for come crashing down around them?

AN INDECENT AFFAIR

AN INDECENT AFFAIR

STEPHANIE JULIAN

MOONLIT NIGHT PUBLISHING

Don't miss updates about new books and sales. Join Stephanie's newsletter on her website at www. stephaniejulian.com.

Don't miss any of the books in the Indecent series:

An Indecent Proposition
An Indecent Affair
An Indecent Arrangement
An Indecent Longing
An Indecent Desire

1

"She brought a date."

"Are you joking?"

"Why would I? She walked in on the arm of some guy who looks like he only leaves his parents' basement to eat."

Tristan Donovan turned to frown at the man who'd suddenly appeared at his side. Adam Oleksy had always been a sneaky bastard, which had saved their asses more than once. He also had a world-class poker face, but Tristan knew when he was bullshitting. Which he wasn't now.

Shit.

"Where are they?"

"Just walked through the front door. I believe your brother may have had a mini stroke."

Tristan's upper lip curled. "Serves the bastard right." His older brother, Philip, didn't deserve Katrina Riley. She was too good for him. Besides, Tristan had already decided he and Adam would have the frosty little lawyer for themselves. Taking her away from Philip would be icing on the cake.

Standing at the bar in the study of Arthur and Angelica Riley's Beacon Hill home, Tristan let his gaze wander over the guests at the Rileys' annual open house. Which was a total misnomer because this was one of the most exclusive events in Boston high society.

Arthur Riley had inherited one of the oldest and most prestigious law firms in Boston and, since the Donovan family had been clients of Riley & McNassett for more than fifty years, they had a standing invitation.

This marked only the second year Tristan had attended.

Last year had been the first.

While Adam ordered a drink, Tristan tried to catch a glimpse of Katrina through the entrance into the parlor, but the doorway only allowed him to view a slice of the great room at the front of the Riley mansion.

In another time, that room would've been called a ballroom, but no one held balls in their homes anymore. At least they weren't pretentious enough to call them that.

"So now what?"

Adam took a sip of his whiskey as he waited for Tristan to answer his question. Adam knew him well enough to know he was formulating another plan. The first plan Katrina had screwed with her date.

But Tristan was nothing if not resourceful. As he worked through various scenarios, he knew there was still only one outcome he would consider: Katrina leaving with him and Adam.

There was no way in hell she was leaving with another man. He'd give her date cab fare if he needed it. But whoever he was, he wasn't walking out the door with Katrina.

"Now I think it's time to introduce ourselves to Kat."

Adam glanced over his shoulder at Tristan, his lips curving in a wry smile. "Sounds kind of like the first plan."

Tristan returned his friend's grin. "It's no different from the first plan. It just means there're going to be two disappointed men instead of one."

"Double the fun," Adam drawled.

Yes, it would be. "Let's move out."

Kat realized her error as soon as Philip Donovan slithered up to her side and proceeded to ignore her every increasingly not-very-subtle attempt to ignore him like he was the plague.

She wanted to run like hell in the other direction, but that would cause a scene, and Angelica Riley did not abide scenes. Especially not by her daughter.

And Kat had no wish to bring any attention to herself here. Though she didn't give a shit what her mother thought, she wouldn't embarrass her dad.

But not even the presence of another man by her side had been enough to deter Philip. He simply ignored Garret as if he weren't even there.

In Philip's eyes, he probably wasn't. Philip only acknowledged people in his own tax bracket as worthy of his attention. Unless, of course, he needed something.

"So I told the governor it wasn't going to happen. I can't believe the man even had the gall to ask."

Kat barely bothered to hide her sigh as Philip continued to yammer on about some deal he was making. Philip ran his father's business, a multibillion-dollar business that was all about profit. She wasn't even completely sure what kind of business they did.

Why couldn't the stock market crash, just a little, so she wouldn't have to put up with this self-important blowhard? In addition to pissing her off, Philip was making Garrett increasing uncomfortable by continuing to ignore him, and that was unacceptable. It was her fault Garrett was here. All her fault that he was enduring what was probably the worst night of his life simply because she'd asked her brother to find her a date for this travesty. Someone who wouldn't expect her to sleep with him at the end of the night but who would at least make it believable that he liked her.

Which was pretty ridiculous in and of itself. Anyone who knew her knew she was unlikable. She worked hard at it.

Kat swallowed a sigh and did her level best not to run screaming. Her dad would worry.

And she certainly didn't want Garrett going back to Erik and telling him his sister was on the verge of a nervous breakdown.

Since Garrett worked for Erik, he'd probably feel duty bound to fill in his boss on everything that happened tonight.

"Of course, the senator and I have played a few rounds so he knew where this was headed. I had to tell him exactly why I thought the deal was not in his best interest."

When she'd first begged Erik to find her someone to bring to this party, she'd thought Philip would be more manageable if he saw she had a date. That he wouldn't assume she was his personal property, granted to him by her mother's approval.

Now she had to worry not only about herself but about

Garrett, a decent guy who didn't deserve to be subjected to Philip.

"And then—"

"Philip, I'm so sorry to interrupt, but would you be a dear and get me a whiskey on the rocks from the bar? I don't see a server anywhere."

That was because she'd made damn sure there weren't any in the immediate vicinity before she'd asked. It was a desperate, childish move, one she wasn't sure Philip was going to fall for. His gaze shot to Garrett for a brief second before Philip smiled and nodded. Apparently, he must've decided that, if she was asking him for his service, she preferred him over Garrett.

Egotistical ass.

"Of course." He smiled, making her want to grimace.

"I'll be back in a minute."

As soon as he was out of earshot, Kat turned to

Garrett. "I am so sorry—"

Garrett laughed, not loud enough to attract attention but with just enough inflection for her to know he wasn't being a prick.

"Kat, hey, no apologies necessary. I knew the score coming into tonight. Erik told me to expect to be bored out of my mind and to be ignored most of the night by the assholes. He also told me his sister needed someone to keep her from going off the deep end. And I've got all day tomorrow and Monday to visit my sister at Boston University. Besides, when Erik asks for a favor, I typically don't decline."

No, her brother had loyal friends who'd stuck by him after his laboratory had been sabotaged and an explosion had nearly ended his life and left him with brutal scars on his face and body.

Erik had people he could turn to, including a best friend and a woman who loved him.

Kat only had Erik.

"Well, I really do appreciate you giving up a night for a stranger. I'm sorry it's just so awful."

Garrett's smile widened. "The drinks are free, the food's great, and my date's beautiful. It's not a total loss."

Her lips parted as she immediately thought to distance herself from him. He was a nice enough guy but— But what?

Garrett was a nice enough guy. At least, he seemed like one. And she trusted her brother wouldn't send some freak on a date with his younger sister. So why couldn't she smile, say thank you for the compliment, and ask him to leave with her? Why couldn't she take him back to her apartment, screw his brains out for the night, then send him on his way tomorrow morning?

Because I'm a coward, that's why.

She blinked and closed her mouth. Then forced herself to take a deep breath. "Thank you for the compliment, Garrett, but—"

"Hey." He held up one hand. "I know the score. It's okay. And I'm not hitting on you. Seriously. It's cool."

She felt a huge weight lift from her shoulders and made a mental note to send her brother a huge thank-you for Garrett. Too bad he wasn't at all her type. Handsome in a boy-next-door fashion with blue eyes, blond hair, and a lean body. Only the dark-framed glasses gave away a hint of his true nature. But they weren't an affectation. Garrett was an electrical engineer with an IQ higher than 150. Since he worked for her brother, he was most definitely a geek.

And she wasn't going there again. Ever.

"Thank you, Garrett." She infused as much warmth as she could into her voice. "I really appreciate—"

"Katrina."

The voice behind her was familiar, and she took a second to compose her expression back into the bland mask she usually wore for these functions. She'd let it slip while she'd been dealing with Philip.

Turning, her lips curved in a smile—that arrested as soon as she caught a glimpse of the men standing behind her. She knew one. The other was a stranger.

Struggling to keep her pleasant smile, she knew it might be a losing proposition if she had to maintain it for long.

"Tristan. How are you?"

"I'm good. It's nice to see you, Kat. How have you been?"

Sucky, actually.

She nodded. "I've been fine. And you?"

"Busy." The word came out clipped and tight, as if he didn't want to waste time on small talk. Which was strange because they'd never shared anything other than small talk.

Truthfully, she tried to avoid even that with Tristan. He made her uncomfortable.

Before she could say something equally short before trying to make her escape, he turned to the man by his side. "Kat, I'd like you to meet Adam Oleksy. Adam is my business partner."

"Kat. It's nice to meet you."

She took the coldly handsome man's outstretched hand

but released it as quickly as possible. If Tristan made her uncomfortable, this man made her want to run in the other direction.

And a very small part of her wanted them to chase her.

She forced herself to hold her ground and hold that smile.

In direct contrast to his brother, Philip, Tristan Donovan was the perfect example of tall, dark, and handsome. He stood at least two inches over six foot, his looks deceivingly bland until he smiled. Then he turned into a heartbreaker with a killer grin and deep green eyes. His dark hair was cut short but not as short as she remembered it being when he'd been in the service.

He was two years older than her, which made him ten years younger than his brother. Who elicited the complete opposite reaction from her.

Philip repulsed her. Tristan...didn't.

Which meant she needed to stay far away.

"Tristan, Adam, this is Garrett. He works with my brother."

"Are you an engineer as well?" Tristan made direct eye contact with Garrett and managed to look truly interested in his response.

"Yes. Electrical. I've worked with Erik since he started the company."

As Tristan and Garrett traded small talk, Adam moved closer. "I understand you're a lawyer."

She forced herself to meet his gaze and hold it. "Yes. And you?"

"I work with Tristan."

Okay, this was going to be a really short conversation.

Not to mention the fact that this man intimidated her.

He was slightly shorter than Tristan and a little broader, which made him look dangerous. If she was casting a James Bond film, he'd be the man standing behind the Russian mobster, cracking his knuckles and looking like a stone-cold killer with those pale blue eyes.

Beautiful eyes, actually. And the longer he held her gaze, the more she realized they weren't cold at all. They burned. Combined with the short reddish-blond hair that still had enough length to show a curl and the faint scar on one perfectly chiseled cheekbone, she couldn't quite catch her breath.

She sucked in air, though she tried not to make it obvious. "Are you enjoying the party?"

"I am now."

She blinked and her lips parted in shock. Had she misunderstood? Or had he just implied that she was the reason he was now enjoying the party?

As she continued to stare in silence, she watched his lips curl into a slight smile.

And heat bloomed low in her belly.

Now she did take a step back, turning toward Garrett at the last second to cover her unease. She didn't think she fooled Adam, though, because his smile widened.

"Garrett, I need to check in with my father.

Gentlemen, it was nice to see you. Thank you for coming."

Adam and Tristan nodded, their gazes never leaving hers.

"We'll be seeing you, Kat."

She heard Tristan's quiet response, and it was all she could do to contain a shiver and continue to walk away at a steady pace. When what she really wanted was to run, though she wasn't sure in which direction. Any way she turned, there was bound to be an obstacle.

Garrett followed at her side as she headed away from the men. She didn't know where she was headed at first, only that she needed to get away before she said or did something she'd regret.

She instinctively turned away from the noise and the lights, heading farther into the house. When she realized she'd cleared the event areas, she stopped and sucked in a breath. They now stood in the hallway that led to the kitchen, deserted at the moment. Thankfully.

"Hey, Kat, are you okay?"

Garrett touched her elbow. He didn't grab her, didn't restrain her in any way, but she still had to fight the urge to yank away.

No, she wasn't okay. Her anxiety level was rising to a critical level, and if she didn't get it knocked down soon, the panic would overwhelm her and she'd either throw up or pass out. And she couldn't do either here.

She'd never hear the end of it from her mother. And her dad would want to rush her to the hospital.

She fought to draw air into her lungs but they felt like they were caught in a vise, unable to inflate. Which would lead to hyperventilation.

"Kat?"

Her stomach rolled and she braced one hand on the wall beside her as the world took a little tilt.

Damn it. This couldn't happen now.

"Hey, what's wrong? Are you having trouble breathing? Kat…"

She heard Garrett talking but it sounded like it was being filtered through water. Like she was drowning.

Stop this. Right now. There's no reason for it. You're a grown woman.

Logical. Every word.

And absolutely no help while she was trying not to pass out.

"Shit, Kat, I'll go get help."

"No!" Blindly, she grabbed for Garrett before he could leave and expose her weakness. She couldn't allow that.

"No, I just need some air. I just—"

Two hands grabbed her shoulders from behind and then she was moving.

"Hang on, Kat. Just a little longer."

Tristan. What—

She tried to breathe in enough so she could speak, but the anxiety attack had its claws in good now. She had no idea where Tristan was taking her, but she couldn't complain. She could do nothing but let him lead her.

Seconds later, cold air slapped at her as Tristan pushed her through the mudroom next to the kitchen and out the door onto the back patio. The cold air threatened to steal what little breath she had left.

"Sit. Head between your knees."

Before she could do anything, Tristan pulled her down until she was seated. But not on a cold metal chair, as she'd been expecting. No, he pulled her onto his lap. The shock made her rear up, but his hand on her head pushed her forward again.

"Breathe in and hold it. Come on, babe. I think you know the drill."

She did but how he knew that… Maybe she didn't want to know.

Instead, she concentrated on not totally embarrassing herself and throwing up what little she had in her stomach. Of course, the more she thought about it, the more nauseated she felt.

"Inhale, Kat. Now."

The force behind Tristan's voice triggered a physical response and she followed his order. And there was no doubt it was an order.

She sucked in a breath, held it for a count of ten then blew it out between her lips as she felt her lungs protest.

Then she took another.

Her stomach heaved but she swallowed it down, drawing in air and holding it until she felt almost lightheaded. Then she released it.

She didn't know how long it took, but finally the anxiety started to ease. And she began to take notice of her surroundings again.

Namely, the fact that she was sitting on Tristan's lap and the hand on her neck that had been keeping her bent forward was now rubbing at the tight muscles.

And that it was close to freezing.

She shivered, and in the next second, Tristan's hand moved and something warm and heavy covered her back and shoulders. A masculine scent infused with sandalwood surrounded her, and she drew in another deep breath. She had the almost undeniable urge to cover her nose with the fabric and inhale again.

Oh my god.

She sat up, embarrassment blasting through her, threatening to steal her breath again. But when she attempted to stand, Tristan wrapped his arms around her waist and held on.

"Stay still for a minute."

She shuddered, though she tried to contain it. "I'm fine now. Please release me."

His arms loosened but he didn't remove them. "I'm not holding you down, but I don't think you should get up yet. Give yourself a moment."

He'd spoken right in her ear, his lips very nearly brushing the shell. She shivered in response, hoping like hell he'd think it was from the cold and not his proximity. "I'm fine—"

"No, you aren't. If you get up too soon, you'll be dizzy. Give yourself a break. Take a minute."

She knew he was right, knew she didn't want to embarrass herself any more than she already had. But if she stayed seated on his lap any longer...

"Kat, hey, deep breath. Keep breathing."

Didn't he realize she wouldn't be able to if she didn't get away from him? Her gaze began to dart around the darkness, looking for an anchor, something for her to focus on, to—

"Katrina. Look at me."

Adam stepped directly in front of her then squatted down until his eyes were level with hers. His pale blue gaze caught and held hers, providing the anchor she needed.

"Breathe in," Adam demanded.

She couldn't not obey. She sucked in air again and held it until he nodded, then released it to draw in another one.

Between Adam's eyes and Tristan's arms, she began to find her center again. And to corral the anxiety back into the dark hole she kept it in.

Finally, Adam smiled. "There you go."

That smile totally transformed him from stone-cold iceman to blue-eyed heartbreaker in a blink.

"Think you can stand now?" Tristan asked.

Tearing her gaze away from Adam's proved almost impossible, but she finally managed and dropped her gaze to look down. She realized she must be wearing Adam's coat.

His bright white shirt shone like a beacon in the dark. "You must be freezing."

"Not that delicate, sweetheart. Keep it on for now."

Then he held out one hand. She took it without thought and let him help her stand, conscious of the fact that Tristan kept his hands on her hips and stood right behind her.

"I think we should probably go back inside before we all turn into blocks of ice." Tristan patted her hips before he released her and took a step away.

She immediately missed his warmth. Which was so damn ridiculous.

More ridiculous than nearly having a meltdown in front of two strangers?

If her mother found out...

"I need to go back inside. I'm so sorry."

Now that the anxiety attack had passed, the anger and humiliation were building back in to take its place. Anger at herself for letting it get that far. Humiliation that she'd had an audience.

She couldn't look at them, couldn't bring herself to meet their eyes and see the pity there.

Poor pitiful Kat. Her brother was strong enough to pull through a horrific explosion, and she's too weak to control her emotions.

She turned sharply, ready to make her escape back to the house, but both men moved with her. Tristan and Adam now stood in front of her, hovering around her, cutting off her view of anything that wasn't them.

If she looked straight ahead, she saw their broad shoulders and chests. If she looked down, she stared at their thighs, which looked amazingly muscular even in suit pants. If she looked up... She couldn't look up and keep her composure.

"Whoa, Kat." Tristan put his hand on her arm. "Slow down."

She tried not to flinch but wasn't completely successful.

Another sign of weakness.

"I'm sorry." She had to take a deep breath before she could continue. "I really need to get back inside."

"What I think you need is to get away."

Tristan didn't release her arm. Instead, he smoothed his hand from her shoulder to her wrist and back again.

Amazingly, the motion soothed her.

"Come with us." Adam's voice. "I could use a change of scenery." *Us.*

Both of them.

Every muscle in her body went rigid, and she stepped away, making no effort to hide her displeasure as she thrust Adam's jacket at him. She didn't wait for him to take it, just let it drop. His quick reflexes allowed him to catch it before it hit the ground.

"I'm going inside now. Thank you for your help in dealing with my...problem. I hope you can be discreet."

"Kat, wait. What the—"

"Good night, gentlemen."

Then she turned on her heel and headed for the door, hoping like hell they didn't follow her.

2

"What the fuck just happened?" Tristan shook his head in response to Adam's question, his expression creased in a frown. "I don't have a clue."

Adam shook his head, staring at the door Kat had disappeared through. They'd scared her, which was the last fucking thing he'd expected.

Tristan had wanted to get her alone, get her to leave with them. Get her in bed between them and show her just how much pleasure they could bring her.

For the past ten years serving together in the Army, he and Tristan had learned a hell of a lot about each other. They'd met at boot camp and, had been pretty much inseparable since. Even though Adam was a punk from a bad Philadelphia neighborhood whose parents had emigrated from Moscow when Adam was two, rich-kid Tristan had recognized a kindred spirit.

Hard partying and arrogant as hell when they'd entered service, they'd developed a bond only men who routinely risked their lives together did. They'd guarded each other's backs, stitched each other's wounds, and shared more than a few nights in close quarters in some pretty dangerous situations.

They knew each other better than they knew themselves, and Adam knew Tristan thought he'd been in love with Kat for years. At least, in love with the idea of Kat. Adam didn't believe in anything as nebulous as love.

Lust, admiration, loyalty. Those were emotions Adam understood. Love was a fairy tale.

But when Tristan talked about Kat, he held her up as a goddess on a pedestal. The quintessential model of unattainable womanhood. And the one who would eventually be his.

Tristan had talked about Kat so much, Adam knew he had to meet the woman who'd captured Tristan's desire simply by the fact of her being.

And make sure she didn't twist Tristan into knots he couldn't untangle.

"Christ, Adam, what the hell happened? She was having a fucking panic attack. Did someone say something to her? I'll fucking kill anyone who hurt her."

Adam tore his gaze away from the door Kat had practically run through to watch Tristan. "I have no idea what might've set her off. I hope to Christ it wasn't us."

Tristan's mouth flattened into a line, but his eyes were shadowed. Adam could see that even in the dim light of the patio.

"Fuck. We need to go after her."

Adam put his hand on Tristan's chest when he would've pushed by. "Give her a few minutes."

Tristan opened his mouth to argue then stopped as he blew out a hard breath. Adam's hand fell away.

"This isn't how I wanted tonight to go," Tristan said.

No, Adam knew how Tristan had wanted this to go.

And Adam would help Tristan however he could.

Because after years of hearing Tristan talk about Kat and showing him the pictures he somehow managed to get, Adam had wanted to meet the woman who'd completely captivated his diamond-hard best friend.

Tristan had talked about her all the time. From basic training to Ranger Indoctrination to their many deployments, she'd been Tristan's favorite subject.

Hell, even when she'd been engaged to her brother's business partner, Tristan hadn't stopped, though he'd switched from talking about how wonderful she was to how she was making such a huge mistake.

The engagement hadn't lasted long thankfully, or Adam would've worried that Tristan would go AWOL so he could talk her out of it. Or kidnap her before the wedding.

Now, Adam watched Tristan consider the problem at hand. Saw his friend's brain work through various scenarios in seconds. That ability made Tristan a natural leader and had helped him move up the ranks at a much faster rate than Adam.

Adam was content being the perfect soldier. Steady. Loyal. Ruthless when needed. The scalpel to Tristan's surgeon.

They worked together like a well-oiled machine. Now, Adam just needed to wait for—

"Something's happened to her." Tristan looked away

from the door and back to him. "That's not the Kat I remember."

"Maybe the Kat you knew didn't really exist."

Tristan had talked so much about how beautiful and brilliant she was that Adam knew she couldn't possibly live up to the hype. No one could. Of course, when he'd badgered Tristan about it, Tristan had smiled and offered up a wager. One Adam hadn't been able to decline.

Now, Tristan shook his head in response to Adam's quiet statement. "No. I haven't seen her for a couple years but something happened. She's...brittle."

"Maybe the engagement."

Tristan sighed again. "Possibly. Maybe."

"Could it have something to do with her brother's accident?"

"From what Erik told me, she helped keep him from withdrawing from the world completely."

"I didn't realize you were that close with her brother."

"We aren't. When Erik was going through rehab, Kat asked me for recommendations for therapists near Erik's home outside of Reading. I hooked him up with Jimmy Cochrane."

"Ah. Jimmy's the SEAL, right?"

"Yeah. Erik and I have kept in touch through email. I haven't heard from him lately, though. Maybe I need to give him a call."

"Maybe."

"In the meantime, we need to do a little reconnaissance."

"Where have you been, Katrina? Disappearing like that was extremely rude."

How Angelica Riley managed to smile while she hissed through her teeth was a mystery. But then, Kat's mother had a long history of hiding an ugly interior behind a beautiful facade.

Angelica had managed to fool Kat's father for all these years into believing she had an actual human heart beating in her chest. But how she'd done it was a mystery on par with who killed Jimmy Hoffa. Kat and Erik had been trying to figure it out for years. They'd never come close.

"Your father and I raised you better. How dare you embarrass us like this."

Well, shit. Her mother was royally pissed. When she started in with "Your father and I...," Kat had learned to keep her mouth shut and ride out the storm. Even though she knew her mother never involved her dad in business like this.

Arthur Riley was one of the smartest men Kat knew. Though he no longer practiced law, he advised some of the world's most influential men on everything from multibillion-dollar deals and international law to world politics and climate change.

Kat had never doubted her dad's love, no matter that she only saw him a few times a week because of his busy schedule.

But Kat doubted her mother had ever felt anything remotely like love, either for her husband or her children. The only thing Angelica Riley loved was her position of power. Over her home, over her life, over her children. At least one of her children, anyway. Erik had managed to escape when he went away to college. Kat hadn't been as lucky. Attending Boston University had meant Kat was close enough for her mother to keep her under her thumb.

Where she'd stayed for far too long.

"I needed a little air, Mother."

But she hadn't been smart enough to keep Garrett by her side when she'd returned. He'd been waiting at the door when she'd practically run back inside. Luckily, he hadn't asked any questions, but she'd needed a little space so she'd sent him for a drink. And that's when her mother had made her move.

"What you need to do is to apologize to Philip Donovan for abandoning him. Honestly, Katrina, I swear you don't have the sense of a gnat. That man wants to marry you and you treat him like a leper. You don't have the luxury of denying him. What other man will be willing to put up with you and your disposition?"

Since this was pretty much what she'd been expecting to hear from her mother, the digs didn't sting like they normally would. Or maybe she'd just gotten better at ignoring them. Either way, she refused to give her mother the satisfaction of a wince or even a blink.

"Maybe I'm not interested in any man, Mother. Have you ever thought of that?"

Angelica didn't bother to respond. "When you apologize to Philip, make sure you make it believable. And smile. Maybe he'll believe you're making an attempt to be pleasant."

Kat let the verbal blows glance off her, taking a deliberate sip of her ginger ale and staring straight ahead. Which made her mother more determined to get under Kat's skin.

Since they hadn't fought this particular battle for several weeks, Kat realized she should've been expecting an attack. She just hadn't thought her mother would do it at a party where other people might hear. Then again, to anyone watching, it probably looked like they were having a regular conversation.

Angelica was smiling, after all. And Kat made sure her expression was a blank, placid mask.

Until Angelica put her arm around Kat's waist and, hidden from view, pinched Kat. Hard. She'd have a bruise there. Wouldn't be the first.

"I don't appreciate being ignored, especially when everything I've done has been for your benefit."

Kat had to bite her tongue against the retort that immediately rose. Her mother did nothing that wasn't for her own benefit. Angelica wanted to tie the Donovan family to the Riley family. That meant offering her daughter up on a platter.

Kat wondered what her mother would think if she told

Angelica she was seriously considering taking the younger Riley son up on his offer to leave with him. And more importantly, making an offer of her own.

An offer so indecent, her mother might never speak to her again.

And wouldn't that be wonderful?

"Excuse me, Mother." Kat turned to give Angelica a bland smile. "I need to find my date."

The idea had been running through her brain since she'd walked away from Tristan and Adam. What would they say if she asked them to take her away?

The thought didn't make her sick to her stomach, and that was a shock. Considering her history, it should have.

Pasting a smile on her face, she moved through the crowd, smiling at guests and shaking hands but never stopping. She knew her mother wouldn't attempt to come after her now. That'd only make a scene.

The anxiety that had nearly suffocated her earlier bubbled in the pit of her stomach, but she managed to keep it tamped down. At least for now.

God, she was a mess. If Tristan and Adam could read her mind, they'd realize what a basket case she was and wouldn't want anything to do with her. She still hadn't come up with a realistic answer for why they wanted her to leave with them.

Maybe she'd totally misread their reaction. Maybe they'd only wanted to help her through the panic attack. Maybe they had White Knight Syndrome and saw only the damsel in distress who needed help. Maybe they were too noble to let her sink by herself.

Tristan had been in the Army. He was used to helping people, and she'd needed help.

No, her past history must be clouding her vision. She'd been an insecure, immature, and frigid girl when she'd accepted her brother's best friend's marriage proposal almost seven years ago. Her engagement to Keegan hadn't lasted, and that had been her fault. She realized that now. Keegan would never have shared her with another man because the only man he shared women with was her brother.

When she'd found out... Well, she'd been insecure,

immature, and frigid. And had nearly had a mental breakdown.

If Keegan had married her, they would've been miserable.

And Keegan and Erik wouldn't have met Julianne and fallen in love with her. The three of them were building a life together in Pennsylvania, and Kat hoped, at least for her brother's sake, that it worked out. Of course, she had her doubts but after what her brother had gone through, she wanted to be wrong.

But until now, she'd *never* considered exploring a threeway relationship herself.

Her mother would scream and rant that it was immoral.

A month ago, she would've thought exactly the same thing.

Now...

Now, she couldn't understand why two gorgeous, successful men who could have any woman in their bed wanted her. Which was why she had to be mistaken. They hadn't wanted her to leave with them. They'd only been trying to help.

The thought had the power to level her. As if someone had handed her a pony or a pink-diamond tiara or a unicorn then took it back with an "Oops, sorry. Not for you." And wasn't that the story of her life?

Wow, pity yourself much?

Keeping the smile on her face through sheer force of will, she headed for the study.

Time to leave. She had to find Garrett and get the hell out of here. If she stayed any longer...

Her lips felt ready to crack. Her cheeks ached. Her temples throbbed.

She wanted to lock the door of her apartment behind her, strip off her clothes, stand under a hot shower for at least twenty minutes then fall into bed and not get out for the rest of the weekend.

"There you are. I've been trying to catch up with you.

Your mother said you were looking for me."

Philip appeared in front of her like her worst nightmare, and her brain stuttered to a stop. She had a brief image of her screaming in his face to get away from her. But that would only prove her mother's theory that she needed professional help. Just as she had when she'd been a teenager.

She managed to hold herself together. "I'm sorry, Philip. She was mistaken. I was actually looking for your brother. Have you seen Tristan?"

The look on Philip's face was priceless. Blank confusion. It gave her time to sidestep him and continue on her way.

And just that fast, she made up her mind.

She scanned the room and found all three men she was looking for standing to one side of the bar. They looked to be having an intense discussion, their attention totally focused on each other. But a split second after she walked into the room, Tristan and Adam looked up. Straight at her. As if they had some sixth sense they'd trained on her.

How wonderful would it be to have someone that interested in her but who didn't want to own her soul?

Stepping up to Garrett's side, she forced a smile.

Adam's gaze narrowed immediately. Tristan's eyebrows rose.

Garrett smiled back, as if in encouragement.

God, how much easier it would be if I were attracted to him.

Then again, nothing in her life had ever been easy.

"So sorry to interrupt, but I'd like to speak to Garrett for a second if you don't mind."

After a second's pause, Adam nodded.

"Of course." Tristan's lips curved into something resembling a smile, but his gaze picked her apart. This time, she refused to back down. "But we'd like to talk to you before you leave. If you don't mind."

Her sex tightened for no reason other than the look on his face, and she was sure he knew it. She managed a smile.

"I'll just be a minute."

She led Garrett to the hallway where she'd nearly lost control earlier, thanked him for his time in the most sincere way she could, and sent him on his way. He didn't seem all that unhappy to be leaving alone, and she wasn't sure if she should be offended or not.

Then she wondered if she truly was losing her mind. Because she was about to do something she never would have thought she'd do.

She was going to be impulsive.

3

"Do you think she'll be back?" Adam asked.

"I'm not sure."

Tristan turned to Adam and watched his friend stare at the door Kat and Garrett had walked through, as if he could make her reappear at will.

To anyone other than Tristan, Adam looked calm, like nothing fazed him. There was a reason he'd earned the nickname Glace. Short for glacial. Most people thought it was because of his eyes.

Those who knew him knew better.

Adam wanted to rip off someone's head right now. Probably Philip's because that's who Tristan blamed for Kat's state of mind.

If Tristan gave the word, Adam would make Philip suffer. Tristan would never hurt his parents by killing his older brother, but that didn't mean he couldn't dream about maiming him. Painfully.

"Maybe you should back off for tonight," Adam suggested.

Tristan shook his head. "We do that, she has time to barricade herself into whatever safe hole she's got."

"What if she bolts anyway?"

"Then we follow."

Adam looked at him with raised brows. "And I suppose you know where she's going to bolt to?" Tristan just stared back.

Adam conceded the unspoken point with a slight shrug. "Of course you do. And you don't think she'll be freaked out when we show up on her doorstep?" "She's going to have to get used to us sometime."

Because Tristan wasn't about to give in and go home.

He'd been waiting too damn long for his chance with her. To show her how much he wanted her. How much pleasure he and Adam could bring her.

He hadn't expected her to need them as much as she did. She'd proved that after nearly passing out from that panic attack earlier.

Now they just needed to convince her of it. And to convince her that, even though what they wanted was unconventional, she should risk it because the rewards would be amazing.

"And if she doesn't?"

Adam had no inflection in his voice at all. Which meant he was thinking too hard.

Tristan looked into Adam's eyes. "You want to throw in the towel?"

"I'm thinking maybe you don't want to run her off by pushing her straight into bed between the two of us."

Tristan took a harder look at Adam, wondering if he'd

missed something because Adam sounded worried. And Adam didn't do worry.

"What are you suggesting?"

A muscle in Adam's jaw started to tic. "That I step back. You make the initial contact."

Tristan raised his brows. "And you'd be okay with that?"

It was Adam's turn to stare at him. But Tristan knew Adam, knew what he was thinking.

Tristan laughed, barely audible even in the silent room.

"That's what I thought."

Adam's mouth tightened, his lips flattening. "Damn it, Tris. This has clusterfuck written all over it."

"No fucking way. Not gonna happen. Don't lose your faith in me now."

"You know I trust you with my life. But this isn't my life we're screwing with. It's—"

Adam cut off, his gaze fixing on a point somewhere over Tristan's shoulder.

Tristan squashed a smile before he turned to watch Kat walk back into the room.

Chin up, back straight, eyes focused straight ahead. She looked confident...except for the fists clenched at her sides.

Tristan turned to stand next to Adam and let her walk to them. They needed her to take those steps.

She stopped just out of touching range.

He hated that she didn't feel comfortable around them, but he didn't think they were the only people she was uncomfortable with. He was pretty sure it was everyone.

He wanted to know why. Wanted to find out everything he could about her. Put her between him and Adam, walk her straight out of the house, and take her home.

Of course, home for him was Philadelphia now. He and Adam had planned to stay with his parents this weekend, but if she agreed, he'd fly them back to Philly tonight. The company jet waited in his family's hangar at a private airport just north of the city. He had it fueled and waiting just in case. They could be wheels up in half an hour and walking through the door of the building he and Adam owned in Center City.

Then again, he figured she'd never agree to accompany them anywhere, much less Philadelphia. And he had no expectation of her asking them back to her place. He was already making a list of suitable hotels in the area when she finally spoke.

"I'd like to leave, and I was wondering if you'd like to accompany me somewhere more private. Now. Without making a fuss and without anyone knowing. Can you make that happen?"

Tristan looked at Adam, who read his mind.

"I'll get our coats." Adam was already moving for the door, but he made sure to nod at Kat before disappearing through the door.

Tristan remained where he was, watching Kat. "Did you drive?"

She took a deep breath. "Yes. My purse is in the coat check." Frowning, she looked over her shoulder. "Damn, I should have thought to get that."

Tristan pulled his phone out of his pocket. "Don't worry about it. Adam will get it. What does it look like?"

She blinked, as if trying to process that information.

"It's black. Leather. Coach."

He had no idea what that meant but he texted Adam.

He'd figure it out. "Where's your car?"

"In the garage behind the house."

"Can we get there without walking through the front room?"

Her eyes narrowed as she thought about that for a second. Her chest was rising and falling at a faster rate, and he could tell her anxiety was rising again.

Stepping forward, he took her hand, gripped it tight in his. She hitched in a breath and held it for several seconds before her lungs began to work again.

"Yes."

Over her shoulder, Tristan caught a glimpse of his brother in the front room, his head turning side to side.

Looking for someone.

Tristan knew exactly who Philip wanted to find.

Since her back was to the door, Kat didn't see his brother hunting for her. The bastard was not going to get what he wanted.

Putting his arm around her shoulders, Tristan steered her toward the one other door he could see in the room.

"Then let's go."

She stiffened against him but didn't fight him when he didn't release her. She allowed him to lead her to the door, but once they were through, she took the lead through two darkened rooms before they finally stopped in a dim hallway beyond the kitchen. He could no longer hear the music from the front of the house.

Retrieving his phone from his pocket, he caught and held her gaze. "Where should I tell Adam to meet us? Should I have him meet us out front?"

He watched her take a deep breath, almost as if she were

gathering her courage. And all those protective urges rose up again. He almost leaned forward to kiss her, to shake her out of this fugue she seemed to be in. Instead, he reined in the urge. He didn't want to lose her now and if he pushed, she'd run.

"Can he get there without being seen?" Her voice had fallen almost to a whisper.

Bending close, he spoke directly into her ear. "We were Rangers, sweetheart. Trust me. No one will even realize he was there."

A delicate shudder ran through her, and he wanted to press her body against his and let her draw on some of his strength. Instead, he waited for her to look up at him.

When she finally did, he grinned because her lips had curved into a small smile. "I'm ready."

Christ, he hoped she meant that because his desire for her had become an almost ravenous beast that wouldn't be denied. He'd never force her, would cut off his own dick if he even considered it, but if she was too fragile for him and Adam to take to bed, he'd want to do serious damage to someone.

He was used to getting what he wanted, and he wanted Kat. And Kat appeared to be on board so this was happening.

And if it didn't happen tonight, well, there was always tomorrow night. Or the night after that...

Kat stopped and Tristan realized they'd reached an outside door in what appeared to be another mudroom. It was too dark to tell for certain but when he looked out the window next to the door, he saw the dim outline of a building across what looked like a small circular courtyard. A covered walkway connected the house to the garage.

Kat reached for the doorknob but paused for a second before turning it. He smiled behind her back, knowing she'd just made a conscious choice to continue.

Shrugging off his suit jacket, he wrapped it around her shoulders. Her dress was in no way revealing, but it definitely wasn't made for subfreezing temperatures.

She flashed him a quick look as she stepped through the door. "My car's just in there."

He kept her moving by wrapping an arm around her shoulders and continuing forward. "Please tell me you have a sedan and not some little sports car. Adam will be grumpy if he has to fold himself into the backseat of some tiny foreign job."

A quick flash of a smile brightened her face. "It's a Jeep Grand Cherokee actually. I'm sure he'll fit."

"I'm sure we all will."

His barely concealed innuendo brought an actual blush to her cheeks, and it struck him then just how much he didn't know about this woman.

He'd wanted her for years but had never had the opportunity to get close to her before.

They'd gone to the same private high school, but he'd been two years ahead and she'd been...young. Untouchable. She'd had two or three girlfriends who she shared a lunch table with but more often than not, she was alone. Almost completely cut off from the rest of the students. She barely spoke to anyone outside of her tiny group of friends, and she'd never dated. At least not that Tristan had ever heard.

And while he'd played lacrosse and wrestled and ran track, she hadn't done a damn thing. No sports, no glee club, no drama club. After graduation, he figured he'd forget about the quiet girl he'd never gotten to know.

But the high school sophomore she'd been when he left for West Point became a beautiful young woman when he'd returned home just before leaving for Ranger school.

They'd met again at a send-off party organized by his parents. His parents had later told him they'd invited her parents, never expecting them to bring their daughter.

Tristan had taken one look and decided she was going to be his.

The first problem, he'd realized, was that her mother wanted Philip as a son-in-law. The second...the girl was a stone-cold block of ice.

But Tristan loved nothing more than a challenge. And stealing her away from his dickhead brother would be icing on the cake.

It'd taken him a few more years than he'd thought it would, but she was here with him now.

He watched her steal one more quick glance over her shoulder before opening the door to the garage.

Matching white BMW sedans occupied two bays. A curvy black Jeep sat in the third at the end. She headed for it, her stride picking up until she was practically running.

Straight for the driver's door.

He almost opened his mouth and insisted he drive but managed to swallow the words. If she wanted to drive, he could control his male instinct to be in control for one night.

Or at least for the next few minutes.

After sliding into the driver's seat, she slipped off her shoes and pulled on a pair of what looked like ballet flats. When he was seated beside her, he held his hands out for her pumps, which she clutched in one hand. Obviously she usually set them on the seat beside her, which meant she wasn't used to having anyone in this seat.

He liked that.

With a slight nod of her head, she handed him her shoes and he turned to put them on the floor behind her.

Weird, but he liked that she trusted him with that small thing. Of course, the real test would come later when he wanted to share much more than space in her car.

She took another shaky breath then hit the remote for the garage door.

Seconds later, she had the car moving, her hands and feet working the gear shift and clutch. The fact that she knew how to drive a stick shift made him ridiculously even hotter for her.

Probably better keep that one to himself. Didn't want her to think he was a complete nutcase.

It took less than a minute for her to pull around to the front of the house, and she nearly stalled the car when Adam stepped from behind a perfectly manicured shrub yards from the front entrance, holding something in his hands.

Stepping on the brake, she caught back a quick gasp by sinking her teeth into her bottom lip, her gaze darting to the rearview mirror as Adam slipped into the backseat.

After a quick breath, she said, "Where are you staying?"

Tristan had hoped she'd invite them back to her apartment, which he knew was across town, practically as far from here as she could get without leaving the city. But he wasn't going to push.

That was fast becoming tonight's mantra.

"Nine Zero," Adam offered from the backseat.

Since they were staying with his family, Tristan had a second to wonder how Adam had pulled the name of that hotel out of thin air.

"A friend of a friend is a shareholder."

Tristan saw Adam pull his phone from his pocket and start to text, no doubt setting up a suite.

"I've never been there."

Kat spoke barely above a whisper but she didn't sound scared. She sounded intrigued.

"Neither have I," Tristan admitted. "I usually stay with my parents when I visit."

As they pulled farther away from the house, he saw her glance several times in the rearview mirror, as if she expected someone to be chasing them down the driveway.

Tomorrow morning, after they woke, he was going to figure out who she was so worried about. Her father? Her mother? His brother?

But that would wait until tomorrow. Tonight, he only wanted to find out what they needed to do to make her scream when she came.

The thought made him smile.

"I've been to the restaurant a few times," she added.

"They have great food."

"Would you like me to order you something from room service and have it delivered to the room?"

A fleeting smile crossed her lips as she glanced into the rearview mirror at Adam. "No, thank you."

"I think I'm going to order a pizza, if you don't mind. No offense to your parents' caterer, but finger food just makes me hungrier."

Silence fell for several seconds and Tristan was about to

initiate more small talk when Kat said, "I'm not in the habit of doing this."

Tristan knew exactly what she was saying and opened his mouth to reassure her that she had nothing to fear from them, but Adam beat him to it.

"We appreciate the fact that you're willing to spend time with us."

Damn. It sometimes amazed Tristan that Adam was able to come up with the exact perfect thing to say in a situation. Usually the guy didn't open his mouth except for one-syllable sentences that usually started with "fuck" and ended with "you."

"Tristan told me you're a lawyer. You work for your father's firm?"

She nodded, looking relieved at the change of topic, and Tristan realized he probably made her more nervous than Adam.

Adam was basically a stranger, which made this a little more anonymous. Tristan was someone she'd known all her life. And was the brother of the man her mother wanted her to marry.

Probably best he step back for a few minutes and let Adam draw her out.

"Yes, I've been there since college. Started as an intern and worked my way up."

"Are you happy there?"

Tristan wondered if Adam would pick up on that tone in her voice. Vulnerable. A little wistful.

She nodded. "I have been."

"But?"

Adam's question hung in the air for a second before she answered, "But I'm not sure I am anymore."

"Then why stay?"

Tristan had to bite his tongue to keep from telling her to get the hell out. Make her own way in the world. He couldn't believe there wouldn't be tons of firms dying to have her. He'd heard she was a damn good attorney but that she practiced mostly business law. His brother had once mentioned in passing that she'd wanted to practice criminal law, but her mother had nixed the idea of Kat having contact with blue-collar criminals. As opposed to the whitecollar ones like his sleazy brother.

"I...have plans for changes in my life."

Tristan couldn't keep quiet any longer. "What kind of plans?"

She stiffened and he cursed himself silently for fucking up Adam's rapport.

Typically Tristan was the talker. He took the meetings, handled the clients, closed the deals. It wasn't that Adam couldn't. He just didn't enjoy it like Tristan. Adam enjoyed the hunt, liked getting his hands dirty.

And as kidnap and ransom specialists, they got their hands dirty. A lot.

Damn it, he should have kept his damn mouth shut, let Adam—

"I'm considering taking a position with another company."

Whoa. Okay. That wasn't what he'd been expecting to hear.

"What company?"

"I'm not at liberty to discuss that. Not yet. But…" She took a deep breath. "It would require me to move."

Out of Boston? Out from under the thumb of her parents?

Kat was twenty-five, well beyond the age where she needed to ask permission of anyone to take a job or move to another city, but Tristan could tell from her expression that this was a huge step for her.

"And where would you move to?" Adam asked.

She paused again, and he could tell she was debating what to tell them. "Philadelphia."

Tristan's mouth nearly dropped open, but he quickly covered any hint of surprise. He and Adam lived and worked in Philadelphia, which she had to know.

"It's a great city," Adam continued. "There's a lot to do."

She nodded. "I've visited a few times. I always enjoy my time there."

Well, damn. He didn't know what to think about that.

Luckily, he didn't have to think about it for long. They pulled to a stop in front of the hotel seconds later. But she didn't pull up to the valet stand. Instead she idled a little farther up the street on the curb.

Now that they were here, he wondered if she'd falter.

Would she tell them she'd changed her mind?

They had her so close to a bed Tristan could almost see that beautiful blonde hair spread out across black silk sheets, her naked pale skin gleaming in low light.

"Why don't you let me go in first? I'll text you the room number."

Adam again, being brilliant.

Tristan wanted to shake himself. He was never this careless, this thoughtless. Good thing Adam had his back tonight because Tristan was totally off his game.

Without waiting for a response, Adam slipped out of the backseat and headed for the door. There wasn't a lot of foot traffic at this time of night, but the hotel was popular and he was sure there'd be people in the lobby.

As he watched her, her gaze followed Adam through the door. And Tristan felt the faint bite of jealousy.

What if she only wanted Adam? Wouldn't that be a kick in the ass?

Well, fuck that. She'd see just how much better it would be with both of them.

"Do you do this often?"

Her voice held the faintest hint of a tremble, but her expression showed nothing. Still, she didn't look at him as she spoke.

And he wanted to see her eyes.

"Are you asking if Adam and I take women to hotel rooms regularly? The answer would be no."

Which was true but not the total picture.

They often shared women. They just didn't do it in hotels.

And even though she was on edge, her mind still worked like a steel trap.

"That sounds suspiciously like prevarication."

Their gazes locked and he found himself unwilling to look away.

Most of his dreams involved staring into those beautiful eyes while he fucked her from beneath and Adam took her ass from behind. He'd wake with an erection so hard it fucking hurt and he'd need to jerk off before he got out of bed.

He was sick of waking up and being pissed off that it was only a dream. Not that he expected that particular dream to come true tonight.

Yes, she'd left with them, and yes, she was still here. He'd almost worried she'd drop them off then speed away and never look back.

But he still worried she would run if they tried to push her too far, too fast. He didn't want to risk that because he wanted more than one night.

So they'd start slow. And it'd be all about her tonight. Even if it killed him, they'd follow her lead. He and Adam had discussed this. They'd worked out all the angles. But they hadn't had all the facts, had they?

"I'm not lying to you, Kat. I won't do that."

Her chin tipped up slightly. "But you're not above *not* telling me everything I need to know, either, are you?"

"And what would you like to know?"

Her eyes narrowed and he could practically see the gears working. He wanted her natural curiosity to win, wanted to see her true nature. He didn't think she let many people see that part of her. And he was pretty sure the reason why she hid that part of herself stemmed from her relationship with her mother. But that definitely wasn't a conversation he wanted to get into now.

"What exactly do you and Adam do for a living?"

"We negotiate hostage settlements and recover kidnapping victims."

Her eyes widened. "I thought you were involved in insurance."

He raised an eyebrow. "Did my brother tell you that?"

She blinked but didn't drop his gaze. "I try not to listen when your brother speaks. I have a habit of wanting to smack him when I do."

"Then that's something we share, but I'd prefer to hit him a little harder. Unfortunately, it'd never be a fair fight."

Her gaze slipped to chest and arms, as if measuring what damage he could inflict. Considering his brother weighed about a hundred and fifty pounds soaking wet and only stood about five-foot-nine, she must've come to the right conclusion.

That Tristan would kick Philip's ass.

He wondered if she'd approve.

"You were in the Army."

He nodded. "Adam and I met in Ranger school. We've been together pretty much since then."

An eyebrow tilted up and he correctly read her look. "We're not lovers. We simply share the same taste in women."

She paused. "So you both like skinny blondes with sharp tongues? And how did you come to realize this?"

Is that how she saw herself? "Maybe I like a challenge. Maybe I like women who speak their own minds, regardless of what anyone else thinks."

Her lips twisted in a slight grimace. "Usually men like women who tell them what they want to hear."

"Then you've been meeting the wrong men."

"And you think you're the right man?"

"I think you'll be surprised at the kind of men we are."

She wanted to say something else. He swore she was practically biting her tongue. So he waited.

Instead, she turned away and stared out the front window.

Patience. Give her some space.

The problem was, he didn't want to wait. Not for anything. He had her almost exactly where he'd dreamed about having her for years. He wanted to push, wanted to reach across the console, wrap his hands around her head, and bring their lips together so he could taste her for the first time.

Impatience was a constant itch under his skin. But he didn't want to risk losing her. Not now. Not when they were so damn close to getting their hands on her.

"So tell me."

Her voice was low but he swore he heard the faintest hint of vulnerability in it. As if she didn't want to be intrigued but couldn't help herself.

"The kind who know how to make a woman feel good."

She didn't respond but he swore he heard her breath hitch. Then his phone vibrated and he pulled it out to read the text.

Room 803

When he looked up, he found Kat staring at him.

"Why don't you go ahead and park? The entrance is right there."

He pointed to the opening that led to the subterranean garage and, with a jerky nod, she put the car in gear and headed into it.

Once she'd found a spot, he barely waited for her to turn off the engine to get out of the Jeep. He stood by the driver's side before the engine shut down completely. Opening the door, he reached for her hand to help her out.

She froze for a second then took his hand as she slid out of the seat and onto her feet.

Without the heels, she barely came up to his chin. And when he put his arm around her shoulders, she fit perfectly against him. He didn't hold her tight, especially when he felt her stiffen. But she didn't pull away, and he considered that another victory.

They reached the elevator without being seen, which he figured would help put her at ease. And when the elevator took them directly to their floor, he wanted to pump his fist in the air.

The warmth of her body seeped into his side, inciting his blood to boil. His chest tightened as he drew in the scent of her perfume.

Christ, if he wasn't careful, the second he had the door closed, he'd have her backed up against it and his hands on those perfect breasts.

But he knew she'd run like a scared rabbit if he pushed her.

Because she wasn't just another hookup. Not to him.

Tristan was only going to be able to maintain his calm for a little longer. And then he hoped like hell that, by that time, Kat wanted him as much as he wanted her. Otherwise, this was going to be an exercise in restraint and futility.

The room was at the end of the hall according to the sign across from the elevator. He turned, keeping a careful eye on Kat to make sure she wasn't freaking out.

What he saw was determination. Not exactly what he wanted to see on the face of a woman he wanted to take to bed.

Desire, anticipation. Hell, he'd settle for plain old lust.

He didn't want to feel like a chore she had to accomplish. Or, worse yet, an obstacle to overcome.

When they reached the door, he had every intention of getting her inside and finding out what the hell was going on with her. They'd sit her down and talk. Adam would realize what Tristan was doing and back him up without missing a step.

The door opened the instant they reached it. Adam had been waiting for them.

Adam waved her in then raised an eyebrow at Tristan when she couldn't see.

Obviously her mood was easy to spot.

Tristan shook his head almost imperceptibly then followed Kat into the room. Adam closed the door behind them then leaned back against it as Kat stopped in the middle of the room. She stood with her back to them, her head turning to check out her surroundings.

He only wanted to look at her.

He was tempted to walk up behind her, wrap his arms around her, and kiss her until she melted against him. She held herself so straight and stiff, she looked almost like a statue. Until she took an audible breath and her shoulders visibly relaxed.

Tristan let himself take a quick look at the room then, trying to see what she saw.

Adam had gotten a suite, so the bedroom was hidden behind one of the doors on the far side of the room. A wall of windows looked out over the cityscape and the river. The furniture felt modern but not cold. Hell, he actually liked it.

Maybe the fact that she couldn't see a bed helped her feel more at ease. Maybe it gave her a little breathing room.

And maybe this is just a completely bad fucking idea.

Adam stepped up to his side and they exchanged a quick glance.

What in the hell do we do now? And will she bolt if we touch her?

They'd inadvertently walked into a minefield, and he had no idea how to navigate it. They'd never dealt with a woman so visibly conflicted about being with them.

The women they'd taken to bed before had been more than willing to accept what they wanted to give. Those women had also been easy to send on their way the next morning, even when they hadn't wanted to go.

Tristan had a feeling he'd be fighting to keep Kat in bed because she'd be the one to say, "Don't call me, I'll call you."

Christ, this was so not how he'd envisioned this night going.

Kat turned then, her gaze flashing at Adam before catching and holding his.

And he nearly spontaneously combusted.

Her expression held undisguised heat, and lust flooded through Tristan's body like a flash flood.

Yes. This was the expression he'd wanted to see. No trace of hesitation, only a desire that made his pulse pound hot and hard through his veins.

What the hell had happened to her nerves?

He knew he should be worried about that, knew he should be thinking farther ahead. But the woman he'd wanted for years stood before him, practically daring him to touch her.

And he couldn't stand not to.

He closed the distance between them, holding her gaze.

She blinked once and took a deep breath, as if she were going under.

Without those fuck-me heels, she had to tip her head back when he got close enough to touch. Her eyes widened, and he checked one last time to make sure he saw no fear or hesitation in her eyes.

When he'd assured himself he didn't, he lowered his mouth to hers and let their lips seal.

Fuck, yes. Finally.

Wrapping one arm around her shoulders and the other around her waist, he pulled her flush against him and kissed her.

Moving his lips against hers, he settled for a gentle, teasing touch. He didn't want to take too much and risk her running scared.

But it was hell reining in his desire. As his lips moved against hers, he had to keep a conscious leash on himself. The fact that she let him kiss her at all made that lust boiling in the pit of his stomach seep through the rest of his body.

He'd managed to keep his cock from stiffening visibly at the party through sheer force of will, but now he was hard as stone and throbbing against the fine wool of his pants.

Just from the touch of her lips against his.

Still conscious of the fact he could scare her off, he didn't press his erection against her like he was dying to. Instead, he flexed the hand on her hip then let it settle against her lower back.

Her dress was deceptively prim, until you realized the back draped, hiding a slit that ran from her neck to her waist. Slipping his hand between the edges of the fabric, he stifled a groan as his fingertips brushed bare skin.

So fucking soft.

He couldn't wait to get the damn dress off her body and see the flesh only hinted at by that slit down her back and the one at her thigh. He was pretty sure he'd seen the hint of a garter there earlier.

As his skin made contact with hers, he felt her shudder then stiffen slightly against him, as if she might pull away.

He took a calculated risk and kissed her harder, coaxing her lips to open so he could slide his tongue between them and finally get a real taste of her.

And had to make a conscious effort not to yank her against him and tear at the fastening of her dress.

Hot. He'd almost expected her to be a little cool, but he was beginning to think that ice-goddess act was just that— an act.

Sure, she continued to hold herself still in front of him, but she wasn't pushing him away.

In fact, she opened her mouth a little wider to give him better access and finally her hands settled on his shoulders. The slight pressure of her fingers as she gripped him burned while the almost tentative touch of her tongue to his caused his lungs to stutter.

He drew back for a brief second to allow them both to catch their breath, but he didn't want to give her time to think now.

He wanted her to lose herself in this kiss. Just like he was. Their lips fused again and this time she opened immediately, her tongue sliding forward to touch his, an active participant.

Yes. This is the woman I want in bed tonight.

Now he took a step forward, closing the tiny bit of distance he'd kept between them.

He sucked in air as her breasts nestled against his chest. Kat was never going to win any wet t-shirt contests and he was usually a breast man. Still, he thought hers were perfect. And when she arched into him, he let the hand he'd kept on her shoulder drag down until it rested on the swell of her right breast.

She broke the kiss this time but didn't move away. Her head dipped as she drew in an audible breath. And when she released it, he felt the brush of it against his hand.

Her chest rose and fell, and he watched the rhythm increase with a rising sense of urgency. The only sound he heard in the room was her breathing. He knew how to control his own, and he knew Adam was, as well.

He hoped they wouldn't need to for much longer. He thought he saw her desire begin to overtake her.

And when she tilted her head up to look at him, he held back a grin.

"Are you planning to do more than kiss me?" she asked.

He lifted one hand to brush his fingers down her neck.

"We plan to do whatever you allow."

Tristan used the plural deliberately and watched her gaze dart over his shoulder to where Adam had settled into a chair close to the door but within full view of them.

Tristan didn't have to look know what Kat saw. Adam sprawled in the chair, his tie undone because he hated wearing them, his jacket tossed somewhere, and his sleeves rolled up.

Kat swallowed hard before meeting Tristan's gaze again. "I've never done anything like this in my life."

Her tone held a hint of frost, but Tristan was beginning to realize she used that to hide behind. At this moment, she was hiding insecurities.

"You're not a virgin."

Her raised brows made his lips quirk in a smile. "No. I hope that doesn't burst your bubble."

Tristan allowed his grin to show. "Honey, my bubble isn't what's about to burst."

Her cheeks turned pink but she held his gaze. "Maybe you need to spell out exactly what you're going to expect tonight."

Seriously? She wanted him to give her an agenda?

"How about multiple orgasms for you? Maybe we should start there."

She blinked, the only outward sign that he might have shocked her. Then again, maybe he was reading her wrong and it was desire that had her sucking in another deep breath.

So he continued. "We want to watch you come. I want to see you come around my fingers at least once. Then I want to watch Adam make you come with his mouth."

Her lips parted on a silent gasp, shock clear in her wide eyes. But the blush on her cheeks deepened and, combined with her rapid breathing, he knew she wasn't frightened.

No, every word he said turned her on just a little more. Then he leaned in, his lips only millimeters from her ear.

"And when you're still panting and your pussy's still clenching, I'm going to sink my cock into you and make you come again before I blow. Then, if you're still willing, Adam will let you ride him."

She sucked in a sharp breath, and he pulled back to determine if he'd gone too far.

The shock still registered in her eyes, but so did the burning desire he'd wanted to see. Without it, he would've had to send her home.

And that would've made him want to tear out some walls. Or beat the shit out of someone, and Adam wasn't up for a round on the mat yet. Not after their last job.

Now he waited because she needed to say the words.

Her gaze held his for several seconds before flicking over his shoulder toward Adam.

When she focused on him again, he realized some of her shock had retreated.

And he started to grin.

4

Kat watched Tristan's mouth curve in a grin and felt her heart pound so hard, she almost couldn't catch her breath.

She should be running for the door. For the life of her, she couldn't figure out why she wasn't.

It'd taken every ounce of her courage to walk out of her parents' home, get in her car with these men, and drive to this hotel.

But some part of her realized that if she didn't do this now, she'd never have the courage to do anything like it ever again.

And she was heartily sick and tired of being afraid.

Afraid that she'd make a mistake. Afraid she'd do something embarrassing. Afraid she'd disappoint her father. Afraid her mother would finally say the words that would make Kat lose her last shred of restraint. And that would not end well. This night... This *one* night... This was for her.

She was going to grab it and take advantage of every last

decadent second. Even if it was the most potentially career- and reputation-shattering experience of her life.

If word got out that she'd left with these men... If someone realized she'd spent the night with two men in a hotel room... Her reputation would be shredded.

Her reputation as an ice princess had been easy to uphold all these years because no man had come close to making her want to step out of her carefully conscribed box, the one she'd been building for years. The one that made her feel safe.

Amazingly, these two men made her feel safe.

And to know that these two men wanted her...she wanted to do a happy dance. But that would be totally undignified and completely un-Kat-like.

She'd look like an idiot.

Maybe they think I'm an easy lay.

No. She dismissed that as bullshit immediately. They'd already seen her let a panic attack get the best of her. How could they think anything about her would be easy?

But here they still stood, looking at her like they wanted to devour her.

It felt...amazing. Like every nerve ending in her body had been electrified. Excitement raged.

It was enough to keep in check the constant anxiety bubbling below her skin.

Two men.

Just the thought that these two men wanted to have sex with her made her light-headed.

And suddenly she realized she didn't know how to continue.

Tristan was waiting for her to make a move. All she had to do was reach for him. They'd brought her this far.

She needed to take that last step.

She drew in a breath and lifted her hand.

Tristan's jaw was covered with dark whiskers, perfectly trimmed and almost soft to the touch. The feel of them against her palm made her shiver. She'd never been with a man who looked so...masculine.

She hadn't lied to him. She wasn't a virgin, but that was only because she'd gone to college.

In college, she'd had two steady boyfriends and a onenight stand that had left her feeling used. Then, in her last year of undergrad, she'd met Keegan, her brother's best friend. And thought she'd found the man she could live with for the rest of her life.

Quiet, stable, steady Keegan who might have loved her forever. Maybe.

But no. She knew their relationship would never have lasted. And she was more pissed off at herself for not realizing that sooner. When she and Keegan had broken off their engagement, no man had interested her enough to break through the shell she'd built. The one she'd needed to protect herself.

These two men interested her.

Tristan and Adam both stood over six feet and, though they weren't over-muscled buffoons, they looked hard.

Tough.

As if, despite the suits they both wore, they were more comfortable in jeans. Or, more likely, fatigues.

She felt small, almost weak, standing in front of Tristan. But he didn't scare her.

He stood perfectly still and let her run her fingertips along his jaw. His gaze locked on hers, his lips parted just a hair as she reached his mouth. A slight hesitation before she touched the tip of her index finger to his firm lower lip. So soft, the rush of his breath warm as he breathed out. Before she could move her finger, he licked her.

Her own lips parted and she shivered in reaction. Her body flushed with heat, erupting from the inside out with a burning desire.

She wanted to give in. Wanted, for tonight, to be a woman who took what she craved.

Staring into Tristan's dark eyes, she sought a little courage. And found it in the warmth of his gaze.

Stepping closer, she let her finger drag against his lip—

And nearly gasped when he opened far enough to catch the tip between his teeth. He barely nipped her, but the effect caused her stomach to tighten and her thighs to clench. Not to mention her sex went wet with anticipation.

The tip of her finger was damp when he released it, and all she could think was how much she wanted to kiss him again.

"Come on, Kat." His voice had a husky quality that made her think of late nights in dark corners of dark bars.

Somewhere she'd never been.

She took the final step to close the distance between them, lifted her mouth to his and pressed their lips together.

Oh God, the heat radiating off him was like the blast of a furnace. She felt like she'd been cold for so long that any hint of warmth made her lose control. And that was something she hadn't done in a very long time.

Until these two men walked into her life.

With their lips meshed, she released a little more of that control…and felt Tristan react with lightning-fast reflexes.

His arms tightened around her and she knew now that he'd been holding back much more than she'd realized.

His arms became steel bands, and the ridge of his erection thrust against her stomach. The sheer size of him should've kicked her back into the panic zone. Instead, she tilted her hips against him, wanting to rub against him and ease the ache building low in her body.

Her clit throbbed and her hands flexed against his shoulders, wanting to tear off his shirt and absorb more of his heat into her.

As if he'd read her mind, he groaned and tilted his head to the side to deepen their kiss. His tongue, until now only flirting with hers, began to demand that she give him what he wanted.

So she did.

He rewarded her by slipping his hands into the back of her dress and spreading his fingers across her bare skin.

Moaning into his mouth, she pressed herself even more tightly against him. His fingers began to stroke her skin. One went up to her dress collar, which was the only thing holding the bodice in place. The other hand slipped lower, fingertips grazing the delicate string of the thong she'd worn so she wouldn't have panty lines.

Tristan stilled then pulled away. Blinking up at him, she couldn't decipher his expression.

Had she done something wrong?

"I'm taking this dress off."

She realized he wasn't asking permission, only giving her a moment to process what he'd said.

Before she could, his fingers had figured out the clasp and released it. The bodice fell to her waist with barely a sound.

She sucked in a sharp breath, her hands automatically moving to cover herself, but Tristan caught them before she could.

"Kat, no."

She felt her body begin to flush. Embarrassment? Or pique at being told no? She didn't know. Whatever the emotion, it quickly turned to heat as Tristan's gaze fell.

His fingers flexed around her wrists, tightening for several seconds before loosening. She heard each breath he sucked in, watched his chest rise and fall with more speed.

"You're beautiful."

The words, "No, I'm not," were on the tip of her tongue but she bit them back.

She knew what she looked like. Skinny, practically flat, no hips. A stick, as her mother was so fond of calling her.

Nothing to really tempt a man into wanting to strip her naked. Yet this man looked as if he couldn't get enough of her.

Probably faking it.

Just the thought made her want to cringe.

Tristan's head popped up and his gaze went straight for hers.

"You're perfect."

Now her lips twisted in a grimace as she dipped her head. "Not at all."

"Bullshit." His immediate denial started a slow burn deep inside her. "Let me show you."

She stilled, waiting for him to do...something.

Anything. But he didn't move.

Confused, she looked up...and found him staring down at her, dark eyes intent.

"Say yes."

His words were a demand she didn't want to disobey. She sucked in a breath. "Yes."

His mouth twisted in a hard grin. "Right answer."

He wrapped one arm around her waist, put the other on her shoulder to arch her back then bent and put his mouth over one nipple.

The shock of his hot mouth on her cool skin made her gasp. Her fingers dug into his shoulders as she lost her bearings, every ounce of her concentration now focused on the sensation of his mouth on her breast.

It felt...mind-altering.

Each swipe of his tongue across the pebbled tip caused her body to shake. Her muscles tightened then loosened and she went light-headed. All from his touch.

How did he manage to undo her with only his mouth?

And should she allow him to continue?

The answer to that last question was a resounding, "God, yes." She wanted more.

Caught against him, she felt his erection press against her mound, causing her sex to clench. Her panties were already wet, and her breasts felt tight and tender.

And his tongue...

Oh my god. No former lover had ever paid so much attention to her breasts. Tristan made her want to give him anything he asked for.

And she couldn't live with herself if that happened.

But for right now, she wasn't going to think about that.

She was going to let Tristan—and Adam—show her one night of unadulterated pleasure.

Tristan moved to her other breast, sucking, nipping, lashing at the nipple with his tongue.

Lust flashed through her, heating her skin until she wanted, *needed* to be naked. Needed him to be naked.

Another first. It typically took her more than a half hour to become aroused to this point. It'd taken Tristan five minutes to make her insane.

Alarm bells began to ring in her head but she ignored them. Time enough for that tomorrow. Tonight was for her. Shaking her head, she opened her eyes to look at

Tristan. His dark head bent over her made her stomach flutter. Releasing one hand from his shoulder, she lifted it to his head and let her fingers run through his short hair. The strands felt thick and a little stiff. She wanted to rub her chin against it. Wanted him to brush his whiskered jaw along her nipples.

Wanted to feel those whiskers against the inside of her thighs.

She shivered and he pulled back, her nipple caught between his teeth. He didn't release her until the very last second, when pleasure would've become pain. With his mouth gone, she did feel some pain.

Lifting his head, he stared down at her. "What do you want, Kat? You need to talk to me."

Could she tell him what she wanted? She'd never been verbal in bed, had always needed complete concentration to get even an iota of pleasure out of the experience. Which should have told her something about those other men.

Even with Keegan—

"I want you to be naked too."

One corner of his mouth quirked into a grin. "Well, then, I guess you need to help me with that."

Setting her on her feet and making sure she was steady, he put some space between them.

She wanted to reach for his shirt and pull him back to her. She felt so exposed with her dress hanging around her waist. But she knew he wasn't going to make this easy for her.

And she didn't want him to.

Lifting her hands to his shirt, she reached for his tie. He'd already loosened it but now she gripped the knot and worked it loose until the strip of silk lay on either side of his shirt buttons. Those were next on her to-do list.

She set to work on those and was pleased to see her fingers shook only a little. As she set the buttons free one by one, she smiled to see the white cotton of his t-shirt come into view. She had no idea why the sight of that plain white cotton made her hornier than she already was.

"Is that as far as you're going?" Tristan's hands settled on her bare hips, just above the waistband of her dress.

She forced herself to lift her head and meet his gaze.

"No. I'm just...admiring your t-shirt."

His eyes narrowed in bemusement. "And why would you do that?"

"Because I think, on the right man, they look sexy as hell."

It was the absolute truth. If he pushed her for more of an explanation, she wouldn't know what to tell him.

Apparently she didn't have to because he laughed, a husky sound that made her thighs clench.

"Honey, you can leave it on if you want but I really want to feel your naked breasts against my skin."

Yes, she wanted that too. She quickly loosened the rest of the buttons and pushed the shirt off his shoulders. He didn't move his hands though and the shirt hung up on his biceps.

When she looked up again, she saw the grin shining in his eyes and she huffed, knowing he wanted her to tell him what she wanted.

Crossing her hands over her chest, she tried to ignore the fact that she was naked from the waist up.

"Put your arms down so I can take off your shirt."

His hands dropped from her waist. "See, that wasn't so hard now, was it?"

If he had any idea... "Your shirt's still not off."

"Go right ahead. I'm waiting on you, babe."

It took her a second to make her arms move. She'd be exposed again. Vulnerable.

But Tristan didn't make her feel uncomfortable. Those were her own insecurities. And she wasn't going to be ruled by them tonight.

She reached for his shirt, her nipples pebbling again as the air hit them. His gaze dropped and this time it was easier to ignore the urge to hide.

Pushing the shirt down his arms, she let it drop to the floor.

Jesus, he looked ridiculously sexy. His now-bare forearms were lightly covered with dark hair and she lifted one hand to run her fingers against his skin.

She had the overwhelming urge to rip away the t-shirt so she could run her hands over the rest of his body.

And why shouldn't she? He'd practically given her free rein.

Hell, if she crooked her finger at Adam, he'd let her do the same to him.

It was a heady feeling, knowing these two men wanted her. She also knew it was only for tonight.

Reaching for his t-shirt, she tugged at it until it released from his waistband. She wanted to slide her hands under the fabric and get her hands on his skin but forced herself to slow down.

First she'd savor, something she didn't get to do a lot of. Then she'd gorge.

"Bend forward. I want this shirt off."

Her tone held a little more of the command she was used to having. Tristan must have heard it because the corners of his mouth curved upward again.

If he ever flat-out smiled at her, she might be in serious trouble.

"Whatever you want."

Before she lost her nerve, she pulled the shirt up his torso and over his head.

When he straightened, she sucked in a breath and held it. *Oh my god. He's beautiful.*

She reached for him, setting her hands on his broad shoulders. His skin radiated heat, which made her want to press her entire body against him. Her dress hanging off her hips felt more like a barrier now than a shield. She only needed to release the clip and zipper at her waist to lose it.

But to do that, she'd have to take her hands off him.

The dress could wait.

Instead, she brushed her hands from his shoulders to his

biceps, the play of muscle beneath the skin drawing her gaze, which quickly moved to his chest.

Tristan must work out on a daily basis because the man didn't have an ounce of fat on him. Only lean, sculpted muscle. No bulges. Just beautiful.

She heard her own breathing, knew they had to realize how turned on she was. Still, Adam remained in the chair and Tristan held steady before her, his chest rising and falling in a steady pace.

How much would it take to make them lose control?

Maybe more than she had. Maybe she just didn't inspire them to—

Her fingers curled and she lifted her hands away, but Tristan grabbed her and spread them across his pecs.

Now, she felt the rapid pace of his heart. And when she looked up into his eyes, she could tell he wasn't as calm as he appeared.

"Don't even think about stopping now."

His voice sounded deep, almost menacing. Amazingly, she felt no fear. Only heat swelling between her thighs.

No, she didn't want to stop.

Brushing her fingertips over his nipples, she felt them stiffen, felt hers tighten in response. She wanted him to put his mouth on her again, but she also wanted to taste him. Leaning forward until her lips were only centimeters away from his skin, she blew against the light coat of dark hair on his chest.

This man didn't manscape and she loved the feel of his chest hair, softer than she'd expected. Then she flicked her tongue against one of his nipples and heard a sharp breath hiss between his lips as he buried one hand in her hair and pressed her closer.

Her hands braced against his abs, she sucked and played with his nipples as he'd done to hers. She'd never wanted to taste a man's chest before, but apparently tonight was going to be full of firsts.

Slightly salty. Warm. Delicious.

She wondered how his cock would taste.

Actually wanting to know was another first.

Her hands shook just thinking about it. Did he want her to?

Of course he did. He was a man.

She realized her hands had fallen to his belt and were trying to work the buckle loose, but she wasn't having much luck.

Pulling away, she looked down to see what the problem was but got distracted by the thrust of his erection through his pants. Her hands followed her gaze down and she had wrapped her fingers around his cock through the material of his pants.

"Jesus, Kat. I'm gonna come if you keep that up."

He sounded deadly serious, even though she wasn't doing anything more than stroking him.

Did she turn him on that much?

She looked up, seeing the blazing sincerity in the tightly drawn planes of his face. She smiled, loving the fact that she pushed him to the edge.

"Unbuckle your pants for me."

"As soon as you drop the dress. Let's give Adam a little more to look at. He's a visual kind of guy."

Her gaze flipped back to Adam...

Who had his pants open and his hand wrapped around his cock, slowly stroking.

The sight arrested her. It should've seemed vulgar. At the very least, it should've been shocking.

Instead it made her even hotter.

She sucked in air because it suddenly seemed in short supply then gasped as Tristan turned her to face Adam, keeping her body directly in front of his own.

She couldn't look away, didn't want to look away.

Behind her, she felt Tristan's hands working at her dress.

With a soft swish, it fell to her feet.

She stood before them in nothing more than a barelythere thong, thigh-high lace stockings, and stilettos.

And felt like the sexiest woman in the world.

Adam's gaze burned as it stroked from her naked breasts to her stomach and lower.

"Lose the thong, Tris." Adam's mouth curved in a hard smile. "Leave the rest."

She sucked in a breath at the icy control in his voice, a direct contrast to his burning gaze.

Behind her, she felt Tristan move closer, the heat of his body intensifying. Her breath caught in her throat as she waited for him to comply with Adam's demand.

Why wasn't she freaking out? She should be. Should be running scared or, at the very least, trying to cover her nudity.

Why did she feel safe here, with these men?

Her eyes locked with Adam's, she could barely keep them open when Tristan hooked his thumbs in the sides of her thongs and pulled them down.

Adam's gaze held hers for long seconds after she felt air

brush against her naked mound. She had the almost over-whelming urge to cover herself but clenched her hands into fists at her sides to resist.

Adam's lips curved in the slightest smile, as if he knew how much effort it took for her to resist her instinctive need to cover up.

Now he did let his gaze drop again, his hand continuing to steadily pump his cock.

Tristan chose that moment to slide his arms around her waist and pull her back against him. Without her heels, the top of her head barely came to his chin, and he seemed so much bigger. Like he could wrap himself around her completely.

Gasping, she realized he was naked. His bare cock nestled against her lower back, her ass plastered against his thighs.

She had the brief thought that she felt cheated, unable to see him. Then his hands flattened across her stomach before one slid up to cup her breast in his palm while he slid his other hand down.

Now she stiffened but not in embarrassment. She froze because she didn't want him to stop.

The hand at her breast engulfed the small mound, tugging at the nipple and sending flashes of almost painful sensation to her pussy. Which he still hadn't touched. His fingers had stopped on her mound, the tips so close to her clit but still not close enough.

"Put your arms around my neck, sweetheart."

She obeyed without thought, realizing only after she'd raised her arms to comply that she was completely vulnera-ble. She trembled, wanting to pull her arms down, but Tristan leaned in and pressed his lips against her neck. Her eyes closed as the most amazing rush of desire swept through her. He made her feel wanted. Not coveted like a prize, but as if he wanted her. The real her.

Which was completely ridiculous because he didn't know her. Not really. Not—

"Breathe, sweetheart." Tristan's breath feathered over her neck as he nipped at her skin, making her shiver. "We won't hurt you."

The rough tone of his voice stroked her almost physically. "Then go faster."

"Oh, I will. When I'm fucking you from behind so you can suck Adam, then I'll go hard and fast. But not yet."

She had to bite back a moan as her gaze locked with Adam's again. His expression tightened even more as he released his cock.

She thought he might join them now, and panic flared. When he didn't make a move to get up, the anxiety died under a rush of sensation as Tristan's hand descended from her mound to her clit.

Already overly sensitive from anticipation, her clit flared with sensation as he caught it between his index and middle fingers and squeezed.

She had to bite her bottom lip to keep from crying out as Tristan began to work her clit until it felt twice its size and she was on the brink of orgasm.

Releasing her breast, Tristan moved his arm to hold her around the waist so she couldn't move her hips. And god, did she want to move. Wanted to writhe against him, make him go faster, harder. Give her what she needed instead of what he wanted to give her.

Apparently he wanted to drive her crazy. And he was

doing a damn good job of it. She felt cut off from reality, her only connection Tristan's hands on her body and Adam's gaze, which had dropped to watch Tristan play with her.

Adam wasn't stroking himself now, but his cock remained in plain view. His hands had moved to his shirt, where he was opening the buttons. His tie had already disappeared and, after he'd opened the last button, he sat forward to shrug out of the shirt. He was also wearing a t-shirt, which quickly followed the shirt and tie to the floor.

Tristan's hands fell into drugging rhythm, pushing her closer to orgasm with every stroke, never pushing her over the edge. But simply looking at Adam made her pussy clench in response.

He had the hard, sculpted body of a man who used his muscles every day and not just in a gym. Tristan looked like a sleek athlete, but Adam looked like a warrior. Even through the haze of desire, she recognized how dangerous this man could be to the wrong person.

And how breathtaking he was to her.

Tristan's upper body had very few marks or blemishes, but Adam had several visible scars. Some so old, they were nothing more than faint lines. Others... Well, those made her want to kiss them better—

Gasping, she clenched her thighs around Tristan's hand, which had slipped back to stroke along the entrance to her sex. She ached for him to part her labia and fuck her with his fingers, to ease just a little of the tension tearing at her control.

She wasn't used to waiting for satisfaction, mainly because she never had to wait on anyone else to give it to her. She'd been taking care of her sexual urges herself for years with toys, which did exactly what she wanted them to do, when she wanted them to do it.

Tristan had his own agenda, his own timetable. And Adam…

He rose from the chair, pants hanging around his waist, his cock so hard it curved upward.

"I think it's time we took this horizontal."

Adam's voice sounded rougher, deeper than it had before. Combined with the motion of Tristan's hand, it made her pussy convulse, so close to orgasm, she wanted to put her hands between her legs and finish herself.

Before she could move, Tristan swung her into his arms and started moving. She barely had time to breathe before he'd pushed through one of the unopened doors.

She couldn't make out anything in the darkness of the room, but Tristan appeared to see just fine.

He took a few steps and stopped as she heard the sound of fabric being ruffled. Then he set her down on a firm mattress covered with baby-soft cotton sheets.

Blinking, she got her eyes to focus, finding Tristan by the side of the bed in front of her and Adam at the foot.

Scrambling to her knees, she reached for Tristan, catching his shoulders and tugging him forward until she could kiss him. The bed sat higher than most, and it allowed her to reach his mouth without straining. She appreciated that.

She also appreciated that he met her almost frantic kiss just as eagerly.

Scooting closer to the edge, she wrapped her arms around his shoulders and pressed her naked body against his. Heat simply radiated off him, and she soaked it in until she didn't feel cold at all.

She had the thought that it would be nice to take her time and run her hands all over Tristan, but the ache between her legs demanded that he cover her body with his and pound into her to ease that ache.

Tristan had other ideas. She moaned as he pulled back, giving her a glimpse of his lopsided grin.

"Lie back, beautiful." Tristan took a step away from the bed, out of reach. "I promise you'll get what you need real soon."

She didn't really believe in promises. Someone always managed to break them.

She didn't want to believe Tristan would break his. And Adam...

Her gaze flashed toward Adam again but he'd moved. For a brief second she thought maybe he'd left, and an indescribable loss swept through her. Then she realized he'd sprawled into the chair by the window, where he could watch.

When will he get sick of watching and join us?

What if he didn't actually want to join and was only there because Tristan wanted him there?

Panic mixed into her other emotions, and she had to consciously push it back. It wasn't hard to do because she wanted what they offered with a greediness she'd never experienced.

Adam stared back through heavily lidded eyes, and she had a brief second to wonder what she could do to entice him onto the bed with her before she felt Tristan's hands on her legs. He smoothed his palms up the back of her calves, and she turned back to look at him just as he was lowering his head.

Oh my god.

His hands shoved under her ass, tilting her to the right angle as his mouth settled over her pussy.

Gasping at the shock of sensation, she thrust her hands into his hair and closed her eyes. Her brain stuttered as she tried to process everything she was feeling and failed miserably.

So she let herself go under. Tristan's mouth and tongue worked together to drive her into a state of desperate arousal. Her muscles strained as he pushed her closer to orgasm. His tongue slicked between her labia, parting the swollen folds to tease at her clutching sheath. Just when she thought he'd give her some relief, he pulled away to nip at her clit.

The frantic beat of her heart pounded in her ears, drowning out the sound of her own moans.

"Tristan. Please."

She knew exactly what she was asking for and so did he. He just wasn't going to give it to her yet. Instead, he sucked at her clit until the little bud felt overstimulated and about to burst.

Then he moved back to her labia, darting his tongue out and stiffening it to fuck her with it.

When another pair of hands grabbed her arms and drew them up and over her head, she cried out, shaking uncontrollably.

Adam.

She hadn't heard him move, hadn't forgotten he was there, but he hadn't touched her and she hadn't been sure he was going to. Now, that extra pair of hands on her body—that sense of the forbidden a second man added to the mix—made her body and mind snap.

Tristan held her hips down as her pussy convulsed in an orgasm she felt down to her toes. Tristan continued to lick at her while she came, and when she opened her mouth and drew in a deep breath, Adam's lips sealed over hers from above.

His kiss was nothing like Tristan's. He didn't ease her into it, didn't give her time to adjust to him before he took what he wanted.

It increased the heat index to another level.

Held down on either end, she couldn't move. And yet she didn't panic. She felt nothing but intense, drugging desire and the innate knowledge that they wouldn't hurt her.

Adam's hard lips parted hers, his tongue sweeping into her mouth to tangle with hers, demanding a response. Demanding she return his kiss rather than simply let him kiss her.

She opened her lips farther and slid her tongue against his. The fact that she'd never responded to anyone the way she was to these two men should have given her pause. Instead, it pushed her to release her fears and doubts and simply respond.

When she moved her head to get a better angle, Adam cut away with a curse but only long enough to rearrange them on the bed.

With a few quick movements, Adam had her on her back with her head on the pillows. In the next second, he sealed their lips again, stretching his naked body along hers.

His bigger, harder frame crushed her into the mattress,

making her gasp, and she sensed Adam's intention to pull back. Before he could, she wrapped her arms around his shoulders and clung to him, kissing him deeper.

Adam immediately took over again, sinking his hands into her hair to angle her head how he wanted. Slanting his mouth over hers, he kissed her with a ravaging demand that made her lower body throb with aching need.

Pressed against him, she felt the thrust of his erection against her thigh. She tried to shift beneath him, tried to get him where she needed him, but he kept her immobile.

Frustrated and overstimulated, she broke the kiss...but only because he let her. She realized that as she wrapped her hands around his neck and felt the leashed strength there.

"I don't want to wait anymore. Now."

Adam's expression barely flickered, as if he were unaffected by what she said, even though she felt the proof of his desire against her body. The thought that he was simply here for sex crossed her mind then vanished when rational thought established itself for a few brief seconds.

Sex is all this is.

Which was wiped away in the next second when Adam rolled them to their sides, exposing her back. Until Tristan pressed his chest against her back.

Her eyes closed as Adam eased slightly away and

Tristan's arms wrapped around her, cupping her breasts in his hands, his mouth fastening onto the tender spot where her neck met her shoulder.

Moaning as her body reacted to Tristan's touch as if she'd touched a live wire, she let her head fall back against Tristan's shoulder.

"Are you ready, Kat? Do you want me to take you now?"

"Yes. Now."

"Soon. I'm going to take you from behind. Just like this, baby. And you're going to suck Adam off while I do it." Uncertainty hit and she drew in a ragged breath.

She'd only given head twice and hadn't really enjoyed it either time. What if she wasn't any good at it? What if—

Her eyes flew open and sought out Adam. He'd moved away, just enough that she could see his face more clearly. She could tell nothing of his thoughts from his expression, but as Tristan began spreading kisses from her shoulder up her neck, Adam reached out to run one finger along her lips.

The simple gesture combined with his steady gaze reassured her in a way she didn't understand.

She could do this. She wanted this, didn't want to be simply the recipient here. She wanted to give too.

Reaching for Adam, she spread one hand on his chest, feeling his strong heartbeat beneath the skin. Skin that had several more scars than she'd seen on Tristan.

One on his left pec that she recognized as a burn.

Another lower on his torso that looked like a puncture.

Several more that appeared to be the result of stitches.

This man looked like he'd been to war, which he had. So had Tristan. Did Tristan have similar scars she hadn't noticed?

And why did it matter now?

Holding Adam's gaze as Tristan continued to hold her tightly against him, nuzzling the skin behind her ear, she slid her hand down Adam's torso until she reached the line of hair that trailed from his belly button to his groin.

Now she used the nail of her forefinger to scratch at his

skin and watched his impressive erection twitch the closer she got to the root of his cock.

"Wrap your fingers around him, babe. Go ahead. Tight."

Tristan shifted behind her, his cock fitting into the seam of her thighs, the tip rubbing against her ass. Wriggling against him, she did what Tristan had told her to do and wrapped her hand around Adam's thick cock. She watched his face as she started to pump him, watched how his gaze narrowed and his mouth tightened. And his cock swelled in her hand.

It became harder to breathe as she let her gaze fall to watch her hand stroking his cock. Her eyes had adjusted to the low light and she saw the fat tip blush a deep red. Heat radiated from the firm shaft, and she wanted to know what he tasted like. Had to know.

She began to move and Adam shifted too, as if he'd known what she was going to do. Maybe he had. Maybe he'd been able to read her expression.

She leaned toward him as he turned toward her and she took him into her mouth on an indrawn breath. His taste hit her tongue as she sucked on the head and let her tongue flick at him.

So masculine. So hot.

"Now I'm going to fuck you, Kat. Just like you wanted."

Adam cupped her head in his hands as Tristan's wrapped around her hips, shifting her into position. Her attention split between pleasuring Adam and Tristan's cock nudging at her sex, she shut down rational thought.

Her cheeks hollowed as she sucked Adam deeper, moaning as Tristan breached her slowly. Hands latching onto Adam's hips, she moaned around him as Tristan worked his way inside her, inch by inch until, finally, he filled her completely.

His cock felt huge, stretching her, making her burn for more. At the same time, she wanted to make Adam burn as badly as she was.

Tristan started to fuck her then, a slow, steady pace that made her body feel almost liquid. Blissful.

And the way Adam's fingers clutched at her head every time she sucked him deeper let her know he enjoyed it.

Enjoyed her.

Behind her, Tristan began to pick up his pace. One of his hands slid down her body to lift her thigh back onto his, spreading her legs and reaching between them to play with her clit. Already overly sensitized, she shuddered, her hips moving back to meet Tristan's on his next thrust.

Tristan groaned, his fingers playing expertly over her clit. His rhythm became a little more erratic, a little faster, harder.

She felt wound tight, waiting...

Adam shuddered, his cock swelling in her mouth.

"Kat."

She heard the warning in Adam's voice. She didn't care. She pulled back to the tip then let the head pop free as she flipped her gaze up to meet his. Lust drew his feature tight, his eyes mere slits.

Her head dipped and she sucked him in again, practically to the back of her throat, and now he released her, his hands curling into the sheets.

Intent on making him come, she played her tongue along his length, her rhythm syncing with Tristan's.

Adam broke first. His low groan signaled his impending orgasm, just before his cock spilled his seed onto her tongue.

The taste, the feel, the sounds, Tristan's fingers on her clit... They all pushed at her until she couldn't hold back anymore, and she came with a moan as Adam continued to twitch against her tongue.

"That's right, baby. That's good. So—"

Tristan slammed his hips against her ass one more time then held himself steady, cock pumping inside her as she finally let Adam slide from her mouth and rested her head against his thigh.

With Tristan's heavy breathing in her ear and Adam's warm thigh against her cheek, she closed her eyes and drifted.

5

Tristan gave her an easy out the next morning.

Adam had cleared the escape route by leaving the bedroom shortly after she'd fallen asleep. Adam didn't sleep much on a good night, so it wasn't unusual for him to be up at all hours.

His absence gave Kat the ability to slip out of bed thinking she wouldn't disturb anyone. Believing they wouldn't hear her or notice.

Tristan continued to pretend to be asleep as she silently opened the door to the living room, collected her clothes, which Adam must've laid out on the couch, then dressed in a rush. Through the door, which she'd left open, he watched her grab her purse and keys from the coffee table in front of the couch and make a beeline for the front door.

Where she stopped. She had her hand on the handle and, even from this distance, he could see her shaking.

Then she turned to look back at the room. Her gaze swept back to the bedroom, where he pretended to be asleep, then to the other door, where Adam probably sat watching television, listening to her every move.

She took her hand off the latch and squeezed it into a fist. And for a brief second, he thought she'd come back. He *wanted* her to come back, wanted her to *choose* to stay.

Instead, she opened the door and slipped out, barely making a sound.

The second the door closed, the other bedroom door opened and Adam emerged, heading straight for Tristan.

Adam pushed open the door then leaned against the jamb, hands shoved in his pants, no shirt, and his hair still mussed from running his hands through it for hours. He stared at Tristan with raised eyebrows as Tristan pushed himself upright.

Tristan knew exactly what Adam was thinking and gave him the answer he knew Adam was going to hate.

"Now we start."

6

"Hey, Kat. How's it going? Everything okay? What's wrong?"

Kat smiled for the first time in two weeks, surprised she still remembered how.

She'd had a rough couple of days and knew she had several more ahead. And the hard part hadn't even started yet.

"It's going. Everything's fine. And there's nothing wrong. I just wanted to call and thank you again for asking Garrett to come with me to the open house. I'm not sure what he told you, but it certainly was no picnic for him.

Please thank him again for me."

On the other end of the line, her brother paused.

Shit. Why hadn't she emailed? Obviously, Erik had heard something in her voice, even though she'd done her damnedest to hide her emotions.

Of course, she'd never been able to hide much from Erik, and she braced for his inevitable third degree.

"Actually," Erik said, "he didn't say a lot, other than the drinks were top-shelf and he appreciated the hotel room for the weekend since it gave him time to visit his sister. But we already had this conversation three days ago so...I'm asking again. What's wrong?"

Her brother was far from stupid even though he could sometimes be the king of the clueless nerds. But he knew her, sometimes better than she wished he would.

It had only been a week since the open house, and since then, she felt as if she'd been racing down a long, dark hallway wearing sunglasses, never sure when something was going to pop out of the shadows and knock her off the path she'd started.

So far nothing had, but now that she'd decided on a plan, she wanted to put it in place before anyone had the chance to deter her.

And Erik was the last person she needed to talk with to set her plan in motion.

"There really is nothing wrong. But... Do you have a few minutes?"

"Of course, just give me a sec."

Erik pulled the phone away from his mouth but she could hear him talking in the background.

"Hey, babe. Tell K I'll be done in a few minutes." A pause. "No, go ahead. You guys start without me." Another pause. "All right, Katnip. What's up?"

She shook her head but didn't say anything about Erik's pet name. She wasn't even sure he realized he'd used it. His brain was probably still focused on his girlfriend Jules, whom he'd obviously been talking to.

"I am interrupting, aren't I?"

"Kat, it's dinner. It's not like it won't be there when we're finished. Now spill."

She glanced at the clock on the wall across from her desk. Hell, it was close to seven and she hadn't noticed. And she still had a mountain of work on her desk.

Sighing, she tossed her pen at the tower of files and leaned back in her chair. "I'm going to take you up on your offer. If it still stands."

Dead silence for a full five seconds. She knew exactly how long because she continued to watch her clock as the second hand ticked by.

"Shit, seriously?" Erik sounded amazed. "Damn, Kat, you should know you don't even have to ask. The job's yours if you want it. Of course it is. But what the hell happened? Did Mom do some—"

"No, no. Nothing happened." At least nothing she wanted to talk about with her brother. "I just think it's time."

Erik snorted. "Well, no shit and duh. You should've been outta that damn law office years ago. You're too damn good for them. Now you'll have your own practice and you can do whatever the hell you want."

Leave it to Erik to make her feel stupid and relieved in the same sentence. Good thing she loved him. Otherwise, she'd have to kill him.

"I needed to do this on my own schedule." She paused.

"But... Thank you."

Erik huffed. "Hey, you don't have to thank me. You're actually giving me exactly what I want. Someone I trust implicitly who knows how I think. It's a no-brainer, Kat."

"And you're sure Keegan will—"

"Stop. Don't even go there. You know he's not going to be

a problem so there's nothing to discuss. As long as you want it, the job's yours. But are you gonna tell me what happened to make you finally get off your ass and make the move? Or will I have to threaten Garrett with unemployment until he spills?"

Erik would never threaten any of his employees over something so trivial. But he'd probably continue to nag her until she told him something plausible.

She just couldn't tell him the truth.

"Something did happen, but it's not something bad. Honestly. I...spoke to someone who gave me a different outlook on my life. Something I needed to hear. It made me see things in a new light and made me realize it's time to make my move."

"And who was this brilliant person who wasn't me?"

Damn, she hated lying to her brother, but there was no way she could tell him what had happened. At least not now. "You don't know them, Erik. And it was a random conversation. I don't think he even realized what he was saying was making such a big impression on me."

Erik huffed. "Well, fine, you don't wanna talk, we won't talk about it. I'm just glad you're finally doing this for you."

Smiling, she nodded, even though she knew Erik couldn't see her. "Me too."

"Great. Now, can you be here in a week? We're kind of in need of a good lawyer."

"You're going to do what?"

Kat watched her dad blink several times as his analytical

brain tried to make sense of the bombshell she'd dropped on him.

"I'm moving to Philadelphia to be closer to Erik since I'll be handling TinMan's account. It's more convenient for me to be located there. Plus, I plan to pursue more…diverse cases than I've been taking up here."

Her dad shook his head, as if trying to make sense of her words. He looked like she'd smashed him across the back of the head with a bat. Confused. Dazed. Totally caught off guard.

"Kat… I'm not sure I know what to say. This seems awfully sudden."

Instead of rushing through an explanation, she sat quietly and waited for her dad to sift through the information. They shared a lot of the same traits.

After several quiet seconds, her father finally said, "Are you sure?"

Of course not. But it was time. "Yes."

Her dad sighed, a wry grin twisting his lips. "I had no idea it'd gotten that bad for you, sweetheart. I know you haven't been happy there but I thought… Oh hell, I had no idea what I thought. Are you sure, though, that this is really right for you?"

"Yes, I'm positive." She had the childish urge to cross her fingers. "It's time to move on, Dad."

"Well, then—"

The door to her father's study flew open, and Kat swung around to see her mother stalk into the room, causing Kat's tension level to flare.

"Don't say another word, Arthur," her mother said. "She's not going anywhere."

Fury and indignation made an awful mess of her stomach. She should've realized her mother would be listening. She honestly believed her mother had the house bugged. Nothing Angelica did would surprise Kat.

But nothing her mother said would change her mind.

"Yes, I am, Mother. I'm moving to Philadelphia."

Kat had spent most of her twenty-five years making sure she never turned her back on her mother. Doing so now was one of the hardest things she'd ever done.

She looked back at her dad with an apologetic twist of her lips. "I already have a real estate agent looking for places, and I'll be going down to view them this weekend."

"You will do no such thing." Her mother's voice was beginning to lose some of that legendary polish, her fury beginning to show around the edges. "You have obligations to fulfill here."

The urge to run for her childhood bedroom on the third floor and crawl behind the chair in the corner, like she used to do as a child, nearly consumed her. Her mother had kept that room exactly as Kat had left it. Erik's room was the same. Almost as if her mother expected them to return someday. It was pretty damn creepy.

Thankfully, she overcame the urge and dredged up every ounce of control she possessed. Then she purposely ignored her mother and continued to talk to her dad.

"Erik and I have already discussed this and I know—"

"Arthur, how can you—"

"—exactly what I'm walking into. I'll—"

"—allow her to ignore everything we've given her—"

"—give myself time to get up to speed on TinMan and then I'll be branching out."

"—and leave you in the lurch like this? This is absurd."

Her dad never took his gaze away from Kat, never spared a glance for his wife. Instead, he smiled and nodded at Kat as he rose from his chair and came around the desk to give her a hug. "I'm going to miss you, sweetheart. I hope Erik knows he's going to be paying you a hell of a lot of money for your expertise."

"Arthur," her mother screeched, the sound like nails on a chalkboard. "Are you serious? This is completely unacceptable."

With a quick smile for her dad, Kat drew in a deep breath and turned to face her mother. Angelica blocked Kat's escape route, her expression livid.

Only months ago, Kate would've caved to her mother's demands, not wanting to rock the boat. She'd never been able to please her mother unless she did exactly what Angelica wanted. And even then, she invariably did something wrong.

And for reasons she'd never been able to understand, her dad, the strongest man she knew, had chosen the path of least resistance with his wife.

Kat couldn't really blame him. Angelica could give Cinderella's stepmother a run for her money. But Kat had learned several things over the years by watching her parents interact.

Her dad listened to her mother's diatribe, let her get it out of her system, then told her what he was going to do and continued on his merry way.

"I've already spoken to Frank," one of the named partners in the firm, "and we've already come to terms. None of my clients or the firm will be inconvenienced in the least. It's a done deal, Mother."

Then Kat headed for the door as her mother stared at her, shock evident on her face.

Well, what do you know? She'd actually shocked her mother into silence.

But as she walked by Angelica, her mother wrapped one hand around her wrist, tight enough to make the bones grind together. Angelica had only ever slapped her once and, frankly, Kat had probably deserved it. She'd been sixteen and had called her mother a bitch. And even if she was, Kat shouldn't have said it to her face.

Of course, Angelica had gotten her revenge. A month in a "mental health rehabilitation clinic" hadn't been far behind.

Now Kat was moving to Philadelphia and there was nothing her mother could do about it. It made her want to dance naked in the streets.

Or look up two very handsome men in Philadelphia.

She stopped by her mother's side and twisted her arm until Angelica released her. "I'll be gone by the end of the week." She took a few more steps to the door before she turned and smiled back at her dad. "Thank you, Dad. I appreciate your understanding." Another level glance at Angelica. "Have a good day, Mother."

Then she walked out the door, leaving Angelica standing in the middle of her dad's study with a dumbstruck expression.

Kat smiled all the way out the front door.

Tristan looked up from his desk, where he'd been making notes, as Adam walked into the room.

He motioned for Adam to sit while he continued to hold his cell to his ear.

"You're sure?" Tristan paused then laughed, and Adam was pretty sure the gruff voice on the other end of the line had just called Tristan a "fucker."

"Yeah, I know." Tristan laughed. "Hey, I appreciate this, man. That case of Macallan is already on its way."

Tristan didn't bother with a goodbye, and Adam knew he must've been talking to Mike Polanski, a former Ranger who now worked for the Boston PD. Mike occasionally provided them with backup when they needed an extra man in the northeast. And he was the only person Adam knew who took some of his payment in good whiskey.

Tristan dropped his phone onto his desk, his grin triumphant.

Adam shook his head. "You look like the lion who just brought down a zebra."

"No zebra. This prey is much prettier."

Shit. "Oh yeah? Finally got the blonde cop to say yes?"

Tristan leaned back in his chair, still smiling. "Wrong blonde. But you know that."

Adam tried not to roll his eyes but lost the battle.

Tristan's grin got wider.

"Just spit it out." Adam dropped into the chair opposite Tristan's desk and used two fingers to rub at the sudden pounding in his temple. "I know you're dying to tell me."

Tristan leaned back in his chair and took a good, long look at Adam. "But you're not all that interested in hearing what I've got to say. Why is that?"

Adam didn't see any sense in lying. "Because I don't think this is going to end the way you want it to."

Tristan's gaze narrowed. "And how do you think I see this ending?"

"With a happily ever after."

Tristan's surprise plainly showed on his face, and Adam wanted to go back to the second he'd walked through the door and do everything differently.

God damn, he should've kept his mouth shut.

He'd watched Tristan go through this before. His best friend had a serious case of white-knight syndrome. And Katrina had enough baggage to fill the cargo hold of an oil tanker.

Adam knew just how much work a woman with emotional problems could be, especially one you cared about. He'd dealt with one his entire life. And he'd sworn to himself he wasn't going to put up with that ever again. Which was why all of his previous relationships with women had been meaningless.

Did that make him a dick? Probably. Did he care? Not really.

That old chestnut "bros before hos" might be politically incorrect but the sentiment behind it was dead-on. Adam wasn't stupid enough to think Tristan would never find a woman to marry and settle down with. The guy still believed in love.

And when Tristan found the woman he thought was the one, Adam would wish him well and step the hell out of the way.

But Adam didn't think Kat was the right woman.

Tristan's gaze narrowed. "And who says that's what

I'm looking for?"

Adam reined in the urge to throttle Tristan and settled for a casual shrug. He knew Tristan wasn't going to listen to him. Tris was too good at rationalization. He'd have an answer for every argument Adam came up with, so Adam had decided he'd let this one play out.

"So, was that Mike?"

"You know it was." Tristan leaned forward in his chair. "But you're not getting off that easy. What makes you think I'm looking to settle down and get married after one night with the woman?"

Well, shit. Tristan had his Commanding Officer face on now.

And that just put Adam's back up.

"Because I know you, Tris. All right? She's just your type."

"And what type is that?"

Fine. Might as well go all in. He crossed his arms over his chest and planted his feet. "Damaged. The kind who need you to fix them. And you just can't resist a challenge."

Tristan's eyebrows raised. "So you're telling me you aren't attracted to her?"

Adam had to restrain the urge to roll his eyes again. "Sure. She's a beauty. Hell, I'll even admit that she intrigues me, but then smart women usually do."

But this one had the potential to do a number on Tristan because of his feelings for her, and Adam had been covering Tristan's back for years.

"So you don't want to see her again?"

Adam's heart began to beat just a little faster at

Tristan's question, but he refused to analyze why at the moment.

"I never said that. Know what? Just forget I said anything. I'm a fucking pessimist. You know that. So what'd Mike want?"

Adam wasn't sure Tristan would let him off the hook that easily.

And he knew he was in big trouble when Tristan began to smile.

"She's coming to Philadelphia tomorrow to look at apartments."

Well, shit.

He saw Tristan's lips quirk and Adam knew he hadn't been able to hide his surprise.

"So she's following through," he said. "Still a long way from actually moving here."

Tristan's grin widened. "She handed in her resignation at the firm earlier this week."

And it just got better. "Good for her. Didn't sound like she enjoyed her job much."

Tristan's grin held. "She's got a reservation at Haven Hotel starting Friday night. Got any plans for the weekend?"

Tristan watched Adam shake his head, his friend's apprehension plain as day on his face.

For the past two weeks, Adam had avoided talking about Kat and the night they'd spent together in Boston. And when Tristan said avoided, he meant wouldn't go there unless he had a gun pointed at his head and even then he'd have to think about it.

Tristan knew Adam's reasons. Hell, he even understood,

for the most part. That didn't mean he was going to cut Adam any slack this time.

Because Tristan knew. After one night, he could say it with absolute certainty.

She was theirs.

Adam stared at him through narrowed eyes, as if he was measuring Tristan for a straitjacket.

"Have you considered the fact that the woman might not want to see us?" Adam's tone held no inflection. "It's not like she didn't slink out of the room the next morning like she'd committed a felony."

"Is that why you haven't mentioned her all week?

Feeling a little brushed off?"

Adam stared back. "Maybe I'm not looking to repeat the same mistake."

Tristan didn't believe that for a second. Kat had not been a mistake. Sure, the woman had baggage but who didn't these days? Hell, Adam kept his close to the chest but he still had it and it was clouding his judgment now.

"Bullshit." Tristan called him on it. "You felt it too.

She's different."

"Jesus, Tris..." Adam started shaking his head. "What the fuck's gotten into you? One night with her and you're ready to get married? Have you lost your mind?"

Good question. One he couldn't answer. He could only say he'd never had a connection to a woman like the one he'd experienced with Kat.

She needed them. She just didn't know it yet.

And they needed her.

"Pretty sure I still have all my faculties. You're just gonna have to trust me on this one, buddy." Adam shook his head but didn't say anything else.

Tristan knew Adam would come around.

And if he didn't...

Tristan dismissed it out of hand. They'd stick this out together, just as they had everything else. Adam would realize Tristan was right. Because Tristan wouldn't allow himself to be wrong.

"So do you have plans for Friday?" Tristan asked.

Adam stared at him, shaking his head. "You're serious?"

"As a heart attack."

"Christ..." Another heavy sigh before Adam sprawled back into the chair. "I guess I'm following you to Haven." Tristan tried not to smile in triumph, and he knew he had to give Adam an out, if he really wanted one.

"That wasn't a command. You know that, right?" Tristan stared straight into Adam's eyes. "You don't have to come with me."

It was Adam's turn to grin, but there was a hard edge to it. "Of course it wasn't. I don't take orders anymore. Not from anyone."

A reminder that when they'd started their company, it had been based on a true partnership. Neither of them could pull rank over the other.

Still, Tristan knew he was right about Kat. He'd just have to wait for Adam to come to that same realization.

"Then you're free to tell me to fuck off."

Adam mulled that over and Tristan knew he was seriously considering letting Tristan go himself. Then Adam shook his head.

"*Shit.* I'll be there. Does she know she's got a date?"

"Not yet."

"So this is a sneak attack?"

"I prefer to think of it as a welcome surprise."

Adam's eyes closed for a brief second. "Of course you do. So what's the strategy?"

Tristan grinned. "Make her realize how much she missed us."

7

Kat sighed as she sank into the secluded booth in Haven Hotel's swanky bar.

She'd been on her feet more today than she'd been in weeks. She'd seen five apartments, six condos, and two town houses in the space of eight hours. She wanted to slip her shoes off but was afraid she might not get them on again.

Yes, she could've gone to her room and had dinner delivered. Instead, she'd told herself not to be a hermit.

Of course, she was still eating alone, but she wasn't sitting alone in her room. What the distinction was... Well, she wasn't going to dwell on that.

After she'd ordered a burger and fries, calories be damned, she'd pulled out her phone and started going through her texts. Apparently being out of touch for most of the day was cause for multiple calls and texts from her mother and several voice messages from the office, all questions about cases. None of which couldn't wait until Monday when she was back in the office for the final week.

She still experienced a little chill when she thought about it.

What if she failed? What if she couldn't hack it alone?

What if she really wasn't that good of a lawyer?

No. Just...no.

That voice of doubt...that was her mother and she'd be damned if she let that woman screw with her life any more than she already had.

With a sigh, she stuck her phone back in her purse and grabbed her tablet. One glance at her overflowing email inbox and she seriously considered tossing both her phone and her tablet in the nearest trashcan.

One more week.

Those few words had become her mantra today every time her phone vibrated with another call or text from her mother. Once she moved, she fully expected her mother to cut her off completely.

The silence would be blissful.

Right now, Angelica Riley was in full Mommy Dearest mode, ranting about how ungrateful she was, how much of a mistake Kat was making, and how she'd never make it on her own.

All of which made her more determined to find a place to live and get the hell out of Boston.

Luckily, she was pretty sure she'd found the perfect condo in Germantown. It actually cost less than she was paying for her apartment in Boston, and it had more square footage, including three bedrooms. More than enough space for her home office. Win-win.

Just more empty space to rattle around in alone.

Damn, she wished her inner pessimist would shut the hell up.

With that, she dug her way into email hell. When her dinner arrived, she gave her server a brief, distracted smile and continued reading.

By the time she'd gotten through nearly two hundred emails, she'd almost finished her burger and was actually thinking about dessert— "Hello, Kat. Can we sit?" *Oh my god, that voice.*

Luckily, she didn't have food in her mouth. She was afraid she might've choked on it.

As it was, she was worried she might hyperventilate.

Tristan and Adam stood at the opening to her booth.

Tristan wore an easy smile that went well with the jeans and chest-clinging Henley. Adam... Holy hell, Adam looked amazing in well-worn jeans and a black long-sleeved t-shirt. Casual had never looked so good on any men before.

She realized her mouth was hanging open and shut it immediately as heat pooled in her gut.

Then, because neither man said anything, she had to ask, "What are you doing here?"

Tristan's smile widened into a grin that she tried not to let fluster her. "I think you know what we're doing here, Kat."

He didn't wait for her response this time. Instead, he slipped into the booth on the opposite side of her and kept sliding around the circular table until he sat only inches from her. Adam followed, sitting directly opposite her.

"So, did you have a productive day?"

A productive day? Her whirling brain tried to make sense of Tristan's question while her body responded to his proximity. Her nipples tightened into points, her lungs had to work harder, and her sex clenched.

Damn it.

When she finally processed his question, her eyes narrowed. "I don't see how that's any of your business. And how exactly did you know I'd be here?"

Tristan continued to grin. "Did you find an apartment?"

Heat flashed through her even though she knew that question should've made him look like a crazy stalker. The only person who knew she was apartment hunting was Erik. How had Tristan found out? Had he talked to Erik? Why?

She realized her mouth was hanging open again and quickly closed it. What the hell was going on?

Adam's expression gave her nothing more to go on. He looked...stoic. Maybe resigned was a better word. As if he didn't want to be here but had agreed to accompany Tristan, who continued to smile and wait for her response.

"Tristan, why are you here?"

He cocked an eyebrow at her. "Dessert?" *Oh.*

Her stomach fluttered and heat raced through her veins. She understood the implication behind that single word, and immediately her brain conjured images of the three of them in that bed in Boston.

Which was exactly what he'd wanted.

Surprisingly, excitement began to bleed through her confusion, intensifying her reaction. Her desire.

Which was so not fair because they knew exactly what they did to her.

"I'm not sure they have what you're looking for here."

"Oh, you'd be surprised what they serve in this hotel."

Tristan's tone shook her to her core. What was it about

this man that pressed her buttons and made her want to strip off all his clothes and jump him right here?

Two weeks ago, she never would have imagined anyone could make her feel like this. Didn't believe anyone could make her want to exchange sexual banter. She didn't know how to do it gracefully, so she simply didn't do it. And, truthfully, she'd never had the opportunity to practice.

Tristan tempted her to do so much she'd never done before.

And then there was Adam...

He sat across from her, arms on the table as if he were completely at ease. But those blue eyes burned with an intensity she feared might incinerate her.

"Maybe I'm not interested in dessert." *Liar, liar, pants on fire.* "I was about to pay my bill and head back to my room. It's been a long day."

Totally the truth. And yet... She wanted them to tell her to stay. Wanted them to *coax* her to stay.

Should she bat her eyes at them? What the hell did that mean anyway? She was afraid she'd look like she had something in her eye.

Should she attempt sexual innuendo? What if she said something stupid or, worse yet, inappropriate? How embarrassing would that be?

No more embarrassing than a twenty-five-year-old woman who doesn't know how to flirt.

Why were they here? Why were they chasing *her*? Of all people, why a woman who'd nearly passed out on them while having a panic attack then snuck out of their bed the next morning like a college girl after a drunken frat party?

"I guarantee we can make your night much more plea-surable," Tristan said.

Oh god. Yes, please.

She so wanted what he was offering. Wanted to reach out and take it with both hands.

Tristan seemed to truly desire her. And Adam... Adam made her want to be the kind of woman he would want.

Someone sexy and fearless and confident.

And why couldn't that be her? She was making a new start. What could it hurt to flirt with these men? To share another night like the one before? She'd enjoyed the hell out of that experience.

Of course, she'd thought that night was the end of their brief relationship. A one-night stand she'd look back on as the start of her independence.

Now Tristan was offering her more than one night.

And she wanted it.

But...was Adam offering the same?

His expression showed nothing, but if she had to guess, she'd say he wasn't all that thrilled to be here. Were they a package deal?

"Why?"

She'd tried to think of a witty comeback to Tristan's offer, but it all boiled down to this one question. Because she truly didn't understand why these men had singled her out.

There was absolutely nothing special about her. Sure, she might have a little more money than the next blonde on their list, but Tristan and Adam weren't hurting financially. She had nothing to offer them other than her sparkling personal-ity, which didn't really sparkle. In fact, she could be a royal bitch. Cold, aloof, and no fun at all. Rigid and unadventurous.

Unless you counted that one night she'd spent with them. Was that person who they were looking for? Could she be that person again?

Across the table, Adam shook his head and turned away, his frustration evident. His reaction confounded her.

Why was he here if she frustrated him?

Then Tristan leaned closer, forcing her attention to turn to him.

"Because I love making you lose control." His voice had dropped almost to a whisper and she had to listen closely to hear him. "Because I love the way you cry out when you come. Because I love watching you suck Adam off. And I know how much you enjoyed that night. You want more and I don't want you to be afraid to admit it.

Come on, Kat. Be adventurous."

Holy hell. She shivered, though she wasn't cold.

No, in the space of a few seconds, Tristan had managed to make her wet and hot and horny as all hell.

She wanted to take what he was offering. Wanted to be that adventurous woman he thought she could be. Wanted to be the type of woman who flirted with two men and left with them to find a bed where they'd spend the night making each other come.

All she had to do was say yes and she knew they'd give it to her.

She swallowed down doubt and said exactly what she was thinking. "You make me want that too."

Tristan smiled like the proverbial cat who caught the

canary, dark eyes narrowing. "Then take us up to your room."

She froze. Could it really be that simple?

"Jesus, Tris. Back off and give the woman a little breathing room."

She blinked and turned to find Adam watching her, his gaze intensely focused. She wanted to squirm, but she also saw a challenge in his eyes.

Before she'd met them, she never would've accepted that challenge.

Come on, you idiot. Be brave. Have fun. At least for one more night.

Another night like the one in Boston, which she hadn't been able to stop thinking about for the past two weeks. "I'm uprooting my entire life in the next few weeks. A new home, a new job." She glanced between the men, making sure they were both listening. And they were, intensely so. "I have no time in my life right now for a relationship."

"Who said anything about a relationship?" Adam's gaze had narrowed, and his expression clearly stated he had no interest in a relationship.

"So neither of you are looking for anything more than sex?"

She flashed a glance at Tristan but all she could see was his desire. It made her wish she had buttons to undo.

"If that's how you want to handle this," Tristan shrugged, "then yeah, it's just sex."

Adam leaned back against the plush cushion, now looking totally at ease, as if he'd gotten exactly what he wanted. A simple sexual affair.

Since this was her first affair, she didn't want to misinterpret anything or leave something to chance. If that made her a control freak...Well, it wouldn't be the worst thing people had called her.

She'd had "frigid bitch" thrown at her a few times. It'd probably been true at that moment. Right now, though, she didn't feel frigid. In fact, she felt damn close to boiling over.

If she allowed herself to be ruled by her libido, it could have catastrophic consequences. Her previous engagement to her brother's best friend had ended in disaster because she'd allowed herself to think with her heart and not her head. Logically, she should've known it would never work with Keegan.

But what Adam and Tristan were offering her... What could be the harm if she knew going in that there was an expiration date to the relationship?

"And is that okay with you, Tristan?"

Tristan's grin never faltered. "I promise to make it the best damn affair you've ever had."

Take what they're offering. Go ahead. You know you want to.

She took a deep breath. "Just to make sure we're on the same page, we're talking solely about sex, correct? This doesn't involve dating or a relationship. Any of the parties involved can nullify the arrangement at any time without repercussions from either of the other two parties."

As she spoke, Tristan's grin widened and even Adam's lips curved at the corners.

She knew she sounded like a lawyer, but that's exactly what she was. Better they know what they were in for before they started down this path.

"Will you talk to me in bed like that, sweetheart?"

Tristan shook his head. "'Cause I gotta say, your lawyer act is making me horny."

Her cheeks flamed and she wanted to curse him but figured it would only make him more determined to tease her. And she just didn't know how to respond to that.

And boy, aren't you just a stick in the mud?

What the hell did these two men see in her? She couldn't help wondering if this was some elaborate ruse. A game they were playing with her.

Who could get the frigid lawyer to crack first? Then they'd exchange bet money and laugh about how gullible she was.

Okay, wow. She really needed to lay off the '80s teen movies on Netflix.

Was it so hard to believe that these two men could simply be attracted to her?

"Kat?"

Adam's quiet question brought her attention back to the men. Her men, if she wanted them. For however long it might last.

She took a deep breath.

"Yes."

Adam felt triumph bleed through him as Kat gave the answer Tristan had been sure she'd give.

Adam hadn't been so sure she'd agree up until the second she said the word.

Now he tried to put that feeling in check.

Yes, he wanted Kat. Yes, he wanted to take her to bed again.

But this wasn't his conquest. This was Tristan's. Adam was only here to cover Tristan's back.

And Kat's obvious reluctance to begin an actual relationship made it even more imperative for Adam to be here.

He knew Tristan. He knew what Tristan wanted from this woman, even if he wouldn't admit it. And he knew damn well Tristan wasn't going to get what he wanted.

Because Adam had had a front row seat to the hell Tristan had in store if he fell for a woman who couldn't love him the way he wanted her to.

But if having Tristan's back meant bedding this woman, he'd make the most of it.

Heartless? Maybe. Right thing to do? Absolutely.

"So...what now?"

The hint of uneasiness in her voice pulled him out of his thoughts, and he took another good look at her.

Her gaze bounced back and forth between him and Tristan, but it lingered longer on Tristan, Adam thought. As if she was afraid of Adam. Or wary of him. Either way, he didn't like it.

When her gaze finally stuck on Tristan and held, Adam switched his focus to Tristan. Who looked perfectly at ease, smiling as if he'd just won the lottery.

"Now, we can either go up to your room, where Adam and I can get you naked and make you scream. Or we can stay and listen to the band for a while. I've seen them before. They're good."

Kat's gaze narrowed. "That sounds suspiciously like a date to me."

Tristan's smile never faltered. "Think of it as foreplay.

Besides, who says we're not going to touch you while we're here?

Kat immediately glanced at the opening to the booth.

Adam followed her gaze, trying to see the room as she might.

Since it was Friday, there were at least a hundred people in the room, either at the bar, in the booths, or at small tables in front of the stage. From their vantage point, Adam realized it would be difficult for anyone to see into the booth unless they were standing right in front of it.

With the low lighting and long skirt on the table, no one would be able to see what they were doing below the table. As if the owners of the hotel had made sure their guests could indulge in illicit activities.

And since Adam knew the owners, he had no doubt that's exactly what they'd been after.

Kat's gaze swung back to Tristan's, and now Adam thought he noticed a hint of fatigue in her expression. He had the insanely stupid urge to wrap her in a blanket and tuck her into bed.

Shit. That was a slippery slope. If there was anything good he'd learned about relationships from his parents, it was that to survive, both individuals needed to be stable enough to hold up their end. When one person couldn't withstand the strain, both would buckle and suck everyone in the immediate vicinity down with them.

Kat wasn't stable. She hid it well but they'd seen how screwed up her foundation was beneath the outward calm at her parents' party.

Tristan didn't need that kind of misery, and Adam sure as hell wasn't going to put up with it. Never again. He'd thought Tristan would get her out of his system after he'd slept with her. Thought they'd move on to a woman who had her shit together and wasn't looking for more than an orgasm or three and bragging rights to spending a night with two men.

Then he realized this was the perfect way to show Tristan how unstable Kat was and why it would be foolish to start any kind of relationship with her. When she ran again after he and Tristan truly put her between them, it'd prove Adam's point without turning him into the bad guy.

Adam slid out of the booth, drawing her startled gaze back to him. Wide-eyed, she watched as he slid back into the booth next to her. For a brief second, he wondered if she was going to move or if he was going to need to give her a push.

A millisecond before he touched her, she shifted away. And found herself that much closer to Tristan, who didn't give an inch.

Nowhere to go, babe. Now what?

Taking a couple of deep breaths, she turned to Tristan. "I'm not exactly sure what you think we can do in this booth."

Tristan's grin turned wicked. "Come closer and let me show you."

She didn't move right away, and Adam couldn't tell if she was playing hard to get or if she was going to push him out of the booth so she could get away from them.

She doesn't have a clue how to play hard to get.

A second later, her straight little nose pointed into the air in a show of backbone. "And if I say no?"

"You haven't yet," Adam pointed out, prodding just a little.

She turned toward him. "No, I haven't."

She faced Adam directly, and he was surprised to see a little fire in her eyes. A little challenge.

He didn't want to be happy about that. But he was.

All right, sweetheart. You want a challenge? You got one.

Sliding closer on the circular bench, he pressed against her side, let his thigh and arm rub against hers. Then, beneath the table, he put his hand on her knee.

She stiffened but didn't move away and never broke eye contact. Those blue eyes looked shadowed in the low light, and he lifted his free hand to stroke his fingers over her cheekbone before he realized he'd done it.

Not a fucking date, remember? It was just fucking.

With that thought in mind, he slid the hand on her thigh higher until he reached her hip. Her stillness intrigued him. Made him remember bits and pieces of a childhood he'd pretty much tried to block out. He and his two younger sisters had managed to come through without physical scars, so why dwell on the past?

Kat appeared to be holding her breath, waiting for him. Too bad for her, he held a master's degree in the fine art of waiting.

"Spread your legs a little, Kat." He leaned just a little closer, watched her eyes widen just a little more. "Let's see how much you can take without begging us to take you up to your room and fuck you."

Heat flushed her cheeks as his finger finally hit their mark. The cotton fabric of her pants felt silky soft against his fingertips. And warm.

He leaned in, his mouth inches from her ear. "I'm going to make you come while you sit here."

Her lips parted and her eyes widened but she didn't move. Instead, she said, "I'm not sure that's possible."

As Adam continued to stroke her thigh, Tristan leaned in to speak in Kat's other ear.

"Anything's possible. But if you're not comfortable, just say the word."

Kat never looked away from Adam's eyes. "I think I shouldn't have to take whatever test Adam is giving."

Adam's lips curled in a grin. There was another spark of that fire he'd noticed before. He didn't want to like it.

"Don't think of it as a test you have to pass," Adam said. "Think of it as a test of your restraint."

Her eyebrows rose slightly. "I think I have a pretty decent handle on my restraint. I haven't smacked you yet, have I?"

Tristan's low laugh made Adam pull away with a grin.

"No, you haven't. So I guess I shouldn't push my luck."

She drew in a slightly shaky breath when his hand finally broke contact with her thigh.

"So you decided to make the move to Philly."

Tristan's question distracted her from the arm he draped around her shoulders as he leaned into the red-velvet back-rest. He made it look like the most natural thing in the world. And for Tristan, it was.

Tristan wasn't afraid to give hugs to guys or girls, young or old. He genuinely liked people, at least those who were likable, and people responded to that.

Of course, Kat didn't look completely comfortable. She looked...as if she didn't know how to accept that kind of easy affection.

Adam had been the same damn way when he'd met Tristan. The bastard had worn him down with time.

"Why Philadelphia?" Adam prompted, though he was pretty sure he knew the answer.

"My brother. I'm going to be working with Erik, but I'll be branching out eventually. I hope to do more defense work, particularly with juveniles."

Huh. He would've figured she'd want to continue corporate work.

"So did you find a place to live?" Tristan's gaze narrowed. "Where is it?"

"Germantown."

Tristan visibly relaxed. "Decent place."

Amazingly, Adam was happy to hear that because *he'd* been worried about her as well. Which was ridiculous. Why the hell did he care where she lived?

"It was number ten on my list of places to see, and I knew as soon as I walked in that it was exactly what I wanted."

"So are you renting or buying?"

Tristan continued to draw her out while Adam tried not to show that he was watching her every move. He'd always been good at reading people. Better than Tristan. Tristan could get anyone to talk to him because he was genuinely interested in what they had to say. Adam couldn't be bothered to fake it because most people he talked to were assholes and he had a low asshole-tolerance level.

But he was damn good at detecting what people hid behind their smiles.

She was hiding something. He just didn't know what.

As the band arrived to start the set, Tristan and Kat fell silent and turned their attention to the stage. Adam continued to study her.

She'd relaxed a bit, wasn't sitting as stiffly as she had before.

He made no attempt to hide his examination, and as the band began its third song, she turned to face him.

"Are you all right?" she asked.

He barely heard her over the band. And when he'd made sense of what she'd said, he took a moment before answering.

Then he leaned in to speak directly into her ear. "I'm sitting in the dark with a beautiful woman. Why wouldn't I be okay?"

Her gaze narrowed. "You look...worried."

His surprise must have shown on his face because her lips quirked into a smile that made his pulse beat just a little bit faster.

"And you look nervous. Why is that?"

She held his gaze and lied with no hint of a tell. "I'm not nervous. It's been a long day. My feet hurt. I have at least fifty emails that need a response by tomorrow morning and I know I'm not going to get to them tonight."

He admired the fact that she didn't let him push her around, but that didn't mean he was going to cut her any slack.

"Maybe we should head up to your room now. Since you're tired. The beds in this place are more than big enough for three."

She blinked and her lips parted to suck in air. Amazingly, she held his gaze. "And do you know that from personal experience?"

His lips curved. "Yes. Is that the answer you wanted?"

She shook her head. "The only answer I want is the truth."

"Does it bother you that Tristan and I have been here before?"

That perfect little nose rose higher in the air. "Why should it? I told you I'm not looking for a relationship." She sucked in a breath. "But the sex was good and I see no reason why we can't have more."

Out of the corner of his eye, Adam saw Tristan's attention focus on him. Trying to figure out what Adam was up to.

Frankly, he wasn't sure. Adam had to hand it to her. She put on a brave face. Maybe the mouse had more of a backbone than he gave her credit for.

And what would that matter?

It shouldn't. It didn't. It was simply an interesting fact.

One he didn't need to dwell on.

Because she was willing and he was horny.

His attraction to her had nothing to do with her personality. She was beautiful and a challenge. And he loved a challenge.

And Tristan would realize soon enough that this woman was definitely not "The One."

In the meantime, why not sit back and enjoy the ride?

With their gazes locked, he put his hand on her thigh again. Lower this time, closer to her knee. Her thighs clenched.

"That night was only an appetizer, Kat." Adam leaned forward until only inches separated their lips. "Are you ready for the full buffet?"

Humor lit in the depths of her eyes and her smile almost caught him off guard. Almost.

"Do you say that to all the girls? Because if you do, I'm thinking you might be lying about all your conquests."

Tristan tried to cover his laughter with a cough but didn't have much luck.

Even Adam could admit it'd been a pretty cheesy line.

But he was surprised she'd called him on it.

"I'm not lying about my experience, sweetheart. And I'm not going to be satisfied with only your mouth this time."

Her breathing became more ragged by the second as he dragged his hand up her thigh. And when he finally reached his destination, he made sure she was staring at him when he dipped his fingers between her legs and pressed against her clit.

She sucked in a harsh gasp, her hands curling into fists on the table.

"Are you wet already? Hell, we didn't even get to the good stuff yet. Do you think I can make you come just like this? With all these people around?"

Her gaze darted away to look out over the small slice of crowd she could see through the opening of the booth again. None of them were looking in their direction.

He watched her throat move as she swallowed then waited for her to turn to face him again.

"Do you think you'll be able to keep from crying out when you come?"

She was breathing so hard now, her breasts quivered beneath her blouse. He wondered what she'd do if he leaned forward to suck at her exposed neck.

As he continued to stroke his fingers over the fabric

covering her sex, he gripped her chin with his free hand and held her still.

Then he kissed her.

He tried to keep it light but the second his lips touched hers, his brain short-circuited. Something about the taste of her drew him in, made him immediately want more.

He still heard the band in the background, but the soft sound she made under her breath hit him like a concussive grenade.

Damn it. He wasn't supposed to be affected like this.

And yet he couldn't help himself.

He sank into that kiss like he'd jumped into the ocean with cement boots. But he wasn't going down alone.

His hand between her legs continued to torment, rubbing and tweaking her clit until her legs spread farther apart to give him more access.

The need to have her completely under his control hit him like the broadside of a bus. He wanted to lift her onto his lap, open his jeans, and fuck her right there.

Holy hell.

He reared back, breaking the kiss and trying to stomp down the lust.

"I think it's time to retire to somewhere more private."

Tristan's quiet voice rang in Adam's ear, and he stole a quick glance at his friend. Tristan had lost his smile. Then he looked down at Kat.

She looked as dazed as he felt.

He wanted to pump his fist in the air. He'd ruffled her feathers, made her aware of the power he had over her. He wanted to see her looking just like this when he had her on her back and was pumping his cock into her as hard as she could take it.

Okay, now was probably a good time to stop and get himself back under control. Yes, he was going to walk out of here with a hard-on. And no, he didn't give a shit. He only wanted to get inside Kat.

Tristan slid out of the booth then held out his hand to help Kat. She took a second to look down at herself before taking Tristan's hand.

She didn't look back to see if Adam followed, and that bothered him enough that he caught up to her side and put a hand low on her back. He wanted to let it slip farther, to caress her ass, but he didn't want anyone else to look at her ass.

Which was pretty damn stupid.

Tristan led them out of the bar and into a nearby alcove where there was a single elevator. There was no one around and they only had to wait a few seconds before the bell dinged and the doors opened.

No one emerged and they stepped into the empty box.

The second the doors closed, Tristan crowded Kat against the back wall and kissed her. Adam moved away so he could see better.

Tristan kissed her like a man possessed. He used both hands to cup her face then held her there and devoured her. And Kat let him. Her hands rose to circle his wrists but she didn't push him away. She simply held on.

Watching Tristan kiss her sobered Adam somewhat. Adam had never seen Tristan act like this with anyone. And Adam had seen Tristan kiss a hell of a lot of women.

What was it about this one?

Adam tried to look at her with a critical eye, but all he saw was the way she responded to Tristan.

Her arms wound around his shoulders, holding him closer. When Adam had kissed her, she'd seemed almost afraid to respond. Maybe because he'd caught her off guard. *And maybe she's just not that into you.*

He'd laugh at himself if he thought he was funny. But was it true? And did he want to know if it was?

Tristan broke away just as the elevator began to slow.

Staring down at Kat, he smiled into her eyes.

"Where's your room, sweetheart? It's time to take this private."

Kate took a deep breath, never taking her eyes off Tristan. "706."

Her voice had a husky quality that made Adam's cock twitch in response. Christ, this had clusterfuck written all over it.

Tristan wrapped his arm around her shoulders and urged her toward the hall. As they turned right, Kat looked directly at him, still leaning against the back of the elevator, and raised an eyebrow at him.

A reluctant smile tugged at his lips. He didn't want to like her. She was definite bad news. And yet...

He pushed off the wall and followed.

8

Kat's stomach was in knots as Tristan guided her down the hallway to her room.

She actually felt more nervous now than she had the last time she'd found herself in this situation. Which was ridiculous.

And it wasn't exactly nerves. She felt almost...giddy. Like a teenager who'd landed the star quarterback *and* the wide receiver as her date for the prom.

And one thought kept going through her head.

They came after me.

She'd been convinced their one night together was going to be the extent of their interaction. Hell, she'd slunk away the next morning like she'd been ashamed of what had happened.

She hadn't been ashamed. Not one bit. But she'd woken up with Tristan curled around her and—

She'd wanted to stay. She'd known she couldn't. And she hadn't known how to handle the morning-after goodbye.

So she'd run, figuring she'd never see them again unless

they bumped into one another accidentally, like at a bar or a restaurant. Which presumed she'd actually *be* at a restaurant or bar.

She knew no one in Philadelphia and had expected to spend a lot of time by herself for the first few months after her move. And she'd been okay with that because it wouldn't have been much different than her life in Boston.

Then Tristan and Adam had appeared at her table. And she'd wanted to pump her fist in the air and do a little victory dance. Close on the heels of that, she wondered what they wanted from her.

Stealing a glance at Tristan now, she easily read the desire on his face. He wanted her.

She wished she had the backbone to ask why. She wished she could relax against him and put her arm around his waist without feeling awkward.

Instead, she walked beside him, stiff and awkward.

As they reached her door, she gave a little thank you to the powers that be that there was no one in the hall. She probably would've turned five shades of red.

Which was ridiculous. She was a grown woman. What she did in private should be of no business to anyone but herself.

Still, she couldn't help but feel she was doing something illicit. Forbidden. And yes, that added to the thrill, didn't it?

Was that why Tristan and Adam did it? For the thrill?

Stealing a glance over her shoulder, she caught sight of Adam following close behind.

His expression was harder to read than Tristan's. No surprise there. She'd already figured out that he rarely showed his emotions. He seemed to be a master at keeping them under wraps. Tristan had no qualms showing her exactly how he felt.

Adam intrigued her. Tristan made her want things she shouldn't. Something more than just sex.

Oh, the sex had been great. At least, she'd thought it had been. But it'd been one night and she'd never expected to see them again. At least, not like this.

She'd thought she'd been a conquest, another notch on their belts. And she'd been okay with that.

She wasn't in the market for a long-term relationship. Not now. Maybe not ever. And Tristan and Adam certainly didn't seem like the kind of men who wanted a woman hanging on them all the time.

Not that she would but—

"Kat? Are you sure you want us to come in with you?"

She blinked and realized they stood at the door to her room. It took a few seconds for Tristan's quiet question to sink in, and when it did, she turned to face him.

Her head tilted to the side. "Do you *want* to come in?"

Tristan's smile had the ability to make butterflies take wing in her stomach. Adam... Well, he wasn't smiling but just a glance from him was enough to make her blood boil.

Please come in.

"I do." Tristan turned to Adam and so did she.

Adam shrugged. "Of course I do." His tone suggested she shouldn't have any doubt about his answer.

Her lips curved into an actual smile, and Adam's gaze narrowed as he stared at her. He looked almost shocked.

Nice to know she had the power to knock him back a step. It made her feel more in control.

Retrieving the keycard from her pants pocket, she slid it

into the door then pushed it open and kept walking through to the small sitting area in front of the windows.

She'd booked a suite, not because she'd expected to be entertaining but because it was all the hotel had available when she'd called.

Now she was grateful for the extra room. These two men took up so much space.

She found she liked that about them, liked that they were strong, muscular.

She also liked how they kept their focus on her. They made her feel special.

"Would you like another drink—oh!"

Tristan had crossed the room in three long strides and covered her mouth again with his. And this kiss was nothing like the others.

It was almost as if he'd given himself permission to let go. So she gave herself up to him.

Wrapping her arms around his neck, she pressed herself against him and let him kiss her. He barely gave her the chance to breathe as he licked his way into her mouth, urging her to kiss him back just as recklessly.

With her eyes closed, she did. Gave herself permission to be the woman who took this kiss and responded to it.

Sinking her hands into the short, dark hair at the back of his head, she pressed him closer, smashed their lips together, and slid her tongue against his in a way she'd never kissed a man before.

And Tristan let her. His hands slid down her sides to her hips, his fingers gripping her hard. She was surprised to find she liked the slight pain. It made her feel connected to him in a way she couldn't explain. Didn't want to explain.

With her eyes closed, Tristan's desire for her felt like a physical force that wrapped around her, enclosed her in a place where they were all that existed.

Until Adam came up behind her and put his hands on her back.

She moaned into Tristan's mouth, fingers clenching in his hair as Adam pulled her shirt from the waistband of her pants then slid his hands beneath the fabric. His hands slid up from her waist, skin against warm skin, then back down, the firm caress making her shiver. On his next upward stroke, he unhooked her bra with one hand.

Tristan pulled away abruptly, leaving her gasping. Taking two steps back, he watched as Adam worked his hands under her now-loose bra and cupped her breasts.

"I think it's only fair that Adam gets to lead this time, don't you think? He's going to take your clothes off so I can see how beautiful you are. I didn't get to see enough last time. Is that okay, Kat?"

Already drowning in sensation, she barely understood Tristan's words. But she understood enough to know he wanted an answer. So she nodded and he smiled.

Good god, when that man smiled she wanted to give him anything he asked for.

And when Adam began to take off her clothes, she couldn't wait to be naked. She wanted Tristan to see her. Wanted Adam to think she was beautiful too. Because when Adam put his hands on her, it almost felt like he worshipped her.

Her gaze locked with Tristan's, she felt Adam work her blouse up her sides.

And when Adam told her to raise her arms, she obeyed

without hesitation. He flipped the blouse over her head in seconds and immediately pushed the bra off her shoulders. She barely had time to feel the air brush against her naked skin before Adam wrapped his arms around her from behind and covered her breasts with his hands, fingers tweaking her nipples, making her eyelids flutter closed for several seconds.

When she opened them again, Tristan had settled on the couch, his gaze still locked onto her. Watching Adam undress her.

Now Adam's hands fell to her pants. He'd already realized they fastened at the side instead of the front and the button gave with little resistance. The zipper fell seconds later.

Then Adam caught the waistbands of her pants and her underwear with his thumbs and shoved them over her ass and down her thighs.

Leaving her in pumps. And completely unattractive knee-high black stockings.

"Go ahead, babe." Adam apparently read her mind. Even though she couldn't see him, she swore she heard his smile in his voice. "Bend over and take them off."

Not thinking, she bent at the waist...and felt Adam's erection pressing through his jeans against her bare ass.

Oh god.

Her eyes closed as she quickly got rid of her shoes and stockings, imagining the scene as the men must see it.

So skinny her hip bones stuck out. Barely enough breasts to fill a B-cup bra. At least her ass wasn't a total failure. That had a little curve to it.

She forced her eyes to stay open as she straightened,

wanted to see Tristan's face. Needed to see if he saw her flaws.

All she saw was desire. Adrenaline shot through her veins, heady and pure.

A second later, Adam's arms wrapped around her, one right under her breasts, the other... The other hand spread over her mound.

That hand pressed her backward until he'd nestled his denim-covered erection between her ass cheeks. He actually had to bend at the knees to do it because he was so tall. And when he straightened, he slid his hand between her legs to rub at her swollen labia.

Moaning, she let her head fall back against Adam's shoulder, one arm lifting to wrap around his nape to steady herself.

His fingers worked their magic on her clit, teasing her, making her writhe against him. His breathing became a harsh echo in her ears just before he bent his head to bite her neck. The shudder that ran through her body nearly made her knees give out, but Adam didn't let her fall. His arm around her chest held her upright as he continued to use his fingers between her legs.

He slipped them back, wetting them in the moisture seeping from her, then took that slickness and spread it to her clit.

It felt...like nothing she'd ever experienced before. None of the other men she'd ever been with had taken so much time with her. She almost felt like she was forcing Adam to cater to her but she hadn't said a word.

She wanted to tell him how much she was enjoying this,

reciprocate in some way. Turning her head, she wanted to kiss him but his mouth was busy laying a path of biting kisses along her shoulder. Those kisses pushed her closer to a state of mindless pleasure.

With no concept of time, she could only breathe and feel. Adam's clothes began to feel rough against her skin, an irritation she wanted removed. And a greediness was beginning to take hold. She wanted Tristan's hands on her body too.

She was so far gone, that thought didn't shock her like it would have before.

Forcing her eyes open, she sought out Tristan, still sitting on the couch. His dark eyes had narrowed to slits, his lips into a flat line. And his erection tented the front of his jeans.

God, she wanted to drop to her knees and taste him. She'd already had Adam's cock in her mouth and had enjoyed the hell out of it. Just thinking about it made her sex contract with aching need.

Adam must have sensed her reaction.

"Are you ready, sweetheart?" He slipped two fingers between her labia and began to fuck her with them. "God, you're wet and tight. You're going to feel amazing around my cock, aren't you?"

She had to swallow before she could form any words.

"So what are you waiting for?"

He bit her earlobe, hard enough that she felt actual pain, which only added to her excitement.

"I'm waiting for you to beg me."

Beg? "Please."

Adam sank his fingers deep inside and stroked against those inner walls. She shook as the sensation sank into her womb. And when he pressed his thumb against her clit, her knees actually did go weak.

"Not very convincing, babe." He bit her neck this time, just below her jaw, making her cry out. "I'm sure you can do better. And when you do, then I'm going to bend you over and fuck you in front of Tris. He got to have you first last time. It's my turn."

She had the fleeting thought she should be offended by something Adam had just said, but her mind was bombarded with images of Adam taking her from behind. The position wasn't one she'd done often, but she knew she'd enjoyed it.

And since it was Adam...

"Please fuck me, Adam."

She felt Adam's deep groan against her back, felt his cock swell even more.

"There you go." His voice rasped against her skin like sandpaper. "That's more like it. Now, bend over and put your hands on the table."

He meant the table in front of the couch where Tristan sat. She'd be looking straight into Tristan's eyes as Adam took her.

She hesitated and Adam slid his fingers from her body to lightly smack her ass. Startled by the sharp sting, she bit back a moan. Her sex ached to be filled again and she took the few steps needed, her gaze glued to Tristan's. He hadn't moved, almost as if he was arrested by the scene. By the sight of her.

Elation fizzed through her blood and her lips curved in a slight smile. Amazingly, she felt no awkwardness as she leaned forward and planted her hands on the wooden tabletop.

Tristan leaned forward until only about a foot separated their lips. She wanted him to kiss her but he held his position.

Behind her, she heard the sound of a zipper releasing and the crinkle of plastic. She sucked in a breath as Adam grabbed her left hip with one hand then rubbed the tip of his cock against her wet pussy lips.

Her lips parted as she drew in a deep breath and Tristan's gaze dropped to watch. But his gaze shot back to hers as Adam thrust forward, burying his cock deep.

Her moan rang throughout the room and her eyes closed as she absorbed the feel of Adam's cock spreading her wide, filling that need and stoking it higher.

Adam had pushed his jeans to his thighs and she felt the thick cotton rub against the backs of her thighs as he grabbed her hips with both hands and pulled her back, sinking even deeper.

Tristan gripped her chin. "Open your eyes, Kat. Come on now. Look at me while he fucks you."

Her eyes flew open as Adam drew back until only the tip of his cock remained inside. Tristan's eyes mesmerized her.

"There you go. Now he'll give you what you need."

Adam snapped his hips forward. The friction of his cock against her tender internal tissues made her tighten around him, increasing the resistance.

"Fuck yeah."

Adam's muttered words served to embolden her, and as he began to fuck her with steady strokes, she began to move as well. Small circles of her hips that caused ripples of contractions through her sex.

She'd already been so close to coming that it only took a few thrusts from Adam to make her groan as a short orgasm seized her. As she shook, Adam held his cock deep as her pussy contracted around him.

It left her wanting more.

"Beautiful." Tristan's voice made her eyes pop open.

She hadn't realized she'd closed them. "Ready for another?" *God, yes, please.*

She couldn't get the words to form, so she nodded and Tristan rubbed his thumb over her lips. Her tongue swept out to lick him and she watched his eyes narrow. He liked that.

He'd probably like her tongue on his cock even more—

Adam began to move again, and every nerve ending in her body caught fire. The blaze tried to consume her and she instinctively tried to contain it.

But Tristan shook his head. "Stop fighting it, Kat. Don't try to control it. Just let go. I swear you'll like it. And when you come again with Adam, I'm going to lay you out on this couch and wind you back up again with my mouth all over your body."

Adam muttered "Jesus Christ" just before he thrust hard, pushing her forward until she almost lost her balance. Tristan's hands settled on her shoulders to hold her steady as Adam's thrusts became faster and more erratic.

"He's gonna come soon, babe." Tristan's voice had dropped to barely a whisper. "He's enjoying your tight pussy too much to last much longer."

The spring that'd been coiling low in her body released,

and this time her arms did give out. Luckily Tristan and Adam were there to hold her up. The contractions of her orgasm reverberated through her entire body, until it seemed that all of her muscles were contracting along with her womb.

It lasted for long seconds, and just as she was starting to wind down, Adam thrust one last time and held deep as he came. She felt his cock pulsing inside her, felt the bite of his fingers against her hips, heard him groan out her name.

And after, she was so tight, it felt almost painful as he withdrew.

She barely had time to blink and straighten before Tristan reached over the table and swept her into his arms.

She felt weightless and boneless as he lifted her off her feet and laid her out on the wide cushions of the huge couch.

The fleeting thought that someone must have designed this couch specifically for sex floated through her mind, but she dismissed that as climax-induced euphoria.

And speaking of euphoria, the look on Tristan's face as he stared down at her caused her pussy to ripple again.

Good god, she must be under some kind of spell, which was such a stupid thought because she didn't believe in magic.

This wasn't magic. It was chemistry.

Something about these two particular men made her body react, as if three explosive chemicals had been shaken together and produced an explosion.

But when she looked into Tristan's eyes... She almost wanted to believe there was something mystical happening between them. The way her body reacted when he ran his fingers from her neck to her belly button... She couldn't imagine it happening with anyone else. And that was a little scary.

"Kat." Tristan's fingers skated back up her body to her breast and tweaked the nipple between two fingers. "What are you thinking?"

"I'm wondering if you're going to take off your clothes."

"Liar." With deliberate movements, he covered her breasts with his hands and molded them with his palms.

"But I'll let that one go."

Oh god, that felt amazing. Her breasts had always been extremely sensitive, but right now she almost believed she could come again if he just continued to do that.

"No, don't close your eyes." Tristan released her breasts, making her moan in complaint. Which turned into a gasp as he dragged them down her body so he could slip one finger into her pussy.

Her eyes flew open as he slowly pumped his finger inside her. It wasn't fair how fast Tristan could push her back into a heightened state of arousal while he looked completely in control.

She wanted to steal some of that control.

"Take off your clothes for me."

It was hard to form a coherent sentence while Tristan continued to play with her. Hard to concentrate on anything except the way he made her feel.

But she didn't want to only take. Tristan and Adam were giving her much more than she gave them.

And she hated feeling like less than an equal partner.

Tristan's grin flirted with his lips as his finger slid free of her body. "What about Adam? Don't you want him naked too?"

She glanced across the table she'd been leaning over only minutes ago and realized Adam wasn't where she'd left him. Rising up onto her elbows, she scanned the room until she found him.

He'd retreated into the shadows near the windows that overlooked Center City.

He looked...forbidding standing there by himself. She had the sense that he'd played his part and now wanted to retreat.

And she realized that's not what *she* wanted. She wanted him to be here, with her.

She'd spent most of her life learning not to ask for anything. To keep what she wanted locked inside because someone could use that against her. Her mother had taught her well.

But here and now, she decided to make a choice.

Leaning against the back cushion of the couch, her breasts pressed to the fabric, she took a deep breath then extended her hand. She had no idea what to say, though, except, "Come back."

Out of the corner of her eye, she saw Tristan grin as Adam's gaze narrowed.

"Why?" Adam's voice made her stomach flutter. "Because I'm not finished with you yet."

His eyebrows curved up and he looked shocked, although he couldn't be as shocked as she was. She couldn't actually believe she'd said that.

Her cheeks burned with a blush, but she refused to drop his gaze and let him off the hook. She had a feeling he wasn't as nonchalant as he fronted.

And if she was pushing herself beyond her normal

boundaries with this affair, then she was going to insist he give her everything.

She let her hand hang there for at least half a minute, just staring at him, until finally he sighed and pushed away from the window. He looked almost angry that she'd called him on his bluff, and she realized he might honestly not want to be here anymore. He'd finished. Maybe that was all—

No. He could've left as soon as Tristan reached for her.

Could've walked out before she had a chance to stop him.

But he hadn't.

When he was within reach, she threw all caution to the wind and grabbed a belt loop on his jeans and tugged him even closer.

"I want you to take your clothes off too."

"You seem to have a lot of demands now."

The hard tone of his voice didn't put her off. It actually made her heart race. "Maybe I just decided to act on them instead of keep them to myself."

Then she moved her hand to his zipper. He hadn't buttoned his jeans after he'd bent her over the table and his zipper was only halfway up. It didn't take more than a tug to lower it all the way.

"You really think you're ready to take us both on at the same time? Do you even know what that means?"

The way Adam said it made it perfectly clear he didn't think she was ready. And he was right.

But she was finished having other people tell her what to do, when to do it, and how.

And the images her brain was conjuring at exactly what he meant made her feel like she'd stepped into a sauna.

Forcing herself to hold Adam's gaze, she nodded. "I know

what it means. And no, I'm not sure I'm ready. But how will I ever know if you disappear?"

His gaze narrowed and she knew he wanted to say something. But then his gaze flipped to Tristan for a brief second and he bit back whatever it was.

After another few seconds, he sighed and gave her a sardonic tip of his fingers. "Your wish. My command."

She blinked, a little shocked to realize Adam had given in. "Now it's a party."

Tristan's voice held a bit of a growl, and she turned back to find him only inches away from her lips. And naked from the waist up. Then his mouth sealed over hers and she closed her eyes and kissed him back.

She may not have had a lot of experience, but Tristan made her feel like she could take risks with him. That she could kiss him and throw her whole self into it. That he wouldn't care if she didn't do it exactly right. Or that she wasn't as practiced as another woman might be.

And Adam... Adam made her want to gain all that experience from Tristan and turn it on him.

Right now, though, Tristan had her pressed against his hot, hard chest, his hands splayed across her back, and her brain wasn't working as well as it had before.

But instead of taking over, he let her direct their show and she needed to think. To figure out which way she needed to tilt her head to get the best access. How to lick at his lips to get him to open. How to slide her tongue against his to make him groan.

While she did that, she let her hands slide down his torso. Over the cut muscles of his abdomen and down to his jeans. She tugged open the button and made quick work of the zipper then shoved her hands into the waistband.

This time she didn't hesitate to push his jeans and tight boxer briefs down over his perfect ass to his thighs.

Since he was kneeling on the couch, that's all the farther they would go so she abandoned them there.

Then she took her courage in both hands and wrapped one of those hands around his erection.

Thick. Hot. Hard. And silky soft. The contradictions entranced her and she stroked him, softly at first until he wrapped one of his own hands around hers and showed her how hard he liked it.

She couldn't believe she wasn't hurting him but when he groaned into her kiss, she gave him what he wanted.

The drag of her flesh against his felt erotic, decadent. And the urge to take him in her mouth as she'd done to Adam before made her pull away from his mouth and lean closer so she could whisper in his ear.

"I want to taste you. Lie back."

She swore she felt a blast of heat race through his body as he pressed his mouth against her neck. She'd probably have a mark there tomorrow, he'd sucked on her so hard. At the moment, she couldn't care less. All she wanted was for him to give her what she wanted.

"I will but while you're sucking me, Adam's going to do the same to you."

Her heart tripped over itself as she contemplated that and found she liked the sound of it. "Okay—oh!"

Adam scooped her up off the couch and headed for the bedroom. "Damn couch is too fucking small. And I'm not letting you get rug burn."

Looping her arms around Adam's shoulders, she tried not to cling when that's all she wanted to do. She'd never had the urge to do that to any other person in her life, had always been proud of her self-sufficiency. Then these two men had bulldozed their way into her life.

Two nights. It'd only taken them two nights to wear away at her hard-won outer shell until they'd wormed their way beneath it.

The thought made her lungs catch and doubt crept in.

But it didn't have a chance to take hold because Adam pushed open the door to the bedroom and practically dumped her on the bed.

She tried to steady herself with her hands, but Adam grabbed her around the waist before she could sit up and set her on her hands and knees.

Before she had a chance to even think about logistics, Tristan had sprawled next to her on the bed, his head propped on the pillows. Naked.

And suddenly, she didn't need to think.

His cock was right there in front of her, waiting for her.

And she wanted—

"Go ahead," Adam said. "Suck him, Kat."

Adam's harsh growl made his words sound that much dirtier. She shivered but not because she didn't like it. No, she liked it way too much.

And without letting her brain trip her up, she leaned forward and licked a path from the base of his balls to the satiny tip.

"Aw, fuck."

That was Tristan and he made her smile just before she

did it again and made him punch his head into the pillows, every muscle in his body going taut.

She repositioned herself a bit then sucked in a breath and took him into her mouth. Her eyes closed as her tongue curled around the head, letting his taste flood her mouth.

She'd never imagined how erotic the taste of a man's cock could be. Couldn't imagine when the thought would've ever occurred to her.

Now...

She took Tristan deeper, letting her tongue slide down the shaft.

Who would've ever thought—

The bed shifted beneath her knees and she pulled away from Tristan, holding her breath, anticipating Adam's touch. When she realized he wasn't moving, she turned to find him on his side, head propped on one hand. Watching her, his gaze intense.

He liked to watch almost as much as he liked to participate, she realized.

"Do you like how he tastes?"

A flush burned her cheeks at his husky tone. She dipped her chin, gaze dropping to the bed. A split second later, Adam had his fingers under her chin and had tilted her head back to look in her eyes.

"There's no embarrassment here. Nothing to be ashamed of."

His voice held a command and she was more than willing to obey.

"Continue."

Dipping her head, she didn't hesitate to comply.

Wrapping her fingers around the base of Tristan's cock,

she slipped the head back into her mouth and gave herself over to the burning lust bubbling in her blood. Concentrating all of her attention on one simple outcome...making Tristan come.

She wanted to get him off, to make him come and make him groan out her name when he did. And she wanted Adam to want her to do the same to him.

So what if she pushed Tristan onto his back and rode him while she sucked Adam?

The thought made her pause, her tongue lapping the head of Tristan's cock.

Should she simply do it? Or should she ask?

No. She didn't need to ask.

Pulling away, she noticed how heavy Tristan's breathing had become, how loud. She liked that. She also liked how he watched her as she straightened, his gaze running up and down her body. He obviously liked what he saw because his cock jerked against his stomach.

Adam watched her as well, his gaze narrowed. She thought she knew what he was thinking. He was waiting to see what she'd do. And she knew he'd be quick to issue another command if he didn't like what she had planned.

Swallowing down a sudden flash of nerves, she looked Tristan right in the eye. "I want to ride you."

Tristan's mouth curved in a wicked grin and Adam rolled off the bed to grab his pants off the floor and dig in his pocket for something before throwing his jeans on the end of the bed.

A condom, which he tossed to Tristan. Tristan caught it in one hand and rolled it on. Then he rolled forward, all those beautiful abdominal muscles clenching, grabbed her around with the waist and lifted her. Her knees automatically fell on either side of Tristan's hips and her hands landed on his hard chest.

Tristan's dark eyes held hers as she settled into another position she'd never found herself in. A position of control.

"All yours, sweetheart."

Tristan continued to hold her hips but he didn't pull or push. He waited as she wrapped a hand around his cock and pulled him back then aligned their bodies.

At the first touch of his cock to the petals of her sex, her lungs contracted and she sucked in air.

God, that felt amazing. Tristan's cock wasn't as thick as Adam's, but he didn't lack for length. She remembered that from the first time. As she slid down his cock, she wondered if she'd be able to take him completely in this position.

It seemed like it took forever to completely engulf him, and when she had him inside, he hit all sorts of amazing spots that made her moan and shiver. She almost didn't want to move but she knew it would be better when she did.

"There you go, Kat." Adam's voice came from right behind her and she realized he'd gotten back onto the bed beside her. "He's all yours. Take him. I want to watch."

She opened her eyes and found Tristan staring at the point where they were connected, but his eyes shut as soon as she began to move.

The look on his face made her feel like the most desired woman on earth. As if he'd never felt anything as arousing. She wanted him to feel even better. And she wanted him to look at her.

She wasn't sure she could speak so she dragged her fingernails down the ridges of his abs. Lightly, barely enough to leave a mark. Just enough for him to groan and for his eyes to flash open.

"Come on, babe. I need you to move." Not want. Need.

She'd never had anyone say he needed her. It made her shiver and clench around him, making him groan. But this time his gaze stayed with hers.

"Ride him, Kat. Now."

The command in Adam's voice stirred conflicting responses. She wanted to do what he told her but her natural inclination was to dig in her heels and deny.

But she didn't want to deny herself.

Using her thigh muscles, she pushed herself up...and moaned at the sensation of his cock stroking against her inner walls.

Her eyes closed and her head fell back as she started a slow rhythm. She didn't want to go too fast, didn't want this to end too quickly, so she dragged herself up his shaft, clenching around him as she rose to the tip. Then she sank back down, moaning at the exquisite sense of fullness.

Beneath her, Tristan groaned and her eyes flew open. She hadn't realized she'd closed hers but now, the sight of him hit her like a shot of adrenaline. Her body shook with it and her fingers clenched into his abs, her nails digging into the muscle and making him pant.

She loved knowing she could affect him like this. That she had the power to make him groan and shake.

The headiness of it made her pick up her rhythm, to ride him faster, to slam down on him harder, watching his expression contort as she fucked him.

Her body inched closer to orgasm with each movement,

until her entire attention was focused inward, at the point where they were connected.

Almost…

"Not yet, Kat."

Adam's voice in her ear nearly made her come. She'd almost forgotten he was there.

No, no, that wasn't right. She hadn't forgotten. His presence had always been at the back of her mind. Knowing he was watching had made everything a little hotter, a little more forbidden, a whole hell of a lot more intense.

She felt like she'd been waiting for him to join them, her body resisting orgasm because she knew he was there.

And this time, she knew he wasn't going to be satisfied with simply watching or having her suck him off.

This time, he'd want…so much more.

Are you ready for that?

Was she?

Beneath her, Tristan had stilled his entire body, except for the rapid rise and fall of his chest. He watched her from beneath heavily lidded eyes, his lips parted and so sexy, she wanted to bite at them.

But behind her…

Behind her, she felt Adam. The heat of his body, the way his breath whispered across her shoulder.

The bed shimmied a bit as he came closer. At least, she hoped he was coming closer. She wanted him closer.

How much closer?

Could she honestly handle what they wanted from her? Before…

Was before. She was no longer that person who'd been

too fragile to come to grips with...well, almost anything in her life.

Now, these two men wanted her like no men had ever wanted her before.

And damn it, she wasn't going to let previous insecurities get in the way of what she wanted.

She wanted this. So badly.

Turning her head until she could just see Adam in her peripheral vision, she licked suddenly dry lips.

"What are you waiting for?"

Both men sucked in audible breaths and her lips curved in a smile. Here, she held power. The heady sensation made her bold.

Her eyelids fluttered closed when Adam's hand fell on her shoulder. He didn't grip her hard but it wouldn't have mattered how he touched her. She still would've felt as if she were drowning in lust, as if it were consuming her.

"I'm waiting for you to be sure, Kat."

She sucked in a deep breath. "I'm sure."

"Then I'm going to take you at your word. If you need me to—"

"I need you to stop talking right now and join us."

No one moved for several seconds until the tension was almost palpable between the three of them.

Then she felt Adam move, and her body responded with an aching shudder that made her pussy grasp Tristan's cock so tightly he groaned. Adam had done nothing more than lean close enough for his mouth to brush against the back of her hair, ruffling the strands. And still it was enough to make her pant.

She sucked in a breath as he came closer, holding it until she felt the brush of his chest against her back.

The heat came off him like a wave, engulfing her. Heightening every sensation. The cool brush of air against her naked nipples, the stiffness of Tristan's cock in her pussy, the hardness of Adam's pecs against her skin.

The man felt like a solid brick wall of muscle behind her. Just as Tristan felt like warm marble beneath her.

Surrounded. The center of their attention.

She felt the seeds of panic begin to flutter, wanting to burst into full-blown anxiety.

And then Adam put his mouth on her neck and bit down.

Adam felt Katrina shake and instinctively knew it wasn't with desire.

Whatever fears she battled to be with them, they were starting to win.

And it pissed him off. He told himself it was because he was right. That she was using Tristan's feelings for her to work out some hidden agenda.

And that was unacceptable. Tristan didn't deserve to be used like that. And Adam wouldn't stand for it.

So he'd break her down and show Tristan why this wasn't a woman he needed in bed. And he'd shore up his own conviction against her as well.

Because—

Releasing his teeth from their gentle hold on her skin, he resisted the urge to force her to bend over Tristan so he could press his cock against the tiny, virgin pucker of her ass. As much as he wanted to take her there, he knew he couldn't do it fast. He had to make sure she was ready. But he'd come prepared...

In the pocket of his jeans he'd stuffed small packets of lube. He hadn't expected to need them. He'd honestly thought she'd turn them down.

So why had he brought them?

Because you wanted *to need them.*

Fuck. His jaw clenched at the thought, but he could admit to himself that it was true.

He wanted to take her like this. Wanted to fuck her ass while Tristan took her pussy. Yes, he got off on this. Big time.

The fact that it was Kat...

Shouldn't make a damn bit of difference.

And yet...

Shutting down that train of thought, he reached for the jeans he tossed at the end of the bed and pulled out one of the packets.

Then he put one hand on Kat's shoulder and pushed her forward. She resisted for a second, her body stiff and unyielding. Then she gave in and sank down. Her head nearly fit under Tristan's chin, even in this position, emphasizing how delicate she appeared.

He almost stopped because he wasn't sure he wouldn't hurt her. She just looked too damn small.

But his hand had already ripped open the packet and he coated the fore and middle fingers of his right hand. Then he dribbled the remainder of the lube between the perfect globes of Kat's ass.

She shivered as the liquid slid down and he wanted to spread her cheeks and see the lube glisten against the virgin pucker of her ass.

He resisted the urge because he knew it might make her uncomfortable to have him hold her open like that. And that had never happened with any of the other women he'd been with.

Closing his eyes briefly, he shoved the thought away and moved closer until he had his cock exactly where he wanted it.

Then he let his slick fingers follow the path the lube had taken. As soon as his finger dipped between her cheeks, she shivered and Tristan wrapped his arms around her back, holding her tight to his chest.

"Do you like that, babe?" Tristan whispered in her ear, his face turned into hers. Adam watched Tris bite her ear and felt her shake again. "Just wait. It gets a whole hell of a lot better."

Adam's gaze immediately shot back to watch his hand turn so his fingers followed the curve of her body. The tips of his fingers barely grazed her labia before he drew them back up to that other, tighter opening.

Smoothing the lube around it, he worked her for several minutes, never breaching her, just massaging the skin. At first, she held herself rigid, her breath rasping from her lungs, but he didn't let up until finally, she arched back toward him.

She only moved a millimeter but his lips curved in a hard grin. *Yes.* She wanted this. Wanted him to— One finger breached that tight opening, only the tip.

Jesus, she was tight here. No way could he take her there. At least not tonight.

But he could make sure she was ready for next time.

His cock, already half hard again, gave a jerk, as if in

protest of being denied. But he would never physically hurt her.

Instead, he wiggled his finger, going deeper but going slow. Loving the way she felt around him, knowing how much better it would feel when he could get his cock into her.

If it ever happens.

Fuck that. It would happen. This wouldn't be the last time they had her.

He slid in another inch and nearly growled when she moaned, the sound muffled with her mouth against Tristan's chest. Tossing the empty plastic packet aside, he put his free hand on her ass and spread her, just enough that he could see where he entered her.

God damn.

He pulled out and went right back in, starting a slow, grinding pump that had her breathing in rhythm with his motion. Sucking in air as he pulled out, exhaling in a harsh release as he pushed back in.

His gaze locked on her body, he watched her hips start to move. Slowly at first but not because she wanted to get away. No, she definitely liked it.

And that pleased him in ways he had no desire to explore right now. Instead, he focused on driving her desire to the next level.

A quick glance at Tristan, who nodded, and then Adam did what he did best. His focus narrowed until he had only one objective: Make Kat give up her control to them.

The hand on her ass began to knead her flesh while his other hand worked her body in a way he knew she'd never experienced before.

Her movements were tentative at first, jerky and uncoordinated. But after a minute or so, her body found its rhythm and her hips moved in a sinuous dance that hardened his cock faster than even the touch of her hand could have.

Beneath her, Tristan's eyes closed and his hands tightened on her hips as he tried not to move. But Adam knew Tristan had to be holding on to his restraint by a thread. The way she moved...

"Next time, Adam's going to take your ass while I fuck your pussy. And you're going to love it."

Adam could barely hear Tristan as he spoke directly into Kat's ear but Kat moaned and shuddered.

"That's right, baby. I'm going to fuck you now and you're going to get a little taste of what it will be like when

Adam gets his cock in your ass at the same time."

"Oh my god."

Her voice had barely any strength but it was infused with lust. Which caused Tristan to move, his hips thrusting into her. Because they'd done this many times before, Adam knew exactly what to do to push her to the edge along with Tristan.

On his next retreat, he added a second finger. Her moan lit through him like lightning and made Tristan groan as his hips pumped faster.

Taking his own cock in hand, Adam gave his desire free rein. Her muscles clenched around his fingers, he felt the second she started to come.

Her moan became a cry that found an answering grunt from Tristan, whose hips snapped several more times before he came as well.

Pulling his fingers free, he jerked himself harder for only

a few more seconds before he came, pumping his seed onto her ass.

Then he let himself sprawl onto the bed and close his eyes.

***

Tristan's chest heaved, lungs sucking in air like he'd been saved from drowning.

Draped over his body, Kat shook with each breath she took.

Shit. Was she okay?

His arms tightened around her as, from lower on the bed, he heard Adam's labored breathing. If his pattern held, Adam would be rolling off the bed in a second.

When Adam remained where he was, Tristan focused again on Kat.

She'd begun to settle, not shaking as much. Her cheek rested against his chest, her skin warm against his. He wanted to close his eyes and fall asleep here and now. But he couldn't do it. Not without her permission.

The last time, she'd left. Hell, she'd practically run for the door the second she'd thought he'd been asleep.

This was her room, her space. Neither he nor Adam would stay unless she allowed it. But he hoped like hell she wouldn't kick them out just yet. Or at all.

The bed shimmied as Adam moved. Tristan figured Adam was getting out of bed but, amazingly, he simply shifted and resettled on the bed. Interesting.

Keeping his eyes open was proving to be a losing battle, but Tristan forced himself to move, shifting Kat until she lay between him and Adam. She didn't protest but she heard her take a deep breath, as if her brain had started moving again. He kind of figured Kat never shut down that brain.

What he wanted to know was why she felt the need to always be on guard. And what he would have to do to get under that guard and bust it open for him and Adam.

But first, he needed to get to the bathroom.

Kissing the top of her head, he moved quickly so she didn't have time to think. Nor did Adam.

"Hang tight, sweetheart. I'm just going to the bathroom. I'll be right back."

Then he caught Adam's eye and moved Kat the few inches needed to put her within Adam's reach. Tristan held back a grin when Adam simply wrapped his arms around Kat and drew her back against his chest.

Kat's eyes drifted open, slits of midnight blue that followed him as he rolled off the bed.

Her fingers curled into loose fists and he saw them flex before she wrapped her hand around Adam's forearm and held tight.

Adam's eyes remained closed but the muscles in his arms flexed, tightening again. Not letting go.

When he returned with a damp towel only a few minutes later, Adam had her tucked more firmly against his chest, her head nestled under his chin.

It shocked the hell out of him that Adam hadn't left yet, and Tristan half expected Adam to get up now that he was back.

When he didn't, Tristan knelt on the bed next to Kat and used the washcloth between her legs. Her eyes had opened again and remained that way, watching his every move.

When he'd finished, Adam took the cloth out of his hands before he could move and used it on her backside.

Which probably explained why Adam hadn't moved yet.

He'd gotten off twice.

If he was lucky, Tristan would get to do the same in the next few hours. Unless she sent them packing.

He couldn't read her expression but he realized she was gearing up to say something.

"Would you hand me that t-shirt?"

Not exactly what he'd expected but he followed the direction of her outstretched arm and saw a black t-shirt neatly folded on the dresser.

With a nod, he did what she'd asked, holding it out to her. When it became obvious she planned to put it on, Adam released her, propping himself up on one elbow to watch her.

The logo on her shirt made Tristan grin. Rancid's band logo. Never in a million years would he have expected her to know who Rancid was, much less be wearing their logo. He wanted to ask, wanted to know this little tidbit about her, but now wasn't the time for that. Later. Definitely later.

When the oversized shirt covered her completely, she sat cross-legged on the bed. And Tristan watched, fascinated, as she shifted from satisfied lover to cool lawyer.

"I know we discussed the possibility of these encounters becoming an affair earlier. I know what you said then. I'd like to know what you're saying now. I'm curious as to whether you're planning to pursue a more...regular relationship."

Her use of the word "regular" triggered a warning in Tristan's brain. Out of the corner of his eye, he saw Adam's gaze narrow and knew his friend had had the same reaction.

Trying to keep his expression neutral, Tristan sat on the

edge of the bed, naked and not caring. If it kept her off balance, good. He had a feeling he was going to need all the help he could get for this conversation.

"And how do you define 'regular'?" Tristan deliberately kept his expression calm though his heart had started to race.

A slight flush crept into her cheeks but she held his gaze. "I'm sorry, perhaps 'regular' was the wrong word choice so maybe I need to be more explicit." She took a breath. "Do you and Adam plan to continue as a team to pursue a...an affair with me?"

Tristan took a moment before answering, watching her closely but seeing nothing in her expression to gauge where she was going with this. "And if I said yes?"

She didn't answer right away. Instead, she began to worry her top lip between her teeth. He wasn't sure she was aware she was doing it, and that alone gave away her state of mind.

He felt a tiny crystal of ice settle deep inside his chest.

"Then I'd have to tell you I may not be able to handle that request. Emotionally."

"And just what the hell does that mean?"

Shit. Tristan heard the brutally frigid tone in Adam's question and watched as Kat felt the bite of it. She flinched, though she tried to hide it.

"It means I don't believe I'm emotionally equipped to handle a relationship with two men."

"And who's talking about a relationship? I thought before we came up here to fuck that we'd agreed this was just sex."

Sonuvabitch. He was going to wring Adam's neck.

Adam had Kat's full attention now, and from the look on his face, he'd reached the end of his fuse. It took Adam's fuse a very long time to burn down but when it did, the explosion would be white-hot and immense.

And he didn't think Kat could handle it.

"Adam—"

Adam cut him off with a sharp hand motion but his gaze never left Kat.

Fuck. Tristan couldn't blame Adam for wanting answers and he had a right to ask any questions he wanted. They were equal partners always. It's how they managed to continue to work together and stay friends.

"Are you going to answer me, Kat? Or are you going to let Tristan tell me not to badger you? Can't you take it?"

Tristan's attention had remained riveted on Kat's expression, and so he saw the second she began to lose it. Her lower lip trembled and she blinked. He figured tears weren't that far behind, something he'd never expected her to use. Although he wasn't entirely sure this was a ploy.

Because as soon as he realized what she was about to do, she blinked, and in the next second, the tears and the trembling stopped. Now, the woman sitting on the bed, who only minutes ago had come around his cock and Adam's fingers, became the frigid bitch his brother had once accused her of being.

But Tristan recognized her reaction for what it was.

Protection. He knew because he'd seen it before.

In Adam. And he knew how Adam had come by it.

Fuck.

He'd seen the signs that night at the party. He'd seen them and he'd deliberately ignored them.

"I believe it's time for you both to go." Her voice held no trace of emotion. "I'd like to retire for the night."

Goddamn it. This was what Tristan feared, what he'd wanted to avoid at all costs.

"I'm sure you would." Adam. Coldly calm. "You've had fun but now it's time for the rabble to clear out. Isn't that right?"

Her gaze shot up to connect with Adam's, her spine straightening. Tristan waited for her to blast Adam. Wanted her to do it. Hell, he wanted to punch the guy himself.

Instead, her voice took on a lifeless tone that made Tristan want to shake her.

"You don't have any idea what I'm thinking. And now I really would like to be alone."

"No problem."

Adam shoved off the bed, the anger Tristan knew he felt concealed in tightly controlled movements as he walked out of the room.

"Kat—"

"And I really," her gaze shot back to Tristan, "don't want to debate the issue."

"Kat. Don't."

That one word seemed to get more of a rise out of her than anything Adam had said. He swore he felt her gaze burning against his skin.

"Don't what, Tristan? Say no? That's exactly what I should've said earlier. Please don't make this ugly. I want you to leave. Now."

He froze, hearing something in her voice that sounded an awful lot like she didn't believe he would. That she was fairly certain he wouldn't.

Shit.

He rose from the bed. "I'll check on you tomorrow, Kat. I want you to answer the phone when I call because if you don't, I'll be back to check on you."

She watched him with wary eyes as he left the room bare-ass naked.

By the time he got to the front room, Adam was nowhere to be seen. Damn good thing because Tristan might've throttled him.

And when he caught up to Adam, maybe that'd be the least of what Tristan did to him.

It'd worked.

Adam closed the door to Kat's hotel room behind him, put his head down and headed for the stairs. He needed to work off some of this tension and seven flights of stairs should help.

Then he needed a bottle of antacids for the pain in his chest.

Damn it.

Rubbing a hand over his breastbone, he wanted to punch something. Maybe he'd hit the gym when he got back to his apartment. He knew he wouldn't be able to sleep.

Maybe not at all tonight.

But he'd done what he'd set out to do. He'd shown Tristan what she was like. Why this would never work. Why she wasn't the woman Tristan thought she was.

Then why did he feel like such a shit?

He'd exposed her flaws, her weaknesses. Exposed why she wasn't right for them.

So why didn't he feel better about the outcome?

Maybe because you took her out at the knees after fucking her practically comatose.

Maybe because your best friend looked like you'd kicked him in the gut and stabbed him in the back.

Adam shook his head. Tristan would get over it. Get over her.

The night seemed to darken around him as he started the long walk home.

9

Adam circled the bag, jabbing with his right, uppercutting with his left.

He'd wrapped his hands but wasn't using gloves. His knuckles hurt like a sonuvabitch but he kept slamming the bag. Occasionally, he brought up his knee for a strike that'd be illegal in a ring but had saved his ass many times on the street and in the field.

He kept up a punishing pace, sweat pouring down his naked upper body and soaking through his shorts.

At one a.m., the gym was empty because it closed at eleven p.m. Adam had a key. The owner had trained Adam since he was ten years old, when he'd found Adam bleeding and cursing in the alley around back. He'd been beaten up by a group of local thugs who'd wanted him to move drugs for them.

Adam had told them to go fuck themselves. The older boys hadn't liked his answer.

They'd thought he just needed a beating to make him fall

into line. He'd told them if he'd wanted to follow in his father's footsteps, he would've asked his uncle for a job.

Then he'd told them who his uncle was and they'd run.

A grin twisting his lips, he threw a roundhouse, letting the impact jolt through every joint. If he kept this up, he'd break his hands. Right now, he didn't give a fuck. He just wanted to beat the shit out of something. Preferably something that fought back.

But that wasn't an option at the moment.

Jab. Hook. Knee smash. Roundhouse.

Fuck.

He jumped away from the bag and shook out his hand.

Damn it, he couldn't afford to break anything. If they got a call about a kidnapping, he needed to be ready to move—

The front door slammed open.

"You fucking sonuvabitch. What the fuck is wrong with you?"

Adam let his forehead drop against the cool leather of the bag for a few seconds before he straightened and turned to meet his best friend head on. Who probably wanted to treat him like a punching bag.

Crossing his arms over his chest, he widened his stance and prepared for the shitstorm.

Tristan stalked across the floor, jaw clenched, lips flat, eyes narrowed. He looked royally pissed. And with good reason.

"How could you possibly treat her like that? Jesus Christ, Adam, you practically cut her open." Yep. He'd been a total ass. No argument.

He also knew himself well enough to know he should keep his mouth shut. If he opened it, he'd say something to make things worse. He also knew if he stayed silent, Tris would get even more pissed off. But at least Tristan would get the chance to vent without Adam digging himself into a deeper hole.

Although right now, he wasn't sure the hole could get deeper. He'd fucked this up way beyond his normal capabilities.

Tris was halfway across the room now, and Adam saw fury burning in his friend's eyes.

"When I left, she looked like she was in shock, for fuck's sake," Tris continued. "But I was afraid if I didn't leave, she'd crack. What the fuck were you thinking?"

That you have no idea what the hell you're getting yourself into with this woman. That you've never had to deal with a woman with major damage. And that you have no idea the hell you're in for.

Adam tightened his jaw so the words wouldn't spill out. Tris needed to get this out of his system before he screwed things up worse by saying the wrong thing. Again.

Of course, not answering just fired up Tris even more.

"And when the *fuck* did you turn into a bully?"

White-hot fury burned like a blowtorch in Adam's gut and he opened his mouth before he could stop himself.

"I'm not a goddamn bully."

Tris' head cocked to the side, his dark eyes narrow and hard. "Then why the fuck did you act like the biggest fucking asshole to Kat?"

Because...he was an asshole. Tris should know that. Should've realized that, no matter how civilized he appeared on the outside, Adam was still pretty much a savage on the inside.

"And don't give me that shit about you being an asshole." Tris sneered at him. "Yeah, you are. But not like this. Never like this."

Tris stopped only a foot away, watching Adam as if he were a target in a sniper scope. Adam didn't like feeling that Tris found him lacking.

It sucked, actually. And he'd brought it on himself.

Tris suddenly turned away, and Adam actually took a step forward to reach for him. He couldn't let him walk away. Not now. Not like this, pissed off and thinking the worst of Adam.

He also couldn't get his brain to form a coherent sentence.

But Tris didn't walk far. He stopped at the trunk holding the boxing gear, threw it open then dug through it. He tossed headgear and gloves at Adam, not bothering to look over his shoulder.

"Put those on."

Without a word, Adam picked up the pieces as Tris took off his shoes, socks, shirt, and t-shirt and put on gloves and headgear as well.

Adam's lips curved in a hard grin as he turned and headed for the ring at the far end of the gym.

Yes. Much better way to settle this.

Turning, Adam climbed into the ring and waited at the center, watching as Tris slid through the ropes and approached.

"Put the fucking headgear on." Tris knocked his gloves together. "I don't want to split your head open. Although you deserve it."

Adam deliberately took his time settling it on his head

and tightening the chin strap. "You don't really think you can get close enough to split my head open, do you?"

Tris didn't rise to the bait, his expression settled into determined lines. His kick-ass-and-take-names face.

Good. Adam didn't want to have to pull his punches tonight. In this state of mind, Tris was a worthy opponent. Most days, Adam would have Tris laid out on the mat in a few minutes. Tonight, with his head so fucked up, Tris might actually be able to hold his own.

Tonight, maybe Adam would let Tris beat the shit out of him.

But he wouldn't make it easy.

Adam barely had time to get his hands up before Tris came at him with a roundhouse that Adam couldn't completely block. The blow glanced off his chin, snapping his head to the side.

Turning back, Adam grinned and threw a body shot that Tris took with barely a grunt.

Adam took a step back. "No rules?"

Tris shrugged and raised his hands. "When do we ever fight with rules? Don't be a pussy."

Then Tris jabbed at Adam's chin, knocking him back two steps.

Adam lifted his glove to wipe at his mouth. It came away bloody. When he grinned, his lip hurt.

"Fine. Let's do this."

Half an hour later, sitting on the sagging wooden bench against the cinderblock wall, Tristan sucked down the last of his water and tossed the bottle at the can fifteen feet away.

It bounced off the side and toppled end over end to the other side of the gym.

Beside him, Adam snorted in amusement. "How the hell are you such a good shot with a pistol when you can't hit the broadside of a barn with a basketball?"

"Because when I take aim with a gun, I mean it. I couldn't care less if I hit the damn can."

Adam shook his head then winced and lifted his hand up to rub at the swelling bruise on his chin. "You landed a few tonight. Mary Alice is going to read you the riot act Monday."

It was Tristan's turn to grimace. Their office manager had been with them since their doors had opened three years ago. Mary Alice Dabrowski had a weak stomach and an aversion to violence that had seemed counterintuitive to the nature of their business.

Instead, she'd turned out to be one of their top assets. She handled frazzled and terrified clients with the right amount of steel and compassion. Problem was, she used those same qualities on them. And even though she was younger by a few years, she acted more like a mother hen than a kid sister.

And because she *was* the kid sister of a good friend who hadn't made it home from Afghanistan, they let her. "It's your own damn fault." Tris turned to look at Adam's split lip. "You probably need stitches."

"Fuck that." A pause then Adam sighed. "I need to apologize."

Tristan huffed in disgust. "Ya think?"

Adam raised his middle finger. How the fucker managed

to make it sarcastic was exactly what made Adam…well, Adam.

"But Tris…"

When Adam didn't continue, Tristan turned, watching Adam struggle to find the words he needed.

Adam never said much. The term "a man of few words" could've been coined just for him. And usually he didn't have to say anything. Tris handled almost all of the client interactions.

Unless the client didn't speak English. The fact that Adam was multilingual usually shocked the hell out of people. They didn't expect a man who looked like him— even when he wore a thousand-dollar suit and custom-made Italian shoes—to be able to switch from English to Russian or German or French or whatever.

But when he needed to, he knew exactly the right words to use. That he struggled now didn't mean he didn't know what to say. Only that he didn't know how to say it because he was worried about Tristan's reaction.

"Do I have to give you another head shot to knock whatever you need to say loose? You know I will if I have to."

Adam sighed and shook his head. "*Shit.*" And one more sigh before Adam looked him straight in the eyes. "I'm out on this one. I'll apologize for treating her like I did. It wasn't fair and it wasn't her fault. But…it isn't going to work and I'm stepping aside."

Shock held Tristan immobile for several seconds while Adam sat quietly beside him. The man knew him better than anyone else in the world, his parents included. He knew Tristan needed time to process because Adam had said the one thing sure to throw him for a loop.

He wanted to step aside.

Bullshit.

Tristan took a breath, reaching for calm. "Okay, I see why you could have some concerns. But you're wrong about her. I know—"

"Tris. Jesus." Adam slammed his hands against the bench then gripped the edges tight. "This isn't about her. It's about *me*. I can't make this work. She needs someone who isn't me."

No. Tristan refused to believe that. "You need to give this some time. Trust me."

Because Tristan wasn't about to give up on this. On *her*.

In high school, he'd been two years ahead of Kat and had run with a different crowd, but their private school had been small and all the students knew each other by name.

He'd been a decent student and an outstanding athlete with a huge group of friends. Kat had been a painfully shy introvert with a near-perfect GPA who'd had maybe three friends. She'd been so far off the popular kids' radar, she could've been invisible.

But not to Tristan. He'd seen something in her, even back then, that had made him want to draw her out, find out what made her tick.

He'd never gotten the chance in high school, but he'd figured he had time. He'd get through West Point and, after graduation, he'd make his move. He'd have a few weeks off before he started Ranger School and she'd be home from college for the summer.

But he hadn't expected her ice to be thicker when he came home. Or that her mother would be grooming her to marry his brother. Or that he wouldn't have as much time to get through to her as he'd thought.

So he'd gone to training without breaking through her shell. Then he'd met Adam and gone through hell. Then he and Adam had started their business and life had gotten in the way.

But through it all, no matter what had happened or who he'd ended up in bed with, he'd never stopped wanting Kat. Had never stopped believing she was the woman he and Adam needed between them.

"And there's that fucking tunnel vision." Adam's voice held even more frustration now. "You need to look at the big picture."

Tris turned to stare at Adam, who continued to stare straight ahead. "I have been mapping this scenario from every angle for the past ten years. We need to stick to the plan."

With a bitter curse, Adam pushed off the bench and headed for the locker room. "Despite popular opinion, you're not a miracle worker, Tris. Not everything you want is going to fall into your lap. And not everyone is always going to give you what you want."

The dig found its target, triggering Tristan's slow-burning fuse. He jumped to his feet and was hot on Adam's heels a split second later.

"Are you seriously telling me you don't want her?"

Adam pushed through the locker room door, shoulders stiff. "I'm telling you it's not going to work. She isn't the woman you think she is. She's *never* going to accept both of us in her bed for anything more than a dirty affair she can write off as an aberration."

No. Tristan knew in his gut that wasn't true. Yes, she might've insinuated that, but she'd been lashing out at Adam's attack. Which had been triggered by her inadvertent offense.

Jesus Christ, what a fucking minefield.

Tristan stopped just inside the door.

Shit. Just… *Shit.* Was he really so blind?

"And the switch is flipped. Hallelujah. He sees the light."

Adam's drawl slammed Tristan out of the crush of his spiraling thoughts. His gaze snapped up to catch Adam's frost-blue eyes studying him.

"I'm taking myself out of the picture, Tris. No harm. No foul. I'll apologize and then I will get the hell out of your way. I am not what this woman needs in her life."

Tristan saw absolute sincerity in Adam's expression, knew Adam believed every word he'd said. He also knew it to be absolute bullshit. But he also knew he wasn't going to win this battle now.

So he said, "If that's what you want."

Adam's eyebrows shot up but Tristan pushed past him, heading for his locker.

In his peripheral vision, he saw Adam staring at him for several seconds before he moved to his locker, only a few away from Tristan's.

"I'll call her tomorrow morning. Apologize."

Tristan nodded. "Fine."

Adam paused for a beat. "So when she's moved in, you'll have a clear playing field."

Tristan nodded again, forcing himself to take his time, even though he wanted to rush to put on his clothes. He needed to think, to map out a direction. He worked better when he had a game plan.

First, if he was going to fix this situation, he needed to talk to someone close to Kat, and there was only one person he knew who fell into that category.

Tristan wasn't used to losing and he wasn't going to start now.

Kat woke late Saturday morning with a pounding headache and an upset stomach.

When she looked at the clock, she realized she'd gotten about three hours of sleep, which accounted for the headache. The upset stomach she wanted to chalk up to food poisoning...which she knew wasn't the culprit.

It was stress, of course. And maybe a little guilt.

She grimaced. Maybe a lot of guilt.

Last night...

Last night, she'd confirmed the fact that she sucked at post-coitus conversation.

Jesus, could she have been any more of a bitch?

Hell, she didn't think she could have if she'd tried.

She'd still been recovering from the most mind-blowing experience of her life and she'd wanted to know if Adam and Tristan were planning to see her again. Maybe take her out on a date.

But for someone who made her living knowing the exact words to use to get what she wanted, she'd picked the absolute worst words last night.

She'd made it sound as if she thought the men were aberrations. As if what they engaged in was wrong. As if she were the biggest, most judgmental prude in the world.

As if she were more like her mother than she could bear.

Another wave of nausea rolled over her.

God, please don't let those men think she was anything like her mother.

She couldn't get the look on Adam's face out of her mind. For a split second, he'd looked like she'd slapped him. Then he'd gone so still, she swore she'd felt a chill coming off him. And his words...so cold.

It'd struck a nerve in her and she'd lashed out.. Just like her mother always did.

Her stomach flipped again and she threw off the covers, ready to run for the bathroom if she needed to. She hated to be sick and fought it back.

Amazingly, after several minutes of deep breathing, the feeling passed.

Maybe she'd learned something from all those shrinks after all.

And maybe I need to call Adam and Tristan and apologize for turning the most amazing sexual experience of my life into something dirty.

She reached for her phone on the bedside table then froze, her hand hovering over the cell.

Maybe they wouldn't want to listen.

Her stomach flipped again, but this time she refused to let it fester.

Yes, she'd panicked last night. Today she'd fix it. She was good at fixing things. Usually for other people, but she was starting a new chapter in her life. She needed to start fixing things for herself.

But do I want to fix this?

She didn't have to think about her answer. "Yes, I do." Her voice sounded weak and it grated on her ears.

Sliding her legs over the side of the bed, she pushed to her feet and shoved her hands in her hair.

First things first.

In the shower, she ran through a checklist. She needed to track down home addresses for Adam and Tristan first. She already had their business address but wasn't sure they'd be in the office on Saturday.

And since she had to return to Boston by Monday night, she needed to do this today. She'd already made plans to meet Erik for dinner, which meant she was driving up to his home tonight. Which also meant she'd be dealing with Keegan and Jules tonight.

The thought didn't immediately make her hyperventilate, so that was both a little shocking and a relief. Usually seeing Keegan made her pucker as if she'd sucked a lemon. Today she couldn't seem to muster any response at all.

Maybe she should cancel now? What if Adam and Tristan—

No, don't get ahead of yourself.

By the time she'd dried her hair and dressed in low-heeled boots, soft jeans, and a soft, figure-hugging sweater that matched her eyes, she had her plan locked down.

Sitting at the small writing desk in her room, she dialed the first number on her list.

Forty minutes later, she had home addresses for Adam and Tristan and an invitation from a local private investi-gator to meet and discuss hiring her on retainer for the firm. DeMarco Investigations had been highly recommended to her by her dad so she'd already decided she was going to jump at the offer. Now, after mapping out the addresses on her phone, she started crafting her apology on the legal pad she carried in her briefcase. And realized after her second use of the word "whereas" that she was absolutely out of her mind.

Her apology sounded like a legal defense. How lame was that?

Setting her pen aside, she turned to stare out the window.

What man wanted to ravage a woman who plotted out her apology on a legal pad and made it sound like a business contract?

She'd have to wing this. Show up at Adam's door and speak from the heart.

Before she keeled over from hyperventilation. Or he shut the door in her face.

Forcing herself out of the chair, she grabbed her purse, threw on her coat, and prepared to do the most daring thing she'd ever done in her life.

And hoped like hell she didn't fall on her face.

10

"Unca Da! Unca Da!"

Smiling at the toddler with his slobbery grin and outstretched arms, Adam snagged his nephew from the floor and tossed him gently into the air.

"Hey, Theo. How goes it, little man?"

The almost-two-year-old babbled something indecipherable, which made Adam shake his head, his lips curving in a grin.

"One of these days, you're gonna give your mom a run for her money. Between you and me, kid, I can't wait." Theo started to laugh, as if he understood.

"Adam, is that you?"

Adam rubbed his nose along Theo's before he answered. "Yeah, Lys. It's me. Where are you?"

"In the kitchen. Of course."

His sister's sharp-edged response made Adam's grin widen, which made Theo pat Adam's cheeks with pudgy hands.

"Uh oh." Adam put Theo on his hip and began to navigate the toy-strewn front room of his sister and brother-in-law's house in Bustleton. "Sounds like Mom's having a bad day. You giving her a hassle, little man?"

"Uncle Adam!"

A high-pitched screech was the only warning he got before a four-year-old with a wild tangle of red curls threw herself at his legs. Luckily, Ariel barely weighed thirty pounds so she made no impact on Adam's balance.

"Hey, my little fish girl. How are you?"

Scooping her up in his free arm, he continued on his way to the kitchen while Ariel told him all about the tea party in her room that he had to attend and Theo babbled.

He was about to ask where his seven-year-old nephew, Ajay, was when he walked into the kitchen and found the kid seated at the table, staring at the floor to avoid the narrow gaze of Adam's older sister, Allysa.

"Hey, sis. How's it going?"

Without taking her gaze away from Ajay, his sister still managed to acknowledge him. "Not so good at the moment. Is it, Ajay?"

The dejected kid chanced a glance at his uncle before deciding he'd probably better not push his luck by appealing to anyone for help.

Apparently, the kid had done it up good this time. Since Adam saw a lot of himself and Ajay's dad, Tosh, in the kid, he could see why Lys looked like she wanted to simultaneously laugh and scream.

Setting Ariel and Theo on their feet, he gave them both a pat on the butt toward the door. They took off without a second prompting.

"What'd you do, bud?"

Adam kept any hint of censure out of his voice, but he didn't let the smile show through either. The kid was seven. How much trouble could he have gotten into?

Then again, by the time Adam was seven... Probably best not to think about that.

"I got into a fight."

Adam gave the kid a once-over, relaxing only when he didn't see any bruises.

"What he won't tell me is why." Lys crossed her arms over her chest and began to tap her foot. And Adam had a major flashback to his mother standing in front of him the exact same way. He tucked that one away to torment Lys with later.

"Why don't you want to tell your mom, kid?"

"She's not gonna understand."

"You wanna tell me what happened?"

Without lifting his head, Ajay nodded.

Lys opened her mouth to protest, but Adam shook his head at her. He didn't do this often, didn't circumvent Lys and Tosh's authority, because these weren't his kids. Ajay had a mother and a father who loved him, but Adam also knew sometimes Ajay needed Adam in a way he didn't need his parents.

And because of the way they'd grown up, Lys got it. She didn't like it but she got it. Lys was a lot like their mom in some ways. She loved her children so strongly that even when they knew they were in deep trouble, they also knew there'd be hugs and kisses later. And probably cookies..

The fact that Ajay didn't want to talk to Lys gave Adam an inkling of what had happened.

So with a deep breath and the admonition that she'd be

in the living room, she left, closing the kitchen door behind her.

Ajay's shoulders sagged just a little lower as he released the breath he'd been holding. Adam snagged the chair next to Ajay's and sat in front of him, leaning back so he didn't loom over the kid.

"Okay. Spill it. What's going on?"

Ajay's gaze finally lifted off the floor and the depth of furious hurt in his eyes made Adam want to hit something. Because he recognized that particular kind of hurt.

"Door's closed, bud. You know the rules. I won't tell anyone what you say to me unless there's blood involved. I promise. And whatever you tell me, I won't get angry about. What happened?"

Ajay's eyes began to fill with tears, but he kept blinking them back because Ajay was too old to cry. At least, that's what Adam's dad, Ajay's grandfather, would say. Only girls got to cry after the age of three. Boys sucked it up and acted like men.

"Tommy Migliorini called my dad a cripple. Said he wore diapers and only sissies and freaks wore diapers."

Adam made a conscious effort to keep his hands from clenching into fists, and he kept quiet because he knew there was more.

"Tommy said my dad couldn't even be a good bad guy and that's why he got his legs cut off."

Shit.

Ajay kept looking at Adam like he had answers for everything. Damn but he wished he did. He had no answers for this because when Adam was a kid, no one would've dared talked to him like this because Adam's father would've fucked them up but good. Mikhail Oleksy had been a damn good bad guy. Still was, if you considered he was one of the highest-ranking Russians in Graterford State Penitentiary.

Reaching across to grab Ajay's hand, Adam squeezed and held on. "Your dad got hurt being a good guy, and don't you ever let anyone tell you different, kid. He's a goddamn hero in my book. He saved your mom's life and he saved Aunt Lea's life, too."

Ajay thought about that for a second. "But you helped too, didn't you?"

Yeah, but not enough. Or else Tosh would still be able to walk.

"I helped. But not like your dad."

And even though he and Tosh would have this fight until they died, Adam would always give Tosh more credit. He'd paid more than his fair share for the hell they'd gone through that night.

"You tell that kid the next time he wants to talk about your dad to ask your Uncle Adam what really happened that night. And if he doesn't like that, you go tell Tommy's dad I want to have a talk. Now, we good?"

With a thoughtful nod, Ajay got up and wrapped his arms around Adam's neck. Adam wanted to squeeze him tight then go pay little Tommy's dad a visit and let him know his kid was spouting bullshit.

Adam figured that'd do more harm than good. In his head, he heard Tristan's sarcastic, "Ya think?" *Bastard.*

"Thanks, Uncle Adam." A pause. "You won't tell Dad, will ya?"

He wouldn't have to. "No, I won't tell him. Now go tell your mom I said you're good."

The boy walked off, head still hanging low. Maybe not as low.

Seconds later, the swinging door from the kitchen into the playroom at the back of the house opened and his brother-in-law wheeled through.

The black look on Tosh's face probably matched Adam's.

"You heard." Adam didn't make it a question.

"Fucking Frankie Migliorini's kid." Tosh shook his head. "Guy was an asshole all through school. Apparently his kid takes after him."

"Kids repeat, you know that."

Tosh sneered as he pulled his wheelchair up to the table, shoving too-long black hair out of glass-green eyes that'd gotten him laid more times than either of them could count. Before he'd married Lys, of course.

"Yeah, yeah. And assholes need to be taught some manners."

Adam didn't disagree. "You want me to—"

"Don't even go there." Tosh's gaze was steady as a rock as he held Adam's. "If I wanna talk to the guy, I'll talk to him. I can take care of myself. I don't need you to fight my battles."

Adam's gaze slipped to the wheelchair his brother-in-law still occasionally used when his prosthetic limbs gave him trouble. The limbs he'd had to wear since he was nineteen and had his legs amputated above the knee.

"I wasn't offering to fight your battles, Tosh."

Tosh dismissed it with a waved hand. "I know that. I also know you can't help yourself. But we both know if you go over there, you'll be punching some asshole in the face. So... what're you doing here this early on a Saturday morning?"

"Can't I stop by to see my family?"

Tosh pulled a couple cans of Coke from the fridge and tossed one at Adam.

"Now I *know* something's wrong. What happened? Case go south on you? You got that look it's something bad. Talk."

"What's going on? What's bad?" Lys walked back into the kitchen, Theo on her hip, headed straight for Adam like a woman on a mission.

Adam knew better than to roll his eyes at his older sister. She'd smack him on the back of the head like he was still Ajay's age. "Nothing happened. Jesus, Lys. Do you listen at the door or what?"

"Don't need to. My house, my brother. I get to listen wherever I want. And I shouldn't have to hear about this stuff secondhand. Now spill."

Lys sat on Tosh's lap, settling back into his chest as Tosh put one hand on her hip and set the baby on his free thigh with the other.

The chair didn't diminish the man one bit. Tosh had stood almost six-four before he'd lost his legs. Hell, the guy looked even bigger now because he worked his upper body like a championship fighter. He also played in a couple of leagues for amputees...hockey, basketball, and a wicked, no-rules rugby that almost always required stitches or at least butterfly bandages after a game.

After Tristan, Tosh and Lys and his younger sister, Lea, were the only people in the world Adam felt safe spilling his guts to. But this... Hell, he didn't even know where to start.

"I met a woman."

Lys' mouth dropped open and her eyes widened until he wanted to smack her on the back of the head. Instead, he sat and waited for the merciless questioning to commence.

Tosh got his shit together first. "Well, damn, it's about fucking time. Who is she?"

Lys smacked Tosh in the chest for the language but never took her eyes off Adam and asked the right question.

"What happened?"

"I'm pretty sure I scared the hell out of her and probably owe her an apology."

Lys immediately shook her head. "Don't. I know what you're thinking. Don't *even* go there, Adam. That's not you. You'd never physically threaten a woman."

"I'm not so sure the woman in question would see it that way."

Lys sneered. "Then she's an idiot."

"No, that's the problem. She's not."

Lys paused, her gaze narrowing. "So who is she?"

Tosh and his sisters were the only family members who knew about Adam's unusual relationship with Tristan. Most of the others figured he and Tris were gay and avoided the subject like it was contagious. Even if they knew the truth, they'd think he was a degenerate. Tosh and Lys didn't. However, Lys thought he was shortchanging himself by not wanting a woman for himself, instead of one he shared with another man.

She didn't understand the benefits or the rewards. And Adam didn't want to have to explain them to his sister. Way too weird.

Tosh got it. Probably because he understood why it was good to have someone you trusted at your back at all times.

So Adam focused on the man he'd looked up to since he was six years old.

"A woman Tristan knows from Boston."

Lys bit her bottom lip as Tosh's gaze narrowed. "Did Tristan have a relationship with her before?"

"No. But he's been after her for years."

"So you never met her until…?"

"A couple weeks ago at a party in Boston."

"And you and Tristan had sex with her?" Apparently Lys had reached the end of her patience. "Do you even like this woman, or are you doing her just because Tristan likes her?"

His immediate aversion to Lys' question must have shown on his face because Lys blinked, shock evident in her expression.

"Wow. You like her. So why is that a problem?"

Shit, did he like Kat? And Jesus Christ, when had he reverted to high school? Hell, even then he wouldn't have reacted like this.

"Yes, I'm attracted to her. She's beautiful. Smart. Successful." And emotionally fucked up.

"And…?" Lys prompted. "What's wrong with her?"

"She's got issues."

Lys rolled her eyes. "Hey, we've all got issues." Adam looked at Tosh, who raised an eyebrow at him.

"You think you're gonna get left out in the cold eventually."

Trust Tosh to get it. Yeah, that was part of it. But the more important part—

"You don't wanna have to deal with her issues," Lys concluded.

Adam held onto Lys' gaze now. "You make me sound like a prick."

Her gaze challenged him. "Were you?"

He sighed and felt his jaw tighten until it hurt. "Yeah."

"And you want to fix it and don't know how."

Adam shook his head. "I told Tris I was out."

"As in, you're not gonna be the third wheel anymore."

Frustrated, Adam rubbed at the fast-tightening muscles in his neck. "I told you, Lys. It doesn't work like that."

At least, it never had before. Then again, neither of them had been as determined about a woman before as Tris was about Kat. And if Adam didn't get on board...

"What?" Lys prompted. "You look like you just got whacked over the head."

He couldn't sit anymore. Pushing to his feet, Adam started to pace.

Lys huffed. "Adam—"

"You're worried about being left out."

Tosh's quiet statement cut off whatever Lys was going to say more effectively than a gag.

Several seconds of silence followed before Adam stopped pacing to lean against the edge of the counter. "I think..." Adam sighed. "Maybe. Yeah."

And he had no fucking clue what to do about it. Or if he should do anything about it.

"Adam." Lys's tone fell into the same rhythm she used to talk to her kids when they were upset. "Do you like this woman?"

Yeah, he did. The problem was...

"You don't think you should," Tosh spoke up again.

"Why?" Now Lys' back went up, as if someone had

outright insulted him. "Does she think she's too good for you?"

When neither he nor Tosh spoke up, Lys continued to stare at him, as if she could read his mind. And it only took her a couple of seconds to come up with her own answer.

The furious look she turned back at Adam made him wince. "Oh... Seriously? That's what you're worried about? Being like Dad?"

He didn't have to answer. Obviously, his expression ratted him out.

Lys was on her feet two seconds later, slapping her palm against the back of his head, and he took it because she was his older sister.

"You are a fu—frigging idiot, you know that?"

No, he didn't know but apparently Lys was more than happy to tell him all about it.

"You're not Dad, Adam. You will never be Dad because you have the one thing he didn't. A moral compass. Dad always excused his behavior by saying he did what he had to do to survive. And maybe part of that's true. But we both know that if he'd really wanted to go legit, he could have. But he didn't. He stayed a criminal because he liked the money and the prestige. But that's not *you*."

Adam had a slight grin on his face by the time his sister wound down. Not because of what she'd said but how she'd said it. She stood in front of him with her hands on her hips, scowl on her face, and utter belief in her eyes. And he knew exactly why he'd come to her.

Straightening, he put his arms around her shoulders and dragged her close for a hug. "You know I love you, even if you are a huge pain in my ass, right?"

Her arms wound around his waist and she squeezed him until he almost had to cry uncle, though he never would. "And you will never be anything other than my baby brother who doesn't think enough of himself. You are worth ten of Dad. Don't ever let anyone make you think you're not. And I wanna meet this chick who makes you doubt yourself. *After* you apologize for being a dick. But I'm the only one who's allowed to call you that."

Adam's grin widened and he stepped back before she decided to smack him again.

"Love you too."

Lys snorted. "Of course you do. Now go apologize and show her you're not just a pretty face."

"I don't think anyone's ever accused Adam of having a pretty face, Lys."

Adam gave Tosh the finger, making sure Theo couldn't see what he was doing. "Back at you."

With a muttered laugh, Tosh got the baby a snack while Lys walked him to the door, stopping him with one hand on his arm before he could make a clean getaway.

"You know I love Tristan, right?"

Adam frowned down at Lys, wondering where she was going with this. "Yeah, of course."

"But you're my brother and I want you to be happy." He shook his head, still not getting her meaning.

"Okay."

Lys huffed. "Tristan isn't your commanding officer anymore, Adam. You don't have to jump when he says jump. You have your own life to live."

"And I am."

Lys just smiled. "But are you living your life for you? Or

just going along for the ride with Tristan? What do *you* want, Adam? I'm not sure you ask yourself that question enough."

Now that she was here, Kat wasn't exactly sure *what* she was doing here.

On the drive over, she'd come up with a million and one ways to say what she wanted to say.

Now, sitting in her rental in front of Adam's home, she couldn't think of one damn thing.

All she kept thinking was, this was not where she'd expected Adam to live. Though it wasn't low-rent, this neighborhood definitely wasn't high-end either.

The streets were clean, trees lined the sidewalks, and the houses were a mix of singles and doubles.

Adam's address was a single, two-story brick. Almost indistinguishable from the other houses along the quiet street.

She'd been expecting a condo in some ritzy, Center City building. Not this quiet slice of middle-class normality.

She didn't know what to make of it.

Didn't really know what to make of Adam.

Then why are you here?

Because she'd treated him abominably last night and she needed to make amends. She'd acted like her mother and she couldn't stand to let him think that's the kind of person she was.

And you're never going to apologize if you continue to sit here.

After a deep breath, she pushed open the door and got out of the car. Walked up to the front door and knocked.

No answer.

Knocked again.

Silence.

She sighed. "Well, of course. That would be too easy, wouldn't it?"

"What would be too easy?"

She couldn't quite contain her startled cry as she spun on her heel. Adam stood in the middle of the walk leading to the front porch, watching her with those ice-blue eyes and absolutely no discernible expression.

And he still managed to be one of the most handsome men she'd ever met.

The thought gave her a jolt. Up until this moment, she'd thought she'd been here simply to apologize and leave.

Liar.

Refusing to listen to that little voice in her head, she tried to force a smile. "Hello, Adam."

He nodded. "Kat. I'm glad you're here."

Really? She blinked. "Why?"

His mouth quirked into a quick grin as he walked toward her. "Because I have an apology to make. But it's too cold to do it out here. Come inside."

Just as he stepped onto the porch, she couldn't help herself. She took a step back. Away from him.

Damn it. She wasn't afraid of him.

Pausing with the key in the lock, Adam turned and caught her gaze. "Or we could stay out—"

"No. I'm sorry. I'm just..." She thought of all the things she could say right now to excuse her behavior then figured it was just better to go with the truth. "I'm not very good with people."

A heartbeat passed before Adam nodded and another faint smile pulled at his lips. "Then you're in good company because neither am I, although you probably figured that out already."

Then he pushed open the door and waved her through.

Amazingly, she didn't need to force herself to go.

She walked into a living room that looked straight out of the handbook for bachelor men. Overstuffed furniture. Huge TV screen with more components than she'd ever seen. A stone fireplace that looked well used.

A large table dominated the dining area toward the back of the room, and she could see a hint of dark wood and stainless steel in the kitchen beyond.

And again, so *not* what she'd been expecting.

"Can I get you something to drink?"

Was it too early for a glass of wine? Probably. "No, thank you. I can't stay long. I just wanted..." What exactly did she want?

To apologize? That's what she'd told herself all the way here. That she needed to apologize. But now that he stood in front of her, she knew why she'd really needed to see him again.

To know if what she'd felt for him last night had been real.

She knew how she felt about Tristan. Tristan was easy. Quick to smile. Quick to laugh. He looked at her and she saw his desire.

Warmth spread outward from low in her body, though she didn't completely trust that feeling. Because when Adam looked at her, she couldn't tell if what she saw in his eyes was desire for her or simply desire for a woman. Any woman.

The way he looked at her now was the perfect example. He watched her so intently she almost felt like a bug under a microscope.

But she also felt her own desire for him heating through her, making her thighs clench and her lungs tighten.

She wanted him to touch her. To grab her and kiss her and bend her over the arm of that couch and take her.

The images in her head made her shaky and short of breath. And hot. And stole her ability to speak.

Adam stood in front of her, waiting. Staring at her with those cool-blue eyes. Eyes she wanted to warm with heat.

She blinked and let her gaze slide away to stare at a spot just over his shoulder.

"I wanted to apologize. I said things I shouldn't have, things I didn't mean. And I wanted you to know—"

"So why did you say them?"

Of course he'd ask the one question she didn't want to answer. Taking a deep breath, she forced herself to meet his gaze again. And saw a hint of that warmth she longed for.

"Because I'm a coward."

Adam's gaze narrowed a fraction of an inch as he took a step closer. She stiffened her spine and held her position. "And what are you afraid of? Because I don't want you to be afraid of me."

There was something in Adam's tone that made her stop and take a closer look at him. Did he think he'd scared her?

"I'm not afraid of you."

Visible relief ran across his expression, and she had a second to wonder why he'd even considered that before he closed the few feet between them, wrapped his hand around her neck, and pulled her flush against him.

She stiffened with shock, even as her body responded with a rush of heat.

"Still not scared?"

No, she wasn't scared. She was far from scared.

Turned on. Horny. Hot. All of the above.

But not scared. Not of him.

He watched her with a gaze that missed nothing. And when she felt her cheeks begin to flush, he leaned in closer.

"You don't have anything to be sorry for. I'm the one who should be making the apology. But all I want to do is kiss you. And you shouldn't let me."

He wanted to kiss her? Then why did he look like that was the last thing in the world he wanted to do? And why shouldn't she let him?

Frustration began to nudge at the desire.

"You're right. I shouldn't. Because I have no idea what game you're playing."

His lips kicked up at the corners and he pulled back a fraction as his hand released her neck to cup her jaw, his thumb rubbing against the corner of her lips.

A short nod, as if he agreed with her, then he stepped back.

She almost followed but managed to contain the urge.

She'd come to apologize and leave, not... Kiss him. Or anything else.

"No games. But I apologize for making you feel like you were played. That wasn't my intention. And it wasn't Tristan's. I hope you won't take it out on him. I don't want you to stop seeing him because of my actions."

Seeing him? Tristan. As in singular. "Do you— Are you saying you won't..."

She didn't know how to finish that thought because she wasn't sure how she wanted him to answer.

Which was bullshit. She knew exactly what she wanted him to say. She didn't want him to step aside. Or away. Or whatever he thought he was doing.

The strength of her immediate denial surprised her. One part of her thought she should be relieved he'd taken the burden of making the choice away from her.

Another, much larger part was angry, hurt, and more than a little disappointed.

This had been a huge mistake. Another in a very long line. When was she ever going to stop—

"Kat."

The sharpness in his tone knocked her out of her thoughts, and her gaze locked with his. Those frosty blue eyes fascinated her. So cold. Or so blazing hot. Especially in bed.

Where he didn't plan to be with her again.

"Of course." She forced a smile, trying to unclench her hands. "I understand. I have another appointment. I need to leave."

Turning on her heel, she headed for the door, blinking away the sudden sting in her eyes.

Stupid, stupid, stupid. Why the hell— "Damn it, Kat. Stop."

But she didn't, not until she had her hand on the doorknob. Glancing over her shoulder, she sucked in a sharp breath. He stood only inches away. He'd followed her so silently, she hadn't known he was there.

Mouth set in a firm line, he stared down at her. His gaze definitely burned now.

So not fair.

Stiffening her resolve, she held his gaze.

"Kat—"

"No. You've said all you need to say. We're finished. I'm leaving."

"Fuck."

"No. Apparently we're not going to be doing that again."

The words were out before she could stop them, and she nearly covered her hand with her mouth to stop more from escaping.

Oh. My. God. Had she seriously said that?

She must have because Adam looked as shocked as she felt. His eyes widened, and she wanted to melt straight into the floor in embarrassment because she knew he'd heard her disappointment.

Turning, she blindly reached for the doorknob again. She was so flustered she didn't realize it was a handle and not a knob. But by the time she figured out that turning wasn't going to do the job, Adam had his hand on her shoulder.

"Kat. Stop."

She did, but only because she refused to embarrass herself anymore. She'd done more than enough of that already.

"Don't leave. Not like this."

She didn't turn and barely stopped herself from trying to shrug his hand off her shoulder. Not because she didn't want him to touch her. But because she did.

And that was unacceptable.

He didn't want her. How humiliating to know he'd had sex with her not because he'd wanted to but only because his best friend had wanted him to.

"I don't think we have anything more to say to one another. Please release me."

"No. We're not finished."

He spoke with such arrogance, Kat felt her blood pressure rise and she had to bite back her immediate response. Which was to tell him to go fuck himself.

And again, that shocked the hell out of her.

Where was all this *emotion* coming from? And how the hell did she contain it? The stress couldn't be good for her.

Then again, stress wasn't all she felt.

The depth of attraction she felt toward Adam disturbed her. He made her want to move closer and step away at the same time.

Instead, she froze, unsure and growing angrier about that with every passing second.

"Kat. I don't want to hurt you."

That made her throw a scornful look over her shoulder at him. "Unless you're going to hit me, you don't have the ability to do that."

Pure revulsion crossed his expression as he took a step away and removed his hand.

She immediately regretted her choice of words.

"Damn it." She sighed. "That didn't come out right. I don't think you're going to hurt me, Adam."

"I'm glad to hear that."

But he didn't sound convinced and she wanted to stomp her foot in pure frustration. She should leave. Now. Before she said something totally ridiculous and made Adam think she was more of a bitch than he probably already did.

Which is why no man will ever want you. You're hopeless.

Her mother's voice echoed through her head, and it hit every sore emotional spot she owned.

She grabbed the door again and managed to get the lever to work this time. But before she was able to open the door more than a few inches, Adam had his hand on it. He didn't close it, but he didn't allow her to open it any farther.

"Wait. Okay? Just…give me a minute. Please. I'm trying not to make a further mess of this."

"I really don't think there's anything more to say."

But she didn't move. They held their positions for several tense seconds until she released the door lever and he pushed the door shut.

Before she lost her courage, she turned to face him, looking up into his face. Seeing his frustration plainly in his expression.

She wanted to laugh at the absurd situation she'd found herself in but wasn't sure if he'd think she'd finally lost it.

Shaking her head, she sighed. "I really am sorry for barging in here today. I blindsided you and that wasn't my intention."

"We didn't exactly get off on the right foot today, did we?"

Her lips twisted into a rueful grimace. "We haven't exactly been on the right foot since we met."

"I'm not so sure about that." His expression took on that intensity she only remembered seeing when they'd been in bed. "There were moments we clicked pretty well."

She sighed again. "Do you do that on purpose to throw me off?"

He looked genuinely confused. "Do what?"

"Make me flustered."

His expression lightened and he almost looked like he was going to smile. "And are you flustered?"

"I've been flustered since the moment I met you and Tristan at the party."

"And still, here you are at my door."

"To apologize for how I acted last night."

"Before or— Damn it." He shook his head. "Damn it. I'm sorry. I'm usually not such a prick."

"Lucky me." She shrugged, trying not to let the hurt show. "I guess there's just something about me that brings it out in you."

Before she realized what he was doing, he'd cupped her cheek with one hand. "This isn't on you. It's me."

The warmth of his skin acted like a drug straight into her bloodstream. Every heartbeat pumped it through her body until she wanted him to lean down and kiss her until she couldn't breathe.

"Kat."

His voice held a definite sexual edge, and her body responded with a surge of heat so strong, she felt sure he could feel it.

Staring up at him, she saw his jaw clench as she focused on his mouth. His lips.

"Kat, maybe you should leave."

"That would be the smart thing to do, wouldn't it?"

And no one would ever accuse her of not doing the smart thing. Until about a week ago when she followed two men to a hotel room.

His thumb brushed against the corner of her mouth, and that same reckless urgency she'd felt the first night they'd met made her swipe at his thumb with her tongue.

"This isn't smart." He moved closer until her eyes closed and she felt his breath whisper against her cheek.

"Do you care?" she asked.

"Part of me really wants to say no."

"And the other part?"

"Is wondering what the hell I'm waiting for." His lips sealed over hers a second later.

She barely had time to breathe before he slid his tongue past her lips to tangle with hers and wrapped an arm around her shoulder to drag her flush against him. Every inch of his heat and hard muscle pressed against a soft point of hers. Tilting her head back, she wound her arms around his waist.

All thought of leaving fled before the rush of lust that consumed her at his taste. Vaguely, she heard her purse hit the floor with a jangle but promptly forgot about it as her hands slid from his back to curve over his ass. His worn jeans cupped the muscled flesh lovingly, and she couldn't stop smoothing her hands over the soft material.

Adam's free hand sank into her hair, curving around her head to guide her into the position he wanted her. Angling her head to the side gave him better access to her mouth, and he kissed her until she thought she might never want to come up for air.

She'd never been kissed like this in her entire life. But then, she'd never met a man like Adam. Had never allowed herself to think a man like Adam or Tristan would want her.

Before… Hell, there was no before. Only here. Only now.

Adam's masterful kiss made her feel as if she was drowning in lust. His lips moved over hers with a purpose that had her pressing closer, rubbing against him.

Tilting her pelvis into his, she tried to get closer, her body moving instinctively. The hard ridge of his erection nudging against her clit made her moan. Made her want more. Harder. Faster.

How did he do it? How did he turn her into this crazy, impossibly horny person she didn't recognize?

Simply by kissing her?

But it wasn't just the way he kissed. It was the way he used his hands. The way he held her tight but didn't make her feel threatened or dominated. The way he kissed her with complete concentration yet still managed to stroke her body into utter surrender.

She wanted him to stroke every inch of her skin with his hands. Wanted to get her hands on him. Just thinking about it made her moan into his mouth.

Adam groaned and pulled away from her mouth but not from her body. "Jesus, Kat." He put his mouth against her neck and sucked on her neck hard enough to make it sting. "This isn't smart."

No, it really wasn't. She tried to pull away, wanted to see his expression, but he wouldn't let her move far enough away. He kept her tight against him, his erection pressing against her stomach, making her want to slip her hands into his jeans and stroke him.

This wasn't why she'd come here.

Wasn't it?

She tried but couldn't catch her breath. His scent surrounded her, making her thighs clench and her sex moisten. She didn't want to stop.

She didn't want to be smart. She wanted to be naked and have Adam pound into her, make her scream his name.

Turning her head, she bit his neck. Not hard, just enough to make him shudder against her. "Fuck."

In the next second, he laced one hand through her hair and tugged. Her head tilted back and he sealed their lips together again.

This time, he demanded so much more. And she was more than willing to give it to him.

She returned his fast-building intensity with her own, her hands working under his shirt until she felt warm skin. Flattening her hands on his back, she pressed him closer, moaning when he settled his hand on her ass and ground his cock against her.

God yes.

The desire to wrap her legs around his waist and rock against him made her frantic. Her fingers dug into his back and she rose onto her toes, trying to make up the height difference. Her breasts felt tender and swollen, aching for his hands to cover them. Or his mouth. His teeth.

Gasping into his mouth as he lifted her off the floor, she wrapped one arm around his shoulders to stabilize herself but had no fear he'd drop her. The arm around her waist felt strong as steel, and the hand on her back made it clear she wasn't going anywhere.

But he was moving and she was pretty sure she knew where he was taking her.

Still kissing her, he carried her to the stairs, navigating as sure-footed as a cat. Every movement rubbed her pelvis against his and finally, she had to break the kiss to catch her breath. Every nerve in her body was energized, every cell straining for something she was fast becoming addicted to.

That should scare the shit out of her. And somewhere

inside her brain, it did. But that part of her brain had been hijacked by the unfamiliar sensation of wanting so badly and having what she wanted within her reach.

When they reached the top of the stairs, Adam stopped, and sudden fear swept through her. She didn't want him to put her down and tell her to think about what she was doing. That he was going to ask her if she was sure and she was going to say no, she wasn't, because that's what he expected to hear.

"One question. Do you want me to stop?"

That had an easy answer. "No."

Leaning close, he spoke directly into her ear. "Good. Because we're about to cross a few lines, and I can't even force myself to care. All I want is you naked and under me."

The pure animal sexuality in his tone hit her like a jolt of adrenaline straight into her bloodstream, wiping out every rational thought in her head.

It was a good thing it only took him a few steps to reach his destination; otherwise, he may have found himself being ravaged by a madwoman.

That's how she felt. Out of control and half-feral. And she couldn't bring herself to care.

"I want that too."

She did. Even if, somewhere in the back of her mind, she knew there would be consequences.

Tristan—

Adam kissed her again, and her brain blanked into a haze of white noise.

She heard his labored breathing and his groan when she opened her mouth and her tongue tangled with his. Setting her on her feet, his fingers worked at her jeans as he walked her backward. Her fingers went to his waistband and it became a race to see who could get the other stripped faster.

Since her fingers felt thick and unwieldy, Adam won that round, undoing her button and zipper and pushing her jeans down to her thighs.

"Take 'em off, sweetheart. Take it all off."

Frustration rumbled in his voice, making her shiver at the depth of need beneath it. She felt all thumbs as she fumbled with the button and zipper but she never hesitated because Adam had stripped off his shirt.

Yes, she'd already seen him naked. Twice.

But before, her attention had been divided. She'd had two gorgeous male bodies to ogle. Now, she could focus her entire attention on Adam.

My god, the man took her breath away. Covered with solid muscle in all the right places. Chest, arms, thighs. A washboard stomach that made her want to drag her nails over the ridges until she felt the wiry hair at his groin.

While she stared, he bared everything.

His erection curved up, thick and ruddy. And so damn tempting.

Her blouse unbuttoned, she abandoned it to reach for him. She curled one hand around his thick cock, entranced by the guttural sound he made.

"You're not naked." He caught her wrist and stopped her from stroking him. "You need to be."

"I think you're capable of finishing the job."

She *so* wanted to torment him as he and Tristan had tormented her, but she didn't want to do something stupid because she wasn't good at this.

And she was sick of feeling not good at things.

As his gaze narrowed at her, she tried to read his expression. Had she sounded demanding instead of enticing? She wanted—

Adam gripped the hem of her sweater and stripped it over her head. She'd taken off her boots and jeans but her underwear remained, though not for long. He stripped off her panties and bra seconds later.

She had to release him to let her bra fall to the floor but immediately reached for him again. Amazing how she was becoming used to having Adam and Tristan see her naked, even after such a short time. Maybe because she could barely think straight when she looked at him.

And practically licked her lips.

Stroking his cock gave her almost as much pleasure as having him stare at her with so much heat in his eyes. He was silky soft yet hard as steel. And right now, he was hers. Only hers. And he stared as though she was the most beautiful woman he'd ever seen. Right now, she felt like it.

Tugging him closer with her hand on his cock, she stepped into him, feeling her knuckles slide against her own skin as she pumped him from base to tip.

She wanted him to use his fingers on her, to stroke her slick labia then slide his fingers inside her aching sheath and fuck her with them. She wanted that so badly, she could barely breathe.

"Christ, Kat. You keep looking at me like that and I'm going to come all over your hand."

She liked the thought that he might not be able to control himself because of her and she smiled. "That's okay.

You can use your fingers on me then."

His blue eyes narrowed. "Is that what you want? You want me to get you off with my hand?"

Deep breath. "Maybe just to start."

One of his huge hands settled on her shoulder. The other on her hip.

"Keep stroking and I'll give you whatever you want."

"Do you like this or—"

"Fuck yes, I like this. Don't stop."

His candid response struck a chord deep inside and her sex clenched. "I need you to put your fingers inside me."

The hand on her shoulder squeezed almost to the point of pain, but in the next second he'd relaxed. Then both hands began to move. The one on her shoulder covered her breast. The one on her hip cupped her sex.

With his mouth at her ear, he said, "You're so damn wet, I'm going to slide right in. Were you thinking about this before you got here? Thinking about me taking you?"

She swallowed hard. "Yes. Even though I was furious with you last night, I couldn't stop thinking about it."

She felt his lips move and she swore he smiled. "We'll discuss that later. First…"

With deliberate strokes, he opened her labia and slid two fingers into her. Her eyes slammed shut at the sensation of being filled. Of getting what she needed.

"Damn, you're wet. But you don't get to slack off, Kat. Come on. Stroke me. That's right. Now take my balls in your other hand. They need attention too."

Yes. Even tightly drawn up against his body, his balls overflowed her palm. She wanted to watch while she stroked him but didn't want to move away because he was using his fingers in ways she'd never believed could be so arousing.

On every inward stroke, he used the tip of one finger to press against a spot high inside her. A spot that made her squirm in pleasure.

"Oh."

"Like that?"

"Yes." Oh god, she liked it so damn much.

"Good. Because I'm going to make you come so damn many times, you're not going to be able to walk for hours." *Yes. Please.*

Her fingers squeezed around his cock and he drew in a hissing breath. Immediately, she loosened her grip but when he slid his fingers inside her again, he nipped at her ear.

"You're fine, baby. I like it rough and I can take it." The implication behind his words made her shiver. Adam pushed her outside her comfort zone and she found she liked it. More than she ever thought she would.

It made her bold. Made her want more than to just take. She wanted to make him beg.

"Then get on the bed."

He pulled his fingers out of her sex so fast she gasped, but in the next second he caught her up in his arms and stalked across the floor to the bed. Practically tossing her on it, she barely had time to blink before he threw himself down beside her on his back.

Reaching for her, he pulled her onto his chest and took her mouth again in a kiss that left her breathless. But as he eased back slightly, she began to find her bearings.

Propping herself on one elbow, she let her free hand settle onto his chest. Sleek, firm muscle. She wanted to pet him. So she did, starting at his shoulder. Over the so-soft hair sprinkled from his pecs to his ridged abdomen. Then down to the soft trail of hair leading from belly button to groin. The hair here was darker than the hair on his head but wiry. Crisp. His stiff erection lay flat against his stomach, long and thick, and she wanted to take him in her mouth.

Before Adam and Tristan, she'd never understood the appeal of blowjobs. Now she realized it took the right man.

Or men, in her case.

Covering his cock with her hand, she watched as she gripped him tight and stroked. He barely slid against her skin. Did he like that?

She glanced up and found him watching her, eyes glittering, nostrils flared. He'd propped himself up on his elbows and his chest rose and fell in harsh bursts. But he looked way too calm. And she felt much too on edge to let him be that calm.

Leaning forward, she licked at the tight tip of his nipple, reveling in the warm, salty taste of his skin. Then she bit him.

And he hissed and flinched, making her smile.

Now, she heard him pant and his cock pulsed in her fist. She felt moisture seep from his cock and slicked her fingers over it, lubricating her grip. Then she worked him harder, taking him at his word that he liked it rough.

Biting her way down his body, she stopped to swirl her tongue into his belly button, heard him groan. The sound lit fire through her blood, making her more and more hungry for his response. Pulling his cock away from his stomach, she took him in her mouth.

His taste hit her tongue, sparking even more hunger deep inside, where she was also aching to have his fingers. But that meant she'd have to reposition herself. And she liked this position. At least for the moment.

So she let that ache build and concentrated on taking him over the edge.

Sucking on the tip, she swirled her tongue around the head, marveling at the heat, the scent, the taste. All of it combined to take her out of herself, to push her into a space where she wasn't her boring old self.

She was a woman who took what she wanted and gave men what they needed.

She drew on him hard then followed her fingers down his shaft until she'd formed a ring around the base of his cock with her thumb and forefinger.

"Tighter." Adam practically panted. "Fuck, that's good."

Yes.

She worked him faster, took him deeper, tightened her fingers around him until she swore he'd have to make her stop. He didn't. He dropped his head back and let her have him.

Her lips felt stretched to their limit, her jaw began to ache, but she didn't stop. She let herself get lost in the rhythm.

Until she heard him groan.

Then she suddenly found herself on her back, staring up at a very determined man.

"I'm not going to come in your mouth." His voice made her shiver. "I'm going to come buried deep inside you. But first, you're going to come on my tongue. And then around my fingers. And then I'm going to make you scream my name when I push my cock inside you."

Oh god, yes, please.

All she could manage was a nod.

In the next second, he'd reached under her legs to grab

her ass and lift her pussy to his mouth. He covered her completely, flicking his tongue against her clit before burying it between her labia. Fucking her with his tongue.

Gasping, she jolted into a sharp orgasm that left her feeling more exposed than ever but also anchored. To him.

Adam's fingers clutched at her ass, holding her stable as he continued to eat at her as her climax wound down. Arching her back, she pushed her mound closer, wanting more.

He gave it to her. His tongue inside her. His teeth against her clit, scraping the tender bundle of nerves until she felt she might implode from the sensation.

Unable to catch her breath and unwilling to stop him so she could, she writhed in his hold and tried to urge the ecstasy to burn through her.

He nearly pushed her over the edge into an orgasm several more times but eased back at the last minute each time. And then he'd start all over until the ache between her thighs became a full-body burn. Every muscle strained for release. Every time his tongue touched her clit, her body leaped to the edge, ready to explode.

And then he sat back on his heels and she nearly screamed in frustration.

"I lied." His voice rumbled deep inside his chest, barely audible yet still managing to make her quake. "I can't wait to get inside you."

Setting her back onto the bad, he leaned to the side, yanked open the bedside table drawer, and grabbed a handful of condoms. Packets fell from his hand until he was left with only one. With his teeth, he ripped it open and rolled on the condom in seconds.

She watched with wide eyes, slightly dazed from being over-sensitized. But she still wanted more.

With the condom in place, he crawled up her body, holding himself over her with his hands planted above her shoulders.

His cock brushed against her mound and her hips lifted up to him.

"Legs around my waist, Kat."

Her legs felt heavy, as if weighted at the ankles, but she wrapped them around him and levered her pelvis closer.

His eyes closed as she rubbed against his cock, but his arms held him rock steady. Reaching for him, she slid her fingers into his hair, dragging her nails against his scalp.

Groaning, he turned his head to give her better access. His cock throbbed between them and she arched into him, trying to align their bodies to get his cock where she needed it. Inside her.

"I need you, Adam."

Turning his head, he pressed an open-mouth kiss against the curve of her neck then bit the tendon, causing her to moan and squirm.

"Good. Because the feeling's mutual."

But he still didn't enter her. Just let her rub against him.

"Damn, you feel amazing." His hot breath blasted against her skin. "I swear I can come just like this."

"Don't. You promised me I'd come around you. I want that."

One small part of her brain was having conniptions over the words coming out of her mouth. The prude part that had been raised by her mother. The part she wanted to wipe out of existence.

The other rejoiced at the freedom she felt here and now.

"Aw hell."

She didn't think he meant those words for her. She wasn't even sure he realized he'd said them aloud.

But as soon as they left his mouth, she felt the change come over him. Like an atmosphere shift before a storm.

He looked down into her eyes, and some primal part of her wanted to give him everything.

She didn't have time to realize how terrifying that should be because in one smooth move he impaled her.

Gasping at the sudden sense of being filled so completely, she slammed her hands against his shoulders and closed her eyes. The reaction was instinctive, unconscious. She didn't want him to stop. She only wanted the chance to catch up.

But Adam wasn't going to give her that time.

"Open your eyes, Kat. I want you to watch me. I want you to know who's making you come."

His tone rumbled and his gaze burned, but she could've sworn she heard a tiny hint of insecurity in his words. Maybe she was reading him wrong. Maybe it was wishful thinking on her part.

Still, it made her lips curve in a slight smile and she moved one of her hands to cup his jaw and lifted her head to press a kiss to his cheek.

"I know who you are, Adam. And I know what I want. Now move."

Between one breath and the next, he sealed their mouths together and followed her order.

As their tongues tangled, he withdrew for a second

before fucking her with a measured pace that pushed her into new heights of pleasure.

Wrapping her arms around his shoulders and tightening her legs around his waist, she held on, gasping incoherent murmurs of encouragement. Her muscles tensed, on the edge of an incandescent pleasure that threatened to steal what was left of her sanity.

Already too far gone to care, she gave herself over to his demand for complete domination.

As if he sensed her capitulation, he adjusted the angle of his thrust and sent her over the edge. Her sex contracted around him, making her cry out at the force of her orgasm.

Pushing him into his own. He came, her name a groan on his lips, sinking down into her.

And making her realize how much she wanted to do this again.

11

Adam rolled onto his back, breathing so heavily he figured the neighbors could hear him.

Kat lay beside him, her breathing almost as loud as his.

Was she shaking?

Without thought, he pulled her against him, filled with triumph when she didn't fight him. But it wasn't close enough. With a little maneuvering, he got her draped over his chest, her head on his shoulder, her arm across his chest, and her leg over his thigh.

And Tristan should be at her back.

Shit. *Shit.*

He needed to be much more coherent to deal with the guilt building in his gut. So for the time being, he might as well simply enjoy the feel of her naked body against his. Enjoy the aftershock of pleasure, the adrenaline high that made him feel like he'd jumped out of a plane.

And enjoy the fact that she'd beaten him to the punch and had come to him first.

"I was planning to track you down today," he said, wanting her to know. "To apologize for my behavior last night."

Her breath hitched before she released it on a sigh. "I guess there's enough blame to go around. I don't enjoy being such a bitch."

"You're not a bitch."

"Hmm. You don't know me well enough to say that conclusively."

Okay, he'd give her that one. "Then let me get to know you better. Let *us* get to know you better."

He wondered how she'd react to him bringing Tristan back into the equation, and when she stiffened, he thought he'd totally fucked this up.

"Does this...what we just did...will this be a problem for Tristan?"

Of course she'd nailed the one part of the equation he really didn't have an answer for. Tristan had been half in love with this woman for years. Hell, he'd been obsessing over her for a decade, at least.

And Adam had taken her alone. Would Tris have a problem? "It shouldn't be."

"But it could be?"

Yeah, it might. But that was something Tris and Adam had to work out. Kat shouldn't have to worry about it.

"No. Because Tris and I won't let it."

Silence fell again, but he knew she was chewing something over in her brain. He let her go for a minute. If she didn't come out and ask what she wanted, he'd push her into it. She needed to know she could ask him...ask *them* anything. Needed to realize that for this relationship to work, she had to be an equal base.

And when she'd shown up earlier today, he'd realized she was stronger than he'd given her credit for last night.

Just when he thought he was going to have to prod her, she pushed herself into a seated position beside him. She covered her lap with the rumpled sheets but didn't go completely prude and cover her breasts. Which was a good thing because she had beautiful breasts. Small but firm and high. If he propped himself on one elbow, he'd be at the perfect level to lean forward and take one of those pale pink nipples between his teeth.

Amazingly, his cock began to stir. He tamped down the urge to pull her over him and take her again.

"So, how is this going to work?"

And there was the lawyer, demanding answers. He wondered what she looked like at her office. Hell, even in a suit with her hair pulled back in a spinster bun, he'd probably still find her fuckable. Maybe more so because he'd seen her like this and knew what she looked like under those clothes.

"Adam?"

She raised her eyebrows at him and he grinned, watching her gaze narrow.

"Okay, here's how it works."

Sitting up, he crossed his legs, not bothering with the blanket. His grin widened as her gaze dipped before she flushed and blinked and met his gaze again.

"Like what you see?"

He couldn't help but tease her. She was the only woman he'd ever felt the need to tease after sex. He liked it.

Her eyebrows lifted. "Yes, actually I do. But you know that so why don't you tell me what I need to know."

He also liked that edge she had. It showed backbone. "Tris might have a different answer, and you'll probably want to ask him the next time you see him, but this is mine. The only way a relationship like this works is without jealousy."

She took a second to think about that before nodding.

"I see how that could be a problem."

"Yeah, it's a huge problem and it's one Tris and I have never had to deal with."

He didn't mention that that was because he'd never formed an emotional attachment to any of the women he'd shared with Tris. And he knew this time was going to be different. For all of them.

"And it's all based on trust," he continued. "You have to trust us not to pull at you like a tug-of-war rope, and we have to trust you not to play us off against one another."

She frowned. "Has that happened before?"

"Yeah. A few times. The women didn't get the outcome they thought they deserved." Which was Tristan siding with them and dropping Adam.

"Did the women know going in that you two were a package deal?"

"We thought we'd made it pretty clear."

"And still they expected you or Tristan to step aside?"

"Basically."

He watched her chew that over for a few seconds. "So...I understand why a woman would find this relationship beneficial. Why do you?"

Good question. And one he wasn't ready to give a

straight answer to because he wasn't sure he wanted to reveal that much of his psyche to her. At least not yet.

"Because it works for me."

Clear-eyed, she stared at him. "Because you don't have to be completely responsible for holding up the male end of the relationship."

Smart woman.

He didn't flinch. "Partly, yeah. Because I know my short-comings."

Her gaze narrowed and he thought she might have something to add to that. Instead, after a few seconds, she nodded. "So now what?"

Good question. "Now we call and ask you out to dinner."

"And who tells Tristan...about today?"

"I do. Like I said. We've done nothing to feel guilty about. There are going to be times we're going to be alone or you're going to be alone with Tris. Jealousy doesn't factor in here."

And he hoped to hell he wasn't lying through his teeth.

Kat dissected her conversation with Adam during the entire hour-and-a-half drive to Erik's place.

Traffic was miserable on the Schuylkill Expressway, crawling then speeding up then slowing to a stop for no apparent reason. Why the hell anyone did this on a regular basis was beyond her comprehension.

But she figured she'd better get used to it if she was going to visit Erik at all.

And she hoped she would. She missed her brother.

He'd been her one true confidant throughout her entire

life, and they knew each other better than anyone else in the world.

He was also the only person in the world she knew who might understand some of the questions she had. Because he was the only other person she knew who was in a three-way relationship. With her ex-fiancé.

And if that wasn't a minefield fraught with enough explosives to level a small city... With a sigh, she released the brake and moved forward another few feet.

By the time she reached Erik's home in Berks County, she'd convinced herself not to say a word to Erik. She loved her brother dearly, but he was a guy. She needed a woman's perspective.

Kat had taken one step onto the porch when the door opened and Jules stepped forward with an apologetic smile on her face.

"Hi, Katrina. Please come in. I'm really sorry but Erik and Keegan are running late. Erik said something about a break-through on some piece of equipment or something. When they start to talk tech stuff, I tend to zone out." She laughed but it sounded strained. "Can I get you something to drink? Let me take your coat. I'll call the guys again and tell them you're here."

So it was just going to be the two of them? Probably why Jules continued to babble. She and her brother's lover hadn't spent a lot of time together alone. Actually, Kat couldn't remember when the two of them had been alone for more than a few seconds.

She didn't blame Keegan for being wary of her reaction to Jules. Kat's engagement to Keegan hadn't ended on the best of terms. Which had been mostly her fault. She knew that now.

Damn, would she ever be normal? She didn't relate well to other women. Probably because she'd never met one who didn't remind her in some way of her mother. Fake.

Haughty. Self-obsessed.

And she'd never had a relationship that hadn't ended in abject failure.

"Katrina?"

Kat realized she'd stopped in the middle of the living room, halfway out of her coat. Blinking, she looked at Jules, who stared at her with nervous worry.

"I'm sorry, Julianne." Kat tried a smile, hoped it didn't look like a grimace. "I'd love a drink, thank you."

Shrugging out of her coat, Kat handed that over to the other woman, noticing how uncomfortable Jules appeared.

Which was all Kat's fault. And so not fair.

"Why don't you go ahead and sit in the living room." Jules disappeared with Kat's coat into Erik's study then reemerged and headed toward the kitchen. "I'll just—"

"If you don't mind, I'll give you a hand."

The shock on Jules' face made Kat want to smile. And shake her head.

At every prior meeting, Kat hadn't really known what to say to Jules. The other woman must've thought Kat wanted nothing to do with her. And despite that, Jules greeted her every time with a cautious but genuine smile.

Now, Jules recovered quickly enough. "Sure. Come on back."

Following along behind the pretty brunette, Kat realized

she had an opportunity here. To build a bridge. She just had to be woman enough to take it.

Shoring up her courage, Kat stopped at the counter as Jules continued to the fridge.

"We've got lemonade or wine. Or beer. Or I can mix you something? Keegan's more of the— Oh, well, I can fix anything you'd like."

Jules looked like she wanted to bite her tongue off at the mention of Keegan, and Kat decided it was time to clear the air so maybe they could move forward. After all, Jules didn't appear to be going anywhere. She made Kat's brother happy, had brought him back into the world after an explosion left him with horrible scarring.

"I think we need a do-over."

Jules' eyes widened and she froze at the refrigerator, leaving the door hanging open. Her mouth opened as if she was going to say something, but nothing emerged.

Okay, Kat probably deserved that. "I realize I'm not the easiest person to get to know."

Jules blinked at her. "Uh…"

"And I'd like to apologize for that."

Jules' expression immediately transformed with compassion. "Oh Kat, there's nothing to—"

"Yes, there is. I've been a bitch and I really don't want to be that anymore."

Gaze narrowing, Jules shut the fridge door. "Kat, did something happen? Are you okay?"

Staring into Jules' dark eyes, Kat saw genuine concern. And the possibility of true friendship. If she made the first move. And didn't make a hash out of it.

"I'm fine. But…yes, something happened. And you're the only person I know who might possibly understand."

"Okay." Jules looked confused but she hadn't turned Kat down or made her feel like an idiot. And Kat knew she had to get over thinking every other woman in the world was like her mother. Or the fake females she'd gone to school with and knew casually in Boston.

"I met two men."

"Okay." Jules stared at her, her expression encouraging her to continue, but Kat knew the other woman hadn't understood exactly what she was saying.

And then Jules' eyes widened again and her mouth actually dropped open for a few seconds before she snapped it closed.

"Oh. Uh, okay. That's…really not what I was… Yeah."

Kat grimaced, trying to find the right words to continue. "I realize this is probably something you never expected to hear from me, but I find myself in a situation I don't understand. And I'd really like to talk to you about it."

Jules simply stared at her for a second before she nodded. "Absolutely. But I really think we need alcohol for this." She opened the fridge again, grabbed a bottle of wine, and waved it in Kat's direction.

Kat nodded, relief flooding through her.

She didn't know what she would have done if Jules had turned her down. Then again, she should've known that the woman living with her brother and his best friend and managing to hold her own between them would be able to handle her.

"So, do you want to tell me about them?"

Setting a glass full of white wine on the island in the center of the kitchen, she pushed it toward Kat.

Taking a deep breath then taking a decent swallow of wine, Kat told Jules everything.

"She's gonna kill us."

Keegan's hands tightened around the wheel as he made the final turn onto the lane leading to Erik's home. They should've left the lab an hour ago, but Keegan had had a breakthrough on the thermal camera he'd been working on for weeks and Erik had told him to keep going. That he'd had time before they had to be home.

"No, she's not. She'll be fine. Besides, Kat's mellowing. She's not gonna go psycho on Jules."

Keegan grimaced, knowing Erik was right. Kat had been different the last few times he'd seen her. Mellow, yes, but... something else. Sad. Depressed.

Hell, he didn't know. He only knew he didn't want Jules to have to deal with Kat for any longer than she had to. Which then made him feel like shit.

"I don't think she's going to hurt Jules, you ass. I just meant Kat's not exactly easy to get along with."

"And Jules knows that. Come on, K. She got me to be kind of civilized. I'm sure she can handle Kat for a few hours."

"'Kind of' being the operative phrase."

"Yeah, fuck you too, K."

Keegan slid a glance at Erik, who grinned at him, his scars mostly hidden in the dark interior of the car. There'd been a time, not too long ago, when Keegan had worried that

Erik might never smile again after the explosion in the lab. And then Erik had seen Jules waitressing a party at their office and had come back to life. Keegan could never repay Jules for that. He could only love her with everything he had and be thankful that she'd taken both him and Erik into her heart.

Of course, if anyone could break through Kat's bomb shelter-thick walls, it was Jules. The woman who'd transformed his and Erik's lives had the kindest heart and the stiffest spine of anyone he knew.

Keegan sighed as he floored the pedal to the floor for the last few hundred yards before slamming to a stop in front of the house. Right next to a white rental that had to be Kat's.

Erik was out of the car in a flash and taking the stairs to the porch two at a time. Keegan caught up to him just before Erik opened the door.

"Do you think I should go home?"

Erik gave him a "you're an idiot" look. "Fuck that. Don't be a pussy."

Keegan gave Erik the finger. "Fine. Let's do this."

Erik took a deep breath and rolled his shoulders as he pushed through the front door into the home he shared with Jules and Keegan, who'd slowly been moving his stuff here from his own home down the road.

They hadn't really talked about which home they were going to keep, but for some reason Jules liked this one better so he and Keegan had figured what the hell. Eventually, they'd figure out what to do with Keegan's place, which he'd built only a mile away.

They'd already talked about expanding this one, adding a study for Keegan and opening up the kitchen a bit more for Jules.

All of which was fine by Erik. As long as it kept Jules and Keegan close, he'd do whatever it took.

Now he could devote a little time to helping Kat get her life in order. Through the first few years of hell after the explosion that had left him emotionally crippled and physically disfigured, Kat and Keegan had been his only constants. Keegan had been his rock of stability. Kat...

Kat had been the one who urged him to push forward when he would've rather curled up in a ball and hid himself in his lab.

Of course, Kat had been more "do as I say, not as I do," which meant she had a pretty decent-size wall surrounding her emotions. And could be a royal bitch when she really put her mind to it.

Shit.

Yeah, he'd told Keegan not to be an ass about leaving Jules and Kat alone together. Now he just had to remind himself that he was right. Kat and Jules were fine. He was sure of it.

Then why are you sweating?

He wasn't. Not really.

Damn it.

Leaving Keegan to close the door, Erik headed straight for the kitchen.

"Hey, Jules. We're home."

"In the kitchen," came the normal-sounding reply.

Throwing a "see, told you" look at Keegan, Erik figuratively crossed his fingers and stepped up his pace, Keegan close on his heels.

Pushing through the swinging door into the kitchen, Erik took a few steps into what had become Jules' domain and stopped.

Jules and Kat sat across from each other at the kitchen table, wineglasses in front of them.

Jules looked fine. Not stressed at all. Relief made him release the breath he hadn't been aware he'd been holding.

Then he turned his attention to Kat. And his gaze narrowed.

His sister looked...guilty. Why the hell did she look guilty?

As he pondered that, he walked over to Jules for a kiss then turned to his sister, drawing her out of her chair and hugging her. It usually took her a second or two to return an embrace, but today she actually hugged him back immediately.

Now he *knew* there was something going on.

"Hey, sis. How's it going?"

Her sister glanced at Jules before meeting his gaze again. "It's going okay."

Then why did he get the feeling he and Keegan had interrupted something?

Out of the corner of his eye, he saw Keegan lean over to kiss Jules as well.

God damn. Maybe he was an idiot. Jesus, Kat and Keegan had been engaged and now Keegan was in a relationship and Kat was still alone, and maybe she didn't want to see Keegan kissing another woman.

But Kat didn't seem to be affected by Keegan and Jules. And that was suspicious as all hell.

"Kat was telling me about the place she found in Philly. It sounds amazing."

Pulling back, Kat smiled at him as she settled back into her chair.

Oh she was definitely hiding something. What the hell?

"Oh yeah?"

Kat nodded. "I'd love to have you all," she included Keegan in her invitation by smiling tentatively at her former fiancé, "come down for dinner after I'm moved in."

Struck dumb, Erik stared at Kat for several seconds before Keegan bailed him out.

"Sounds great. Where is it?"

For the next minute, Jules, Keegan, and Kat sedately discussed her new home until finally Erik shook his head.

"Okay, time out." He formed his hand into a T and all eyes turned to stare at him. "Kat, what the hell? What's going on?"

Jules was the first to recover. "Erik, that's no way to talk to your—"

"Jules, it's okay." Kat slid a brief smile in Jules' direction before she looked back at Erik. "I've been picking Jules' brain about a few things. And before you go ballistic and jump to all the wrong conclusions, I'll tell you it's about a guy." She stopped to bite her top lip, a sure sign she was uncomfortable. "Well, it's about two guys." As Kat started to explain, Erik's gaze narrowed.

Sonuvabitch.

That totally explained the voice mail he'd gotten earlier today.

Looks like he was going to make a trip to Philly sooner than Kat expected.

"I'm coming. Jesus, Adam, stop pounding on the damn door."

Tristan yanked open his front door Sunday morning, fully expecting to find Adam.

When he didn't, the face didn't immediately register except for the fact that the guy had gone through some serious shit.

Which clicked into place exactly who stood on his doorstep.

"Erik. Hey, how are you?"

Tristan automatically stuck his hand out to shake, and Erik Riley took it with a slight smile on his scarred face. "Tristan. It's been awhile."

"Yeah. Yeah, it has. Shit, come in." Tristan moved away from the door so Erik could walk through. "Sorry. I was expecting someone else. How've you been?"

Erik shrugged and grinned, making the scars on his face twist. "You mean, besides the explosion and nearly dying and the scars and the rehab? Not bad, actually." When Erik stopped in the middle of Tristan's living room and stared at him with a raised eyebrow, the one on the side of his face without scars, Tristan's brain blanked.

Completely.

"Uh... Glad to hear it."

Erik actually laughed. "And I'm glad to still be here to say it. I know I told you before, but I wanted to thank you again for hooking me up with Jimmy Cochrane."

The former SEAL Tristan had pointed Erik toward after the explosion. Jimmy had lost an eye and a foot in Afghanistan and now worked as a therapist, mostly with fellow veterans.

"I was glad to help."

Erik's smile widened, but now Tristan didn't see much humor in it. And suddenly, he realized why Erik was here.

Oh shit.

"So, Tristan. You wanna tell me what the fuck your intentions are toward my sister? Because I gotta tell ya, if you and your buddy screw her over, I will tear your hearts out."

Tristan's back went stiff at the implied insult in Erik's words, and he had to rein in his immediate reaction to tell Erik to fuck off.

Because if Tristan had a sister, he imagined he'd feel pretty much the same. If two guys with his and Adam's reputations started pursuing her, he'd probably want to rip their heads off, too.

So he bit his tongue and gave serious thought to his response. Erik deserved that.

"We have no intention of screwing over your sister.

I've had a thing for Kat since high school. This is the first I've been able to act on it since then. And I intend to continue to see her."

"You and Adam Oleksy."

Tristan nodded. "You did your homework."

Erik's arms crossed over his chest. "Damn right I did. And I'm here to tell you, if you mess with her head, I will find ways to destroy you that you will never see coming.

And I don't mean physically. Kat's not like other women. She's got—"

Erik's mouth snapped shut and he grimaced. But Tristan knew where the other man was going. Kat had issues. Tristan knew that. But they weren't going to stop him because he also saw the sweetness beneath the prickly exterior.

"I'm not—"

Another series of loud knocks interrupted Tristan's response, and this time he knew it was Adam.

"Hold that thought." Tristan moved to the door.

"Because you're going to get to take us both on at once."

Standing at Tristan's front door, Adam had been thinking about what the hell to say to his best friend since yesterday.

He'd actually been relieved when Tristan had gotten called out of town to consult on a job yesterday. After a night's sleep, Adam felt he had a better perspective.

He hadn't been expecting Tristan to answer the door and put a hand in his face, shutting Adam off before he even opened his mouth.

"I've got company. And yeah, you're gonna want to be here for this."

Tristan stepped away from the entrance to allow Adam to walk through. He didn't get more than two feet inside Tristan's condo when he realized there was someone standing in Tristan's living room. Someone who looked like he'd been caught in an IED explosion.

"Adam, this is Erik Riley. Erik, Adam Oleksy. Great, introductions complete. Now, before we spill blood, does anyone want alcohol? I know it's only a little after nine but I have the feeling I'm going to need a shot at least."

Erik Riley. As in Kat's brother. Who didn't look real happy at the moment.

Adam nodded at Tristan then closed the door behind him.

Alcohol sounded good because it was time to face some music.

And hopefully none of them would need a trip to the emergency room afterward.

***

Kat ran her hands down the skirt of her dress, wondering if she should change.

Not because she thought her dress was too fancy but because she'd never worn anything like it before.

It was casual. Soft, dark blue with embroidery around the hems. A little retro with its low waistline and scooped neck and silky fabric that clung to her minimal curves and made her feel feminine.

She'd spent part of the day at the King of Prussia malls, wandering the stores, her mind mostly on the phone call she'd gotten earlier.

From Tristan. He and Adam wanted to take her out tonight.

Unless she preferred to stay in and order room service.

She'd opted for Plan B. Mainly because she hadn't wanted to have this conversation in a restaurant where anyone might overhear them.

And yes, maybe because she simply wanted to be alone

with them. Where they could do whatever they pleased, whenever they pleased.

The flutter in her stomach became an entire herd of pterodactyls. Of should that be flock?

And really, what did it matter? They'd be here any minute.

She turned to look at the room. The hotel had gorgeous furnishings and nothing was out of place. A few small candles burned on the small dining table in front of the windows, and she'd only lit two other lights in the suite. One by the door, the other in her bedroom. She'd left the door to the bedroom cracked so a hint of light spilled out.

Now all she needed were the men.

Her talk with Jules had been enlightening, and she felt she had a better handle on the dynamics of a three-way relationship.

Unless they were coming to tell her, sorry, this isn't going to work, it's been great and thanks for the memories but time to move on.

Those pterodactyls became T. rexes, shaking her confidence.

Maybe she should start on the wine—

The knock at the door startled her, even though she'd been expecting it.

Okay. Deep breath.

She opened the door, a smile on her lips.

Which quickly froze at the sight of Tristan and Adam.

Dressed in casual slacks, a pale blue button-down for Tristan, and a long-sleeved black t-shirt for Adam, she'd never seen any more handsome men in her life.

And they were here for her.

Her smile widened and Tristan's lips curved in an answering grin, one echoed by Adam, although his was muted.

She didn't let that worry her. She was beginning to read them both a little better, and she knew Adam could hide so much.

"Hi. Come in."

"Hey, Kat." As he walked in, Tristan leaned down and brushed a kiss across her mouth, making her long for more.

"Thanks for having us over."

Adam followed on his heels, leaning down as well but brushing his lips against her cheek. "You look beautiful."

Her heart stuttered at Adam's straightforward comment, and heat rushed along her skin when he followed his kiss with a brush of his finger against her jaw.

Her smile widened as she shut the door behind Adam, shutting out the rest of the world.

"Would you like something to drink? I've got—"

"We'd actually like to talk to you first," Tristan said. "If that's okay with you."

Her mood plummeted. *Shit. Oh shit. This isn't going to end well.*

She held on to her smile for dear life. "Of course. Do you want to sit—"

"What I want," Tristan said, "is for you to understand exactly where you stand in this relationship."

She froze. "And where's that?"

"Directly between us. Naked."

12

Kat's mouth dropped open at Tristan's bald statement.

Naked and between them.

Oh god, yes. That sounded wonderful.

She wanted that. And everything that went with it. All she needed was the courage to take what they offered.

Go ahead. Do it. Say yes.

Tristan watched her, his expression intent and a challenge in his eyes. From the very first, he'd been upfront about exactly what he wanted. Which was her.

Nothing in her life had prepared her for Tristan. No one had ever pursued her with such straightforward commitment. It made her ache for everything he wanted to give her.

At the same time, it made her wary of giving herself over to him and having the rug pulled out from under her later.

That was a game her mother liked to play. Give with one hand and take away with the other.

Kat had learned to be wary of anyone who offered her

anything with no visible strings attached. There were always strings. Something else her mother had taught her.

Her gaze skipped to Adam, who had all sorts of hidden strings. She wasn't sure she had the necessary tools to deal with him. He held his emotions so closely in check, she sometimes wondered if he felt anything at all. Well, anything besides lust.

If they continued this affair, she'd have to learn to deal with that. And decide if she could live with a man who only wanted her sexually.

If Adam didn't commit... If he was only in it for the short-term...

Could she live with knowing she would be only a bed partner to him?

Can you live with knowing you didn't even try?

She'd regret it every single day.

"I want that too."

Tristan's immediate smile lit him up, stealing the air from her lungs. His expression transformed into one of a man who'd gotten exactly what he wanted. Which was *her*. The thought made excitement sizzle and pop along her nerves.

Then she slid another glance at Adam, and panic nipped at her confidence.

"It's just..." She struggled to pick the right words. "I'm just not sure I know how to do...this."

Tristan shook his head. "There's no right or wrong.

We'll figure out what works for us as we go."

She nodded, but Tristan's statement didn't exactly make her feel better. She liked having a plan. Liked knowing what was expected of her. Where she fit into the scheme of things.

"Kat."

Adam's voice made her blink before her gaze flipped to him.

"Yes?"

"*We* want this. Both of us."

Adam stared at her just as intently as Tristan had seconds ago. But his eyes lacked the warmth Tristan's held.

Or did they?

She couldn't read Adam. As much as she tried, as much as she wanted to, she didn't know what he was thinking. The only thing she was sure of was Adam's desire for her. That was clear as day.

Frustration bit at her. Would it always be like this?

Would she always be lacking something in Adam's eyes?

And did it matter, if she found what she needed in Tristan's? "Do you? How can I know that for sure?"

Adam's chin lifted. "You can't. You can only trust me when I say that I wouldn't be here if I didn't want to be."

She absolutely believed that. She also knew that Adam's bond to Tristan was so strong, Adam might accept her into his bed simply because he knew that's what Tristan wanted.

Except that didn't explain yesterday's encounter.

"Did you tell him?"

The question escaped before she could bite her tongue.

She wanted to take back the words immediately. Glancing at Tristan, he didn't look shocked or surprised as Adam nodded.

Thank god.

That pressing weight on her shoulders suddenly felt twenty times lighter.

"Good. That's...good. I don't want there to be secrets."

With a widening grin, Tristan took a step closer. "I'm glad we're on the same page. Adam and I know each other. We trust each other. You're not a prize we're competing for.

You're the woman we want to make love to."

Desire heated her blood at the warmth in Tristan's eyes. Her fingers itched with the urge to reach out and run her fingers along Tristan's strong jaw. To feel the slight abrasion of his whiskers against her skin. To let her fingers run down his neck to the broad muscles of his chest. Wanted to strip off his shirt and press her naked body against his.

She wanted Adam to plaster himself against her back, grip her hips with his hands and bite her neck so hard he left a mark.

Her gaze flipped to Adam, who'd held his ground.

"But you have to understand," Adam said. "I'm not Tristan. I'm not easy."

Amazingly, Adam's blunt statement made her smile. As her lips curved, Adam's expression lost some of its darkness.

"I've actually been able to pick that up on my own."

Tristan cut the distance between them by another step, and her heart skipped a couple of beats.

"So are you ready to eat?' Tristan asked.

She blinked. "You want to eat first?"

Tristan's grin widened and even Adam's lips curved.

Reaching for her hand, Tristan squeezed her fingers then rubbed his thumb over her knuckles. "We're not just interested in sex."

Neither was she. But relationships were fraught with even more pitfalls than "just sex."

"Okay."

"Kat."

She looked at Adam.

"Yes?"

"Do you want to eat?"

She did. Her stomach rumbled at the thought. "Dinner. Yes. Let's order dinner."

"Or would you rather we lay you out on the table and show you why you won't be sorry you said yes?"

Her breath stuttered in her chest as her gaze slid to the table for a brief second before locking back onto Adam's gaze.

"Oh hell, Kat." Adam's voice held a rough note.

"You're gonna kill us."

She started as Tristan's hands landed on her hips. She hadn't seen him move. Now, he pressed his body fully against hers, just before he dropped his mouth over hers and kissed her.

Yes, this. This is good. This is amazing.

Tristan's kiss encouraged her to melt into him. Give herself over to the heat of his body as it seeped through her clothes and sank into her skin. When his tongue licked at her lips, she opened her mouth to let him in, her hands reaching for his shoulders to pull him even closer.

Drugged with passion, she felt her body grow heavier with each flick of his tongue against hers, every time he moved his hands up and down her arms.

Then Adam did exactly what she'd wanted only seconds earlier. He pressed himself against her back and put his mouth on her neck, nipping at the tendon and stringing tiny bites to just below her ear.

Moaning, she pressed more closely into Tristan. Which

caused Adam to crowd against her until she felt completely enclosed between them.

Her knees quivered, but she knew Adam and Tristan wouldn't let her fall. Two pairs of hands kept her on her feet.

With a groan, Tristan broke away and took a step back. But Adam remained at her back, one arm sliding around her shoulders, the other around her waist, keeping her back pressed against him, his erection nestled against her back.

"So. Dinner." Tristan smiled. "Don't kill us but I already ordered for all of us so the food could be sent up right away."

Amazingly, she didn't care. Her inner control freak seemed to have been kissed into submission. At least for the time being.

"How'd you know what I'd like?"

Tristan shrugged. "I ordered a selection. Pasta, steak, chicken, salad. Chocolate and fruit for dessert. I figured we can share. Just watch out for Adam. He's a carnivore."

"But I know how to share." Adam's voice rumbled in her ear. "And I don't bite." He paused. "Unless you ask me to."

Hyperaware of the heat of Adam's body surrounding her and her own internal heat fueled by Tristan's smile, she shivered.

"Okay. Dinner."

"Good choice." Adam nipped at her earlobe with his teeth. "You're gonna need the sustenance for later."

She'd barely sucked in a breath when Adam released her. "Come on, I'll help you set the table while Tris calls for the food to be sent up."

Tristan turned toward the phone on the table and she turned to follow Adam to the tiny kitchen, her brain curiously quiet. As if she'd reached her overload point and it'd shut down. So she concentrated on the task at hand.

China plates and crystal glasses in the cabinet. Linen napkins and heavy silverware in the drawer.

Adam passed the glasses to her then piled the napkins and silverware on plates. Her attention shifted to his hands.

She wanted those big, capable hands on her.

They worked in silence to set the small table, Tristan's low rumble in the background the only sound except for the clink of china and silver.

When they finished, Adam held out a chair for her and she took it.

"Do you mind if I turn on some music?" Adam nodded to the small entertainment system on the table.

Something to fill the silence? "Of course not."

She was actually curious to find out what type of music he liked or if he'd simply play a station she'd already programmed. She watched him consider the screen for a second before turning the dial. And when he finally hit play, she smiled when she heard Frank Sinatra.

He caught her smiling and raised an eyebrow at her. "Okay?"

She nodded. "My dad loves Sinatra. He plays him when he works at home. I spent a lot of time as a kid in his office." Usually tucked in a chair with a book. Trying to stay out of her mother's critical sights.

Adam slid into the chair opposite her as Tristan joined them, taking the chair next to her.

"I always liked your dad," Tristan said. "Smart guy."

She smiled. "Brilliant guy, actually." Which was why she'd never understand why he'd married her mother. "He and Erik used to play these weird math logic games and I'd just sit and watch, totally lost."

"Math was never my strong suit." Adam shook his head. "Nearly flunked out of high school because I hated it so much. Luckily, the Philadelphia school system is more interested in getting kids *out* of school than keeping them in."

She watched Adam carefully. "So you grew up here?"

He nodded, his gaze locked to hers. "Born and raised.

My parents immigrated before my sisters and I were born."

"From Russia?"

"Moscow, yeah. We already had family here."

And since she'd done her homework, she knew who his family was. What she didn't know was if he wanted to tell her that his father was in jail for attempted murder and his uncle reputedly ran the Russian mob in Philadelphia.

"But you already know that, don't you?"

She tried not to feel guilty about having the DeMarcos do a background check on Adam. But she needed to be smart. Needed to do what was best for her.

And Adam didn't look angry.

"Yes, I know about your father. And your uncle. But

I'd rather know more about you. Not them."

She saw him digest that info, consider it. Then he nodded.

"I joined the army because I hated school and couldn't imagine spending another four years torturing myself simply to get a degree in a subject that meant nothing to me." He paused, and she saw him make a conscious decision about what to say next. "And in my junior year in high school, a rival family decided my sisters would make great pawns in their turf war against my uncle and father. My brother-in-law lost his legs below the knees when he and I went to get them back."

Oh god. That hadn't been in the report.

She had no idea what to say. "I'm so sorry."

Adam's jaw clenched as if he wanted to say something else

"What he always fails to mention," Tristan cut in, "is that he nearly died that night too." Tristan's voice held almost no inflection but his eyes were flint-hard. "He was shot. The bullet grazed his lungs and his spine. And he still managed to drag Tosh and carry his youngest sister out of a gunfight."

Adam didn't react to Tristan's interjection. "And Tosh still lost his legs."

"But he's still here, and so are your sisters."

Adam slid Tristan a cool glance, and Kat had a feeling this was a long-running argument between them, something she wasn't yet privy to. And she wanted to be included. In everything.

"A year later, the threat was neutralized, my sisters were safe, and I needed to find something to do with my life that didn't involve street gangs or...other illegal activities. So I enlisted."

He made it sound so cut and dried when she knew it couldn't be. She had so many questions. So much she wanted to know. And yet she didn't want to pry, to cause him any more pain. And he definitely felt pain as he brought this all up again.

"Did you enjoy being in the army?"

A flicker of surprise crossed his expression. "Yeah, I did. And I was good at it."

"Because he's a sneaky bastard." Tristan deliberately needled Adam. "And he's a decent shot."

Adam's mouth curved in a grin. "Better shot than you."

Tristan rolled his eyes. "Now you're just fooling yourself."

Kat smiled, watching their banter as if it were a tennis match. Sliding off her shoes, she tucked her legs under her and leaned back in the chair. As she resettled, she noticed both men return their attention to her.

"How did you meet?"

Her curiosity grew, fueled by the interplay between them. They knew each other so well, they'd developed a shorthand. She wanted to learn it, wanted to be on the inside with them.

When Tristan smiled at her, she felt drawn inside that small circle.

"When the newly minted Second Lieutenant got assigned to my platoon." Adam's smile widened. "Fresh out of West Point and already a Grade-A prick."

Tristan didn't look at all offended by Adam's dig. "I may have had a somewhat elevated opinion of myself at the time."

"Lucky for us, you proved yourself in the desert."

She knew they'd served in the Middle East for several years, but it had been more of an abstract concept than a fact. Now, her stomach clutched at the thought that one or both of them could have been killed. Which was ridiculous because they were here now. Safe and sound.

But would they always be?

"Can I ask about your work?"

She had their complete attention again, their focus a little unnerving. Adam's so intense, Tristan's so...inviting.

He nodded. "Of course."

"We just need you to understand that we have confidentiality issues," Adam interjected. "Just like you do with clients."

She nodded. "I understand. So...what exactly do you do?"

"We run a private security firm." Tristan's tone implied it was that simple. Which she knew it wasn't, thanks to the DeMarcos.

"Which means..."

Tristan paused to think about his answer, but Adam leaned forward, tapping his finger on the table to get her attention.

"Maybe you should tell us what you already know.

Then we'll fill in the holes."

Would they understand that she'd had them investigated only because she was curious about them? And not that she was prying into their business? Was there even a distinction to be made there?

"I know you provide security services, but you also do something called kidnap and recovery."

Adam's eyebrows rose but he didn't look surprised.

"That's not something we put on our website."

"I didn't get that from your website."

"No, you had us investigated."

Adam didn't sound angry so she nodded. How would they take that?

A second later, Adam's lips curled in a tiny grin and Tristan outright laughed.

"Good for you, sweetheart," Adam murmured.

"Another woman would've just taken us at our word."

"I like to know who I'm dealing with."

"Good policy to have." Tristan cocked his head to the side then, his gaze narrowing. "And did you get the answers you were looking for?"

"Not really, no."

Tristan spread his hands and leaned back in his chair.

"Then go ahead and ask. Anything you want."

She paused, getting her thoughts in order. But the knock at the door scattered them.

Adam stood and turned to answer the door but not before letting his fingers trail across her jaw, further distracting her. "Hold that thought."

While Adam got the cart, Tristan said, "Corkscrew," before he got up and headed back to the kitchen.

She watched the men take care of things, wordlessly working in tandem, as if they knew, without words, exactly what each of them needed to do.

She didn't have close friends, not on the level of Tristan and Adam's friendship, and she'd never had that closeness with anyone. Some of that she could attribute to her mother and her control. The rest was all on her. *Snap out of it.*

"Can I help?"

Adam handed her a dish from the cart, and together, they filled the small table to overflowing.

Kat shook her head, a bemused smile curving her lips.

"Are we really going to eat all of this food?"

"I didn't know him back then, but Adam's nickname during basic was Coney Island." Tristan laughed at the confused look she gave him. "Ever seen the hot dog eating contest on the Fourth of July?"

"No."

"Those guys can pack away, like, fifty hot dogs in five minutes. It's pretty disgusting, actually. Adam can eat for hours and never get full. It's like his legs are hollow."

Adam shrugged as he took his seat. "I've got a high metabolism."

"You're a freak of nature, man."

Tristan and Adam continued to trade good-natured barbs as they dished out the food, including her as if she'd always been a part of their little circle. She was content to watch them, not contributing much, though they never made her feel shut out.

By the time they'd finished the main courses and one and a half bottles of wine, she'd almost forgotten she still had questions.

Adam hadn't. As the conversation wound down after

Tristan's explanation of the difference between Rangers and SEALs, Adam set his fork down and pinned her with his gaze.

"So...what else do you want to know?"

"Wait." Tristan set a glass of chocolate mousse in front of her. "I think we're going to need chocolate for this one."

She wasn't sure she could eat another bite, but the confection looked amazing.

Adam snorted. "Tristan has the sweet tooth of a teenage girl."

"Better than the crap you eat. Sour Patch Kids." Tristan smiled at her. "Seriously. He can eat an entire bag in one sitting."

"We all have our vices," Adam drawled as he dismissed

Tristan with a roll of his eyes before he nodded at her. "Go ahead. Ask anything you want."

Now, she wasn't sure she wanted to know the answer. She enjoyed being in this little cocoon where the rest of the world didn't exist. Where it was only the three of them. If they started talking about their dangerous jobs… *Get a backbone.*

"So…kidnap and recovery. What exactly does that mean?"

Tristan and Adam exchanged a quick glance.

"It means exactly what it sounds like," Adam said. "We recover kidnap victims. Usually in foreign countries. We've been doing more work in Central and South America lately because they're hot spots. We also get a lot of work in

Russia because of my family ties there."

"And by recover, you mean…"

"We bring them out by whatever means necessary," Tristan continued. "Sometimes it only takes a briefcase full of money. Sometimes we have to use other methods. But we're good at our jobs. And usually a damn sight better than the idiots who think all they have to do is snatch an

American and the money will pour in."

Other methods. "So you still get shot at on a regular basis?"

"Not regularly." Adam shrugged. "But, yeah, as our business grows and our reputation gets around, we've been getting more work, and occasionally there're circumstances out of our control."

"But Kat," Tristan cut in as she tried to digest the fact that the men she was starting to care a great deal about put themselves in serious danger. "We're damn good at what we do."

The confidence in Tristan's expression was mirrored in Adam's, making them even more undeniably sexy. It didn't calm the unease making her chest ache, but it did refocus her on the here-and-now and not on the what-might-be. "Have you ever not recovered someone?"

Adam nodded. "Yeah, and it sucks. Sometimes shit happens and no matter what you do, it's not gonna change things. But Tris is right. We're good at what we do."

Tristan smiled. "And now we have something to look forward to when we get back."

He meant her. The thought made her feel like she'd swallowed a gallon of Pop Rocks, fizzy and giddy.

And horny.

She blinked, but apparently not fast enough to hide her reaction from Adam.

Resting his elbow on the table, Adam leaned closer.

"Do you know what I'm looking forward to now?" She swallowed hard, lungs struggling to draw in air. *Yes.*

"No."

Out of the corner of her eye, she saw Tristan grin.

"Yeah, you do. Same thing I'm looking forward to." She took a deep breath. "And that is?"

"You know." Adam leaned back in his chair again, arms crossed over his chest. "Come on, Kat. Don't run scared now."

Was that how he saw her? Did he really think she was scared?

Was she scared?

No, not scared. Not exactly. "I'm not running. I'm just not sure..."

"Not sure of what?' Tristan prompted when she paused.

"Not sure I can play this game."

Tristan's smile never dimmed. "It's not a game. And yes, you can. Say it, Kat."

Yes, she could. She only needed to say the words.

"I want you naked and on the bed."

Adam's sudden grin took her breath away. "That's a good start, babe. But Tris and I are more interested in the scenario where you're naked and on the bed."

Ah, negotiation. Now, this she understood. "Are we going to negotiate who gets what first?"

Tristan leaned back as well, mimicking Adam's pose. She wondered if they even realized they mirrored each other so well. "You like to bargain."

It's all she knew. "Is that bad?"

"No, it's not." Shaking his head, Tristan sighed. "Okay. So, let's bargain."

"What are the stakes?"

"Exactly what you think," Tristan said. "We want you in bed. If this is how it needs to happen, I can handle that. But I warn you. We're going to end up with exactly what we want. Which is you in bed between us."

Which is exactly what she wanted. But the thought that they were willing to play with her made her want to play hard to get.

She sat up a little straighter in her chair. "And what do I get out of this deal?"

"Two men dedicated to your pleasure?" Tristan said.

"Multiple orgasms?" Adam drawled.

Oh my god, yes, please. "Can you guarantee that?"

Tristan and Adam exchanged a glance. In unison, they said, "Yes."

It suddenly became extremely hard to breathe, and she could no longer hold their gazes. Or stay seated. Pushing to her feet, she started to collect the dishes.

Neither man said anything. They stacked their dishes and passed them to her. She piled them on the cart as Tristan came up behind her with the glasses. Adam flanked her with the food platters then pushed the cart out the door.

As he did, Tristan put his arms around her and pulled her into his body.

She went with a hitch in her breath, her arms winding around his waist. When she met his gaze, her heart skipped a beat at the heat in his eyes.

"I want to strip that dress off you so I can see your gorgeous body. Then I'll get on my knees and lick you to an orgasm while Adam holds you against him so he can play with your breasts and suck on your neck."

The images he conjured made her shiver. She wanted to say how much she wanted the same thing, but no words would come. The heat in his eyes singed them all away.

So much for being an equal on this playing field. But she wasn't about to simply give in.

"It comes off over my head. But if you're taking off my dress, I want you both to lose your clothes, as well."

Adam reached for her skirt, gathering the fabric in his hands until it bunched at her waist. "Jeans have to stay, babe. If mine go, I'm gonna bend you over and take you in seconds. I have very little self-control around you. "

How could he make her hotter and more sentimental with the same few words?

In front of her, Tristan had already shrugged out of his shirt and was throwing it at the nearest piece of furniture. She had no idea if it made it or not because Adam tugged her dress up.

She only had a second to realize this probably wasn't the sexiest way of stripping, but she lost that thought when she caught sight of Tristan's grin.

"I knew you weren't wearing a bra."

She blushed, the response automatic. "I don't really need one."

"I'd like to tell you to never wear one, but I don't want other men looking at you and getting ideas." Tristan's smile widened. "Come closer, babe."

She didn't have time to obey because Adam was at her back, nudging her forward. He'd lost his shirt as well, and his bare chest pressed against her shoulders, hard abdomen against her back. And his iron-hard erection pressing against her ass.

Already burning from the inside out because of the heat in Tristan's eyes, she leaned forward and pressed her mouth to Tristan's chest.

His hands fell on her shoulders as she sucked on his nipple, playing her teeth over it. Adam's hands tightened on her hips as he bent to bite at her shoulder.

Her body trembled under a flood of emotion. Desire. Lust. And a fierce tenderness that should've been so at odds with the other two and wasn't.

That tenderness made her slow when she wanted to go

faster, to make them go faster. Her body wanted Tristan's hands on her breasts, wanted Adam's between her legs.

As if she'd spoken aloud, Adam's fingers teased at her thighs, getting her to spread them so he could stroke them along the lips of her sex, already slick and puffy.

Adam groaned against her shoulder, where he'd pressed his lips. His hand tightened on her hip as he spread her labia and found her clit. He flicked it, sending a sharp, almost painful shaft of pleasure through her lower body.

She pulled away from Tristan, not wanting to bite him inadvertently, a definitely possibility when Adam continue to play with her clit, circling and tapping and flicking until she wasn't sure she'd be able to stand for much longer.

While Adam teased her below, Tristan bent to put his mouth on her breasts. He tugged on her nipples with his teeth, as she'd been doing to him.

And that quick, she lost the upper hand, if she'd ever had it to begin with.

It didn't matter. Not one bit.

Because they made her feel like a goddess being worshipped.

One hand clutched at Tristan's shoulder while the other reached behind her to wrap around Adam's neck.

Connecting them.

Adam turned his head to kiss her palm before sliding the hand on her hip around her front and pressing her ass more firmly against his cock.

"Right here, babe. We're gonna take you right here." Adam's voice raised the hair on her arms. "Then we'll take you into the bedroom and spread you out."

"Good. Just hurry."

Tristan had already begun to work on his jeans and they were gone in a blink, his hands rolling a condom into place.

"Arms around my neck, Kat. Trust us. We've got you." She didn't doubt.

Winding her arms around Tristan's neck, she felt her feet leave the floor as he lifted her. His thick cock brushed against her stomach then the tip pushed against her entrance as her legs automatically went around his waist.

Gravity was her friend as she slid onto his cock, feeling him stretch her pussy until she moaned.

Rolling her hips, she took him deeper, lifting her face for his kiss. As Tristan sealed their lips together, she felt Adam at her back once again.

She tensed, her experience at this still so minimal. But she knew how incredibly intense the pleasure would be so she forced herself to relax and let Tristan and Adam take care of her.

As Adam began to press inside her, Tristan pulled out, just enough to give Adam room to maneuver. Which he did.

Their rhythm quickly drove her to the brink of orgasm. The dual penetration held a bite of pain with the pleasure, so good it made her want to cry out.

She bit back the urge but wasn't able to totally contain the sound.

Tristan broke away to press her head against his shoulder, groaning as he sank deep again.

Behind her, Adam's body gave off heat like an oven, and his harsh breath echoed in her ears as he laid his forehead against the crown of her head.

She had a second to think about how amazingly in tune they were before her body divorced itself from her brain and let pleasure race through her veins and spur both men to follow her.

"I have to go back tomorrow." Yawning, Kat leaned over to check the clock on the bedside table. "Actually, this morning. I need to leave by six."

Behind her, Tristan slept on his side, one hand on her hip, his steady breathing ruffling the hair on the top of her head. Keeping her voice to a whisper, she spoke to Adam, lying on his back next to her. One arm behind his head, the other lay beside her, his fingers entwined with hers. His eyes were closed but she knew he was awake. He kept rubbing his thumb over her knuckles in tiny circles that sent shivers all through her.

"When will you be back?" His voice barely registered as sound but she heard him clearly. Probably because she hung on his every word.

"Friday's my last day. I plan to have dinner with my dad Friday night then leave Saturday morning with as much of my stuff as I can carry in my car. The movers will bring the rest."

"So what time will you be free for dinner Saturday?"

Her lips curved in a wide smile. "I'd have you over but I won't have any furniture. Or any way to cook. I guess we could do a picnic on the floor."

He turned to look at her, and she could see his slight smile in the dim glow coming from the light in the bathroom.

"We'll figure something out before then."

Another yawn caught her off guard, but she knew she wouldn't get any sleep before she needed to leave. And she'd rather lie here and talk to Adam anyway. "Do you have plans for the week?"

"A few system installations to oversee. A personal security detail Wednesday for a Swiss banker and his suitcase."

"You're providing security for a suitcase?"

"Pays the bills."

"Are you going to talk all morning?" Tristan's voice sounded from behind her. "Or are we going to spend the next few hours making sure you're good and sweaty before you have to leave?"

Then Tristan bit her neck and pressed his erection against her ass.

Adam turned onto his side and slid closer until she could barely breathe. Behind her, Tristan left for a second before turning back, lifting her leg over his thigh and sliding his cock between her legs.

"Oh, god, yes."

13

"Adam, we need to gear up. Got a call from Daniel Sinclair. Sinotec has a K&R."

Tristan stuck his head into Adam's office Friday morning, expecting to see Adam with his attention completely focused on his monitor.

Instead, he stood at the window, one hand splayed on the glass. Fog spread out around his hand as flurries drifted by outside.

"Adam, hey. Did you hear me?"

"Hmm?" Adam turned, his attention obviously somewhere other than here and now. "What's up?"

"Phone call. Job. Airport. Gotta go."

"Shit." Adam shook his head. "Sorry. Didn't hear the phone."

Tristan raised an eyebrow at him. "So I gathered.

Wanna tell me what's wrong?"

"Nothing's wrong. Where're we going?"

Tristan didn't look convinced but he didn't push. "Colombia. Engineer disappeared last night, ransom demand came in this morning. Seems pretty straight-forward."

Nodding, Adam turned back to his computer, shut down whatever was on his screen, and turned off the monitor. "Okay. Sure. Where are we going?"

Now Tristan knew Adam wasn't all here. "Already told you. Colombia. You want to tell me what's going on before we head into the jungle and I get shot because you're supposed to have my back and your brain's previously engaged?"

As if he'd flipped a switch, Tristan now had Adam's full attention. But where Tristan was expecting Adam to flip him the bird or something equally obscene, Adam merely grimaced.

"Sorry. Shit." Adam sighed, rubbing a hand over his neck. "Got an email from my dad. It sounds like there's a deal in the works that might get him cut loose early."

Whoa. No wonder Adam looked freaked out. "Okay, I'll give Eddie Danielson—"

Adam grimaced. "No. Fuck that. I'll be fine. Just giving you a heads-up."

"Adam—"

"Tris." Adam held his gaze. "I'll be fine. You know I'd rather be working anyway."

True. Adam worked better under severe pressure than anyone Tristan had ever known. Adam's ability to compart-mentalize and narrow his focus to one item of business at a time made him the perfect partner for Tristan's ability to take in the big picture.

"Then get your kit." Tristan slapped his hand against the doorframe. "I chartered a flight. We leave in fifteen for the airport."

Adam nodded, his gaze skipping out the window again.

"Are you going to call her?"

Wow, okay. That had come out of nowhere. Tristan knew who Adam was talking about, but he couldn't quite believe it. And holy shit. It made Tristan want to pump his fist in the air. "Can you do it? I still have to set up transportation in Bogota. Tell her we should be back by

Saturday."

Adam grunted, which Tristan took to mean "Okay." Could just as well have been "Fuck you." Tristan left before Adam could say anything else.

And then, even though he felt like an idiot, he waited in the hall, just beyond Adam's office door, until he heard Adam say, "Hey, it's Adam. Listen, Tris and I got a call.

We're leaving in an hour."

Kat swore she felt her heart skip a beat. "Am I allowed to ask where you're going?"

"You can ask. I can't say." Adam paused, as if he were putting some thought into what he said next. "You don't need to worry, Kat. We'll be fine."

Kat had just finished her final interview with the senior partners, who'd smiled and wished her well.

In the midst of packing the last of her boxes and making sure her former assistant had everything he needed, her phone rang. She'd smiled as she recognized the number, and her assistant had looked so dumbstruck, Kat had actually laughed at him as she waved him out of the room.

The smile hadn't lasted long.

Now, the bitter fear sinking through her blood made it hard for her to breathe.

"Okay. Thank you for calling. I guess...I'll wait to hear from you."

"And you will. Seriously, Kat. There's nothing to worry about. We'll see you soon."

She forced herself to smile even though she knew he couldn't see it. "I'm sure I'll have more than enough to keep me busy. I do have a new home to move into, after all."

"And we'll be there to help you move furniture wherever the hell you want it."

That brought a real smile to her lips. "Sounds like you've done this before."

"I have two sisters who've moved more than three times each. I think I can handle lugging your couch around a few square feet."

"I'm going to hold you to that."

Adam paused, as if he'd heard the fear in her voice.

"Kat."

"I'm sorry, Adam. I have to go. I need to meet my dad for dinner in an hour, and I have a few more things to wrap up here. Take care. You and Tristan."

She heard his frustrated sigh loud and clear. "We'll talk to you soon. Think of us, babe."

The phone clicked dead in her ear.

Sinking into her desk chair, she stared out the window at the cityscape, so different from the view from her new office in Philadelphia.

That office wasn't nearly as large, the view not nearly as grand.

She was basically starting from scratch. She had one

major client, which was her brother's business. It was enough to float her, but while she was good at corporate law, she wanted to branch out. She wanted to work with children, for children. No, there was no money in it, but the law had never been about money for her. It was about using her skills to help people who needed it. And now she had the time and the means to do it.

But it meant upending her entire life. And she'd never been good at change.

Now she was dealing with a relationship with two men, moving her entire life to a new city, and starting a new business.

Enough to give anyone second thoughts. Or a panic attack.

Her chest started to tighten and her stomach rolled. She began her breathing techniques but was already reaching for the Ativan in her drawer.

You're not even strong enough to control your panic attacks. How the hell are you ever going to manage your own business and hold your own between two men?

Her mother's voice in her head made her stomach flip again. Swallowing down the nausea, she closed her eyes and fought through the attack.

When she reopened them, five minutes had passed and her hands literally ached from clenching the arms of her chair.

But she wasn't running for the bathroom to throw up so she considered this a win.

Maybe you have more backbone than you give yourself credit for.

She held tight to that thought as she left the building,

glancing back only once and then only to wave goodbye to the doorman. She'd be early to the restaurant where she was meeting her dad, but she could use a drink and a few quiet minutes to herself at the bar.

Which never materialized because the second she walked in, she saw Phillip Donovan. As if he'd been waiting for her.

"Katrina, I'm so glad I ran into you. Why don't we grab a table? I'd like to talk to you."

With a polite smile, she took a step away, forcing him to release the hold he had on her elbow. "I'm sorry, Phillip.

I don't have time. I'm meeting my dad for dinner."

Hell, even if she wasn't, she would've lied through her teeth to avoid spending any more time with him than she had to.

Phillip smiled as if he had a secret. "And I'm sure you'd rather your father didn't know you're sleeping with two men so you'll spare me a few minutes."

Shock at Phillip's blunt statement zapped her into a frozen silence that allowed Phillip's smile to grow.

He took her elbow again and began to lead her toward the back of the bar, where secluded tables hid in the dark shadows. She took a few steps before she stopped, not quite yanking her arm from Phillip's grip but not allowing him to force her.

Surprise made him look like a fish out of water, gaping at her. As if he thought she'd been cowed.

A month ago, she might have been. Tonight... She wasn't in the mood to put up with his shit.

"I'll spare you two minutes." She looked him straight in the eyes. "At the bar where you can buy me a drink."

Then she turned her back on him and walked to the bar. He had no choice but to follow or look foolish. And Phillip hated to look foolish.

Even though her heart pounded a mile a minute, she took a seat and waited for him to join her.

The bartender appeared instantly and took their order. As soon as he moved out of hearing range, Kat turned to him. "What do you want, Phillip?"

He lifted a brow at her. "You. I thought I'd made that clear."

"That's not going to happen." Sincerity rang in her voice because she knew that for a fact.

"I wouldn't be too quick to say that."

Phillip looked so sure, but she'd dealt with men like this all her life. And of course she'd dealt with her mother.

"Actually, I do know that for a fact. Now, what exactly were you planning to blackmail me with? The fact that I'm seeing two men? There are women who would give me a medal for bagging two of the hottest men on the planet. Men who served their country heroically. Men who continue to make a difference in the world. Instead of a man who believes that money and social standing are more important than actual humans."

Phillip laughed, though there was no amusement in his tone and his expression had hardened with every one of her words. "How idealistic of you. I had no idea you had that in you. Your mother obviously has no idea how far you've fallen."

"And I'm not in the mood to spar. This conversation is over, Phillip."

"Not quite. Just this last thing to think about, since I will honestly hate to see you destroyed by my brother. Do you know why Tristan and Adam share this…arrangement?"

He made the last word sound like the filthiest swear word. "No, but I suppose you're going to tell me. Make it fast because I'm leaving in thirty seconds."

He reached into his pocket, threw some money on the bar, a sly smile on his lips. "Ask them about Diane." He tipped his glass at her. "Don't say I didn't warn you."

He walked away, glass in hand, stopping farther down the bar to talk to someone.

Kat tried not to let her unease show. Told herself Phillip was simply being an ass, a common state of being for him.

Of course, everyone had relationships in their past that'd gone wrong, ended badly. No one could avoid it. She and Keegan made an excellent case in point. Tristan and Adam would be no different.

"Kat, honey, you look lost in thought. I hope nothing's wrong."

Her head popped up to see her dad standing next to her. She'd completely missed his arrival.

Forcing a smile, she gave her dad a hug and maybe she clung a little too long.

"Hey, sweetheart. What's wrong?"

He patted her back, awkwardly, though he didn't push her away. The first few years after she'd hit puberty, her dad hadn't known how to show his affection. Considering he'd never been overly demonstrative to begin with, it had seemed almost as if he didn't want to touch her for fear of any sense of impropriety.

And that she blamed squarely on her mother.

"You're too old for that," her mother would say when Kat

would hug her dad. Her mother's voice had dripped with so much disdain, Kat had felt almost dirty. It had colored her relationship with her father and so much more.

Christ, her mother had so much shit to answer for.

"Why did you marry her?"

The words escaped before she could stop them, and she regretted them the instant her dad stiffened.

As she pulled away, gaze down as she shook her head, she wanted to smack herself.

"I'm sorry. I'm—"

"Kat, come on. Let's get our table."

His voice held a gentle tone she remembered from child-hood, one that nearly brought tears to her eyes. Since her emotions were already running riot, it didn't help her contain them and she really was worried she'd burst into tears.

Which was ridiculous. She should be angry. At Phillip. At her mother. Hell, she should turn some of that blame on herself. She allowed her mother to continue to drag her down, even after she'd assured herself she wouldn't.

Forcing her chin up, she nodded and let him lead her into the dining room. As they passed Phillip, she made sure she made eye contact, refusing to let him think he'd gotten to her.

Almost every table was taken, but she could hear only a slight murmur. In this place, people didn't raise their voices and there were no children.

And no one broke down in an emotional wreck.

By the time they were settled, Kat had her emotions back under rigid control.

"All right, Kat. Tell me what's going on."

Her dad looked concerned, and that was the last thing she wanted.

She'd wanted to leave for Philadelphia on a high note. A fresh start. Not rehashing old wounds and past hurts. Or worried about the bullshit Phillip was spewing.

But she loved her dad. She considered him her only true parent. Sure, he had his faults, but he wasn't a self-absorbed diva bitch who used her daughter like a chess piece.

"I'm starting over in a new city. I'm leaving everything I know and taking a huge leap of faith that I'll be able to make it on my own. It's a little scary."

He raised an eyebrow at her, and it struck her then how much Erik looked like him. Did people see her mother when they looked at her? Oh god, she hoped not.

"But that's not everything." He sighed. "I wish you felt you could confide in me, but I guess that ship has sailed, hasn't it? Your mother ruined any chance of that."

Shock made her mouth drop open and then she couldn't help herself. "Then why have you stayed with her for so long?"

Her dad's rueful expression made unexpected tears gather in her eyes. "Because fighting her for custody would've made more of a mess. And she wasn't always the way she is now. She only started getting….bad when you became a teenager."

Her dad held up a hand before she could respond. "I'm not saying you were to blame. Not at all. I'm saying your mother has some deep-seated emotional issues of her own. You've met your grandparents." His wry tone spoke volumes. "They have a lot to answer for where your mother is concerned. And that's being kind."

Yes, she'd figured out years ago that her mother's parents were cold-blooded creatures who valued wealth and status above everything. "I guess I should be glad I didn't have to grow up with them."

Her dad nodded gravely. "If I'd divorced your mom, there was a very real possibility that would've happened. They would have fought me and my family with every resource to keep their claws into you and Erik. As it happened, it didn't come to that."

Because he had had sacrificed himself for the past twenty-six years.

"Don't look so horrified." Her dad shook his head. "Like I said, your mother isn't a monster. She is merely the product of her upbringing. She does have a heart. In her own way, she loves us. And she honestly believes everything she's done has been for your benefit."

"By putting me in a mental institution for a month?"

Her dad grimaced. "Sweetheart, to be honest, I actually thought you'd benefit from that. You've always been..." He sighed, as if unable to find the words he wanted.

"Emotionally insecure. Every little thing would set you off."

She wanted to argue that was bullshit. That it was her mother who'd made her the way she was, but she bit back the words.

Because he was right. She'd been emotionally unstable, too easily hurt by every little thing. A black look from her mother had sent her fleeing for her room when she was twelve. A distracted "Just a minute" from her dad would've been tantamount to a complete dismissal.

That wasn't saying her mother wasn't a cold bitch. It just

meant Kat was old enough now to realize her own faults, as well as others.

"But afterward," her dad continued, "you became… distant. A little tougher. I thought that was good. You need a bit of a tough shell to get along in the world today. But you simply managed to hide the brittle part underneath, didn't you?"

Kat tried to hide her amazement that her seemingly clueless dad had figured that out, but obviously something must have shown in her expression because he shook his head and dropped his gaze, embarrassment a slight tinge of red on his cheeks.

"I'm sorry, sweetheart." He shook his head. "I don't mean to make you uncomfortable."

He caught her gaze again and she saw his love for her.

She'd never doubted that.

"You're not, Dad. And you're not wrong. But I'm working on that."

Now he smiled outright. "I know. I've seen the change in you recently. Do you want to tell me what that's about?"

Did she? *Could* she tell her dad about her relationship with two men? Erik was in the exact same relationship, but he was a guy and there were different rules for guys. There always were.

"You can tell me anything, Kat. Anything at all. No judgment here."

Ah. "You've heard."

His faint smile told her everything. "Phillip Donovan isn't exactly known for his discretion. He's got the brain of an emotionally stunted eight-year-old. He couldn't wait to enlighten me about his brother's *depravities*. That's his word, by the way. Not mine."

"But you think it's wrong, don't you?"

"I had a mistress for years." He dropped that bombshell so casually, it took Kat several seconds to process it, and by that time, he'd continued. "Your mother knew. Hell, she actually approved. So long as I kept it discreet, she was happy to farm out the sexual side of our relationship. You and your brother were young. You were three when I met her. Our affair lasted ten years. The problem came when your mother realized I'd fallen in love with the other woman."

Kat blinked, unable to form a coherent question. She wasn't completely sure her dad wanted her to ask questions. He continued as if he was relating his latest day at work.

"I considered divorcing your mother, but I knew she'd make it impossible for me to see you or Erik. Her family had enough money to tie me up in court until you were eighteen. Then she told me she loved me. That she'd always loved me and couldn't live without me. And I stayed, which eventually drove away a woman I truly loved."

Tears burned her eyes but she blinked them away.

"You did that for us. For me and Erik."

"I did it for me, too. Because I didn't want to lose my children. Because I believed your mother. And I know you're going to find this hard to believe, but I love your mother. Love really doesn't have rules, honey. You love who you love and you hope like hell they can love you back in a way that works for both of you. Or all of you."

She bit her lip, so many questions bouncing around her brain. "Are you sorry? That you didn't stay with her, the other woman? That you stayed with my mother?"

"Does it make me a bad person to say I'm sorry I couldn't keep her as well as my family?"

Kat shook her head, a bemused smile curving her lips. "No. I completely understand that. But...what if I can't make it work either?"

Her dad shook his head. "The situations are completely different. Tristan and Adam already know how this type of relationship works. I was of the opinion that it would never work for me. And, knowing your mother, it wouldn't have."

"But what if I don't know how it works?"

It was the question that had been nagging at her brain for the past week, and it was the one she hadn't been able to ask Jules. Jules didn't know her well enough to tell her what she needed to know.

Her dad reached across the table and patted her hand, as if trying to comfort her. "Erik always had to figure out how things worked. We'd find him taking apart lamps and TVs." Chuckling, he shook his head. "Lost a couple of microwaves before we realized he was experimenting with them. You look at something from every angle before you make a move. That can be dangerous because sometimes you look at something for too long and decide it's not worth the trouble. And it should be. Sometimes the risks are worth taking even if everyone else thinks you're crazy."

She nodded, knowing everything he'd said was completely valid. "But there's so much more to lose."

"True. But, honey, think about how much more you can gain."

She wished that was all she could think about. Wished all she could focus on was the fact that two men wanted her.

That fact still had the power to make her shake her head in amazement.

"So you think I should? Be with them?"

"I think only you know what you want. And what's right for you. But once you make that decision, don't let anyone tell you you made the wrong choice. The only person who can tell you that is yourself. You're the only one living in your head. Don't let anyone else in there. There's usually only room for one."

Smiling now, she nodded and watched her dad's expression lighten, as well.

"Now." Her dad rapped the table with his knuckles, as if declaring that portion of their meeting at an end. "What are we drinking to celebrate this new phase of your life? I think tequila shots might be in order."

***

She regretted those shots the next morning when her phone rang a little after seven a.m.

Temples pounding and her mouth dry, she reached for the phone and the bottle of water she'd put on her bedside table last night.

Expecting to hear an unfamiliar voice telling her the movers were arriving in seconds, she was disoriented when she realized she knew the voice that said, "Kat."

"Tristan?"

"Yeah. Hey, sorry to call so early but...I didn't want you hear this from anyone else."

"Hear what?"

Tristan paused and Kat yawned, blinking to bring her

brain into focus. And when she did, she realized Tristan hadn't continued.

"Tristan? What's wrong?"

She heard him sigh clearly through the phone line. And her stomach rolled as fear sank in.

"Adam's in the hospital. He's going to be fine."

Her brain began to spin, latching on to the words "Adam" and "hospital."

"What happened? Was he in an accident?"

"No, it wasn't an accident. And he really is going to be fine. He's a tough bastard." Another sigh and she heard the weariness in Tristan's voice now. "He doesn't know I called and he's gonna be pissed as hell that I did before you got here, but I figured you should know before someone else got to you."

"Got to me? Tristan, I don't understand. Why is Adam in the hospital?"

"We had a job go a little sideways yesterday."

"Sideways?"

"Yeah. Look, let me charter you a flight out of Boston. Can you be ready to leave in an hour?"

Her brain totally blanked until everything she needed to do came back in a rush. "The movers are supposed to be here any minute and I was planning to drive down—"

"I'll have someone there in half an hour to take care of your car and handle the movers. And I can have you at the hospital less than three hours from now."

Her breath stuttered in her lungs. "Oh god, Tristan. How bad is he?"

"He's fine. He was never in any danger."

"Danger? In danger of what? Dying?"

"Shit, I'm totally fucking this up." Tristan sighed. "Seriously, he's fine. I just thought… Damn it. I just thought you should know before you got down here. I didn't want you to be surprised."

She wasn't surprised. She was shocked. And terrified.

And she wanted to be there. Right now.

"Okay. Yes. I want to be there as soon as possible." She swore she heard Tristan sigh in relief. "Good. Great. I'll have someone there in thirty minutes. I'll pick you up at the airport. We're anxious to see you, sweetheart. We've missed you. I know Adam will be happy to see you."

"Is he really okay?"

"He's fine. Honestly. Damn, I fucked this up. Everything's fine. I'm glad you'll be here sooner rather than later. I'll see you soon, babe. I'll text you the name and a picture of the man who'll drive your car down and take care of the movers."

"All right. Tristan?"

"Yeah, babe?'

"I missed you. Both of you."

"We missed you, too. Hey, Kat. Deep breath.

Everything's fine. We just want you here. Now."

The next few hours passed in a breathless whirl as Tristan's friend arrived and took charge.

Kellan Douglas listened intently, navy blue eyes pinning her with laser focus as she gave him the details about the movers and handed over the keys to her car.

With his buzz-cut dark hair and bulging muscles, he should've made her nervous, but the fact that Tristan trusted him made it okay. And if he made it possible for her to be in Philadelphia that much faster, so much the better.

She didn't have time to analyze or even breathe, really, until she had herself buckled into the small jet Tristan had chartered.

She'd never been on a private plane before, would've been so much more interested in her surroundings if her fear for Adam hadn't been building.

Yes, Tristan had told her Adam was fine. But he'd never explained what had happened. And the unknown was now making her crazy. Had he been shot? Stabbed? Fallen off a cliff? What?

She didn't even know where they'd been. If she asked, would they tell her? Could they tell her? Probably not. She imagined there were all sorts of confidentiality clauses involved in the work they did.

Did this happen a lot? In their line of business, she imagined it might.

She'd done research on the kind of business they ran and knew that the danger they faced in a recovery situation was very real. And possibly deadly.

She just hadn't let herself think about those possibilities in relation to Tristan and Adam. Which presented a serious flaw in her rationale about their relationship.

Luckily, the flight from Boston to Philly wasn't long enough for her to work herself into a full-blown panic attack. It helped that her head was still spinning from the speed at which she'd left that morning. She'd had no time to reflect on the fact that she really was leaving behind her entire life and picking up in a new city.

When the plane landed and the copilot, who'd met her when she'd arrived, told her she could deplane, she found herself not at the main terminal but at a private hangar. And by the time she reached the middle of the stairs, Tristan was waiting for her.

He must have come from the hangar but she hadn't noticed. She'd been too worried about tripping down the stairs in her haste to get off the plane because all of a sudden he was just there.

Arms crossed over his chest, exhaustion clearly evident on his face, which hadn't seen a razor for a couple of days. And smiling, not fake or forced, but a true smile that told her he was happy to see her.

She had a second to wonder if she should throw her arms around his shoulders or if that would seem too clingy before he grabbed her into his arms two steps from the bottom and hugged her tight. Her arms immediately wrapped around his neck and tightened until she thought she might be choking him.

But Tristan didn't complain, and she turned her face into his neck, trying to hide the fact that she was dangerously close to crying.

"Hey, Kat. Damn, I fucking missed you."

"I missed you, too."

Tristan huffed out a laugh and dragged her even closer.

"Glad to hear it."

Easing his grip on her, he put a hand under her chin and tilted her face back so he could look into her eyes. He didn't say anything about the tears she knew he saw. Instead, he used his thumbs to wipe them away then lowered his mouth and kissed her.

It was an all-consuming, volcano-hot kiss that made her want to plaster herself against him and let him have his way with her. Any way he wanted her.

He kissed her as if he hadn't seen her in months and he was starved for her. Dying to taste her. Longing to rip off her clothes and find a flat surface to push her up against or lay her on.

Dropping the tote she'd hastily packed before leaving Boston, she thrust her fingers in his hair and held him even closer.

Someone cleared their throat behind them and Tristan reluctantly released her, drawing back after one more lingering press of his lips against hers.

"Nice to see you again, Tris. Tell Adam I'll check in with him later today."

Blinking out of the fog in her head his kisses created, Kat turned to find the female pilot behind her. Smiling at Tris as if she knew him well. And why would she need to check in with Adam?

The pretty redhead wore navy pants and a white button-down shirt and looked like the sweetest girl-next-door Kat had ever seen.

And if she continued to smile at Tristan with that warmth in her eyes, Kat was going to have to hurt her.

"Thanks, Mandy. Appreciate you and Drew getting her here so fast."

"Anything for you, Lieutenant. You know that."

Oh, there had definitely been something going on there.

The strength of her jealousy took her by surprise, and she had to turn away and stare in the opposite direction. It was such an unusual reaction, she wasn't exactly sure how to deal with it. She'd never had anyone to be jealous of before.

It was...disconcerting. And that was putting it mildly.

A second later Mandy walked away, and Tristan grabbed

Kat's overnight bag and put an arm around her shoulders as he got her moving toward the hangar.

"It'll take maybe half an hour to get to the hospital. He's already bitching about when he can get discharged. The bullet grazed his head and knocked him out for a few hours. The only reason he's still in the hospital is because he got a concussion when he fell and hit his head. He's got a pretty decent bruise on the side of his face and he's missing some hair around the area where he was hit. Otherwise, he really is fine."

Tristan's calm tone almost hid the reveal that Adam had been shot. But her brain finally caught up and her breath caught in her throat.

"Bullet. You're saying Adam was shot."

He tried to cover it but she felt him wince. "Not exactly. I mean, yeah, there was a bullet involved, but it's not like he actually got shot. It just...grazed him."

It got harder to breathe as her lungs contracted in fear even as she tried to hold on to the fact that Adam was fine.

"Does this happen a lot?"

Tristan didn't answer right away as he pressed the remote in his hand and the car parked at the side of the hangar bleated once then fell silent. When they were settled in his SUV and he'd gotten them headed toward the exit, he continued.

"Not a lot, no. But," he sighed and shook his head. "I gotta be honest. It does happen sometimes. What we do isn't without risk, but we're good at what we do and that minimizes the risk."

She let his words run through her head as he headed toward the highway and back to the city. Everything he'd said sounded so rational. Hell, she could walk out her door one morning and get hit by a bus.

But she didn't typically walk straight into traffic, which was basically what Adam and Tristan did for a living.

"Kat?"

She blinked, turning to focus on Tristan. He was frowning at the road, hands clenched around the wheel.

"Yes?"

"He's fine."

Yes, he was. They both were. And if she was going to continue this relationship, she needed to come to grips with the fact that they weren't going to change their careers simply because she couldn't handle their dangerous jobs.

They'd lived through a war. The possibility that they could've been killed had been so much higher then.

And yet, she knew if something happened to either of them, she'd be an emotional wreck. Unless she learned to deal.

Starting here and now.

"Good. I'm glad he's okay. Will he be in the hospital long?"

Tristan slid her a glance, gaze narrowed as if he wasn't sure he trusted her calm tone. "Actually, he should be released today. Told him I'd pick him up this morning. I didn't tell him about flying you down, but I know he'll be glad to see you. He still thinks you'll be here tonight."

"So you were just going to spring me on him?"

Tristan's grin made her stomach tighten. How the hell did he do that? Even with all the stress of the morning, he still made her body tingle with a smile.

"Yeah, but he's gonna be thrilled. Trust me."

She did trust him. Sometimes she found it hard to believe but Tristan made it easy. Adam was still tough to read sometimes, but she was determined to make this relationship work so she'd find a way.

Adam sat on the hospital bed, foot tapping, knee bouncing.

Tristan had promised to pick him up this morning so he'd promised Tristan he'd stay until he showed.

But if Tris didn't get here soon, Adam was going to break down and call his sister to come get him. Yes, he could sign himself out and get a taxi, but his damn head hurt bad enough that he figured he'd take the few extra hours of down time.

Kat would be here tonight, and he had plans that didn't involve a migraine. He hadn't decided how to explain the stitches, but he'd figure out something. Or he'd leave it to Tristan. Tris would find some way to sugarcoat it so she wouldn't freak out when the words "bullet" and "head" were used in the same sentence.

Hell, it was little more than a scratch, but he wasn't sure Kat would recognize the distinction and he didn't want to be the cause of a panic attack.

And where the *fuck* was Tristan?

He looked at the clock, as if he hadn't done it five times in the last two minutes.

Shit.

His phone rang and he grabbed for it, hoping like hell it was Tris.

Fuck.

Not Tris. Christ, he didn't need this. Not now.

He thought about letting it go to voicemail, but he knew he'd have to deal with this situation sooner or later. He'd prefer never, but he wasn't one to stick his head in the sand.

With a sigh, he answered.

"Yeah?"

"Hey, is that any way to say hello to your father? Adam, your mother raised you better."

Adam grimaced. Yes, she had. And for all his faults, the man on the other end of the phone was his father.

"Dad. How's it going?"

"Better than yesterday, which you would know if you returned my calls."

Adam rubbed at the building ache between his eyes. "I was out of the country yesterday on a job."

"My boy, the superhero."

Amazingly, there wasn't a trace of sarcasm in his Mickey Oleksy's voice. Only pride. And right there was the dilemma that had plagued Adam for years.

"Not a hero. Just doing my job."

"Bullshit. What have I always told you? Whatever you are, whatever you want to be, you gotta own it."

And damn if his dad wasn't right. "I know, Dad."

"Good. Now...I'm getting out Monday."

Adam had known it was coming. He still felt like he'd been sucker punched.

His dad huffed. "Shocked, aren't ya?"

"No. Just... What happened?"

"We'll discuss it Monday. Carve out some time to talk to your old man, okay?"

"Does Mom know?"

"Of course. She's the first person I told."

He said it like it was a given, and Adam made a mental note to check in with his mom as soon as possible.

"Sure, Dad. We'll talk Monday."

"Good."

"Do you need to be picked up?"

"Nah. I don't want you picking me up at the prison. You know that. Your uncle's coming."

And his dad would be right back in the life. Adam's headache took a turn toward migraine.

He sighed. "Dad—"

"Dime's up, son. I'll see you Monday."

The line went dead and Adam had the almost overwhelming urge to toss his phone at the wall or the door or anywhere else.

Fucking hell.

Sitting on the bed, hands on his knees, head down, he took a couple of deep breaths, trying not to let the stress settle in.

Obviously his dad had rolled on someone to get released early. Jesus, he hoped it wasn't anyone who'd come after his family again. He honestly wasn't sure he could keep himself from going medieval and tearing people apart. He'd managed to rein himself in fourteen years ago. Now... Yeah, he was older and wiser, but he'd also been trained in how to do the most amount of damage with the least amount of visibility.

Shit.

He heard footsteps approaching, a man and woman from the sound. When they stopped outside his door, he figured the nurse was back with the doctor to release him.

He looked up and it took him two seconds to realize it wasn't a nurse.

"Kat."

He was off the bed in a split second, arms around her shoulders, yanking her against him. He sealed their lips together and kissed her, hard, until he had to pull back or risk passing out from lack of oxygen.

"I thought you weren't coming 'til later today."

"I had a little help getting here earlier." Her gaze flicked to Tristan, who'd come up beside her, smiling like the cat who ate the canary. "Are you okay?"

"I'm fine. What did he tell you?"

She raised her eyebrows at him. "That you were shot but not really and it wasn't bad and you were fine."

"Which I am. And ready to get the hell out of here."

Hell, he felt a hundred times better now that she was here. "Tris, go see if you can find the damn nurse with the release papers, will you? I wanna go home."

14

They went to Adam's house.

Tristan had packed a bag before he'd left for the airport, and he carried that and Kat's tote into Adam's small house.

Adam liked it out here, away from the hustle of Center City but still only minutes from the office.

Tristan liked Adam's place. It felt like a home, not just a house.

But it'd be too small for the three of them.

Maybe they could find a bigger place, somewhere in Fairmount or maybe Manayunk—

Getting way the hell ahead of yourself, aren't you?

Yeah, but damn, it was really nice to think about.

As Adam ushered Kat through the door and into the living room, Tristan watched Adam. He looked a hell of a lot better than he had last night when Tristan had carried him out of that hellhole of a Colombian village.

There'd been so much damn blood all over both of them that he'd had their office manager burn their clothes. She hadn't blinked, but that might've been because she'd been almost paralyzed by the sight of Adam's hair turned nearly maroon.

"Why don't you sit down?" Kat said, a worried frown marring her forehead. "You look pale. Are you sure you feel okay?"

Adam sank onto the couch, and Tristan knew he was fighting a migraine. The fact that Adam didn't give her a hassle told Tristan it was going to be a bad one.

"He's getting a migraine. I'll get his pills."

And when Adam didn't tell him to fuck off, he didn't need them, Tristan knew it was already pretty bad.

"Can I do anything?"

Kat had lowered her voice to just above a whisper and eased onto the cushion next to Adam, who looked even whiter than he had when they'd left the hospital.

Maybe he should've pushed harder for Adam to stay in the hospital another night, but he knew Adam. He would've told Tristan what he wanted to hear then he'd have checked himself out and left on his own.

Besides, seeing Kat was good for him. Now to get rid of the migraine...

Tristan left to retrieve Adam's pills from the bathroom on the second floor. By the time he found them, he heard Kat's voice in the hall. She must've coaxed Adam into bed. Which was where he'd wanted them to end up anyway. But what he'd had planned wasn't going to happen. At least not now.

Adam needed to sleep this off. Hell, Tristan could use a little downtime himself. The travel and the trouble they'd run into were catching up with him fast, and he felt fatigue starting to crash down on him.

He got to the bedroom in time to see Adam drop his shirt on the floor, jeans already gone. Tristan winced at the bruises on Adam's back. And heard Kat's quiet gasp as Adam turned and she caught sight of them, as well.

Adam either didn't notice her reaction or was too tired to respond. He crawled into bed and closed his eyes.

"Here, take this before you pass out."

Adam cracked an eye and took the pill and the glass of water.

"I'll be fine in a few hours. Tell her."

"I will. Get some sleep. We'll talk about your stupidity later."

That brought a faint smile to Adam's lips then Tristan turned and hustled Kat out the door and back downstairs.

Heading for the couch, Tristan sank into the cushions, though he tried not to close his eyes. If he did, he'd be out cold.

Instead, he tracked Kat as she moved to stand next to him.

The wry smile on her face intrigued the hell out of him.

"You look like you could do with a few hours of sleep too." She settled herself on the cushion next to him.

"I'd rather spend that time with you."

Her smile brightened. "I'm glad to hear that. I also think you should've saved the money to charter that plane because neither of you is going to be awake in a few seconds."

A yawn caught him by surprise and Kat chuckled.

"See?"

He returned her smile with a tired grin. "Best money I've spent all year if you're here when I wake up."

The warmth in her gaze told him he'd said the right words.

"And so I will be. Why don't you close your eyes and get some sleep?"

"Yes, ma'am."

Before she could get up, he stretched out on the couch and put his head in her lap. "Remote's on the table. I'm just gonna close my eyes for a few minutes."

The last thing he felt before he fell asleep was Kat's fingers trailing through his hair.

Kat felt Tristan drift off seconds after his head hit her thigh.

Staring down at him, she let her fingers drift through his short, dark hair and took a deep breath. It felt like the first she'd been able to manage since getting on the plane this morning.

So many emotions rioted through her, she wasn't sure where to start to sort them out.

Amazingly, she wasn't having any anxiety, probably because there was just too much to process. Then again, maybe she was finally learning to control it.

Wouldn't that be nice? To be able to do normal things without the fear that she'd have to run for the bathroom before she got sick when an attack hit her.

Maybe she'd simply found two men who made her fight that much harder to overcome her limitations.

One of whom had gotten shot yesterday.

And there was the fear. But she figured that was pretty normal when someone you cared about had been in danger.

And that was definitely something she needed to come to grips with.

But not right now.

Grabbing the remote from the side table, careful not to jostle Tristan, she flipped through stations until she found something inane to watch. A Scooby-Doo movie on Cartoon Network. Perfect.

However, when the movie ended two hours later, restlessness set in.

She wanted to check on Adam.

Tristan was so deeply asleep, he barely moved when she slid out from under his head, replacing her thigh with a pillow.

Upstairs, she checked on Adam, still asleep and sprawled across as much of the bed as he possibly could be. The wound on his head stood out sharply against his blond hair. A few centimeters—

No. She took a deep breath. He was fine.

Back downstairs, she looked around the clean, bright living room, checked out the mostly undecorated dining room, noticed a study near the back of the house then headed for the kitchen.

Tristan, at least, would probably be hungry when he woke. She liked to cook though she didn't do it a lot. And she loved to bake.

It took her fifteen minutes to go through Adam's fridge and cabinets, figuring out what he had and what she could make from it. Surprisingly, he had a fully stocked kitchen.

Apparently, he liked to cook too.

She had just turned on the stove to bring the vegetables

and chicken to a boil to make stock for soup when she heard the front door open.

She froze for a second before she heard a woman's voice call for Adam.

Taking a deep breath, she headed out to the front room to find a blond woman grimacing over Tristan.

When the woman caught sight of Kat, her bright blue eyes widened, and Kat realized this had to be a relative of Adam's. Probably a sister.

"Oh wow. Hi." She lowered her voice to barely a whisper, drawing Kat closer so she could hear. "I'm Lea. Adam's sister. I didn't realize they were back. Or that they had company. Are you Kat?"

Stunned that this woman knew her name, Kat took Lea's outstretched hand.

"Yes, I am. I, ah, just got here this morning. I've got a pot about to boil over." Kat waved toward the kitchen.

"Can we—"

"Oh sure." Lea's smile widened. "No problem."

"Ooh, smells good." Lea moved toward the stove to sniff at the pot then turned back toward Kat with a huge grin. "Sorry, you're probably wondering how I know who you are. Adam made the mistake of telling our sister about you and, well, she can't keep her mouth shut. She's gonna be *so* upset that I got to meet you first. So where's Adam?"

Kat blinked at the rapid-fire speech, realizing that this motormouth was younger than she'd first realized, probably no more than twenty. "Upstairs. Sleeping off a migraine."

Lea grimaced. "He's gonna be miserable when he wakes up. Just a heads-up. So, what do you do, Kat?"

Amazingly, Kat didn't take offense to Lea's digging. And

she was definitely digging. Her bright eyes shone with interest, and she couldn't contain her smile. If she hadn't looked so much like Adam, Kat would've wondered at the family connection. Then again, she and Erik were nothing at all alike personality-wise.

"I'm a lawyer opening my own office in the city. I just moved here from Boston."

"Cool." Lea headed for the fridge and pulled out a soda, totally comfortable in Adam's home. And why shouldn't she be? "So how'd you meet Adam?"

Trying not to show her unease at that question, Kat figured simple was better. "Through Tristan. Tristan and I have known each other since high school."

"So you're dating both of them, huh? My sister gets a little freaked about that, but I think more power to ya, sister. If you can keep up with them, why shouldn't you have two guys at your beck and call?" Lea paused long enough to tap on each of the ingredients on the table. "Are you making brownies too? Adam's got a huge sweet tooth. Feed him sugar and you'll never be able to get rid of him."

Kat's smile spread as Lea finally wound down and gave Kat an apologetic smile.

"Sorry. Adam's always bitching about how I never shut up." She shrugged. "You'll get used to me."

Kat chuckled. "I'm sure I will. Would you like to help me with these? You can interrogate me while you cream the butter."

"And a sense of humor, too." Lea's grin reappeared. "Okay, I think I can handle mixing. So tell me about your law practice. What kind of law? I'm going to Temple but I'm still undeclared. I like math but I'd love to study music."

The next couple of hours flew by, much to Kat's surprise. It usually took her months to warm up to someone new, because most of the people she dealt with had secrets they either wanted her to help them keep or they didn't want her to know.

Lea was an open book and a literal gusher of knowledge about her brother and Tristan. Kat tried not to pump her for information, but all she had to do was mention Adam's or Tristan's names and Lea would go off on a story.

It almost felt like cheating, getting to know Adam through the eyes of someone who loved him unconditionally and had known him most of his entire life.

The Adam Lea knew was overprotective and so fiercely loyal you couldn't help but love him despite the fact that he'd made her social life "hell."

That hadn't stopped Lea from dating. At the moment, she wasn't seeing anyone on a regular basis, but that didn't mean she wasn't going out. Apparently, she went out almost every night.

A social butterfly, Kat's mother would've called her, with a sneer to make sure you knew she disapproved. Kat envied Lea the fact that she enjoyed the hell out of life.

"So you and Tris when to school together?"

Now sitting on top of the counter watching Kat mix biscuit batter, munching a carrot, Lea had decided it was Kat's turn to reciprocate.

"Tristan and I grew up in the same neighborhood in Boston, though we didn't really hang out then."

"But you wanted to?" Lea's smile made Kat grin. "I mean, who wouldn't, right?"

"Of course. Every girl in school wanted him. But I'm

pretty sure he never knew I existed. He was two grades ahead of me and only dated girls his own age. Or older."

"Well, that's no surprise. The man is totally hot. I have to admit to having a crush on him."

"You wouldn't be the only one."

"Now, why you like my brother..." Lea laughed at Kat's raised eyebrows. "I guess he's okay. He can be kinda intense, though. Just don't take any of his crap and you'll be fine."

"And what crap," said a deep, masculine voice, "would that be?"

"Tris!"

Lea jumped off the counter and into Tristan's arms, giving him a tight hug that he returned by lifting her off her feet and kissing her on the cheek.

He looked so much more rested than he had two hours ago when he'd closed his eyes.

"Hey, sunshine. How's it going?"

Setting Lea back on her feet, Tris came for Kat, leaning down for a kiss that was decidedly not brotherly. In fact, she thought her toes might actually be curling. She almost put her arms around his neck until she realized she still held the wooden spoon she'd been using to mix the batter and her other hand was covered in flour.

That didn't mean she didn't return his kiss. And regret that it wasn't longer.

Until she remembered Lea was watching. And she still didn't care.

When he pulled back, she followed him until he kissed her again, his lips curving in a smile when he finally pulled away.

"You look rested."

He leaned closer and spoke directly into her ear. "And you look good enough to eat."

A blush burned her cheeks and she heard Lea fake cough. "All right, I can take a hint. I just stopped to say hi to Adam because he called Friday and I wasn't able to get back to him. So I'm just gonna head out—"

"Are you sure you don't want to stay for dinner? I cooked enough for an army."

Kat caught Tristan's wry grin and she wondered if she'd overstepped before he turned to Lea.

"Stay, Lea. Adam'll be happy to see you when he gets up. But I gotta warn you. He was hurt on the job yesterday and spent the night in the hospital. He's fine, hon. He's got a hard head, but he's got some stitches and he looks a little rougher than usual."

Lea's smile dimmed a little. "Did he tell Mom yet?"

"I don't think so."

Sighing, Lea reached for the phone in her back pocket. "Then I better warn her before my cousin tells her. Rach works in the billing department at Penn. She's gonna be on the phone to my mom as soon as she sees Adam's name in the system. And trust me, you don't want my mom to find out from anyone else."

"He told me he wanted to tell her himself. I thought that meant he was gonna call."

"If I didn't know, my mom doesn't know 'cause she definitely would've called Lys and me."

"Damn it. Yeah, call your mom and warn her." Tris turned to Kat. "Why don't you go up and see if you can wake him? He's not gonna want to wake up and find his mom here freaking out."

"Are you sure I should?"

A teasing light shone in Tristan's eyes. "Better you than me. He won't tear your head off. He'd probably try to punch me. And he'd only hurt himself."

The warmth in Kat's gut spread and she nodded, setting down the spoon and wiping her hands. "So I'm the sacrificial lamb?"

Tristan smile spread. "Absolutely. He'll be pissed he slept so long as it is."

Since she wanted to check on him anyway, she left, knowing that Lea watched her until she was out of sight.

She liked feeling as if they were building something permanent. Just thinking about a long-term relationship made her happy. Giddy, actually.

She didn't do giddy, but she could get used it...if she could get used to the fact that Tristan or Adam could be taken from her at any time.

Maybe this morning had proved she had the strength to believe everything would work out.

Smiling, she eased open the door to Adam's room. She tried not to make a sound but something must have alerted him because his head turned and his eyes opened.

Like Tristan, he looked much better for having slept, and she breathed a sigh of relief.

Easing up on his elbows, Adam shook his head. "I can't believe I didn't notice you get out of bed. I was looking forward to waking up with you here."

And there was that giddiness again, making her stomach flip and her lungs tight. "How are you feeling?"

She walked to the bed, not hesitating at all to sit on the side and reach for the hand he held out to her. Which he used to tug her down for a hard kiss. "Better. Is someone downstairs?"

"Your sister, Lea."

Adam rolled his eyes, though his smile was indulgent. "She's nosy as hell. You're lucky she didn't text my mom and my other sister the second she realized you were here. Otherwise, there'd be three Oleksy women here."

"I like her."

"Good. So do I, even though she's got a big mouth."

"She's sweet."

"Yeah, when she wants something. She's already snowed you under, hasn't she?"

Kat turned her nose up at him, determined to meet Adam's playful mood with her own. She was just so damn happy he seemed to be feeling better. "Maybe you're just a grump."

His gaze sharpened. "Yeah, I can be. I *am*, most of the time."

Leaning down to kiss the frown forming on his lips, she let herself linger for long seconds, loving the fact that Adam's lips clung to hers when she pulled back. "Then I'll guess we'll have to work on that."

"I guess so."

She stood. "Now, go take a shower then come downstairs. You need to eat."

"I'll be your slave forever if you feed me."

She laughed, liking the sound of that. "Then prepare to worship at my feet."

He didn't laugh like she'd expected. Instead, his expression became thoughtful. "All right, babe. Let me get a shower and I'll be down in a few minutes."

"So, I like her. Wasn't sure I was gonna at first. She seems a little stiff, but she loosens up after a few minutes."

Tristan shook his head at Lea, who he'd been more than happy to adopt as his little sister the first time he'd visited Philly with Adam. She'd been a young teen, awkward and giggly and so damn girly. Adam adored the hell out of her and so did Tristan. So for her to like Kat meant a hell of a lot.

"Lys told me Adam was all screwed up over this girl."

"Wait, Adam talked to Lys about Kat?"

"Dude." Lea cocked an eyebrow at him, looking so much like Adam that Tristan had to laugh. "How long have you known my family? Of course he told Lys. You know he had to get Lys and Tosh's approval. And you know Lys tells me everything because she can't keep her mouth shut."

Since he and Phillip had never been more than passing acquaintances growing up, not only because of the age gap but because Tristan had realized Phillip was a dick by the time he was ten, Tristan had been amazed when he saw how Adam talked to his sisters. The soldier he'd gotten to know and respect and like was a totally different person around Lys and Lea. And when those sisters began to treat him like another brother, Tristan had returned their unconditional affection.

But it'd meant he'd had to learn to deal with nosy sisters. He found he enjoyed the hell out of it.

And so did Adam. Adam also trusted Lys' judgment in almost everything, except his love life. For Adam to have talked to Lys about Kat...

Well, the Devil probably wondered why it was snowing in hell.

"So what'd he say?"

The floor creaked above them and Lea grinned. "I guess you can ask him yourself in a few minutes. And don't worry. I'm not gonna hang around all night. I just want to say hi to Adam then I'll leave you to your own nasty devices."

Tristan was still smiling when Kat returned a few minutes later.

"Adam will be down in a few minutes. He's taking a shower. Will you stay to eat with us, Lea?"

"Sure, if you don't mind. I take free food wherever I can find it."

The doorbell rang and Lea hopped off the counter where she'd been perched. "I'll get it. It's probably Lys. She's got some kind of ESP where Adam and I are concerned. She always knows when something's wrong." But it wasn't Lys.

"Alea. You get prettier every time I see you."

"Uncle David, hey. How are you?"

Shit.

Tristan was out of his seat and halfway to the front door before he realized he'd moved. Kat's startled "Tristan, what's wrong?" caught him after he'd left the kitchen.

Adam's gonna go ballistic.

"I'm good, sweetheart, but I hear Adam's been in some trouble. Ah, Tristan. Why am I not surprised to see you here?"

"David."

Tristan didn't waste empty friendly greetings on David Oleksy. David knew he wouldn't mean it.

In his late fifties, David looked every one of those years.

His silver-white hair and the Oleksy blue eyes gave him a grandfatherly appearance that was deceptive as hell.

David didn't have kids, which was probably the smartest decision the guy had ever made. His wife had died of cancer more than thirty years ago, and he'd never remarried because he was married to his business. A huge, illegal business.

"Tristan." The head of the Philadelphia Russian mob nodded at Tristan, his smile holding genuine warmth.

David liked Tristan and Tristan had to admit David was a likable guy, if you could get past the fact that he should be in jail. Then again, Tristan knew several politicians who had fewer scruples than David.

"How are you? You weren't hurt, too, were you?"

"No. I'm fine. And Adam is, too. The bullet only grazed him."

David nodded and Tristan figured Adam's uncle already knew that. "Is he sleeping it off?"

"Yeah."

"Good. I'm glad to hear he's okay." David nodded, smiled at Lea, and turned to go, but he didn't get far.

"Uncle David. What are you doing here? Is Dad okay?"

Tristan caught back a sigh as Adam practically stomped down the stairs and headed for the door.

David nodded. "Yeah, yeah. He's fine. He said he talked to you this morning, but he thought you sounded off so he wanted me to check. You didn't tell him you were hurt."

Adam walked over to his uncle, taking his hand and the rough hug David gave him, as well.

Tristan knew how conflicted Adam was about his family. And how much he loved them. Tristan couldn't honestly say the same about his own. He couldn't say he loved his brother. He was too much of a dick. He did love his parents, though they were more likely to give him an awkward pat on the back than a hug.

"Because I'm fine. He doesn't need to worry."

"And you know he does." David glanced at Lea before smiling. "So, I've checked in and I can report that you're fine."

Something else passed between Adam and his uncle, something they both acknowledged with a nod, then David turned and headed for the still-open door.

"Adam, a few minutes of your time on the porch, please. Lea, tell your mom I'll see her soon. Love to Lys and the kids."

Adam exchanged a quick glance with Tristan before he followed David out the door.

Tristan wanted to follow, but he knew what that look meant.

Don't follow and no questions. Not now. Not in front of Lea. And especially not Kat. Who walked out of the kitchen at that moment with a smile.

"So are we ready to eat?"

"You talked to your dad, yes?"

Adam swallowed back a sigh but appreciated the fact that his uncle didn't drag this out. He wanted to get back inside.

"Yeah. He told me he's getting out Monday."

David turned, gaze narrowed. "Did he also tell you he's coming out with a price on his head?"

Adam ground his teeth to stop the flow of obscenities.

"No, he failed to mention that."

"Figured." David sighed. "I don't think the Guerra family

will come after anyone but your father. Hell, I'm not even sure they'll come after him. They've got too many problems of their own in-house to worry about additional charges for one of their lieutenants already doing time. Still,

I thought you deserved a heads-up."

"Thanks."

"You know I'll do whatever I have to keep this shit from rolling downhill. But if your dad finally goes through with his threat to retire... Well, there's gonna be some changes."

Adam heard the unspoken question in David's words and started to shake his head, before he stopped with a grimace as he felt an ice pick of pain cut through his head.

"No, Uncle David. The answer's always gonna be no."

David's smile spread. "Yeah, I know that, kid. I really do. Still, I had to ask. You're family."

Yeah, they were. And that was both a blessing and a curse for the Oleksy clan.

"You'll let me know if Dad needs anything, right?" Adam held out his hand. "Because you know he won't ask himself."

David took his hand and used it to draw Adam in for a hug. "You'll be my first call. Take care, kid. I'd hate to have to travel to South America. Too damn hot down there."

And Adam knew David would be on the first plane to Columbia if Adam didn't recover from his injuries. He'd take out an entire guerilla army for his family. What he'd done to the rival family who'd taken Alyssa and Lea when they'd been younger had merely cemented David's perpetual warning to everyone.

Fuck with my family and I will destroy you.

Adam couldn't exactly find fault with that. So he shook his uncle's hand and watched him walk to the big black

Cadillac sitting by the curb. Adam nodded to the deceptively unobtrusive man sitting on the bumper, waiting for David.

Max Burdanov, David's personal guard. The guy was a year older than Adam, and they'd known each other all their lives. They'd been mistaken for brothers as children, but where Adam's hair had stayed blond, Max's had darkened to auburn. And unlike Adam, who knew he looked the part of a Russian mobster, Max looked like a clean-cut Harvard business graduate, which he was.

Why Max had gone to work for his uncle after graduation still made Adam's head spin in confusion. Then again, Max's dad, like Adam's, worked for David and had for decades. Rumor had it David was grooming Max for his job. David was no dummy and Max was brilliant. And he appeared to want the job.

So who was Adam to judge? He'd been taking lives in defense of the United States for years. Sanctioned killings, but he killed just the same. Hell, Adam wasn't sure Max had ever used the gun he carried at his back.

And now his head really was starting to throb.

Shit.

For sixty seconds, he allowed the frustration to eat at him. Ever since he'd learned his dad had lied about being a real estate agent, that same frustration had lurked in his gut. It never subsided, never disappeared, and sometimes, like now, it got the better of him. He wanted to scream, wanted to pound something into pulp.

And he couldn't. He had to hold it together to make sure he didn't upset his sister. Or Kat.

And what the fuck was he going to tell Tristan?

Jesus Christ. What a fucking mess.

Kat noticed the tension between Adam and Tristan as soon as Adam came back inside.

Both men seemed a little preoccupied, which didn't surprise her. But she could tell there was something else, something…off.

Lea helped by being a chatterbox, talking about everything from TV and movies to friends and family. Nothing heavy. Kat was pretty sure that was deliberate. Lea might seem like a ditzy young woman, but Kat realized she had a deliberate plan behind every story, which was to make Adam smile. And Lea took her job quite seriously.

Adam made an effort to smile and respond, and Kat could tell he only did it for Lea.

But Lea left soon after dinner.

Tristan insisted he would clean up, that she and Adam should put their feet up. Adam because he was injured and Kat because she'd cooked.

She was sure Adam wouldn't have sat unless she did, so she led him back to that huge u-shaped sectional couch, where he sank down with a barely concealed grimace.

Sitting next to him, she frowned as she looked him over.

"Are you sure you're feeling okay?"

That blue, blue gaze narrowed up at her. "I'm fine." But he wasn't. "You can barely keep your eyes open.

Why don't you go upstairs and lie down?"

"I don't want to go upstairs."

His heated gaze made it clear exactly why he didn't want to go upstairs. She had to laugh. "You are in no shape to do anything but sleep."

His head fell back on the couch cushion. "I hate to admit it, but I think you're right. Move back into the corner, sweetheart."

She did as he asked then, with a heavy sigh, he shifted until he'd spread out on one section of the couch and laid his head on her lap. Her hand immediately went to brush through his hair, carefully avoiding the stitches in his scalp.

From the kitchen she heard pots and pans clanging and the occasional tinkle of glass.

Adam's breathing leveled out in seconds and his entire body relaxed, his head resting heavily on her thigh.

She smiled ruefully. This wasn't how she'd expected this night to end. Then again, she wasn't unhappy. Quite the opposite.

Closing her eyes, she let herself drift, enjoying the weight of Adam's head on her leg, the warmth of his body seeping through her clothes and into her skin.

She wasn't exactly asleep so she heard Tristan come out of the kitchen and stand by the couch. Opening her eyes, she met Tristan's dark gaze.

The sun had gone down while they were eating, and Tristan had turned out most of the rest of the lights. Only a soft glow from the kitchen enabled her to see him.

"Hey."

"He's asleep." Tristan didn't make it a question.

"Dinner was great."

"I'm glad you enjoyed. Thanks for cleaning up."

He eased onto the cushion at the opposite end of the sectional, just far enough away that she couldn't reach him.

"Wanna show me how thankful?"

She laughed quietly at his teasing leer. "Adam's asleep.

He needs the rest."

Tristan's brows rose. "And I'm not suggesting we wake him. I also don't want to wait until he wakes up."

Her breath hitched, but she was starting to get used to this whole teasing thing and she kinda liked it. Batting her eyes, she said, "Wait for what?"

His smiled widened as the look in his eyes smoldered. "Come over here and I'll tell you."

She wanted to. So badly. And yet... She stared down at Adam. "What if he wakes up?"

"He'll be happy to watch."

Aching need hit her low in the gut. She wanted Adam to watch. Wanted Tristan to take her right here, right now.

"Come over here and kiss me, Kat."

She stared at him for a few seconds longer, feeling her own mouth curve into a grin and heat pulse between her legs.

Carefully, she grabbed a throw pillow and replaced it for her thigh, scooting away slowly so she didn't wake Adam.

Then, instead of going directly to Tristan, she turned and headed for the windows. She pulled the curtains closed then checked the lock on the front door.

Tristan never took his eyes off her, and when she finally stood in front of him, she couldn't help but notice his erection pushing against the zipper of his jeans.

"Will you strip for me?"

Tristan's husky question made her thighs clench. She heard so much desire in his voice. For her. She wanted to give him anything he asked for.

Instead of speaking, she let her fingers drift to the button of her jeans. The hem of her t-shirt barely covered the waistband so Tristan could see the button pop open and watch as she lowered the zipper.

Moving her hands to the waistband, she dragged the jeans down, careful not to take her underwear with them. She knew Tristan had a thing for lingerie, and she'd made sure to wear the prettiest set she owned.

She'd never thought she'd have so much fun shopping for extravagant, expensive lingerie, but the boutique in Haven Hotel had been irresistible. Now, she couldn't wait to see its effect on Tristan.

Since she'd taken her shoes off earlier, she made sure her socks disappeared with her jeans then straightened to find Tristan's gaze leisurely making its way up her body.

He raised his eyebrows when her hands gripped the hem of her shirt but hesitated.

"Do you want me to beg?" His wry tone matched his smile. "Because, trust me, I will. And then I'll make you pay for making me beg. You'll enjoy it, though. I'll make sure of it."

"Then you should definitely beg."

He leaned forward, gaze burning. "Please, sweetheart. Please take off your shirt."

"Just the shirt?"

"If the bra matches the panties, then yeah, just the shirt. Because I definitely want to fuck you while you're wearing them."

It wasn't like she hadn't heard him use that language before, but combined with the ridge in his jeans and the look in his eyes, she could've melted with lust on the spot. But she wasn't finished teasing him yet.

Dragging the shirt up her body, she pulled it over her

head, dropped it to the floor then let her hands rest on her hips. "Your turn."

He didn't move right away. Instead, his gaze strolled up her body, staring at her breasts long enough to make her nipples peak until they tingled.

"Just so you know, I think this might be my favorite set, so I'm gonna try damn hard not to rip it off. But if I do, I'll replace it. I might have to do that a few times before I learn to restrain myself."

God. How did the man bring her to the brink of an orgasm with a few words? She was so wet, her thighs felt slick.

Which could be because the panties were crotchless. She couldn't wait for him to discover that. She wanted to drive him crazy, wanted him to lose himself in her just as she did with him.

But Tristan had much more control over his emotions than Adam. Adam might seem like he was all icy restraint, but when you pushed him, you saw the ice crack. She loved watching Adam lose his grip.

She wanted to see Tristan lose his.

"Why don't you start with the shirt? I love your chest."

Was that a blush on his cheeks? Yes, it was. She didn't have long to smile about it though because he sat forward and yanked his shirt over his head.

And now she had an amazing view of his chest as he leaned back into the couch. Broad, strong. She wanted to bite at his tiny nipples then lick them. Wanted to straddle his lap and kiss him while she rubbed her pussy all over his cock before impaling herself on it.

Just thinking about it made her stomach tighten with anticipation.

Tristan must have seen something of her thoughts in her expression because he grinned at her…and reached for his jeans.

"You wanna help me with these?"

She crossed her arms beneath her breasts and watched Tristan's gaze drop. So he wasn't as controlled as he fronted. "No, I think you're doing just fine on your own."

Nodding, he popped the button and released the zipper then crunched forward just enough to get them down his legs. Which made his abs do amazing things.

And made her mouth dry from anticipation.

Then he lay there, completely nude and so beautiful, she wanted to stare for hours. She also wanted to lick him from his ankles to the tip of his stiff cock.

"Whatever you're thinking, please go right ahead and indulge yourself."

She reached for her own control and found it fraying. "And what if I told you I wanted you," she took a breath, "to play with yourself so I could watch? Would you do that for me?"

His smile widened. "You mean like this?"

Reaching between his legs, he cupped his balls with one hand and wrapped the other around his cock. The image was so much more arousing than she ever could've imagined. She tingled from head to toe and everywhere in between.

His hands moved slowly, squeezing tighter than she'd believe comfortable. But he certainly didn't seem to be in any pain. No, he looked like he wanted to devour her as he played with himself.

His cock stiffened and swelled, the head turning a deep red that enticed her closer. She took two steps forward before stopping again.

Then, making sure their gazes were locked, she went to her knees between his legs. Laying her hands on his thighs, she pushed them apart to make room for her then scooted forward.

Above her, she heard Tristan's breathing become harsher, and his fingers formed a ring around the base of his cock and squeezed. She took the opportunity to lean forward and opened her mouth around him.

As he groaned, she sucked on the head, his flesh hot against her tongue. So hot. So arousing.

For several long minutes, she sucked on his cock, hands braced on his taut thighs as she took him deep, sliding her tongue along his length, then going back to the tip.

She lost herself in the motion and his taste and the sheer eroticism of the motion. She wanted to make him lose control, but Tristan had something else in mind.

With a growl, he grabbed her shoulders and pushed her back until she had to release him.

Blinking up at him, she got a quick glimpse of the muscle in his jaw pulsing and the narrowed slit of his eyes before he grabbed her under the arms and lifted her onto the couch, knees spread on either side of his thighs.

Rolling on a condom, he didn't waste time with teasing, his intent plainly obvious when he held his cock straight with one hand and used his other to pull her down onto it.

They both groaned at the sensation, Kat stretched so tight around Tristan's hard erection. Head falling back, she didn't have time to process the roil of emotion and sensation before he leaned back and began to fuck her. Fast and hard.

Her hands grabbed his shoulders to hold herself steady, and eventually she caught the rhythm, driving down as he drove up. The base of his cock hit her clit, and with each contact, her body tightened even more.

She only needed—

Tristan leaned forward and kissed her, thrusting his tongue into her mouth as he pulled her down and held her, rocking her back and forth on his cock until she came with a cry.

A second later, Tristan groaned and she felt his cock pulse deep inside her.

It took her at least a minute to recover, her body going boneless until she lay panting against his chest, listening to his heart pound.

Finally, she heard Tristan draw in a breath.

"I like the panties. I think I'm going to buy you ten dozen pairs, and that's all you're going to wear from now on."

She could barely breathe but still he made her smile.

"I don't think I'll be able to wear them to work. Too distracting."

"So are you." Tristan pressed his lips to the top of her head. "And—"

"That's the best damn cure for a migraine I have ever seen," Adam drawled, and Kat turned her head to see him staring at them, sitting up now. "Come here and let me show you how much better I feel." And she did.

15

Kat hurried through the lobby of the office building, slipping into an elevator just before the doors closed.

Catching sight of herself in the mirrored doors, she smiled.

Happiness would do that to you.

For the past two weeks, she, Tristan, and Adam had been together more than they'd been apart.

During the day, she spent hours familiarizing herself with TinMan's accounts. Her brother's business ate up most of her time, but she'd been able to make some headway with the bar association about *pro bono* work for local children's services.

At night, they switched off sleeping wherever they happened to land that night. They'd been spending a lot of time at her new place though they weren't sleeping there because her queen bed wasn't big enough for the three of them. They ended up at Adam's most often because it was closest to her place.

She'd already decided to get a king-size bed by next week.

The bell dinged and the doors opened. It was close to nine at night, but the guys had told her to meet them here.

Something had come up.

Mary Alice, their office manager, was nowhere to be found when Kat opened the door to their office. Which was probably a good thing when she heard Adam telling Tristan to "Back the fuck off."

At the top of his lungs.

She'd never heard Adam that angry, that pissed off.

"You fucking promised me this wouldn't happen.

Goddamn it, Adam. When the fuck are you going to fucking learn?"

And she'd never heard Tristan talk like that to anyone. Ever. What the hell was going on?

She didn't want to eavesdrop, but they'd known she was on her way.

Should she leave and wait in the hall?

What were they arguing about?

"You sonuvabitch. How the hell can you even ask that? Christ, Tris, it's my family."

"And here I thought we were building one of our own."

"So because you can't stand yours means I have to give up mine to do that? I can't. And I won't. You know that."

"But you can't get drawn into this shit. I can't help you with this."

"Did I fucking ask you to help? I don't *want* your fucking help. That's the goddamn point. I don't want to drag anyone else into this."

A pause and Kat realized she was holding her breath.

"Goddammit, Adam. We're partners. Isn't this what we swore we wouldn't do? That we wouldn't let this shit come between us? You can't fucking do this."

"And you know damn well I have to do this. And we both know we can't drag Kat into this."

"Christ, don't you think I fucking know that?"

"Then this is the only solution. I step the fuck out, here and in her bed, until everything else settles."

"And you expect me to just let you do it? Alone?"

"Yes. This isn't your fight."

"Oh no. No *fucking* way. Don't even throw that shit in my face. This isn't your fight either. But you're allowing yourself to get drawn into it."

"How can I not? This is just going to keep going in a fucking circle unless I help him get the hell out." Another pause.

Kat had begun to put the pieces together, and she believed she'd come up with the correct answer. Neither Tristan nor Adam had breathed a word of it, but Kat had heard from Janey DeMarco that Adam's father had been released from jail right after she'd moved here.

Janey hadn't had any details of the reason he was released early, but Kat assumed he'd cut some kind of deal.

"Christ almighty—"

"No. Tris, listen to me. This is my problem. My family. I'll clean it up."

"So you expect me to just sit on the sidelines and watch you get drawn into this shit? Like we're just fucking acquaintances? That's not fucking happening."

"You're not my goddamn keeper."

"No, I'm your goddamn best friend. I thought you weren't going to do this lone wolf shit anymore."

"Oh, fuck you, Tris. Just... *Shit.* I can't do this and worry about Kat being collateral damage. And I don't want to have to worry about you getting fucking dead because of my family."

Another pause. No sound came from the office at all, but she heard her own labored breathing clear as day. She couldn't believe they didn't hear her from in there.

Finally, she heard something that sounded a hell of a lot like someone's fist hitting the wall.

"What the fuck am I supposed to tell Kat?"

"Tell her whatever the hell you think she should hear. I just don't want her anywhere near this shit. I don't want her anywhere near me now."

Pain pierced her straight through her gut.

If she looked at this rationally, she could maybe understand where Adam was coming from. But emotionally, she wanted to crawl in a hole and cry until she had no tears left.

She wanted to leave. Now. Before they discovered her. And yet she couldn't leave and let them lie to her later. To have them lie and knowing that they had... She wasn't sure she'd be able to forgive them.

Taking a deep breath, she forced herself to take the first step toward Tristan's office. She faltered for a second but put one foot in front of the other.

"You can't tell her anything. If anyone found out she knew..."

"I know. Goddamn it—"

Kat pushed open the door to Tristan's office.

"There's no need to tell me anything."

Tristan and Adam whipped around to stare at her. Shock on Tristan's face and sick frustration on Adam's. She immediately wanted to go to them. Reach up and smooth the lines away from Tristan's forehead and kiss Adam's lips until he didn't look like he wanted to punch the walls.

But she couldn't. Not if she was going to give them the out they needed. And they needed one desperately.

Tristan started to reach for her. "Kat—"

"No." She shook her head and held up her hand to stop him from coming closer. "No, please don't lie. I heard enough to know what's going on. And I'm going to give you exactly what you want."

Tristan grimaced. "Kat, wait—"

"No. I don't want to hear it. You need me out of the way so I'm taking myself out of the equation."

"Goddammit, Kat—"

"Stop." Adam's voice cut through Tristan's like a knife and his blue gaze was crystal clear. "Yes, you need to be far away from this."

"Then you're going to get your wish. When you're finished, maybe I'll still be waiting."

Tristan looked like he'd been gut-punched. Only the muscle leaping in Adam's jaw gave away his frustration.

"But you've both taught me that I'm worth one hell of a lot more than I've given myself credit for. I've learned to love you both and that is something I never would have believed possible. But I'm not going to wait forever."

She turned and headed for the door then turned just before she walked through.

"I just hope you realize we're stronger together before there's nothing left of us to salvage."

16

"Hello, Kat. How've you been?"

Kat looked up from the paperwork spread across her desk on a rainy Wednesday morning and found the last person she'd expected standing in the doorway of her office.

"Keegan." She blinked, dumbfounded. "What are you doing here?"

Her former fiancé's mouth curved in a wry grin. "Nice to see you too."

Shocked at the sight of him, she tried to think of something to say. Anything that didn't include the words, "What are you doing here?"

"Oh." Shaking off her confusion, she stood. "I'm sorry. I don't mean to be rude." She just couldn't seem to help it when he was around, and that really needed to stop. "Please have a seat. What can I do for you?"

He shook his head, taking a few steps closer then stopping, as if he wasn't sure he should get closer. "Can't stay long. I'm in town for a meeting with one of our contractors."

He held up a manila envelope. "We found a few other files stuffed in a desk that Erik thought you should have. Since I had this meeting, I offered to drop them off."

She realized she'd frozen in place, as if she were afraid of him. And that was just stupid. Giving herself a mental shake, she tried a smile and found it wasn't that hard to do. Stepping around her desk, she took the envelope from his outstretched hand. "Okay. Thank you for bringing them."

She expected him to turn and leave immediately, but he didn't. Instead, he let his gaze travel around her office.

"The place looks great." His gaze connected with hers again. "How's everything going?"

Small talk? Really? Okay, she could do that, too. "It's going as well as can be expected, I guess. Thank you for asking."

"You're welcome."

Now an awkward silence fell, and Kat had no idea what the hell to say as Keegan continued to stare at her expectantly.

What did he want to hear? She didn't have a clue. It wasn't like she and Keegan were best buddies and she was going to confess all her secrets.

There was no way she was going to tell him about her horrible weekend. About how miserable she'd been because she hadn't heard from either Tristan or Adam. How she'd spent nearly ten hours a day for the past three days in her office then returned to her condo to eat in front of the television and read through more files.

She wouldn't blame him for thinking he was lucky he'd escaped marrying her.

And wow. She really knew how to throw herself a pity party, didn't she?

But the fact was she hadn't heard from either Tristan or Adam all week. And it was playing havoc with her brain.

How long was she supposed to wait for them? Why hadn't they called? Was she going to lose them?

Had she ever really had them?

"Kat… Are you okay? Is something wrong?" Keegan's voice snapped her back to her office.

"Wrong?" Yes, lots of things were wrong. Tristan and Adam had deserted her, that's what was wrong. "No. Nothing's wrong. I'm fine. Thank you for dropping off the files. Is there anything else I can do for you?"

Keegan's gaze narrowed. Probably due to the sharp edge of her tone. It wasn't directed at him. At least not purposely. It just seemed as if everything that'd been going right with her life had been snatched away in seconds, and she was back to being alone and miserable.

Had Tristan and Adam changed their minds about being with her? Had she been right to walk out? Or had she lost the men who'd come to mean so much to her?

"Kat?"

Her gaze snapped back to Keegan, and the rush of emotion that blazed through her was almost sickening.

Jealousy, fear. Bitter and nasty and totally unwarranted.

And Keegan didn't deserve it.

Her stomach rolled, she felt so awful about her reaction.

His gaze narrowed at her and he took a step forward.

"Hey, did something happen?"

Yes, something had happened, but she really did *not* want to talk about this with her former fiancé who'd found true love and practically radiated happiness and contentment.

Shoving back every negative thought and hurtful emotion, she dug up another smile for Keegan. "I'm fine. Really. I've just been spending some long days trying to get up to speed, and it's catching up with me. I didn't mean to snap at you."

Keegan's frown actually deepened and, for a second, she thought he might push. Try to get her to open up to him. She wasn't sure she could hold herself together if he did. And that wouldn't be good for either of them.

With a barely concealed sigh, Keegan nodded and turned, heading for the door.

She felt like she needed to say something, anything, to make things better. "Tell Jules I said hello. And Erik."

Keegan stopped at the door then turned, and now he wore a smile. "Jules wants you to call. She wants you to come for dinner."

A week ago, she would've picked up her phone the second Keegan left and made that call. She liked Jules.

This week... Just thinking about talking to the other woman made her want to cry.

"Tell her thanks and I'll call when I get a chance. Like I said, I've been so busy..."

Keegan nodded, though he looked completely uncon-vinced. "No problem. Take care, Kat. You look like you could use some sleep."

Smiling again, she nodded, biting her tongue to keep from breaking down into tears in front of him.

"That's on my to-do list. Just as soon as I have everything in order."

She tried for normal, hoped like hell she fooled him because otherwise...

Jesus, she was a pitiful mess, wasn't she?

Keegan disappeared into the elevator, and she retreated back to her office.

Dropping into the chair behind her desk, she set the files on top of the pile still waiting to be read. She'd made a huge dent in those files this week. Because she'd done nothing but work.

And think about Adam and Tristan.

Maybe she should make the first move.

She *had* walked out on them. Told them she was taking herself out of the equation so Adam could take care of his family obligations.

Maybe he hadn't done that yet.

Or maybe they'd decided she was too much work.

That was the blow that continued to hit the hardest because she *was* too much work and she knew it.

And maybe now they thought so too.

17

"Adam, I gotta ask one last time. Are you sure about this?"

Sliding a holster over his shoulders, Adam took a deep breath as he reached for his gun and his fast-fading calm.

His jaw wanted to lock against answering Tristan's question, but Tristan was here, standing beside him when he didn't have to. The guy deserved an answer. Hell, he deserved a hell of a lot more than an answer.

"Yeah. I'm sure I have to do this. No, I'm not sure it's a good idea. Yes, this could be a total disaster. No, I can't back out. Yes, I think you should stay the *fuck* out of this. And no, I know you won't. Does that answer all your questions?"

Tristan sighed and scrubbed a hand through his hair for what had to be the hundredth time in the past five minutes before he grabbed his suit coat off the closest chair.

Adam wanted to rip the coat out of Tristan's hands and forbid him to go to this meeting.

Hell, he'd tried to do just that. Several times. Tristan had finally taken to giving him the finger to get Adam to shut up.

Now, Tristan flipped the coat over his shoulder and stuck his arm in, concealing the holster under his arm.

He hoped like hell they didn't need them, but he wasn't leaving without it.

They both had concealed-carry permits. Of course, if they used their guns in the commission of a crime, it wouldn't fucking matter. They'd still get arrested. And that kind of exposure would *not* be a good thing in their line of work. It would destroy everything they'd built.

Hell, one of them should be staying the fuck out of this. But Tristan wouldn't be swayed.

Fuck.

Adam reached for his suit coat as well, hiding his gun and holster.

Of course, their office manager, Mary Alice, would notice. The girl had sharp eyes. He knew she'd realized something was going on, but she hadn't asked any questions. Yet. Probably because she knew she wouldn't get any answers.

The fewer people who knew, the better. He hadn't told his sisters, hadn't mentioned a word to Tosh.

Hell, he wished he'd been able to spare Kat—

He shoved the thought away. It'd been two weeks since she'd walked out of this office. Two weeks and neither of them had spoken to her.

If he started thinking about her now, he'd just get pissed off and that wouldn't be good for anyone. He needed to maintain a cool head this morning. Otherwise, things could become a clusterfuck in seconds.

And Adam figured he was going to need to keep his dad in line so they didn't set off a war.

"Adam, you have a visitor."

Mary Alice's voice came through the intercom, and the tone set Adam on edge right away. That was her disapproving voice. After the past three years with her in the office, Tristan and Adam had grown to have a healthy respect for that tone.

Even though she was only twenty-three, Mary Alice had no trouble making men bend to her wishes. Raised with three older brothers who'd adored her only slightly more than they'd tormented and sheltered her, she should've been a tomboy or a wallflower.

Instead, she was a fiercely feminine fireball with red hair, green eyes, and a mouth like a sailor who'd been devastated by the death of her oldest brother fighting overseas. Instead of retiring with Tristan and Adam and going into business with them, John Matthew had re-upped.

And been declared KIA on a mission that remained classified. Not even Tristan, who had friends in every level of the armed services, could find out more.

Hell, if *this* situation went sideways, Tristan wouldn't have enough pull to get them free.

Which was why Adam was seriously considering cold-cocking the guy and leaving him tied up in the closet. Tristan would be pissed as hell but—

"Don't even think about it." Tristan's voice was little more than a growl. "I know that look. Do *not* piss me off by trying to ditch me."

Adam gave Tris the finger as he headed for the reception area. "Let me get rid of whoever this is and then we'll leave."

Pulling open his office door, the first thing Adam saw was Mary Alice, standing inches away, back ramrod straight.

As if she were guarding the door.

Frowning, Adam looked over her shoulder and saw Max Burdanov. Dark suit. Perfect hair. Handsome face. Innocuous smile.

Harvard Law grad exterior camouflaging the street brawler he'd once been.

Mary Alice was an amazing judge of character, however. She obviously sensed the submerged air of danger surrounding Max.

Adam put his hand on her shoulder and squeezed, trying to reassure her, even though he knew Max's appearance here probably wasn't good. Hell, there was no "probably" about it.

"Thank you, Mary Alice. Max, come on in."

Mary Alice turned to give Adam a narrow-eyed frown. Too damn smart for her own good. She knew something was going on. She simply hadn't pieced things together yet. But she would. And when she did, he had a feeling they'd need to find another office manager because she would be royally pissed. And hurt. With good reason.

And that would totally suck.

One problem at a time.

Max walked forward, his gaze locked on Mary Alice. When he stopped only inches away from her, she had to tilt her head back to maintain eye contact. But she didn't back down an inch.

Adam found himself smiling. She was like a Chihuahua facing off against a Doberman. And if she *ever* realized he'd just compared her to a dog, she would find a way to make him pay that would be painful and excruciatingly embar-rassing.

And he wouldn't blame her.

Why she was facing off against Max, though, was mystifying.

Did she know who he was? Why he was here?

He and Tristan had been careful not to let anything slip to Mary Alice about what was going down with his father. They didn't want her to know anything in case this all went to hell.

And speaking of…

Adam stepped around Mary Alice to hold out his hand.

"Why don't we talk in my office?"

"Sure." Max took his hand, his smile as slick as his custom-made suit and handmade Italian shoes. "I just need a few minutes of your time."

Out of the corner of his eye, Adam saw Tris stiffen. Mary Alice must have noticed as well because she turned to look at Tristan, her gaze calculating. As if she could figure out what was going on just by looking at him.

Fuck.

He waved Max through. "Sure."

Nodding at their office manager, a hint of a smile playing on his lips, Max walked into Adam's office. Tristan followed, leaving Adam to deal with Mary Alice.

Who turned to him with her arms crossed over her chest and her eyebrows raised in expectation.

She was going to be sorely disappointed.

"Don't ask." Adam stared straight into her eyes. "Just don't. I can't tell you anything, and even if I could, I wouldn't. You're not getting involved. No chance in hell. Go back to your desk. Do what you do to keep us running smoothly every day. And know we couldn't do what we do without you."

Her eyebrows rose even higher. "And that's supposed to placate me? Adam, do you think I'm stupid? Do you think I don't know something's going on? Something big? And now the man taking over your uncle's so-called," she actually made little air quote motions with her fingers, "'business' strolls into your office like he just hired you and you're going to close the door in my face? Jesus, Adam. I thought you were smarter than this."

He'd started to shake his head about halfway through her tirade, and when she finally finished, he felt like he'd rattled something loose.

He should've realized Mary Alice would know exactly who Max was. The woman was way too smart for her own good. "Then you should understand why I'm not telling you a goddamn thing. It's in your best interest to be totally in the dark."

"Adam—"

"Mally, don't."

The use of her brothers' pet name stopped her cold. Adam had never pulled that card on her before. Never felt he'd had to use it. But he couldn't let this touch her.

Which made him think of Kat, which was something he tried really hard not to do because when he did...

He'd almost broken down and called several times. He'd told himself he was going to call for Tristan's sake. Tris had been edgier than Adam had ever seen him. Quick to snap and unable to sit still. Not at all like himself.

And it was all Adam's fault. He should've made Tristan

stay the hell away from this, but when Tris put his mind to something, he didn't back down.

But there was no way in hell he'd let Mary Alice get tainted by this.

Mary Alice huffed, drawing his attention back to her.

Her green eyes blazed with frustration and a hint of fury. *Tough. It's for her own good.*

With a muted growl, she turned on her heel. "Fine. I'm going out to get coffee. I have no idea how long I'll be. And

I'm not bringing you back any."

She strode toward the door, red curls swinging along her shoulders as she practically slammed the door behind her.

A sick ache in the pit of his stomach made him want to punch the wall.

One more day of this lead ball lying in the pit of his stomach. Only one more day until this was settled and everyone could move the fuck on.

Christ. At least he hoped like hell this was finished at the end of the day.

Because Max had brought trouble. He'd bet his life on it.

With a suppressed growl, he turned back for his office, slamming the door shut behind him.

"All right, Max. What the fuck is going on now?"

Kat tossed the local section of the *Philadelphia Inquirer* at her desk.

For the past two weeks, since she'd walked out of Tristan and Adam's office, she'd been scouring the paper but she hadn't read a word in any article to indicate unrest in the local criminal scene. Which was a totally ridiculous thing to be thinking about.

When had her life taken such a surreal turn?

At least she didn't have to think hard about the answer to that. She knew the exact moment. The night she'd left her parents' house with Tristan and Adam. Which she was beginning to believe was the biggest mistake she'd made in her life.

After her conversation with Keegan Wednesday, she realized she'd put her life on hold for Tristan and Adam.

Neither of them had asked her to do that. She'd made that decision totally on her own.

So she only had herself to blame for being as miserable as she was.

With a sigh, she pushed to her feet from her desk chair, stretching her back as she walked to the window and stared out at a city where she still felt like a stranger.

Would she ever hear from Tristan and Adam again?

They'd said they'd call. At the time, she'd walked away, hurt. But she'd had no cause to doubt that they wouldn't.

Now, doubts ate away at her self-confidence at every turn.

And in the back of her head, she kept hearing her mother's voice, questioning her every move.

Her mother would have a heart attack if she caught wind of any of this. Frankly, Kat was shocked Angelica hadn't shown up at her door, screaming about Kat's association with a family of known criminals and demanding she return home before she caused her family any more embarrassment.

She was actually beginning to be concerned that her

mother hadn't made any contact at all. Kat was waiting for the other shoe to drop where Angelica was concerned. No way did she believe her mother would resign herself to losing this battle of wills with her daughter.

With a sigh, Kat pulled a file from the massive pile on her desk. TinMan Biometrics needed her attention—

The front door of her office opened, and her head popped up in surprise. She had no clients scheduled, and she hadn't yet hired an assistant. She'd been meaning to do so this week, but something had always interrupted.

Which meant, right now, she was completely alone.

Jumping up from behind her desk, she hurried into the reception area. There were only five rooms in her office suite: reception, her private office, a meeting room, bathroom, and a small storage space.

The man standing in the center of her front room looked like he could bench-press a truck. He wore cargo pants that he most definitely had not bought at a local department store. She had a feeling they were military grade. His white t-shirt was pristine, the color a high contrast to his bronze skin.

His facial features spoke of Latino and Asian ancestors, the mix unusual and highly striking. The longer she stared, the more handsome he became. Until she realized she'd been staring for several seconds.

She forced herself to speak. "Can I help you?"

He nodded. "Ms. Riley."

It wasn't a question. This man knew who she was.

"Yes?"

"Jesse Kanawata. Max Burdanov sent me."

Max Burdanov. The name sounded familiar but—

"Mr. Burdanov works with David Oleksy."

Her heart skipped a beat and she took an involuntary step forward. "Are Tristan and Adam okay?"

The words were out of her mouth before she processed the complete thought. Her heart began to race and her lungs constricted.

Jesse nodded, his expression impassive. "As far as I know, they're fine. Mr. Burdanov merely likes to take all angles into consideration when dealing with an unknown situation. He asked me to keep you company today."

She blinked, her brain playing out scenarios as she asked, "And what exactly does that mean?"

A corner of Jesse's full mouth kicked up. "It means exactly what you think it means."

So, whatever was going on with Adam's family, it was happening today.

Her heart began to pound a little harder. "Then why are you here and not with Mr. Burdanov?"

More importantly, why was he not providing backup for Adam and Tristan?

Now she saw the faintest hint of annoyance cross his features, which she didn't think was directed at her. "Because Mr. Burdanov asked me to spend the day with you."

Which meant Mr. Burdanov thought she might be in danger. "Do Adam and Tristan know you're here?"

He shook his head. "Frankly, I'm pretty sure I'm wasting my time here. And, no offense, but I'm not real happy to be babysitting today."

Well, she *was* offended by his statement, but after that

brief flare of indignation, she realized something else. "So why are you standing in my office, Mr. Kanatawa?"

His mouth twisted with that tiny smile again. "Actually I should be watching your building from the street. Gives me a better view of who's coming and going."

"Then what are you doing *inside* my office?"

He paused as if thinking about his answer, and Kat swore if he played more word games with her, she was going to start screaming. "I wasn't told explicitly to watch from outside."

Frustration made her clench her fists even as she took a deep breath and asked one more question. "So *why* are you here, Mr. Kanatawa?"

"Because when Max asks me to watch over a woman, I watch over a woman, no questions asked."

His answer stymied her because he said it without a trace of sarcasm. Straightforward, no bullshit.

She frowned at him. "I don't know what to say to that."

He shrugged, clearly not caring how she responded. "You don't need to say anything. If you've got work to do, go ahead and do it. I'll be in the hall."

No, that would never work. She wasn't the only tenant on this floor. There were four other offices, including one for a therapist who dealt primarily with young children.

One look at this man and some of those kids would run screaming. It wasn't that he was scary-looking, but he was big.

"You don't need to sit in the hall."

"Yeah, I do. Because if I sit in here, you're not gonna be able to help yourself and you're gonna grill me. And I'm not gonna tell you anything because I can't. And because you don't honestly want to know." He turned to go.

She followed him, her hand reaching for his arm but not quite touching. "Wait. Please."

Jesse stopped and turned to face her again, one eyebrow raised.

She imagined he cowed a lot of people with that look. But Kat had been learning how to deal with strong men.

"I'd appreciate it if you'd stay here. I'd feel...safer."

He raised the other brow then he began to smile and shake his head. "Adam always did go for the smart ones. And I gotta hand it to you. You almost made that sound like you really are scared."

She was. She was frightened. Just not for herself. She released her bottom lip from between her teeth. "So you'll stay?"

He shrugged, as if it didn't matter. "Sure. What the hell. It's gonna snow, and I'd rather not freeze my ass off in the car. Or scare the natives in the hall."

Kat quickly erased her smile. "Then you're welcome. I was in the middle of something in my office. Do you want to sit in there with me?"

Another wry grin. "Sure. But why don't you just go ahead and ask?"

She sat behind her desk again and waited until he'd taken the chair across from her. "If you're so sure what I'm going to ask, why don't you simply go ahead and tell me?"

He laughed. "Maybe because this is more fun."

She couldn't quite contain her own grin, even though her worry about Adam and Tristan had started to grow.

"Well then, I wouldn't want to interrupt your fun."

"Oh yeah, I definitely understand what Adam sees in you."

Okay, he was right. She did want to grill him. "So you've known Adam for a while?"

Max shook his head, but she knew it wasn't in answer to her question. He was commenting on his participation in this conversation. "You could say that. We went to school together."

"High school?"

"Since first grade."

"And you work for his uncle now?"

"I work with Max. Max works for David."

"There's a distinction?"

Jesse's grin disappeared. "There's about to be."

Tristan wanted to pace. It bugged the shit out of him that he couldn't.

No, he had to look cool, confident, and ready to kick someone's ass at the drop of a hat while he stood behind Adam.

It wasn't the position giving him the problem. He had no trouble watching Adam's back. It was the feeling that he was out of his depth in this environment.

He really fucking hated that.

He also fucking hated the fact that Adam hadn't immediately turned down Max's offer. The one he'd made at their office before they'd come here.

Shit.

He forced himself to take another look around the room.

Ten men stood against the walls, encircling the six men sitting at the round table in the center. The room was big enough that Tristan couldn't exactly hear what was being said. Even though they were speaking in Russian and he only understood a few words of the language, he figured that was a good thing.

He wanted absolutely no knowledge of what was going on.

Adam stood directly behind his dad, looking so much like Mickey, Tristan had to control the urge to shake his head. He'd never really seen the resemblance before. Now he wondered if that was because he hadn't wanted to.

Adam looked right at home there, but Tristan knew it was all an act. David and Mickey, however, were *not* putting on an act. For them, this could be the start of lives lived without looking over their shoulders. Without fear of someone trying to kill them for so-called business purposes. Hell, Max's position was even more delicate.

David and Mickey wanted out. Max wanted something that was going to be even more difficult to attain.

Respectability.

Across the table sat three men Tristan had never seen before. He didn't know their names. He figured he didn't want to. They'd addressed Mickey and David in Russian when they'd walked in the door and had continued in Russian since.

The five men they'd brought with them hadn't said a word. Neither had Adam, Tristan, or the other three men David had brought.

The men at the table had kept up a steady conversation for the past hour. No one had raised their voice; no one laughed. There had been a brief moment where the men around the table had smiled, but that had passed quickly and they were back to negotiations. At least, that's what Tristan imagined was happening.

Suddenly, one of the men on the other side of the table leaned forward and the tension in the room tripled. Adam and his uncle's men straightened. The men on the other side of the room straightened.

Mickey moved his arm on the table, but David put his hand on his brother's forearm, stilling his movement. David said a few words.

And everyone relaxed. That appeared to be the end of that.

The negotiations continued for another fifteen minutes before David sat back in his chair and extended his hand to the slightly younger man on the other side of the table.

Without hesitation, that man took it and shook. Then he stood and shook Mickey's hand, saying a few words. Mickey replied with a nod but kept his mouth shut, an amazing feat.

Then the man took Max's hand and said more than a few words. Max nodded but didn't say anything.

Then the other party walked out of the room. And the palpable tension dissipated.

Tristan felt like he could finally suck in a deep breath, but when he turned to Adam, he realized he'd missed something. Something important.

Adam's expression looked like it was carved from stone as he closed the few steps between him and his father and slammed his fists on the table next to Mickey.

"Damn it, Dad. Why the hell didn't you tell me?"

Mickey sighed hard as he stood. "Because I knew this is

how you'd react. I told you, Adam. I'd never let any of this touch you and I meant it."

"But—"

"No buts. David and I talked about this and this is the only way it works."

Adam looked at a loss for words, but Tristan knew his brain was moving fast. "Does Mom know?"

Mickey's expression twisted with offense. "Of course your mother knows. And the agreement doesn't apply to her. She could've stayed. She can come back and visit whenever she wants. Hell, we're keeping the house."

"But you and David have to move back to fucking Russia! Jesus, Dad—"

"Adam. Enough."

Mickey sliced his hand through the air between them, cutting off whatever Adam was going to say. Adam was a grown man, but he was still his father's son and he treated Mickey with a loving respect. Even though the man had been in prison for the past five years. Even though the man had been a criminal since he'd been a kid growing up in the Moscow slums.

Tristan didn't always understand Adam and Mickey's relationship, but he couldn't fault Adam for loving his father.

"I know it's a shock," Mickey finally continued. "Hell, your sisters are gonna be furious and Lea... Well, she's the one part of this your mother and I fought over."

Oh Christ. Lea was barely twenty, and her mom was moving halfway across the world. Yes, she now lived on her own in an apartment close to Temple University. Still—

"We want her to come with us, but we don't think that's going to happen. So she's going to need you more than ever."

Adam looked like he wanted to swear and rage, but his jaw locked. Tristan knew Adam wouldn't go off in front of Max and his men. He'd internalize it all.

Max's offer made a hell of a lot more sense now. It also explained why he'd told Adam to take his time and think it over before giving his answer.

Tristan had been shocked when Max had offered Adam a job as head of security for the new corporation Max was creating. Tristan had never considered that Adam would take Max up on it. He'd never thought Adam would break up their partnership.

But now Tristan realized why Max had offered Adam the position. Because it kept the Olesky name tied to the legitimate side of the businesses.

Max and David stood in the farthest corner. David had his hand on the younger man's shoulder and was speaking so low, Tristan couldn't hear a word he was saying. Max kept nodding, his expression completely focused on David.

Tristan didn't envy the burden Max had just taken onto his shoulders. Even if everything worked the way Adam had explained to Tristan before they'd gone into the meeting, Max still had the biggest mountain to climb by taking a select few of David's businesses legit. And without David to run interference...

Yeah. Not a job Tristan wanted.

But what if Adam wanted what Max had offered?

Fuck.

What Tristan really wanted was to call Kat. Tell her they were coming to pick her up and she should be prepared to spend the weekend—at least—at Adam's. In bed. Naked.

Yeah, maybe he should ask first. And be prepared for a little resistance. They hadn't talked to her for two weeks.

Tristan had nearly broken down and called her more than once, but he'd managed to convince himself the separation was the best way to keep her out of this.

He couldn't fucking wait to see her.

He hoped like hell she was just as glad to see them.

Jesse stationed himself between the window and the door in her office and tried to make himself invisible.

He wasn't entirely effective. He was simply too big to ignore, but he was almost preternaturally still. Which was a distraction all on its own. Still, she forced herself to work, to fall into the safety of what she knew.

Which was the law.

When her cell phone rang, the noise startled her. She realized she'd been reading for more than an hour, losing herself in her first pro bono case.

Her gasp caused Jesse to turn and look at her with raised eyebrows.

She managed not to pull a face at him as she picked up her cell, but she couldn't hide her sigh when she saw the caller ID.

"Hello, Mother. How are you?" Amazingly, her voice sounded steady.

"Katrina. I'm surprised to find I'm still listed in your contacts."

Jesse had stood the second he heard "mother" come out

of her mouth and was already at the door by the time Angelica started in on her.

She was pretty sure, though, that he'd heard the first part of Angelica's high-pitched screed. A month's worth of pent-up frustration and anger made her mother sound even more shrewish than usual.

"Have you been enjoying yourself, Katrina? I hope your new life is everything you hoped it would be." And it devolved from there.

For twenty minutes, her mother berated her for every decision she'd made since the party. Took Kat to task for deserting her family, for being so selfish as to make a new life for herself in a new city.

How dare Kat make Angelica worry because Kat wasn't where she could get to her every day? How awful that Angelica had been taken to the hospital because she couldn't sleep because of Kat's desertion.

Twenty minutes. Kat watched the clock the entire time.

Her heart rate increased, her chest tightened, and her stomach rolled. She felt the panic attack build every time her mother's voice rose to a screech. At the twenty-minute mark, she began to hyperventilate.

Good thing she was sitting down. Even so, she might need to put her head between her knees before she passed out.

So why are you still listening to her?

Why indeed? She could hang up at any time.

She took a deep breath then another.

Closing her eyes, she focused on lowering her heart rate. And ignoring her mother.

Amazingly, she found it wasn't that difficult to simply

tune out Angelica. All she needed was to think about something else.

About the fact that she was making it on her own. Running her own business and doing the kind of law she'd always wanted, rather than working for a huge firm and being told what cases to handle.

Or the fact that she wasn't a broken mess because the men she'd been seeing appeared to have abandoned her.

She'd found a strength she'd never known she had.

Good for me.

And she didn't have to take this anymore.

"Mother, I'm going to hang up now."

She'd interrupted Angelica in mid-sentence, something about how ungrateful Kat was.

Kat heard her mother audibly inhale and didn't even flinch when Angelica started in again.

"How dare you treat me like this? I am your mother.

What gives you the right—"

"I have work to do. Work that I enjoy. Which you would know if you'd thought to ask. I've enjoyed decorating my new home. Again, something you would know if you'd asked. But you haven't. It's all about you. It's always about you. And I think... No, I *know* I'm not going to do this with you anymore."

"Katrina, what are you—"

"I'm saying goodbye, Mother. I'd really appreciate it if you didn't call back unless you actually want to have a conversation instead of this one-sided bitchfest."

"Katrina! How dare—"

"Goodbye, Mother."

She hung up the phone before she heard Angelica say another word.

A minute passed as she stared out the window, waiting for the phone to ring again. Part of her wanted to jump up and down and do a victory dance when it didn't. The other part wanted to be able to shed a few tears at her loss.

Although what exactly she'd lost was a mystery.

She'd never really had a mother, not the kind she'd wanted. Maybe she could mourn the fact that her mother would never be what Kat needed her to be. Or maybe that she'd finally stood up for herself and there was no one around to celebrate with her.

The quiet knock on her open office door startled a gasp out of her. She panicked for a moment before she remembered she wasn't alone.

Jesse stood there, his expression bland. But his gaze had lost that hard sheen.

"My mom wanted me to be a doctor," he said.

Kat shook her head, convinced she hadn't heard him correctly. "I'm sorry?"

"My mom." Jesse leaned against the door, hands in his pockets. "She wanted me to be a doctor. I had other plans. When I was twenty-one, she nearly died. Breast cancer. She wanted me to promise her I'd go back to school and get my degree. I couldn't do it. To this day, she continues to tell me how disappointed she is that I disregarded her deathbed wish. I keep telling her she hasn't died yet so there's still time for me to change my mind."

Kat had no idea what to say to Jesse's comment, so she simply nodded and watched as his lips curve into a smile. And wow, the man really was handsome.

Which only served to make her miss her guys more.

He shrugged. "Just an observation. Everybody's got family issues."

She thought of several responses but finally settled on the truth. "My mother doesn't like me very much. Never has. I'm not the daughter she expected me to be."

Jesse laughed. "Hell, no one can live up to their parents' expectations. If we did, what would they have to bitch about for the rest of their lives?"

Kat couldn't help but return his smile, even though she shook her head as she did.

"I think—"

The opening strains of "Hell's Bells" cut her off, and Jesse dug into his pants for his phone, holding up an index finger as he looked at the screen then answered.

"Yeah."

His expression didn't change and he didn't say anything else, but when he took the phone away from his ear and slipped it back into his pants, she knew whatever had happened was over.

"So, you free to get some dinner?"

The question was so unexpected, she actually froze, lips parted as her brain stuttered over an answer.

"Uh, thank you for the invitation but I think..."

"You're gonna wait for another offer."

She nodded though she wasn't sure she was. "Yes, I think I am."

"No problem." He headed for the door then turned back just before he left her office. "Just don't let them make you wait too long."

"I'm calling."

Adam's hands clenched into fists, the knuckles cracking. "I'm not sure I'm gonna be decent company tonight."

"I don't give a shit." Tristan's voice held pure command. "Get over yourself. I'm not fucking waiting."

Adam practically bit through his tongue before he told Tristan to go fuck himself, but he couldn't deny he wanted to see Kat as much as Tristan did.

They'd returned to their office after the meeting, a little before noon. Mary Alice was still gone.

Tristan hadn't said more than a couple of words the entire time, and Adam hadn't said anything at all. He had too damn much on his mind.

His dad had been banished. Christ, that sounded medieval but it was true. And his mother along with him.

His sisters would be devastated.

Lea was only twenty. She needed her mother. But Lea and Alyssa would be heartbroken to be separated if Lea decided to go with their parents. And he...

He didn't want to lose more than half his family in one swoop.

Fuck.

"Adam."

He needed to talk to his mom, needed to talk to Tosh and Lys.

"Adam. God damn it."

Fuck. *"What?"*

Tristan looked almost as frustrated as Adam felt as they stood in Adam's office. "We need to call Kat."

"Then call her. You're right. You need to see her. I've got to talk to my mom and dad. Figure out how to handle the house. We need to figure out where Lea's going to live. Where—"

"Adam."

"Jesus Christ, Tristan." He wanted to scream but barely held himself in check as he took a deep breath. "I can't fucking deal with anything else right now."

Tristan's jaw looked ready to crack. "Kat isn't something you have to deal with. She's the woman we need here, between us. We promised her we'd call. I'm not going back on that."

"I don't expect you to. Call her. I'm not saying you shouldn't. I'm saying I can't deal with one more damn thing right now."

Tristan closed the distance between them, stopping just out of reach. "That's where you're wrong. You do need her. *We* need her. This thing with your dad is just a goddamn excuse."

Maybe. *Fuck.* Probably. Still... "And what about Max's offer? What the fuck am I supposed to do about that?"

Tristan just stood there, staring at him, every breath an audible huff. "What the hell do you want to do about it?"

Adam ran a hand through his hair, fighting the urge to tear it out. "If I fucking knew what the hell I wanted, don't you think I'd tell you?"

Adam watched Tristan take a deep breath and visibly relax. How the hell he managed it, Adam wished he knew.

"Look." Tristan's voice had lowered and his tone gentled, as if he'd taken a Valium. "I know this is a shock. I get it. All right? But we owe it to Kat to call her."

"Then call her. I just need...a little space."

Tristan fell silent for too long before he said, "Space."

"Damn it, Tris. Give me a fucking break!"

Tristan opened his mouth to respond then snapped it shut and turned away, pacing back to the door. He stood facing out of Adam's office, his ramrod straight back proof enough of his agitation.

But Adam had too much on his mind already. Tris was a big boy. He'd deal.

Finally, Tristan turned and faced him. "You need a break?" He took a deep breath. "Yeah, I get it. It's been a rough day. But Adam... Try not to let it fuck with your head any more than it already has. Because you're gonna lose even more than you think you have already."

Tristan turned and left. Adam continued to stare at the door but he clearly heard Tristan, now in his office.

"Kat. It's Tristan. How are you?"

The ache started somewhere in his chest at the sound of her name. Adam could barely hear her voice from where he stood but what little he did hear made him ache with desire. And not just physical desire, though that was part of it.

No, it was the desire to simply be with her. Hold her.

But he knew he'd be pretty shitty company right now. She needed more from him than he'd be able to give right now. And he'd want to take everything she had.

It wouldn't be fair. Not to anyone.

Better if he just stayed the fuck out of everyone's way.

He shut the door to his office because he didn't want to hear any more.

Now, the silence closed around him like a void. He was

tempted to turn on some music simply to fill the dead space. But he knew music would just annoy him.

Hell, everything would annoy him right now. He felt like he was going to crawl out of his skin. Walking to the window, he stared down into the street. People rushed around with somewhere to go, looking like they had a purpose.

Christ, why the hell did he feel like everything was coming down around him when, for the first time, he should feel like a weight had been lifted off his shoulders?

His dad was finally getting out of the illegal life he'd been living for years. He should be thrilled. He should be— "I'm leaving."

Adam spun to see Tristan in the doorway, his expression tightly controlled.

"Come with me."

There was a command in Tristan's voice that made Adam bristle. And made the former soldier in him want to obey.

"No. Better for everyone if I just...don't. Not now."

"Bullshit." Tristan's voice had a sharp edge. "It's not better for anyone. But you want to be a dick? Fine. Be a dick. But you are fucking up the best thing that's ever happened to you. I'm just not going to let you fuck it up for me too."

Then he left. No tantrum, no slamming doors.

Nothing.

Just left.

Adam wanted to bang his head against the glass window in frustration.

Tristan decided to walk to Kat's office.

Yeah, it was more than a mile away, but he figured he could use the time to think through the frustration.

And if he showed up at her door looking like he wanted to hit something, well... He wouldn't blame her if she turned him away.

He really didn't want her to turn him away. He wanted her to welcome him back with open arms. Press her beautiful body against his and kiss him until they couldn't breathe.

He was sick of being lonely, sick of wanting her so damn badly and not having her.

Goddamn Adam—

Shit. He pulled up short in the middle of the sidewalk, causing the older woman behind him to nearly run into him. With a suppressed curse and a quick sidestep, he mumbled an apology, but she'd already passed him and never looked back.

Maybe he was the one who needed to get his shit together. Maybe Adam had had the right idea to take a little time.

But Tristan wasn't the one who needed time to figure out what he wanted. He knew exactly what he wanted.

Kat.

Except it wasn't supposed to be just the two of them.

It was supposed to be three.

What the hell would he do if Adam didn't come around? What would *they* do?

He knew one thing for sure. He wasn't giving up Kat.

But would Kat only want him?

He and Adam had been a package deal. They'd told her she'd have both of them.

Fuck.

Pushing away from the wall of the building he'd been standing beside for at least a minute now, he started walking again, this time a little slower.

You know what? Fuck this self-doubt. No more. I need to find a way to fix it, not dwell on it.

Usually, he and Adam fixed things together. If they had a problem, Adam was like a dog with a bone, working at it until he had a solution.

Okay, so Adam needed a little time to get his head on straight. Tristan would give him a couple of days. Then he'd make damn sure Adam got with the program.

With a plan in place, Tristan looked around...and realized he'd just walked by Kat's office building.

With a sigh, he turned back and headed inside. The elevator opened after only a few seconds and the man exiting gave him a brief nod before moving around him.

The guy's snarky smile made Tristan do a double take.

What the fuck? Did he know him?

Tristan figured if he'd met him before, he would've remembered. The guy definitely looked memorable.

Before Tristan could turn, the guy was gone.

Christ, every little thing was making him twitch today.

Fuck it. He only needed to focus on Kat.

He took the elevator to her floor, unable to keep from pacing, even in the confines of the elevator.

As soon as the doors opened, he made straight for her office. He barely got through the door when she appeared directly in front of him.

Her eyes widened as he stopped in front of her, and her mouth opened to speak but he didn't give her the chance.

Wrapping his hand around her neck, he urged her closer then dropped his mouth over hers. Their lips sealed and Tristan groaned at the contact. Kat trembled against him then stilled.

He wanted her hands on him, wanted—

Finally, she moved. Wrapped her arms around his shoulders and pressed her body against his.

Yes.

Prizing open her lips, he kissed her deep and hard. Tangled their tongues together and let her taste seep into him. Weaving one hand through her hair, he tugged, tilting her head back to get a better angle on her mouth. His other hand fell to her waist and pulled her even closer.

His cock, already hard and straining for her, fit into the notch of her thighs. He needed to be closer, wanted to be naked and horizontal with her beneath him. Wanted—

He pulled back to suck in a breath and heard Kat do the same.

"Tris—"

He kissed her again, putting his hands around her waist and lifting her against him, her feet inches off the floor. Then he began to walk forward until he had her back against the wall. She made a soft sound as she made contact, but it turned into a moan as she opened her mouth even wider and slid her tongue against his.

Jesus, he could kiss her for hours and not get enough of her. Her taste intoxicated him. Lifting her higher, he wanted her to wrap her legs around her waist but realized her skirt was too tight. So he stepped closer.

Now, as his mouth moved over hers, the tip of his cock brushed against her mound, sending a shock of sensation tearing through him. He thrust his hips forward and up, pressing even more tightly against her.

With a moan, Kat tore her mouth away from his, her hands sliding into his hair and tugging until he opened his eyes.

"Tris."

She looked at him with those blue eyes, and he wanted to give her anything she desired.

"I fucking missed you," he said.

Her soft smile made him even harder. "I missed you, too."

Then she looked over his shoulder and quickly looked back.

Grimacing, Tristan shook his head. "He's not here."

He couldn't hide the edge in his tone and wanted to take back the words immediately. He didn't want to take his anger at Adam out on Kat.

"Sorry. Damn it. I'm not mad at you."

"So why are you mad at Adam?"

Setting her on her feet, Tristan sucked in a sharp breath and tried not to let his frustration get the better of him.

"Because he's an ass." And that was totally unfair. Tristan took a step back, running a hand through his hair and reaching for calm. "Sorry. Jesus, I'm sorry. I didn't mean that."

Kat stared up at him, concern clearly visible on her face. "Tristan? What happened today?"

Hell, he wasn't really sure and he wasn't sure what he should be telling Kat because, damn it, it was Adam's story to tell.

When he didn't respond, she frowned. "Is Adam okay? Are *you* okay?"

Was he? Shit, he wasn't really sure. "Adam's fine. Physically. We both are."

"Then why are you here alone?"

He wasn't alone. He was here with her. He gritted his teeth so the words didn't escape.

Did she not want him if Adam wasn't part of the deal?

"Tristan? Did something happen between you and Adam?"

Yeah, something had happened. He just didn't know what exactly or how to fix it.

"No. Nothing happened. Adam's just…got a lot of stuff to deal with right now."

"With his family?"

"Yeah."

She sucked her bottom lip between her teeth and started to chew on it, like she did when she was thinking. Her brow furrowed and she looked like she had more to say.

But after a few seconds, she sighed and her lips curved in an almost rueful smile. "I am glad to see you."

Thank Christ for that. "Me too, sweetheart."

Cupping her chin in his hand, he leaned down to kiss her again, slower and not as frantically as before. He let himself savor her this time. Because if this was the last time—

No. Fuck that. He wasn't going to allow himself to think like that. Instead, he'd use this time to show her exactly why she shouldn't give up on him.

"Do you have any appointments scheduled for the rest of the day?"

She shook her head, a question in her eyes.

His mouth curved into a grin. "I missed you."

She smiled sweetly. "I missed you, too."

"I want you."

Her smile turned a little naughty as she leaned closer.

"Me too."

Bending down, he nipped at her earlobe, taking it between his teeth and tugging until he felt her shiver. "Can I have you? Right here. Now. On your desk. I want to bend you over it and take you from behind."

Her lips parted and he heard her suck in a breath. Her gaze went a little hazy, as if she'd focused on something inside her head. Then she blinked and refocused.

"Lock the front door and I'll let you."

Every word felt like the stroke of her hand on his cock.

And the look in her eyes... Holy hell. He'd come in seconds.

Without saying a word, he turned and headed back to the front door. He made sure it was closed tightly then slid home the deadbolt and made sure the lock on the knob was activated, as well.

And when he walked back into her office, he felt like he'd been sucker punched.

She'd backed up to the desk, leaning her ass against it and crossing her arms under her breasts, forcing them up and making them strain against the buttons on her blouse.

Her outfit was straight-up lawyer garb. Thin black skirt that fell below her knees. White silk blouse that buttoned up the front. She'd only left two buttons undone. Hell, she even wore pearls. They were black but still pearls.

The look totally worked on her.

Her hair hung loose around her shoulders, though, framing her beautiful face and making him want to twist it around his fingers again. It looked a little tousled from earlier and he definitely liked that.

"Turn around."

His voice sounded like he had gravel in his throat and she swallowed hard at the sound. She actually reached for the pearls with one hand and fingered them for a second before she stood and turned, resting her hand palms down on the desktop.

God damn, the woman had a beautiful ass. He wanted to strip her naked and caress every inch of her body.

But he knew he didn't have the time to take this slow.

Or make it last, for that matter.

He wanted her too damn much to make himself wait.

Reaching for her hips, he slid his hands down the outside of her thighs then slowly began to gather up her skirt. When he had the hem in his fists, he lifted the skirt to her waist, revealing the skimpy beige silk undies that barely covered her ass.

Later, he'd go to his knees, spread her legs, and eat her pussy. Right now, if he put his mouth on her there, he'd come without getting inside her. And he wanted to come inside her.

Now, he put one hand on her shoulder and pushed her forward. "Bend over, honey."

She didn't hesitate. Spreading her arms out on the desk, she wriggled her ass once and made him groan.

Ripping the wallet out of his back pocket, he grabbed the condom then tossed the wallet on her desk. He unbuckled his belt, snagged the zipper then shoved his pants and underwear down around his hips. Seconds later, he had the condom rolled on and the tip of his cock poised at her entrance.

Jesus, she was wet. He saw the slick gleam of desire on her pussy.

And her ass... So pale and sleek. He grabbed her hips and pushed forward, burying his cock inside.

She moaned and rolled back against him, sending him even deeper. She clenched him like a fist, squeezing until he couldn't stay still.

He fucked her hard, hips pistoning. The friction created by their bodies electrified him from the root of his cock to the tips of his toes, which curled in his shoes.

Every muscle in his body sang with desire, and every brain cell rang with the knowledge that she was his again.

"Tristan."

She breathed out his name, her pussy rippling around him.

He leaned closer, breathing in her scent. "Kat, baby. Come on."

He wasn't quite sure where he wanted her to go. He only knew he wanted her with him.

Sliding one hand around to her front, he arrowed straight for her clit. Before he even touched her, she shivered, rocking her ass back against him.

Her smooth skin pressed against his thighs, silky and warm. Her back arched, and he ran his free hand up her back and curled his fingers over her shoulder. Then he let himself go.

Every thrust forward made his balls slap against her ass, the motion almost as arousing as the sensation of her pussy tightening around his cock.

He heard her heavy breathing as clearly as he heard his own, saw her knuckles go white as she gripped the edge of the desk.

He wanted her to be out of control. Needed her to give up control completely to him.

She gasped and he froze, afraid he'd hurt her.

"No!" She released one hand from the desk to reach behind and grab his hip. "Oh god, don't stop."

He obeyed with a groan. Anything for her. He'd do anything—

She cried out, her voice a hoarse rasp, and he felt her come around him. The sensation tripped his own orgasm, and it ripped through his body with devastating effect. Every nerve ending lit up. Every muscle went lax with satisfaction until he had to put his hands on the desk so he didn't fall forward and hurt her.

When he finally shook off the glaze over his eyesight, he saw Kat lying boneless on the desk, her back rising with each shuddering breath.

Quickly, he pulled out, yanked off the condom, and tossed it in the trash can to the side of her desk. Then he pulled his pants up, leaving them open, and lifted her into his arms and sat on the small couch along the wall.

She wrapped her arms around his shoulders and let her head fall into the curve of his neck where her breath brushed against his skin.

She felt so damn good in his arms. He never wanted her to be out of them for more than a couple of hours.

Okay, eight hours, max. They still had to work. And if not his then...

Goddamn Adam. He should be here.

"Kat, you okay?"

"Fine. Just..." Her lips pressed against his neck and he shivered, arms tightened around her. "Trying to catch my breath."

Yeah, he knew the feeling. But his wasn't as easy to control. Especially when rational thought began to creep in again.

He loved her. He wanted to tell her. Needed to tell her.

And yet, he knew something was missing.

Someone was missing.

"So can you tell me what happened?"

Sighing, he let his head fall back onto the couch cushion and stared at the ceiling. She felt perfect right here.

This felt right. Not complete, but right.

And maybe you're going to have to learn to live with perfect but not complete.

No. He didn't accept that. He wouldn't.

"Adam found out his parents have to move back to Russia as part of the deal to get his father out of the life.

He's taking it hard."

Her fingers stroked along his neck. "I guess that's understandable."

"Yeah, but he's letting it fuck with his head, and we can't let him do that."

"Are you telling me he doesn't want to be here? With me? With...us?"

Pulling back, Tristan put his hand under her chin and lifted until he could meet her eyes. "He wants to be here. Trust me on that. He just doesn't think he should be because he thinks he has to take care of everything else. That somehow this is his fault."

Her brow furrowed. "What do you mean, his fault?"

"I mean he thinks his dad made these plans because it's what Adam has wanted all his life. For his dad to go straight. And now that he has what he wanted, his family's being ripped apart. So he feels responsible."

She didn't say anything else, but Tristan could practically hear her thinking. He just didn't know what to tell her to reassure her.

Shifting on his lap until she could look up at him without straining her neck, Kat stared into his eyes, hers filled with uncertainty.

He wanted to kiss it away, make her understand he wasn't going anywhere. And that he'd make good on the promises he'd made to himself and to her, although he'd never told her directly.

"Come to dinner with me tonight."

He tried not to make it sound like an order, but her brows rose and he knew he hadn't succeeded. But she didn't say anything. Nodding, she rose, fixing her skirt as she did. Then she deliberately bent to pick up something from the floor. When she rose, her underwear dangled from one finger.

He didn't bother to hide his smile as he stood, zipped his pants and buckled his belt, then tucked his shirt in.

Bending down, he kissed her again. Soft and unhurried, no rush now because she hadn't turned him away.

Closing her eyes, she leaned into him and kissed him back, arms wrapping around his waist, hands sliding over his ass and pressing him forward.

She flicked at his lips with her tongue, a leisurely lick that made his heart race.

"Yes to dinner."

She paused, and he knew she wanted to say more. Then she must have thought better of it.

"Now," she smiled, "I really do have work to finish so you have to go."

"I'll pick you up at seven. Wear something fancy. We'll go to Haven."

"Okay. See you then."

And if he had his way, they wouldn't be going without Adam.

"Adam, sweetheart, I know this is a shock. But you've got to understand. This was a joint decision between your father and me. We decided on the best course of action for everyone involved, and this is the only way it worked. We need you to be on board. Your sisters are going to need you now, especially Lea."

Adam watched his mother's gray eyes fill with tears, and impotent anger made him grit his teeth against the obscenities crowding his tongue.

Damn it. He wasn't upset with his mother. And he'd gotten over his anger at his dad.

So where the hell was this burning rage coming from?

He should be happy. Hell, he should be ecstatic. His dad was finally leaving the life. Getting out. Something he'd been dreaming about since he'd been seven and discovered what his dad did when he left their house at all hours of the day.

"Truth be told," his mom continued, "I'm actually looking forward to seeing Moscow again. It's been years since I visited my mother's grave. And your grandfather has been sick and unable to travel the past few years. He'll be coming to live with your dad and me. My sisters have taken care of him for years. Now it's my turn."

Jesus, his mom continued to turn the screws. Smiling at him with such a mixture of sadness and joy, his mom could still pass for forty even though she was close to fifty-five. Blonde, her face unlined, and her body only slightly rounded, she looked like the ideal of the American woman. Her favorite stores were Macy's and Saks. She loved her Starbucks mocha latte. Did they have those in Moscow?

"And it's not like you won't be able to come and visit." Her gaze entreated him to see that this wasn't the end of the world. "There are so many things I want to show you in *my* city. I can't wait for you to meet my sisters and your cousins and your granddad. And I'll be traveling back and forth so much, you'll soon decide I'm being a pain in the ass."

His mother would never be a burden. His father...

Adam turned to his dad, sitting next to his wife on the couch in the house Adam had grown up in. While his dad's "business" had allowed his mother to gut the house and make it her own several times over, they'd never moved from their predominantly Russian neighborhood. His father had occasionally made noises about moving to the Main Line, but it'd never happened.

Adam used to think his dad had figured they were safer here, where the men they hired to keep them safe also lived. But he'd realized in the past few years that, if his mom had wanted to move, his dad would've had them in a new house the next week.

He hadn't realized until now how much his mom missed

her homeland. Staying in their neighborhood had allowed her to maintain that connection.

Still...

"Have you told the girls anything?"

Now his mom's tears rolled down her cheeks, and Adam wanted to kick himself for mentioning them. But he figured if they were going to have this conversation, they might as well get it all out now. His dad reached over and took his mom's hand, clasping it tightly.

He should just let it go. All of it. Make the best out of the situation. Send his parents off with a party and a smile. Give Lea free rein in one of the spare bedrooms in his house so she didn't feel completely abandoned.

Help Lys and Tosh with the kids more, pick up the slack that would be left behind in his mom's absence.

His mom's sigh cut through his thoughts, and his gaze snapped back to see her shaking her head.

"No. But they'll be here in an hour. We wanted to talk to you first. And now that we have... I want to hear about this girl you're seeing."

Christ, he swore he should have whiplash. And since he'd been trying not to think of Kat at all, now he could think of nothing else.

"Shouldn't we be talking about what to do with the house?"

His mother looked puzzled. "What do you mean? We're not doing anything with the house. Where else would I stay when I come to visit?"

The noose around his neck loosened a little, and he realized how tightly wound he was. He realized his dad had mentioned keeping the house after the meeting. Adam just hadn't processed it then.

"Adam." His dad's voice was as serious as Adam had ever heard it. "We're not abandoning you."

Shit. "That's not what I meant."

"No, but it's what you thought." His dad shook his head. "I'm not blaming you, son. I know things haven't always worked out the way you've wanted them too. I've tried to keep my business from affecting you, but I know that wasn't always possible. I've always been so damn proud of you for your service. And for the man you've become. But you can't be all things to everyone. It just doesn't work. Sometimes you really do have to look out for yourself."

"So." His mom leaned forward, a gleam in her eyes.

"Tell me about this girl."

18

Adam walked into the office around five that day, unsure if Tristan was there.

His brain hadn't stopped spinning. He'd been thinking about what to say since he'd left his parents' house two hours ago.

His sisters had arrived not long after his mom had started grilling him about Kat. They'd started crying shortly after their parents began to explain, but they hadn't been as devastated as Adam had thought they'd be.

Yes, Lea had been thrown for a loop, but she'd recovered faster than he'd expected. And the fact that his baby sister was no longer a child hit him squarely in the chest.

Lys took it harder than any of them, but after their mom assured her she'd be back several times a year, including Christmas, Lys finally stopped crying.

And the weight on Adam's chest had alleviated somewhat. Now the guilt over how he'd dealt with Tristan started to bite him in the ass.

Christ, he'd been a prick.

He knew what he needed to say to fix things with Tristan. Knew what he needed to do to mend the relationship with Kat.

That only left the offer from Max. And that one... Damn it, that one wasn't so clear-cut. But it should be.

"Nice of you to drop by."

The sarcasm seeping from Mary Alice's greeting brought a smile to his face as he closed the front door behind him.

Even with all the shit still filtering through his head, he huffed out a quick laugh for the girl leaning against her desk in the front room of their offices.

"Nice to see you, too, Mally."

Her nose wrinkled in disdain but he saw the hurt in her eyes. "Tristan was back earlier but he's gone again."

"Then why are you still here?"

She tilted that adorable nose in the air. "Because I wanted to be here if you came by. I was worried about you."

Damn, the girl was sweet. He loved her like a sister. Considered her part of his family.

Like Tristan.

Like Kat.

But his relationship with Mary Alice was much less complicated than his relationship with Kat.

With a sigh, he leaned next to her on the desk, mirroring her stance. "You want to know what happened?"

She raised an eyebrow at him, her expression clearly telling him he was an idiot for asking. "Do you want to tell me?"

He shook his head. "It's not that I *don't* want to tell you. I just needed to figure out the situation."

"And did you figure it out?"

"Some of it. I still got a few things I need to work through."

She nudged his shoulder with hers. "So spell it out for me."

He shouldn't drag her into this. None of it was her problem. And yet... She'd asked and he needed a sounding board. And everything was a done deal. The papers signed, handshakes exchanged.

"My dad's being exiled back to Russia. My mom's going with him. My dad can't come back. My mom's free to travel. My sisters are handling it better than I am. Hell, I think Lea might actually be looking forward to being on her own. I feel like...everything's breaking apart and I'm not sure how to handle it."

She snorted. "Gee, that's such a shock."

Well, hell. "Thanks, kid. Here I thought you were going to be all supportive and shit."

Mary Alice laughed and laid her head on Adam's shoulder. "You know I love you, right? Even though sometimes you're more trouble than you're worth. You can be so damn stubborn, it makes the people around you want to shoot you."

He tried not to squirm as her barbs hit home. He knew she wasn't being mean. It wasn't in her nature. He also knew she was absolutely right.

"So why do you put up with me?"

She rolled her eyes. "Because you're also the one person everyone relies on to get them through to the end. Do you know when John Matthew died, you were the only person who realized I wasn't handling it? Everyone else just thought I was dealing like I always do. It's the curse of the overly stubborn. We box all the crap up inside and think we're handling it when really we're just not dealing with it at all. Really easy to see in everyone else. Not so easy to see in ourselves."

He'd started to smile halfway through her speech. "So when did you become such a philosophizer?"

She laughed, loud and long. "Damn, you did watch 'Dodgeball.' Told you you'd like it. And I'm just naturally brilliant. It's why you hired me."

They'd hired her because they'd promised her dead brother they'd take care of her if anything ever happened to him. Yes, she had two other brothers but they were in the service, as well, and stationed now in Germany and Africa.

When John Matthew had died, Tristan and Adam had gone to his funeral and told Mary Alice to quit her dead-end job at the dry cleaners and report for work at their office the next day.

Actually, Tristan had wanted to coddle her. He'd wanted her to take a week off first. Adam had shot that down and told her to show up the next day and not to be late.

She'd arrived five minutes early and left a half hour late and had taken only six weeks of vacation and three sick days since.

"Tristan looked pretty pissed when he left. He did say he'd see me Monday. And that I should go home."

But she'd waited for him, to make sure he was okay. He put his arm around her shoulders and pulled her in for a hug.

"And we've never regretted it. All right, Mally. Go home. I have a few things to do here then I'm heading out too."

"Will I see you Monday?"

Her expression became more serious now, as if she was worried she might not see him again.

"Of course. I'm not going anywhere."

Mary Alice bounced away from the desk then turned to him with a smile. "Good. I've gotten used to your grumpy moods."

She smacked a kiss on his cheek, leaving him smiling. He leaned against the desk for a little while longer, listening to her pack up for the day then call out a goodbye.

When the door closed behind her, he turned to look out the window, making plans.

"It's almost as if you knew I was coming and dressed for the occasion. You look beautiful, Katrina."

Kat had the overwhelming urge to slam the door in Phillip Donovan's smug face, but she was so dumbfounded by his presence that she froze.

"I'm glad I caught you at home," he continued as he brushed by her and walked into her living room. As if she'd invited him. "Your mother was worried about you. She said you didn't sound like yourself on the phone and she knew I was in Washington for the weekend so she asked me to check in on you."

A blast of icy wind blew by her, prompting her to close the door or she would have left it open. She *so* did not want to be alone with this man. The only thing keeping her from screaming at him to get the hell out of her home was the fact that Tristan was due to show up in ten minutes.

And even though she didn't want to spend any amount

of time with this man at all, she was more than a little curious what he'd do when his brother arrived.

She had a brief daydream about Tristan punching Phillip right in his smirking mouth. Or maybe in his slightly paunchy gut.

Wait, what had he said?

"My *mother* asked you to come?"

Strolling through her living room, Phillip headed toward the window looking out onto the street.

He turned and smiled at her, looking so smug, she wanted to punch him herself. Which would solve nothing, she realized. Maybe it was a good thing he'd shown up. He'd get to see her with Tristan and maybe then Phillip would realize it was never going to work between them. Not in a million years.

And what had her mother told him? That was as good as any place to start.

"Yes. She's afraid you might have been...agitated."

Agitated. Yes, that was a good word. She had been. But Phillip made it sound like she was sick. "My mother and I spoke today. She was being irrational so I ended the conversation. Something I should have done a long time ago."

Phillip's expression froze in surprise for a second before he regained that haughty look she wanted to wipe off his face.

She could see behind his smile now. She knew he thought she'd be easily cowed by his arrival and the conversation she'd had with her mother. He hadn't expected to find a woman with a backbone. Her mother had probably told him she was an emotional mess after speaking to her on the phone and had sent him in to pick up the pieces.

And now she finally had the chance to put him in his place. And the backbone to go through with it.

"Angelica was worried you might have had another... break with reality."

She had to laugh. Couldn't help herself. "Seriously? Is that what she said? You really are a jerk, aren't you, Phillip?"

His mouth opened and the surprise on his face made her want to continue to laugh.

Clueless. He was absolutely clueless.

He honestly thought he'd show up, browbeat her with her mother's concerns about her having a nervous break-down, and fall into his arms.

The knock at her door made her grin uncontrollably at Tristan's perfect timing.

"Hold that thought." She winked at him and almost missed the look of moronic disbelief on his face as she turned toward the door. But it was there and it made her continue to smile as she answered the door.

She grinned at Tristan, so damn happy to see him. Tall, dark, gorgeous, and smiling at her like he worshipped her.

Wrapping his arms around her shoulders, he drew her into his body, pressing her against him and kissing her like he hadn't seen her in days.

When he finally let her up for air, his grin had turned a little wicked. And she realized he knew Phillip was here.

"So, sweetheart. You ready to leave?"

"Absolutely. Your brother was just leaving. Weren't you, Phillip?"

She turned to look over her shoulder at her unwanted visitor, catching sight of the frustration and jealousy consuming him.

Tristan acknowledged his brother with a nod but didn't say a word, simply waited patiently by her side.

Phillip obviously didn't know how to deal with the situation. She'd never considered herself a violent person, but she totally wanted Phillip to take a swing at Tristan.

Only because she knew he'd never land the punch. And Tristan would most definitely land his.

Then again, Phillip was a coward. A blowhard and a bully, as well. Which was probably why he'd gotten along so well with her mother. They recognized kindred spirits.

Phillip started toward them, and she could see his brain grinding away with every single step. By the time he'd gotten to the door, she and Tristan, still with his arm around her shoulders, had stepped aside.

Kat wasn't at all worried about a physical attack from Phillip. He wasn't that type of man. His abuse was verbal and emotional. And he proved that the second he stopped in the doorway.

"I take it you never asked him about Diane. Pity. You'll eventually regret it. Have a nice night."

Tristan stiffened beside her as his brother walked out of sight and she left his side to close the door. When she turned back to him, he looked furious.

"That son-of-a-bitch."

Kat leaned her back against the closed door, watching Tristan try to get his anger under control. Yes, she remembered Phillip had told her to ask about Diane. She hadn't because, frankly, there'd been too much other stuff going on. And because she honestly believed Phillip had been trying to stir up trouble.

Apparently she was right.

"Do you want to talk about it?" she asked.

Tristan's eyes closed and it took him a good ten seconds before he sucked in a deep breath and opened his eyes again.

"No, I really don't. But I will because that bastard brought it up."

"Is it really that bad?"

"Yeah, it's bad. But not for the reasons that son-of-a-bitch wants you to believe."

Grabbing Tristan's hands, she tugged him toward the couch. "Tell me. We have a few minutes before we have to leave to make our reservations."

"I know how this is going to sound, which is why we don't talk about it. Ever." Another sigh as he sat. "Diane was a woman Adam and I met a few years ago. She seemed to know the score, knew how to deal with the relationship with Adam and me. She seemed to have it all together. She was a financial consultant, worked for some huge firm in King of Prussia. Everything went well for a while until she wanted to move in with us. Both of us. Get a place, do the whole happy family thing. Sounded great." He paused.

"Until I balked."

"Why?'

"Because she wasn't the woman I wanted to spend the rest of my life with."

His gaze burned as he stared at her, and she knew he was making a statement about her. Declaring feelings he hadn't yet spoken out loud.

"When I told her, she went on a tear. Trashed my apartment. Slashed Adam's tires. Made a couple of anonymous complaints to the police about abuse and how Adam and I were degenerates and mentally ill. Turns out she was the one who was ill."

Kat swallowed hard, not really sure she wanted to hear the rest of the story.

Instead, she nodded for him to continue.

"She ended up in the Temple psych ward for a month. They ultimately determined she had more than one issue to deal with. She'd been having trouble at work. She'd cut off all ties with her family because she thought they didn't support her. She'd been dealing with emotional problems all her life, but when I told her we were done, it pushed her over the edge. She had a mental break, spent several months in the psych ward."

Kat heard the repressed pain in his voice, the guilt. But she didn't hear any hesitation. As if he thought she might not be able to handle it. As if he thought she was in any way like his former lover.

And it was that, more than anything, that made her sit in his lap and put her arm around his shoulders.

"It wasn't your fault."

"Logically, yeah, I know that. Emotionally, I thought it was all my fault. Adam took it hard and I blamed myself for his depression, too. We didn't speak for weeks about anything that wasn't business related, and I figured our relationship was over then. That I'd killed it. Good thing we're both stubborn SOBs."

"I certainly am glad of that. So what happened to bring you back together?"

"You."

"Me? Why?"

"Because Phillip called to gloat that you were going to

say yes to his marriage proposal. And I knew he wasn't the right man for you. Hell, Kat, I've pretty much been in love with you since high school. We just never got the timing right. But I knew I couldn't let Phillip anywhere near you. He doesn't deserve you. Adam and I don't deserve you either, but I love you, Kat. If you tell me to turn and walk, I'll do it. I won't become some crazy stalker and make your life miserable. But I don't want to live my life without you. We need you. Adam and I. He's got some shit to work out but he needs us to support him now. We can't let him cut himself off."

Kat hadn't stopped smiling since he'd said the "L" word the first time. It welded shut some broken piece inside that she hadn't realized she needed fixed.

Now, she leaned forward and kissed Tristan. Softly, gently. No tongue.

Just a vow.

"I love you, too."

Tristan's grin reappeared. "Thank Christ for that."

When he kissed her this time, it was much longer and with a lot of tongue. And it definitely wasn't long enough.

She wanted more but he set her on her feet as he rose to his.

"Come on, babe. Let's head out before I decide to see what you've got on under this pretty dress. I'm kind of hoping for nothing. But I told Adam we would meet him at the restaurant, and I really want to believe he's going to show up there."

So did Kat. She wanted her fairytale ending. Hell, if everything worked out the way she hoped it would, she was going to get two princes instead of one.

And, damn it, she wanted both. Call her selfish. She didn't care.

If Adam didn't show tonight, she damn well wasn't going to take it sitting down.

Maybe lying down...

"I really love this hotel. It's so beautiful."

"The owners are friends. I'll introduce you sometime. But tonight I want you all to myself."

Kat stared at Tristan over the top of the leather-bound menu. "You don't think he's going to show, do you?"

Tristan sighed, shaking his head. "Honestly, I have no idea. But don't worry, I have plans for you tonight, and nothing is going to get in my way."

The sound of his voice made her panties damp. How did he manage that? "And I'm so looking forward to your plans. But behave for now. I need to eat before we...retire for the night."

Tristan's eyes had a sharp gleam in them now. "We could always have dinner sent to our room. I booked us a suite for tonight."

"Really? You only live a couple of minutes from here."

"Because you've never seen anything like this room. You're gonna love it. Trust me."

"I do. Trust you. Completely."

But she wished...

No, no more of that. She was going to be grateful for what she had tonight. Which was Tristan, all to herself. "Glad to hear it."

"So tell me about this room."

She didn't want to think about Adam not being here, about the hole she definitely felt at his absence.

Tristan's grin definitely made her want to squirm in her seat. "Nope, not spoiling the surprise. So, what are you having?"

For the next hour, Tristan made it his mission to tease, flatter, and flirt. And make her long for dinner to be over so they could get to the best part of the evening. The part where they were naked.

She kept her concentration focused on Tristan, but occasionally her mind wandered and she looked for Adam.

Who never appeared.

Finally, when their server asked if they'd like dessert, Tristan declined.

"If we want dessert later, we'll order up room service. Okay with you?"

She nodded but once the server left with a smile on her face, Kat leaned forward. "I want chocolate mousse so I can slather it on your body and lick it off."

Tristan blinked, his mouth opening as if he were going to say something then closing before he did. Instead, he grabbed the check, signed it, and stood, reaching for her.

"I apologize now if I accidentally rip that dress getting it off you. But you're definitely going to pay for the hard-on I'm not going to be able to hide on the way out."

She laughed. "Then I'll just have to take it off for you."

Groaning under his breath, he helped her to her feet. "You're going to kill me, sweetheart, I swear. When the hell did you turn into a tease? Not that I don't like it. But damn, my cock's already throbbing."

Laughing as they left the dining room, she leaned over to speak into his ear as they stopped at the elevator. "That's the sweetest thing you could say. You know how to make a woman feel good."

"I am going to make you beg me to let you come."

Then he gave her a little push toward the open elevator door and followed her in.

They didn't say anything else as they took the elevator to the fifth floor.

Kat could barely catch her breath, she was so turned on. Not even the fact that Adam wasn't here could dampen her enthusiasm.

When they finally reached the room, Tristan opened the door and let her walk in ahead of him.

Soft lighting showed off certain areas of the room, and what she saw took her breath away.

"Oh my god, Tristan. This is gorgeous."

"The owners recently renovated the rooms on this floor with different themes. This one's called the Sultan's Harem."

And she could see why. Colorful silk fabric draped the walls, and jewel-toned chaise lounges and billowy pillows filled the space. The low table in the center of the room was meant to be used for things other than eating, if the rings on each leg were any indication. The floors were covered with oriental rugs, and brightly colored gauze hung from the ceiling to drape around certain areas.

"Wow, the sex you can have in this room…"

Tristan laughed as he came up behind her and wrapped his arms around her waist.

"Great observations. So let's have some. I've been dying for you for the past two weeks."

Movement from behind one of the gauze panels made her gasp, and Tristan stiffened for a second before she felt him relax. It actually took her a second to realize Tristan had recognized who was there.

"I hope you know I've been lost without you, too." Adam stepped into the light near the center of the room.

"And I hope you can forgive me for being a complete ass."

Behind her, Tristan stilled, as if he were waiting for her answer just as much as Adam.

Which made sense, she supposed.

But she needed answers. She needed him to talk to her.

"Are you willing to tell me why you were acting like an ass?"

He dipped his head for a brief second. "Not going to let me off the hook easily, are you?"

"Not really, no. Do you think I should?"

"Not really. So what do you want to hear first? My explanation? Or do you want me to skip straight to begging for your forgiveness?"

She glanced over her shoulder at Tristan, who stared at Adam with a narrowed gaze. He barely moved, but she heard agitation in every indrawn breath.

"I only want you to talk to me."

Adam grimaced. "That's never been one of my strong suits."

She opened her mouth to respond but he continued before she could.

"But for you," his gaze flicked to Tristan for the briefest second, "I'll try."

Adam began closing the distance between them. "I love my dad. He's far from perfect. Actually, he's pretty much as far from perfect as you can get. But I never once doubted that he loved me. That's actually his one best quality. He loves his family and, except for one time, he's never let the shit he deals with touch us. I was never afraid of him. And he never once hinted that he wanted me to follow in his footsteps."

Adam stood just out of arms' reach now, close enough that she had to tilt her head back to look at him.

The sadness in his eyes made her want to wrap her arms around him, but she waited, realizing he'd stopped where he had for a reason.

"The only thing I ever wanted was for him to be out of the life. Now he is and he's leaving and taking my mom away from their grandchildren and my sisters. I feel like I'm getting the one thing I've always wanted but at the expense of everyone else in my life." He finally took those few steps to bring him into her reach. "Including the woman I love and my best friend."

Tears welled at the leashed emotion in his voice, and she reached for his hand then. "You know it's not your fault, don't you? About your dad? And I'm not going to hold any of that against you. I love you, Adam. I don't want to spend any more nights alone."

The joyful look on Adam's face made her light up inside, but she hurried on because she needed to finish this first. "I've realized how lonely I've been all these years, and I don't want to be alone anymore. You and Tristan showed me how much better life is when I have the two of you by my side. I never thought I'd find a man who'd love me just the way I am, but then I found two and I felt like I'd won the lottery."

Adam shook his head. "We're no prize, sweetheart. Tristan and I are the ones who should be getting on our knees to thank you for being with us. I know it's not always going to be roses and candlelight. You already know I can be a miserable jerk and Tristan has his moments."

Behind her, she heard Tristan huff. "I'll admit to being difficult. Occasionally."

Adam's gaze transferred to Tristan. "I've made up my mind about Max's offer. We'll make a counteroffer. You and me. We'll figure that part out. Together."

Behind her, she felt Tristan nod, and Kat realized that whatever had been messed up between them had just been forgiven.

"We can discuss that 'occasionally' part later," Adam continued. "Right now, I want to show Kat how sorry I am for being such a prick."

She barely had time to suck in a breath before Adam stepped straight against her and bent to kiss her.

He stole her breath and her ability to think straight as his lips moved over hers and his hands flattened on her back, pulling her against him.

The heat of his body seared her, raising her blood pressure and making her heart pound against her ribs. Her hands gripped his shoulders and she rose onto her toes to get closer.

He kissed her like he'd almost lost her. Like he couldn't quite believe she was here and he wasn't going to let her get away again.

She was fine with that.

She was more than fine with that.

As if he'd read her mind, he groaned and let his hands slide down her arms to her hands, where he laced their fingers together then brought them to his hips.

"I want you naked and I'm sure Tristan won't object. Can we strip you, sweetheart? I'm dying to have you on top of me with my cock buried inside you. And I know Tristan is dying to take your ass. Can we have you? We promise you won't regret it. I can't promise that we'll never piss you off or make you sad or worried. Sometimes our jobs are dangerous. But we're good at them."

And she'd show them she could deal with that. "I understand. I don't want you to give up anything for me. I just want to be part of your lives, however you'll have me."

"We'll have you anyway we can get you."

Tristan's hands landed on her hips and he pressed against her back. His erection nestled against her ass, and she shivered as she realized she could have this always. Have them always.

That's what they were offering. And that's what she wanted.

With one hand on Adam's hip pulling him closer and the other reaching behind for Tristan, she nodded, rubbing her nose against the scruff on Adam's chin.

"And I want to give myself to you. I love you. Both of you. I never thought I'd say those words to anyone, but you two have made me see my life has so much more to offer. That there don't have to be so many rules and there are no obstacles we can't overcome together."

"We'll try to never let you regret your decision." Adam's hands began to gather her skirt, gradually exposing her thighs.

"You know you can just take the dress off. The zipper's in the back."

"Tris, you heard the lady."

"Yes, I did."

Tristan had her zipper released in seconds. Adam tugged at the skirt and the dress dropped to the floor around her feet.

Both men sucked in air and Tristan actually groaned.

"Hell, I am definitely buying stock in that damn lingerie shop."

She shivered with reaction to Adam's gruff statement, loving how his gaze traveled over her body with a hunger she'd come to crave.

"I never dressed this way for anyone, not even myself. Never wanted to. Only for you."

"And we'll make sure you know just how grateful we are."

Tristan smoothed his hands over her shoulders as Adam lifted one of his to run his finger over the swell of her breast pushing past the pale pink lace trim on the bra.

She barely felt Tristan unhook the bra, but Adam obviously knew what Tristan was doing and hooked his finger in the front to draw it away the second Tristan released it.

She'd already realized they loved having her mostly naked between them. She also realized they focused so much on her that they didn't bother to remove their own clothes.

Unless she insisted. Right now she didn't have the patience to strip them herself.

"I want you both naked. Now."

Adam's mouth twisted in a sexy grin. "I think we can accommodate that."

She felt movement at her back and turned to find Tristan already doing away with his shirt.

"The least you can do is give me a hand with my pants, sweetheart."

The gleam in Tristan's eyes made her thighs clench and her pussy even wetter.

She unbuckled his belt by touch, leaning forward to press kisses along Tristan's chest as she undid the button on his pants, slid down the zipper and pushed his pants to the floor.

"I think I need a little help too, babe."

Adam pulled her back to face him, pulling her hands to his pants and thrusting his hands into her hair to lift her face.

He kissed her breathless, but she still managed to get his jeans undone, even though her fingers shook and her body tried to absorb all the sensations at once.

Her hardened nipples brushed against Adam's chest as her hands curled around his stiff cock. The warm flesh made her moan, and when Tristan leaned against her from behind to bite at her neck, she swore she came.

Adam's fingers slid between her legs and played along her wet folds before sinking inside and stroking her.

"You're ready now, aren't you, babe?"

"Yes. Right now."

In the next second, Tristan scooped her into his arms and nodded in Adam's direction. "Bed's there."

Adam moved toward it then kicked off his shoes and stripped away the rest of his clothes.

She had a brief glimpse of him laid out on the bed like the sexiest male pinup she'd ever seen before Tristan set her on her knees directly over Adam's hips.

"Sorry," Adam muttered as he pulled her head down to seal their lips. She didn't have any idea what he was apologizing for until she heard fabric tearing and pulled away to look at him with mock dismay.

"I'll buy you ten more," Adam said. "Just take me in now."

With a little shimmy, she felt the tip of Adam's cock brush against her lips and shifted until he was lodged firmly. Then she pushed her chest up with her hands on Adam's stomach and sank onto him until he was lodged deep.

Eyes closed, she stilled, enjoying the feel of him stretching her wide. Adam's hands covered her breasts, tweaking her nipples with his fingers and tormenting her with sharp pleasure until she couldn't stay still.

She also couldn't go slow. She rode him hard and fast, building the friction to a level that made her long for release.

So when Tristan grabbed her hips, forcing her to stay still, impaled on Adam's cock, she moaned and let Adam wrap his arms around her and hold her against his chest.

She felt the bed shift as Tristan positioned himself behind her, felt the cool slickness of lube on his fingers as he rubbed his fingers between her cheeks.

Her pussy clenched in anticipation and Adam huffed, as if in pain. She knew he wasn't. He'd liked that. She did it again.

And felt him tighten all over.

"Fuck, Tris. Hurry up."

"You know I can't."

Tristan's voice sounded strained but in the next second, she felt his cock press against her ass, forging ahead slowly but surely.

When they were both buried inside her, Tristan bent to kiss her between her shoulder blades.

"Now."

They began a wickedly controlled rhythm that soon had her begging them for release.

"Soon, baby," Tristan whispered in her ear. "And always."

She came with a muffled cry, the sharp pulse in her lower body spreading ecstasy through her entire being.

Her world narrowed down to these two men who held her so tightly she could barely breathe. But she knew they'd never let her falter.

Adam followed her with a groan, his cock pumping inside her pussy. Tristan wasn't far behind, his body tense as he gritted out her name.

Long seconds later, Tristan eased out of her and dropped onto the mattress next to Adam, still holding to her tightly.

After at least a minute, Adam released her to let her slide to the mattress between them.

Where she planned to stay forever.

Don't miss the next story in the series! Find out who Mary Alice falls for in An Indecent Arrangement.

AN INDECENT ARRANGEMENT
TWO BAD BOYS TRYING TO GO LEGIT. ONE GOOD GIRL WHO COULD BE THEIR DOWNFALL.

Max and Jesse grew up on the streets of Philadelphia, working for the city's most successful crime boss before going straight. They're inseparable, their friendship honed by danger. They share everything, including a burning desire for the same woman. But an affair, while they're still untangling themselves from their past, could be dangerous, not only to their friendship but to their lives. And to hers.

Mary Alice has always walked the straight and narrow, but her secret craving for Max and Jesse is fast becoming an obsession. They don't fit into her safe little world of family, friends and work. That doesn't stop her from wanting these intensely sexual men who fascinate her. When fate hands her an opening, Mary Alice proposes an indecent arrangement guaranteed to rock their worlds.

Their powerfully erotic relationship is shattered in an instant. Jesse and Max stand united even though they're miserable without her. Mally is hurt and angry but she's not ready to give up on them. She has to make them understand that they're safer together. And that she's tougher than they realize.

ALSO BY STEPHANIE JULIAN

WICKED & CHARMING

Seducing Whitney

Claiming Ellie

Sharing Brianna

INDECENT

An Indecent Proposition

An Indecent Affair

An Indecent Arrangement

An Indecent Longing

An Indecent Desire

SALON GAMES

Invite Me In

Reserve My Nights

Expose My Desire

Keep My Secrets

Rock My Heart

FAST ICE

Bylines & Blue Lines

Hard Lines & Goal Lines

Deadlines & Red Lines

REDTAILS HOCKEY

The Brick Wall

The Grinder

The Enforcer

The Instigator

The Playboy

The D-Man

The Machine

LOVERS UNDERCOVER

Lovers & Lies

Sinners & Secrets

Beauty & Brains

Thieves & Thrills

FORGOTTEN GODDESSES

What A Goddess Wants

How to Worship A Goddess

When A Goddess Falls

Where A Goddess Belongs

DARKLY ENCHANTED

Spell Bound

Moon Bound

MAGICAL SEDUCTION

Seduced by Magic

Seduced in Shadow

Seduced & Ensnared

Seduced & Enchanted

Seduced by Chaos

Seduced by Danger

Moonlight Seduction

LUCANI LOVERS

Kiss of Moonlight

Visions of Moonlight

Edge of Moonlight

Temptation in Moonlight

Grace in Moonlight

Shades of Moonlight

ABOUT THE AUTHOR

Stephanie Julian is a USA Today and New York Times best-selling author of contemporary romance and romantasy.

Copyright © 2014 by Stephanie Julian

All rights reserved.

No part of this book may be reproduced in any form or by any electronic or mechanical means, including information storage and retrieval systems, without written permission from the author, except for the use of brief quotations in a book review.

www.ingramcontent.com/pod-product-compliance
Lightning Source LLC
Chambersburg PA
CBHW030143200726
48285CB00004BC/1398